Fallam's Secret

Also by Denise Giardina

Fallam's Secret

Denise Giardina

W. W. Norton & Company

New York   London

For information about permission to reproduce selections from this book, write to Permissions, W. W. Norton & Company, Inc., 500 Fifth Avenue, New York, NY 10110

Manufacturing by The Haddon Craftsmen, Inc.
Book design by Lovedog Studio
Production manager: Anna Oler

LIBRARY OF CONGRESS CATALOGING-IN-PUBLICATION DATA
Giardina, Denise, 1951– .
Fallam's Secret / by Denise Giardina.
p. cm.
ISBN 978-0-393-33695-5
1. Americans—England—Fiction. 2. Young women—Fiction. 3. Time travel—Fiction. 4. Great Britain—History—Commonwealth and Protectorate, 1649–1660—Fiction. 7. West Virginia—Fiction. I. Title.

PS3557.I136 F35 2003
813'.54—dc21   2002015942

W. W. Norton & Company, Inc., 500 Fifth Avenue, New York, N.Y. 10110
www.wwnorton.com

W. W. Norton & Company Ltd., Castle House, 75/76 Wells Street,
London W1T 3QT

1 2 3 4 5 6 7 8 9 0

IN MEMORY OF LAURA FORMAN

Contents

THANKS TO Jane Gelfman, Amy Cherry, David Wohl, Sherry Wolford, Arla Ralston, Colleen Anderson, Ancella Bickley, Julie Pratt, Arline Thorn, Sarah Sullivan, Jim and Judy Lewis, Gordon Simmons, Grace Edwards, Kate Long, John Richards, Barbara Ladner, Jack Magan, Tod Ralstin, Hazo Carter, Juris Lidaka, Barbara Bayes, Cathy Pleska, Al Peery, Chuck Wyrostock, Rosalie Blau, Leona Giardina, and Phyllis Giardina.

Author's note: I will not attempt to re-create word for word the speech of characters in the seventeenth century. Suffice it to say that Lydde Falcone's training in seventeenth-century drama came to her aid. Once she picked up certain inflections she became more easy with the speech of the past and even slipped into the manner of it herself, as though back on the stage again and performing an improv version of *As You Like It* or *The Winter's Tale,* but with a slight flavor of the talk she'd heard from old people back home in the mountains of West Virginia.

Part One

The Fire

TIME, UNCLE JOHN explained to Lydde over supper, is like pasta. Not a straight hard length of supermarket spaghetti, but pasta cooked and poured into the colander, then tumbled into a bowl, heaped and tangled and layered. He gestured to his own steaming plate of carbonara when he said it, fork aloft and trailing strands of spaghetti. He had cooked the meal himself, because Aunt Lavinia only did roasts.

Uncle John fell in love with Italian food as a boy, at the same time his older sister Margaret fell in love with an Italian immigrant. Margaret and John were the pampered children of the superintendent of a West Virginia coal camp and lived in the big house on the hill. Margaret was only sixteen when she met Carlo Falcone.

Carlo was twenty-two, a coal miner whose father had been killed in the mines. He lived with his widowed mother and youngest sister in a four-room shack in Tally Hollow. Nine-year-old John was Margaret's cover when she snuck out of the house to meet Carlo. John was a restless boy, and to give their mother some peace and quiet, Margaret offered to take him places in the evenings. The place they went was the Falcone house, where Carlo's Sicilian mother sat John at the kitchen table and fed him heaps of pasta slick with tomatoes and olive oil, and sometimes a little cup of red wine to go with it, while Margaret and Carlo courted in the front room.

That's how Uncle John came to love Italian food. He loved time because he just did, and when he grew up he became a professor of physics.

Most of what Lydde knew of her family came from Uncle John and Aunt Lavinia. Uncle John told her the story of how her parents met at the dime store in Lafayette, when Carlo wandered by the ladies' wear department as Margaret was choosing a dress and suggested she try the green one instead of the brown one she held in her hand. John had emerged from the toy department across the aisle, clutching a model airplane kit, to find his sister twirling before a mirror in the green dress, her face flushed. A dark young man sat on a red vinyl chair and watched her intently. Margaret bribed John with a chocolate soda to keep him from telling.

When Lydde was older, Aunt Lavinia told her how Carlo and a pregnant Margaret had eloped to Virginia, where there was no waiting period for a marriage license. The courting sessions in Tally Hollow had moved from the front room to the bedroom with the passive approval of Mama Falcone, who thought her boy richly deserved a Boss Man's daughter. Carlo and Margaret returned from Virginia to confront her family with the indisputable results. Margaret was disowned, and Carlo took a job at Boomer coal camp, since his new father-in-law refused to hire him.

·   ·   ·

WHAT did Lydde actually remember, what did she know of her family that didn't come secondhand? Precious little. She recalled there had been other children, all older than she was. She remembered chickens in pens behind the house, frightening her with their clawing and gabbling, and her father in the yard running a board into a buzz saw. He seemed angry. On the mountainside winter trees loomed, stripped of leaves, their branches joined together like claws holding hands. Someone picked Lydde up and carried her inside.

She had no memory of someone called Mother. But she recalled a smiling face close to hers, singing to her, a lullaby, *when the bough breaks the cradle will fall, and down will come Lydde, cradle and all.*

Aunt Lavinia showed Lydde pictures and asked, "Who do you remember? Anyone?"

Lydde studied the photographs and then pointed to a girl with delicate arched eyebrows and long dark hair.

"That's Mary," said Aunt Lavinia. "Your oldest sister. By the time you came along, Margaret was covered up with children, so Mary took charge of you. She hauled you around everywhere with her."

"She sang to me," Lydde said, not really remembering, but knowing. "And she told me stories."

Lydde's other memory was of a faraway house of red and gold flame, so pretty she wanted to touch it.

CARLO Falcone, inevitably called Carl by his West Virginia neighbors, had come to America as a child in 1918. Poverty brought his family across the ocean, but also trouble with the Black Hand, which had been antagonized by Carlo's father. Carlo was seven, and furious. He left behind a small sharecropped farm on the coast of Sicily, an impossibly blue Mediterranean cove, olive trees and lemon trees and vineyards, and worst of all, a beloved donkey. In return he got a tiny house in a dusty coal camp, cheek by jowl with other houses, winters of blackened slush and bitter cold, fruit and vegetables from tin cans. Poor then in every way. He would never get over so much loss, never.

Carlo returned to Sicily during World War II with U.S. Army intelligence.

"The war was a terrible time for him," said Uncle John, who also served in Sicily. "Something happened he would never talk about. Whatever it was, they pulled him out and sent him to a British unit headed for the mainland. For his own safety, I'm guessing."

With money Margaret saved from his Army pay, Carlo bought thirty acres of cove—half of it relatively flat, the rest hillside—halfway up Fallam Mountain near the head of Shades o' Death Creek. The land skirted the edge of the ancient New River Gorge and, unusual in that part of West Virginia, included the mineral rights as well. Security, Carlo told Uncle John. There'll be no mining around me.

Until Uncle John and Aunt Lavinia moved into Roundbottom Farm just down the mountain, Margaret was unhappy with Carlo's choice. There were rumors among the neighbors that Carlo's property was haunted. It was told that just after the Revolution, a boy was out scything in the cove near the head of the creek. He failed to see his little sister playing in the tall grass and accidentally cut off her head. When the boy realized what he had done, he tore off in a frenzy the quarter mile along a spit of land that narrowed and narrowed until it ended in a prow of rock surrounded on three sides by a sheer drop into the Gorge. Fallam Point. The distraught boy threw himself over. That was how Shades o' Death Creek got its name.

The New River Gorge was rimmed with rock cliffs like jaws set with gray teeth. When Lydde was a child she imagined someone had flung himself off each of them.

CARLO Falcone had no time for ghosts. He named his West Virginia cove Montefalco, Falcon's Mount. In addition to including his own name, it recalled to him the Umbrian village of Montefalco he'd seen while driving a British army jeep through the Vale of Spoleto after its liberation by the partisans. That was a part of Italy where the mafia seemed not yet to reach, and so it was heaven to Carlo. *Italia senza cosa nostra,* like West Virginia without coal, he told Uncle John. He'd stopped in Montefalco for a rest, to look around, and the only way to escape the swarm of begging children was to duck into the church. There he'd found medieval wall paintings, scenes from the life of Christ transposed from Palestine to a green mountainscape like that of Umbria or West Virginia. And in the crypt, a mummy of a twelfth century bishop. Carlo had briefly felt peace and something like joy in a ravaged Italy, in that church. Back outside, he walked the village, leaving packets of chocolate in his wake, studying the place. He was invited into someone's home for a meal of polenta and grilled fenocchio.

When he bought his land on Fallam Mountain, he knew he wanted more than a house. He wanted to recreate Italy.

He went about it bit by bit, in the hours he could spare from setting up his own construction business. The house first, hardwood floors and wood-beamed ceilings from trees he felled to clear the site. The outside was stucco with elaborate textured swirls, two stories topped with a roof of red tile. Below the house he put up a small stone barn and dreamed of importing donkeys from Sicily. One weekend he built a donkey cart and painted it the traditional bright Sicilian hues, red green blue yellow. He wasn't an artist who could paint scenes like those on the most elaborate carts in Sicily, so he contented himself with stripes of color. *For the bambinos,* he said. He built a stone smokehouse for the prosciutto and pancetta he would put up from his own pigs. Behind the house he planted roma tomatoes and an herb garden, basil and parsley and oregano. He built retaining walls and planted grapevines, *Treviano* for vinegar, *Trebbiano* and *Sciava* for wine. Would they thrive in West Virginia? He would never know.

·   ·   ·

LYDDE was the last of six children. She used to say their names like a litany. Louis Mary Grace Dominic Jane Lydde. The boys to honor their father's Sicilian uncles, the girls their mother's Cabell ancestors. Louis to Lydde, she would say for short as she dug through the ruins of their house with a stick.

All the children had dark hair, like their father. All but Lydde had his dark eyes as well. Lydde's eyes were gray like her mother's.

Several months before the fire, the five older children had their school pictures taken. They gave wallet-sized copies to Uncle John and Aunt Lavinia, and Lydde inherited them when she went away to college.

In the photos, each child's expression was serious, as though the school photographer forbade everyone to smile. Or perhaps he possessed a manner that intimidated the children, unlike the photographer who years later would tease Lydde into a pose of wide-eyed goofiness, much to Uncle John's amusement.

Louis had a long face, short hair brushed back from his forehead, and thick Sicilian eyebrows. Mary was thirteen. Her hair was long, parted in the middle, and held back with a barrette. Eleven-year-old Grace had thick unruly hair and was biting her lip. Her eyes were enormous. Dominic wore bangs across his forehead and was the one closest to breaking into a mischievous grin. He had on overalls and his ears stuck out. Jane was only six, with a tiny bow mouth, and she was looking away, upset, as though about to scold someone off camera. Or perhaps she was frightened.

Lydde thought they were beautiful, but they seemed to know something very sad.

When Lydde was grown, she carried the photos in her wallet. She didn't have children. But sometimes, in England or on airplanes, when strangers asked, she would pull out her wallet and say, Here are my children. If the strangers noted the boys' rough shirts and the old-fashioned dresses of the girls, they didn't say.

.   .   .

CHRISTMAS Eve, 1948. The younger children had been coaxed to bed early by Louis and Mary, because two-year-old Lydde was sick. Mary had tried to sing Lydde to sleep, but the baby fretted and wouldn't go down.

"She can sleep with me," Mary offered.

But Jane and Grace put up a fuss, for Mary had promised to tell them stories until they fell asleep, and they had to fall asleep soon or they were afraid Santa Claus wouldn't come. So Margaret retired early, taking Lydde into bed with her. Carlo stayed below in the dining room and set out Santa gifts around a Christmas tree glittery with shredded aluminum icicles. There was one present for each child—a charm bracelet for Mary, dolls for Grace and Jane, a red Schwinn bicycle for Dominic, Louis's two-volume set of Shakespeare (he was the bookish one), and Lydde's teddy bear.

Margaret banged on her bedroom wall once to quiet the boys, for Dominic had sneaked a glimpse of a bicycle wheel through the banister railing and was bouncing on his bed with excitement. Just as the baby was finally falling off to sleep, Margaret heard a thump on the roof above. Jane heard it too and yelled, "Santa Claus!" Mary tried to shush her.

Carlo paused, screwdriver in hand, and looked up, but decided a tree limb must have blown onto the house. He finished assembling Dominic's bicycle, turned out the lights, and climbed the stairs to bed.

He woke to the smoke and flames, the screams of Margaret and the children. He didn't think he'd slept long, or really slept at all, only slipped briefly into a moment of unconsciousness. Margaret held up the phone from beside the bed. As from a great distance, Carlo heard her crying that the line was dead. When he tried to describe later what it had been like, he lapsed into the broken English of his childhood.

Margaret scream from the hall, grab the little one. I go through smoke for the children. Them up and running back and forth gathering up their things. No time for that, no time. Follow me! Grab Dominic by the collar of his pajamas and drag him downstairs, miss a step in the thick smoke and twist my ankle. I lose hold of Dominic. He run to back of the house calling for his bike! No time! Margaret go after him but I grab her and pull her out the front door I turn the children are on the stairs the flames come down the front of the house and I see their shadows through the flames following Dominic to the back. I think they will make the back door. Margaret push the baby to me and run back I put the baby down and follow but so does the baby. Who know she can run so fast on those little legs? Margaret is back in the house I yell they will make it out the back. I pick up the baby and take her back away. The front of the house fall in. All so quick. Like that.

Like that.

Carlo carried baby Lydde around to the back of the house, which was now totally engulfed in flames. Red and gold, so pretty, Lydde recalled. Carlo thought to find the children huddling together after having escaped out the back kitchen door, he was sure he had seen them come down the stairs and flee after Dominic, Louis and Mary each with one of the young ones. He dreaded to tell them their mother had disappeared back into the flames.

They weren't there. That was when Carlo fell to his knees and waited until fear and grief and the gray dawn of Christmas morning drove him down the mountain to Uncle John and Aunt Lavinia at Roundbottom Farm.

THE fire department came in time to survey the smoldering ruins, the police arrived to investigate, hearses waited to take away the bodies. Carlo returned to the scene with Uncle John while Aunt Lavinia looked after Lydde.

"He seemed to have aged overnight," Uncle John told Lydde later. "There were patches of gray in his hair I hadn't noticed before, and a singed spot on the side of his head. Most of his eyebrows were gone, and the right side of his face was raw. He got more of the flame than he realized. He wept on my shoulder when they brought Margaret's body out to a hearse. He blamed himself. Shameful that a woman had gone back in the house while he cowered outside with the baby. Not that he could have done anything else, not with you to deal with. Anyway he would have died too. But maybe that's what he wanted."

Uncle John tried to coax Carlo back down the mountain so he wouldn't have to watch the removal of the bodies of the children. But Carlo refused to budge. So they stood and stood while a light rain fell among the hissing gray frosted timbers and scorched cinderblocks. Watched as rubble was hauled out. Identified the twisted metal frame that had been Dominic's new bike, the blackened spine of the Christmas tree. The hearses waited, empty.

Then they heard a fireman remark as he carried away a sodden bundle of books, "The fire wasn't as hot at the back. It must have started up front somewhere."

He began to toss the books onto a pile of rubble, but Carlo roused himself suddenly and said, "Let me see those."

There were two thick volumes, browned around all four edges, missing their binding and stinking of smoke. And yet, as Carlo and Uncle John turned the brittle pages, an area of print at the center of each page could clearly be read. *Out out brief candle I come not to bury Caesar there are more things in heaven and earth Horatio . . .* Louis's *Complete Works of William Shakespeare.*

Carlo looked at Uncle John and said, "The children. They aren't here. Something else has happened to them."

"Carlo." Uncle John put his hand on his brother-in-law's shoulder. "In a fire like that—"

Carlo shook off the hand. "They would find bodies. You know I'm right, you and I saw bodies incinerated by firefights in Sicilian cellars and still something was left. Here they found my Margaret. They found these books. My son's books." He wheeled and ran, flailing his arms like a madman, grabbing this fireman, that policeman, crying, "My children! My children! They aren't dead! You must find them!"

No one found them, though they raked the coals for days looking for anything, a fragment of a limb, a skull, a finger. Nothing.

They found other things. Scraps of furniture. Bits of dishes. A metal canister that might have held gasoline. The fire chief told the local newspaper he refused to speculate on the cause of the blaze.

They found the phone line outside the house cut through.

The police came and went at Roundbottom Farm. They thought it unlikely the Falcone children would have escaped the fire at Montefalco, because where would they be? Why would they have run off?

They regarded Carlo with suspicion and without telling him searched the area for newly dug graves, but found nothing. And then there was the matter of the cut phone line, and the fact that Carlo had carried baby Lydde from the house. If Carlo Falcone was a man intent on doing away with his family, why had he done that? At last they concluded there was no evidence against him, and charges were never brought.

Still Carlo haunted the local state police barracks. Someone has my children, he insisted.

Who? the police asked, bewildered. And why would anyone do that?

Uncle John was present the first time the police asked that question. Carlo had looked like he'd seen a ghost, Uncle John told Lydde. He hadn't answered, except to sit back in his chair and whisper, My God.

"Did he think someone kidnapped them?" Lydde asked.

Uncle John nodded. "That's why he left, to look for them."

Lydde was never quite convinced when Uncle John said this. She thought her father left to get away from her, because she had kept him from returning to the fire, because she had survived.

"Do you think they were kidnapped?"

"I don't know," Uncle John said. "Maybe it had something to do with what happened in Sicily when he was in the Army. But sometimes I think something else happened too."

They had this conversation when Lydde was ten, when Uncle John and Aunt Lavinia thought she was old enough to know. Uncle John didn't say what else he thought might have happened. Carlo would never talk about what happened in Sicily that might have to do with the disappearances. The police decided the Falcone children had stopped at the Christmas tree to rescue presents and been incinerated when the roof fell on them, but Uncle John, the scientist, scoffed at that. "We found the spine of the Christmas tree. And even a crematorium leaves something behind." He'd shake his head.

Lydde grew frustrated at the lack of answers. At first she was afraid to visit the ruins. But at ten—for Lydde the age when she dared her fears—she went to look for herself, scraping through the ruins with a long sturdy stick she kept for the purpose, hoping to find a clue someone had overlooked. One October day she trudged up Shades o' Death Creek, stick in hand. She was conducting her search meticulously, a few inches at a time. Uncle John had described the layout of the house and she had memorized the location of each room. It was an exercise in spatial imagination, invisible rooms existing in height width depth and time past.

That day Lydde was digging in a corner that on one level had been the living room and on another her brothers' bedroom. Now all was collapsed in a thin layer of ash, which she patiently loosened. Never mind that the ruins had been sifted and sifted and sifted yet again. They had missed something, Lydde was sure of it. And she was right.

What she found was a corner of silvery metal, which gradually emerged, after much scraping, as a cigarette lighter. She wiped it carefully with the sleeve of her sweatshirt and carried it home in the pocket of her jeans. Uncle John and Aunt Lavinia, seated at their kitchen table, turned it over and over, passed it back and forth.

"Is it my dad's?" Lydde asked.

"No," Uncle John said. "He never uses a lighter, only matches. I don't know—"

"Maybe it was Louis's," Aunt Lavinia said.

They both looked at her in surprise.

"He was sneaking smokes," she explained. "I caught him once when he was doing some work for me in the garden, and he begged me not to tell. I don't think Carl would have minded in those days, but you know how Margaret was. She told Louis eighteen was old enough to start smelling like tobacco."

Lydde didn't know how Margaret was, but she didn't point this out. They sat and passed the lighter back and forth like a talisman.

"Do you think that's how the fire started?"

"A fourteen-year-old boy doesn't start fires," Uncle John said. "Not Louis. He was a good, smart kid."

"Maybe one of the little ones got ahold of it," Aunt Lavinia said.

But Uncle John shook his head again and Lydde thought he was right. She fiddled with the lighter and couldn't even get it going herself.

"It won't be working now," Aunt Lavinia said.

But Uncle John took it from Lydde and flicked it. A pearl of flame perched atop the silver rectangle. Fire from fire.

CARLO Falcone came and went. Came again and left again. He would stop by Roundbottom Farm twice a year like clockwork, once in July and once right after Christmas. Never on Christmas Eve or Christmas Day. Never.

Lydde didn't ask where he was living, just sneaked a glimpse at his license plate. Each time it was different, Florida, New Jersey, Louisiana. The last time was Nevada.

Carlo was a tall, lean man, stooped as if he were older, with graying black hair, a long, crooked nose, and, for the last few years, eyeglasses. He would have cut a romantic figure, Lydde supposed, when he was twenty-two and Margaret Cabell fell in love with him.

He would say very little when he arrived, only hug Lydde. His hugs were not enveloping, just an arm around her shoulder, pulling her to lean against him for a brief moment. Nothing else, not even a touching of cheeks. As she got older, she resisted him and turned away from the pained look on his face. He would watch her with his eyes, everywhere she went. She avoided him as much as possible. She feared him, as he did her. Neither wanted to know what the other might regret, or what blame the other assigned. Carlo would not touch Lydde again until he was ready to leave. Then he would put his hand awkwardly on her shoulder. "Poppa loves you, *bambina,*" he would say. "You are all I have left."

Not nearly enough, Lydde would think. For either of us. And Carlo would disappear just as surely as the past.

LYDDE poked through the charred foundation of Montefalco until she was sixteen and word came of Carlo's death in Nevada. He'd been on the highway driving toward California. Probably spent a night on the town in Vegas. Probably fell asleep. Ended in a ditch alongside the road, where his car caught fire and burned, sometime in the early morning hours. A trucker had seen the flames and found him.

Enough, Lydde thought. Now I can forget it all. I will be a different person. I will go away to school somewhere that is not the New River Gorge. I will be something no one expects. She even thought she might change her name, though she never did.

Lydde Falcone. The last.

Chapter 2

The Mystery Hole

U<small>NCLE</small> J<small>OHN</small> <small>WAS</small> six feet tall. At little Gauley Bridge High School that had been enough to play center on the basketball team, despite a dollop of clumsiness. He carried a slight stoop through his adult life. By the time Lydde was a teenager, Uncle John had a shock of brown hair that didn't thin in front even after it turned gray, but a bald circle gradually appeared on the crown of his head, like a tonsure. All this made him look like what he was, a physics professor, and what he was not, a medieval monk.

Roundbottom Farm was a mile down Fallam Mountain from Montefalco, isolated at the end of a dirt track that snaked into the Gorge from the highway. Uncle John and Aunt Lavinia had been at Roundbottom Farm less than a year when the house at Montefalco burned. They had met when John took a literature class at West Virginia Tech while completing the undergraduate work interrupted by the war. Lavinia was a new instructor and uncertain in her first job.

She assigned twice as much reading as she should have. But the class of veterans tolerated this, for after their ordeal they could not even think to complain about bookwork. Lavinia was a petite woman from a wealthy Charleston family, who wore wool skirts, cashmere sweaters, and a string of pearls in the classroom. She soon had her students standing beside their desks and reading Andrew Marvell aloud. Former Lieutenant John Cabell addressed the poems to her, and they fell in love.

When Lydde came into their lives, Uncle John was absent part of each week, at Ohio University finishing his dissertation in quantum physics while continuing to teach part-time at West Virginia Tech. The unexpected presence of an active two-year-old on top of his stunned grief for his sister Margaret caused him a number of sleepless nights.

"The timing is tough," he told Aunt Lavinia as they lay side by side in bed, staring at the ceiling.

"No," Aunt Lavinia said. "It's perfect."

"How could that be? It's so hard on you. You're here by yourself half the week, and even when I'm home, I'm holed up in my study."

"Exactly," she said. "I've been to Dr. Brook. I've got fibroid tumors. He says I should have a hysterectomy."

When Uncle John was silent, she added, "I can't give you a child, John."

He sensed she was crying and wiped her cheek with a thumb, then pulled her close. His own tears left damp spots in her hair. They listened as Lydde, asleep in a crib across the room, babbled in her sleep.

"She could be ours," Aunt Lavinia said.

"Don't get too attached," Uncle John warned. "Carlo will want her back after he's come to terms with all this."

"No, he won't," Aunt Lavinia said. "Whatever it takes to raise a child has been killed in him."

She was right.

.   .   .

THEY were different—Uncle John the dreamer, Aunt Lavinia the practical one—but both were independent and they gave each other plenty of room. After finishing his dissertation, Uncle John had time to nurture an obsession for ancient mathematicians he developed during the war, when he had been stationed in Britain, then North Africa, then Sicily. He read all he could about the Druids, the ancient Egyptians and Arabs, and the Mayans. Incredible mathematicians and astronomers, he told Aunt Lavinia. He had a notion that those ancient cultures might have spread farther than anyone suspected, that North American Indians had been in touch with them. An old man in Lafayette who claimed to be part Indian said his grandfather told stories of monks who crossed the ocean in reed boats and settled in the New River Gorge, that they scratched runes on the walls of caves. Uncle John decided to search the caves on Fallam Mountain for any markings that might remain.

"What if you find them?" Aunt Lavinia said, looking up briefly from the storybook she was reading to Lydde. "You won't be able to read them." Aunt Lavinia was not much interested in what she considered outlandish ideas, and only liked outdoor activities that produced tangible results, like gardening.

Uncle John shook his head and smiled as he pulled on his field jacket. "Then I'll get some good exercise out of it," he said. He headed up the dirt road, then turned into the woods, making for a rock outcropping shaped like a giant clamshell that hung just below the highway.

When he returned, he was so silent and shaken that Aunt Lavinia was alarmed. "What did you find?" she asked.

"Nothing," he said at first. When she persisted, he admitted that was not quite true. "I found a skeleton," he said.

"Good Lord!" Aunt Lavinia exclaimed. "You should call the police."

"No," Uncle John said. "It's an old skeleton, been there a long time. Probably an Indian. I don't think it would be right to disturb it or cart it off to some museum. It seems at rest."

For a while Aunt Lavinia insisted, but finally Uncle John said, "No. I don't want anyone going up there and messing around. I'll go back and say a prayer over it, if that will make you feel better. Otherwise that cave should be left alone."

He played with Lydde while Aunt Lavinia cooked supper, crossing the living room on all fours while the child clung to his back. When he tired, he pretended to buck so that she slid gently to the floor, then he caught her up in his arms.

"You know, Lydde," he whispered, his face close to hers, "I just may have an idea what happened to your brothers and sisters."

Lydde squealed with delight and pinched his nose.

THE New River is ancient, the oldest in the world, Uncle John was fond of claiming.

"It's silly to call it the New," Lydde said once with a child's logic.

Uncle John only shrugged. "That's not its real name," he said.

After that Lydde just called it the River.

The River runs north. It is littered with boulders the size of houses and cuts its way through worn humps of mountains so ancient them-selves that the River is indeed new to them. On some stretches there are rapids and every summer flotillas of bright yellow rafts filled with tourists ride the watery roller coaster. But that came later. When Uncle John and Aunt Lavinia moved to Roundbottom Farm, the River was empty save for the occasional fisherman.

Deep in a West Virginia hollow, you cannot see much of the moun-tain that shelters you. There were two ways to see Fallam Mountain properly. Lydde could ride in Uncle John's car across the River on a low highway bridge and up the flank of the mountain on the other side, Gauley Mountain. Partway up a winding road stood a rock out-crop Uncle John called the Overlook. It wasn't far from Roundbottom Farm but too dangerous to walk along the narrow shoulder of the switchback pavement.

The other view, from Fallam Point, was Lydde's favorite, even though they had to walk across Montefalco cove to reach it. Lydde liked that the only way to reach the Point was a path through the woods past stands of dark green rhododendron thick and tall as church walls. Sitting on the rock at the Point's end was like flying through the air on the back of a stone bird. This was where Uncle John and Aunt Lavinia took her when they were in the mood for a long walk, and told her stories about her family, and about the New River Gorge. Standing on the narrow nub of Fallam Point was, Uncle John said, like being an ant and perching on a person's outstretched fingertip to gaze at his or her head. Or heads, in this case. From the Point, Fallam appeared to be several mountains. But all was serpentine Fallam, with its folds and coves and cliffs. Beyond Fallam came Black and Droop and Sewell and on, a tangle of peaks seeming to stretch into infinity.

On the wall in Uncle John's study was a print of two men in rough garb standing in a formal pose on a rock outcrop, the mountains falling in waves behind them. Below them was the River. These were the explorers Thomas Batts and Robert Fallam, the first Englishmen to see the New River and its mountains, in 1671. Lydde learned about Batts and Fallam in school. Robert Fallam kept a journal and in it he wrote, *It was a pleasing tho' dreadful sight to see the mountains and Hills as if piled one upon another.*

From the house at Roundbottom Lydde could only see the wall of Fallam Mountain close on three sides, not the mountain whole. But her bedroom was on the back corner of the second floor, the southeast corner, wedged into those three sides of Fallam like a puzzle piece about to be locked in place.

ROUNDBOTTOM Farm sat at the bottom of a chute where Shades o' Death Creek bumped and dumped its way down Fallam Mountain, creating stairsteps of little waterfalls as it went. The property included some bottomland along the River where corn once grew, and there were gnarled fruit trees on a shelf of land around the mountain's curve. But such a fine house had not been supported by meager farmland. It was a miller's place. The old mill had burned down long before, but the house had stood since 1840. It was wood and solid, three stories high and odd because its porch did not wrap around the house but instead hid in a recess on the ground floor, walled in on three sides. Double doors were built into each wall and in the summer Aunt Lavinia threw them open to the breeze.

The house had other odd features. The built-in bookcase in the living room pulled away from the wall on a hinged door. Each bedroom had a large walk-in closet, which Aunt Lavinia said was unusual for houses of the time period.

"Why?" the ever-curious Lydde asked.

"They didn't have that many clothes to keep," Aunt Lavinia replied.

"Then what did they put in the closets?"

"People," Aunt Lavinia said.

Roundbottom Farm had been a stop on the Underground Railroad, Aunt Lavinia explained. "That's why your Uncle John's study has a little door in the wall. It's a secret hiding place. You could put a bed or desk in front of it and no one would know it was there."

Uncle John's study was nestled at the top of the house beneath the eaves. Lydde loved the way the roof sloped and caressed the windows. She wasn't allowed in the study while Uncle John was working. But fifteen minutes before supper was ready she would be sent to call him. She would charge up the stairs and then play in the secret room behind the little door, or explore the study while Uncle John put away his work. Papers and books were always stacked on every flat space, the overflow from a massive file cabinet and floor-to-ceiling bookshelves at one end of the room.

The wall opposite the bookshelves held several frames. The centerpiece was a large print of a painting by Salvador Dalí—*Christus*

Hypercubus, or Jesus Christ crucified on a tesseract. Uncle John said a tesseract was an unraveled hypercube.

"Dalí's trying to visualize the fourth dimension," he said.

Lydde thought of height, width, and depth. "What's the fourth dimension?"

"Time."

The Dalí looked to her like a neon cross she'd seen outside a Pentecostal church near Lafayette. She liked the word *tesseract* and the way Jesus looked like he was floating in air and might just fall off the cross instead of being stuck on.

Below the Dalí painting was a photograph of a circular hole blasted from ribbed rock. A small man stood beside the opening to show scale. *Hawks Nest Tunnel,* read the caption. Hawks Nest was just two miles downriver from Roundbottom Farm.

Beneath this was an antique print of an English church. *Old St. Pancras Parish Church, Norchester.* Lydde thought Pancras was a silly name.

And finally there was the print of Batts and Fallam discovering the New River in 1671.

The prints were flanked by a framed pair of quotations done up by Aunt Lavinia in calligraphy, one of her hobbies.

> *Magic is any sufficiently advanced technology.*
> —Arthur C. Clarke

And—

> *There are more things in heaven and earth, Horatio,*
> *than are dreamt of in our philosophy.*
> —William Shakespeare

Lydde learned later that each object on the wall had a purpose, and each was connected one to the other.

. . .

LYDDE was a dreamy child, stubborn and independent, happier entertaining herself than hanging out in a group. She played sandlot football and baseball. She had a handful of friends, mostly boys who treated her like a sister, and she seemed to require no more. Aunt Lavinia dutifully enrolled her in Girl Scouts and guitar lessons, and drove her to youth meetings at the Episcopal church. There were intermittent enthusiasms—Appalachian clog dance lessons, chess—that Lydde pursued for a time and then dropped. Sometimes the three of them would turn off the television and act out scenes from Shakespeare, Lydde playing Hamlet or Henry the Fifth while Uncle John and Aunt Lavinia held down all the supporting roles. But she liked best to curl up with a book or walk in the gorge with Uncle John.

They never went to the clamshell rock. Uncle John owned everything up to the highway right-of-way, and he had erected a plywood barrier around the cave. Lydde forgot the outcrop and ignored the site as she made her way up Fallam Mountain to the ruins of Montefalco. The cave was left untouched, as Uncle John wished, for twenty years. But the New River Gorge was gaining a reputation for tourism, drawing visitors for whitewater rafting and rock climbing, and Uncle John was afraid someone would stumble onto "his" cave and tear down the makeshift barricade.

By then Lydde had graduated from college and was living abroad, leaving Uncle John and Aunt Lavinia to reinvent themselves. Uncle John decided to build on top of the clamshell cave as a way of keeping people out. This made sense to Lavinia. If the cave's entrance was covered by a building and only Uncle John had the key, the skeleton would be undisturbed. What she didn't understand was why the building must be what she referred to as a "tourist trap." For Uncle John had decided to build an attraction for paying visitors that would defy gravity.

"Why spend your time on something like that?" she asked one morning over breakfast.

He shrugged. "It will bring in a little extra cash," he said.

"Not enough to even notice."

Uncle John sipped his coffee. "I think it would be fun," he said. "The only bad thing about living here at Roundbottom is we don't get many visitors. And with Lydde away it's awful quiet. Besides, it would be inspiring for my work."

Aunt Lavinia snorted. "Fleecing tourists would inspire your work?"

"Not fleecing tourists. Observing people as their sense of reality is confounded. Demonstrating over and over that what we think we experience is not what's real at all. It would get my juices flowing, the way writers take walks in the woods to get their creativity jump-started."

Aunt Lavinia shook her head. There were times, she realized, when she didn't understand her husband at all. But she enjoyed humoring him, so she watched good-naturedly as the Mystery Hole took shape.

Uncle John had tenure and no longer taught summer term. He hired some of his students to help with his new project. They took a backhoe to the site between the highway and the clamshell cave, and dug all one summer, then poured concrete. By the time school started, the building, an old Quonset hut reinforced with a frame of logs, was up. Uncle John worked on the interior during his spare time that winter. No one helped with that part, and he sometimes worked alone into the night. In May of 1971 the Mystery Hole opened for business.

At its heart the Mystery Hole was a simple room built foursquare into the bedrock of lower Fallam Mountain. But Uncle John had designed the room so that it appeared to defy gravity. It was turned on its side so that what should have been the floor appeared to be a wall, and furniture had been nailed to a wall so that it appeared to be the floor. Exposed to the light, the secret of the Mystery Hole would have been simple, an architectural version of Donald O'Connor dancing on the walls in *Singin' In The Rain*. But underground, with nothing to help with orientation, the Mystery Hole did indeed seem to defy gravity. A warning, perhaps, against taking things out of context.

The Mystery Hole became something of a cult favorite and was open at Uncle John's whim only, so that part of its charm was in bragging that one had actually gotten in. Visitors reached the underground room by filing past the "Rules of the Hole"—NO SMOKING NO SHOVING NO RUNNING—and along a passageway that twisted and turned until it was hard to say which way was up and which way was down. When people finally stepped inside the chamber, they were ushered to a bench and urged to sit cautiously. Except the back of the bench was what would have been the floor and what appeared to be the floor would have been the far wall aboveground. The "walls" were decorated with a variety of black light posters and the lights were doused for a time to allow for a few minutes of glow-in-the-dark and Rolling Stones music.

Then the lights came up, a red door opened, and Uncle John popped out, trying not to show how carefully he was walking. He performed a variety of gravity-defying feats such as pouring water up into a cup, and placing a ball at the foot of a ramp and letting it go to roll uphill on its own. When the show was done, the disoriented visitors heaved themselves from their seats with great difficulty and staggered against gravity up the exit ramp.

Uncle John accumulated the Hole's decorations over the years. Unusual hubcaps, shined to a fault, covered one outside wall, and metal pie tins, each bearing a brightly colored letter spelling MYSTERY HOLE, were nailed to the entrance. A life-sized plastic gorilla, arm upraised and fangs bared, crowned the roof. A hand-painted sign above the door proclaimed, SEE THE MYSTERY HOLE, and another along the porch railing added,

SEE FOR YOURSELF
NATURE'S BEAUTY SEEMS TO HAVE GONE AND
LOST ITS BALANCE

Down from the building, the gorge plummeted out of sight past a rock cliff, and beyond the River continued to complain in a low moan as it gnawed its way through rock.

LYDDE played Ado Annie in her high school's production of *Oklahoma!* and was hooked on acting. She went to Duke University on scholarship with a double major in history and theater. In her happiest moments she stood in the wings waiting for her entrance, so charged with nervous energy that she bounced on tiptoe as though on the end of a diving board, then launched herself onstage, plunging through heavy air into another dimension, a parallel universe of dust-mote light with a black sky above and scuffed wooden boards for a ground.

Her senior year she was off to London for an exchange program in Elizabethan theater. Aunt Lavinia and Uncle John took her to meet the train for New York. She sat between them, wearing jeans, Keds, and a white Duke T-shirt. All her belongings were stuffed into a long canvas duffel bag, for she had not yet begun to accumulate things and still possessed the turtlelike freedom of the young and the homeless. A thick white fog filled the Gorge and muffled the sounds of rushing water and birdsong.

Lydde climbed aboard the train in the West Virginia dawn after hugging her tearful aunt and uncle, and read *Howards End* in paperback and dreamed out the window at passing mountains and fields and city neighborhoods dense and tiny as scale models, dozed through a New Jersey night until she woke on cue to black-and-gold Manhattan soaring on the horizon. There she boarded a plane for London, and her new life.

LONDON in those days was a dowdy city, despite Carnaby Street and the British music revolution. Lydde liked it at once. People were not stylish, their houses were small and cold, with radiators that clanked and windows that rattled when the wind blew. The popular new restaurants were those that badly mimicked American diners; there people sat with knife and fork in hand, cutting properly away at burgers in buns. Greasy fish-and-chip papers blew about in the wind and the gutters were littered with fruit peels and cigarette butts. It was fine by Lydde. She would have been put off by neatness and intimidated by glitz.

By day she attended classes. Most nights she went to plays, cheap standing-room-only tickets. She memorized the names of the theaters and made a litany of them to recite on her solitary walks—

Adelphi Albany Aldwych
Duchess DukeofYork Garrick
St.Martins Strand Wyndhams.

Best of all, the Royal Court. They were musty, most of them, some with atrophied balconies once for the nobility and now unused, others plain. In nooks and crannies of the basement and upper stairwells, glasses of wine were served at dark oak bars that reminded her of the altar rail and communion cup at All Saints Episcopal Church back home. Gielgud and Richardson and Olivier, Bates and Schofield, Dench and the Redgraves passed like a parade of the hallowed. She watched them over and over, studying their gestures and intonation, went back to her room and jotted down the details in a notebook.

At the end of the year, Lydde auditioned at the Royal Academy of Dramatic Arts and was accepted. When she called home with the news, Aunt Lavinia wailed, "You'll never come back."

Lydde cried as well. She had not seen her aunt and uncle, or the mountains, in nine months. But she wanted to stay in London.

"Can you call Duke and have them mail me my diploma?" she asked. "And could you ship my books?"

"Won't you miss the mountains?" Uncle John asked in his turn.

"I already do," she said. "And I miss you. But the theater here—I can't explain it. If you want to be a priest, this is the Vatican."

"America has theater," he stubbornly insisted.

"I know," Lydde said. "But I want something that can't be taken away."

"They can't take the mountains."

"No," Lydde agreed. "But you know what I mean."

He did. More than anyone he knew how it had hurt her to see her father come and go. And all the rest. It was Uncle John who found Lydde up the hollow, by herself, scraping through burned ruins with her stick.

Thirty years later, when he went to England for the last of his periodic visits, he told Lydde he had been wrong about the mountains.

LYDDE was never famous, nor wanted to be. She was a character actress, no Judi Dench or Vanessa Redgrave. She liked the smaller parts, cozy and warm as a pair of bedroom slippers. While the leads carried the burden of the reviews and the audience, Lydde lounged in the dressing rooms reading magazines, gossiping. For a few moments suspended in time she plunged onstage, and now and then she stole the show.

She started out in improv with Joan Littlewood in the East End. But she left after a time, drawn to Shakespeare. Two years with the Royal Shakespeare Company at Stratford, a year at the Young Vic, parts in the West End, but as much time spent in Hammersmith, Reading, Birmingham, Edinburgh, Bristol. Anywhere to pay the bills.

Actors, like athletes, have superstitions. On Lydde's first opening night she began a habit she never relinquished. Before going to the dressing rooms, she walked the interior of the theater in street clothes. She went to the top of the dress circle and walked the length of the rows, one after another, like a labyrinth, then down to the stalls, and finally back to one of the wings and onto the stage, where she stood a moment staring up at the top of the dress circle from whence she had begun her pilgrimage. Lydde learned later that Aborigines in Australia go on walkabout, singing the stories of their Ancestor, and that's something of what she felt she was doing, walking the story into existence so she could then inhabit the part properly. All she knew was it worked.

Lydde's first and biggest break came early in 1974. She was facing eviction from her Clerkenwell flat. The hot young director Phil Dunleavy was mounting a production of *Henry IV Part One* at the Royal Court and talking all around about spitting in the face of the Shakespeare establishment.

"The only reason to keep doing Shakespeare," Dunleavy told the *Guardian,* "is if you can find a way to subvert him."

Bullshit, Lydde thought, then checked the pitiful state of her bankbook, toted up the number of failed auditions she'd had recently, and wondered how far Mr. Dunleavy was really willing to go.

In West Virginia she had been a tomboy, which was easy there. You didn't find many little girls into frilly dresses and patent leather shoes. In the days before the audition she dreamed herself back to the New River, climbing rock faces, launching herself off the side of Fallam Mountain while clinging to a gnarled grapevine, wrestling boys to a draw. Scrabbling around burned ruins with a stick in her hand.

She cut her hair short and strode into the audition wearing jeans, an oversized sweatshirt, and her best hillbilly swagger.

Dunleavy looked startled, then amused, as she stood in front of him. He left his seat and came up onto the stage. "Err—but aren't you a woman?" he finally asked.

Lydde raised her chin and stared him down for a moment. Then she said, "'Do not think so; you shall not find it so. And God forgive them that so much have swayed your majesty's good thoughts away from me.'" She leaned closer. "'I will redeem all this on Percy's head, and in the closing of some glorious day be bold to tell you that I— am—your—son.'"

His eyes narrowed and he stood still, wondering whether to laugh or to tell her to stop wasting his time. Then he looked down at his script and said, "Act One, Scene Two. 'Now, Hal, what time of day is it, lad?'"

Lydde found the place and replied, "'Thou art so fat-witted with drinking of old sack, and unbuttoning thee after supper, and sleeping upon benches after noon, that thou hast forgotten to demand that truly which thou wouldst truly know.'"

He smiled and said, "You've got a good rich voice. You could almost fool me. But really—"

"'The *fico* for thee then,'" she interrupted, and thrust her finger in an obscene gesture so abrupt Dunleavy took a step back.

He waved at the AD standing nearby—"Get a sword over here." And when she had it in hand—"Draw on me."

Lydde did, and set the point neatly at his throat. "'Thou owest God a death,'" she said with venom.

Dunleavy turned abruptly and left the stage, followed by the AD. They stood in the front row arguing and Lydde stepped downstage to listen.

"Innovation is one thing," the AD was saying, "but this would be a joke."

Lydde yelled, "Do you know how old Hal was?"

They turned and looked at her.

"He was fourteen," she answered her own question, "when he fought in that battle."

"Pardon me," the AD said, "but we're having a conference here."

"His voice was just changing," she persisted, ignoring the AD and focusing on Dunleavy. "He wasn't an irresponsible prince, he was a kid fighting for his life. Acting goofy sometimes, but then so damn charismatic he couldn't help but rally the troops. You'll never get a guy in his twenties to pull that off." She pointed the sword at the AD. "'Think not, Percy, to share glory with me any more.'"

He threw up his hands. "Right, Phil, do you want to see the rest of them or not?"

"Of course," Dunleavy said. He gestured Lydde offstage. "Someone will call you."

She wavered a moment, leaning on the sword, then dropped it and sauntered offstage, unable to let go. When she was just out of sight, he called her back.

"Just curious," he said. "Are you American?"

"You bet."

"I thought so. Only an American woman can walk that way. So bold it's almost heartbreaking."

A week later he called to tell Lydde she had the part. And he asked her to dinner.

The relationship only lasted a couple of months. Lydde realized quickly that Phil, a tall lanky man with a wisp of red beard, liked her better as Hal than as Lydde. When Lydde told him they wouldn't work as a couple, he told her she would have made a great lesbian.

"Too bad," she said. "I've never had the remotest interest in women."

But Lydde wasn't doing so well with men either, she had to admit. She wasn't sure if she had an incorrigible independent streak toughened by abandonment or if she was just too picky. She ran from safe, sweet guys because they seemed boring or wimpy. But she let herself be swept off her feet by jerks who turned out to be sleeping with two other women at the same time. She fell hard for gay men, and fended off married men, who seemed to find her intriguing because she wasn't like their wives, but who were clearly not ready to leave those wives, and wouldn't really have wanted her if they were.

Prince Hal was the hardest role Lydde had to quit, and not only because of the great reviews and her sole Olivier Award nomination. Every night she sat before her dressing room mirror, her face surrounded by a circle of lights while the makeup man applied dark smudges beneath her eyes. Her black hair had been cut to its medieval male pudding-bowl length, the back of her neck shaved to the base of her skull. With her high cheekbones, pale complexion, and large gray eyes, Lydde looked like the photograph of her lost oldest brother Louis. Out on the street she sometimes left off her makeup and lipstick and passed for male, once even going into a men's loo (but leaving at once because of the stench of urine). She looked often into mirrors—a handsome boy. She was falling in love with her own face.

LYDDE moved back and forth between London and New York. Some years she rented an efficiency in the East Village while she worked at Joseph Papp's Public Theater, others she stayed in London or moved about among the English provinces. It was a nomad's life like her father's had been, and not one that lent itself to establishing relationships.

Twenty-three years passed. In middle age, acting roles for women were fewer and the competition fiercer. At last Lydde left London, which she could no longer afford, to become director of the Repertory Theater in Norchester, a small cathedral city near the Channel in the southwest of England. Uncle John came for what would be his last visit. He was alone. Aunt Lavinia was visiting a sister in Arizona and Uncle John didn't care for Arizona—too hot and brown; or the sister—too much of a snob. Besides, he said on the telephone, he had to talk to Lydde in person.

When she picked him up at Heathrow, he slumped beside her in the seat, blasted by jet lag. She was shocked at how he had aged, though she shouldn't have been. He was in his seventies, and she had not seen him in two years. He looked as pale as an overexposed photograph.

Lydde reached over and squeezed his hand. He smiled. "So, how's the job?" he asked.

"It's okay," she said, trying to sound enthusiastic. "I get to choose the plays, and I direct two a year. There's a lot of paperwork, grant applications and so forth."

"Any acting?"

Lydde shook her head. "Two plays in four years. None in London."

"Directing's not the same, is it?"

"No. I miss acting terribly."

"You still want to stay in England?"

She took her time answering because she knew he was going to try to talk her into going back to West Virginia. But she finally admitted, "It's funny, but my home was the stage. Without that, I'm not as comfortable here. I feel at loose ends. I suppose that makes me sound a bit barmy, not at home in the real world. But other actors know what I mean."

"'Barmy.' That sounds British. You need to spend some time in West Virginia."

"Uncle John, don't start."

"Lavinia wanted to see you," he said, "but she wasn't interested in coming to England again. She said last time we were here it looked too much like America."

"Is that why you didn't bring her along this time?"

"I wanted you to myself," he said, and patted her arm. Then he nodded off for the rest of the way. But he woke when they reached Norchester and looked around eagerly. "Amazing," he murmured, "that you would end up here. But maybe not so amazing."

"What do you mean?" she asked.

Then he clammed up.

THE first day he did little but sleep off the jet lag. The next day he slept in, but Lydde left work early and returned home to make him lunch. She was in fortunate circumstances—the flat provided by the Rep took up the ground floor of a restored Jacobean building alongside Priory Park, and in the evening she could look out the window and fancy she saw the shades of friars wandering among the trees.

"Did you know," Uncle John said as they ate roast turkey sandwiches, "this building used to be the jail?"

"Really? How did you know?"

"Did some research before I got here."

After lunch they went for a walk. Norchester was a pretty cathedral town. Its river, the Pye, was placid, with swans and ducks passing in majestic flotillas and brightly painted houseboats moored to the shore. South of the city the river opened into an estuary that had once been a working port but was now given over to pleasure craft. It was said Joseph of Arimathea first set foot on British soil nearby, leaving deep prints in the wet sand as he trekked the half mile when the tide was out. He was on his way to Glastonbury with the Holy Grail, and a ruined abbey named for him crowned a cliff to Norchester's southeast.

Uncle John stopped often on the riverbank to stare at the spires of the cathedral or stand in an intersection to study a row of black-and-white buildings which once might have housed candlers and coppersmiths but now were Pizza Hut, a Waterstone bookstore, and a real estate agency. Then he leaned on Lydde's arm and gestured north along the Pye.

"Let's mosey on up that way. I'd like to see what's there now."

"What do you mean, 'now'?" Lydde asked.

Uncle John actually blushed. "I don't mean anything special," he said.

Lydde was more disconcerted by his response than by his initial slip, if that was what it had been. For that was what he seemed to think it was. She tried to tease him. "If I didn't know better, I'd think you've been to Norchester before."

"Let's walk," he said.

She put her arm through his and guided him along the shaded river path.

"When I was a kid," she said, "you used to have a print on your study wall, an old church here in Norchester. St. Pancras."

"I still have it," he said. He refused to meet her eyes, as though this were some sort of guilty admission.

"Why Norchester?" Lydde asked.

He didn't answer.

"Because I was thinking about it after I moved here," she continued. "I thought it was a coincidence too that I ended up here. And I asked about St. Pancras Church, and sure enough, there's a St. Pancras. You walk out Eastgate Street about a mile beyond the old medieval walls. But it didn't look anything like your picture and the cornerstone says it was built in the 1800s."

He sighed. "The old church burned," he said. Lydde waited out another silence and he finally added, "Who knows why things interest us? When your mom and I were kids, our mother told us her ancestors came from Norchester. It just stuck in my mind, that's all."

"And the picture of the church?"

"Your Aunt Lavinia found it in an antique shop one vacation we took to the Outer Banks when you were little. She knew about the connection and bought it for my birthday."

Lydde didn't quite believe him, or at least didn't think he was telling her everything. She had always known Uncle John to be direct with her and it was plain when he was not. They went on in silence past a footbridge spanning the Pye into a residential neighborhood. He was walking more slowly, as though tiring, but when Lydde glanced at his face it was not weariness she saw but a mixture of anticipation and reluctance. Then he stopped. "There," he said. He was staring at a rambling Tudor house set in a deep-walled garden which backed onto the riverbank. Only the gabled roof and upper floor were visible.

"Yes," Lydde said. "Soane's Croft."

He smiled slightly.

"It's a tourist attraction," she added. "It belonged to a doctor back in the seventeenth century and they've preserved a lot of the old medical implements. Plus there's a little restaurant and a nice garden where you can buy fresh herbs. Keeps with the medical theme, I guess."

"You've been inside?" He was still staring at the house.

"Once to poke around. Doing the tourist thing when I first moved here. And I've had lunch there lots of times. The food's very good. You want to stop in?"

They had reached a heavy iron gate set in the wall at the back of the house and were peering through at a large garden with beds of roses, columbine, and wisteria. A few tourists were wandering the gravel paths with cameras round their necks. Uncle John shook his head suddenly and backed away. "No," he said. "Doesn't interest me."

Right, Lydde thought.

THE next day Uncle John's mood seemed to lift. They had mornings together, then he went off on his own in the afternoons while Lydde was at the theater. In the evenings he came to the plays or stayed in Lydde's flat with a book. One night he ushered her inside with an excitement he had obviously been hoarding until her return.

"Have you spent much time in the cathedral?" he asked.

Lydde smiled and said, "I'm there almost every Sunday."

This caught him by surprise. Uncle John was senior warden of All Saints, Lafayette, in the county seat back home. But he'd given up trying to get Lydde there once she hit high school, and she hadn't mentioned church since she'd been in England.

"I started back in London a couple of years ago," she said, "and I just kept it up. Don't get me wrong, I'm still a skeptic. But it's a lovely cathedral, this one. If there is a God, He'd like this cathedral."

She didn't tell him how important it had become to her to be there on Sunday for the Eucharist. Lydde didn't like sounding holy, even to Uncle John, and anyway it wasn't really holiness she felt. It was much like the stage, which she missed desperately, the feeling of stepping through an invisible curtain into a parallel world, another existence, and participating in the great stories as they played out in all their tragedy and joy. That was what Lydde felt as the priests moved from lectern to pulpit to altar.

Uncle John was looking pleased. "Have you read all the cathedral memorials?" he asked.

Like most old English churches, Norchester Cathedral was covered floor to ceiling with memorial plaques in the nave, the chapels, the cloisters, and every other odd place.

Lydde raised her eyebrows. "All of them? That would take forever. Anyway there's nobody there I'd be familiar with."

"Don't be so sure," he said with a Cheshire cat smile. "Come with me tomorrow morning?"

So next morning Lydde went with him through the ancient archway that opened into Southgate Street, and down the narrow lane into the cathedral close. Inside the nave of the cathedral he stopped.

"This is interesting," he said. "A labyrinth." He pointed to an engraving in the stone floor. It was as though he were a tour guide.

"I know," she said. "Older even than the one at Chartres."

"And an older pattern. A carryover from the Celts, maybe." He stepped to the edge. "Let's walk it first. Put us in the mood for my big surprise."

Labyrinths look like mazes. Except a maze is a puzzle, with dead ends leading to confusion, backtracking, getting lost. A labyrinth will lead you along its winding paths, around the edge of the circle, then inward, seeming sometimes to carry you away from the center so you think you are lost, but in reality leading you on and in to the heart. There you stop and think or pray or resolve or just breathe, then you are led out again, retracing your steps, until you are back where you started. The Chartres labyrinth is cruciform, with its four quarters ornate as the petals of a flower. At Norchester the labyrinth was plain by comparison, only the path outlined, a two-dimensional ball of yarn. They walked slowly, silently, and Lydde felt herself grow peaceful.

Afterward Uncle John said, "Every physicist should do that now and then."

"Why?" Lydde asked, but he was already heading for the cloister.

"Here," he said, and stopped. They were standing by one of the arches that opened onto the green rectangle of the cloister garden. Just above eye level a clutch of cherubs guarded an engraved plaque.

In Memoriam
Robert James Fallam
Born March 3, 1623 Died February 15, 1702
He served his King in the New World
Beloved father

"Our Robert Fallam?" Lydde asked.

Uncle John nodded. "Batts and Fallam, first Englishmen to reach our mountains. And to see the rivers flowing west. Robert Fallam was from Norchester and came back here after his adventures." He pointed. "And below is the mystery."

For there was more. After a fulsome description of his "beloved mother" Elizabeth, the son who had placed the memorial added his uncle.

Noah Henry Fallam
dissenter
Born September 16, 1625
Lost in the wilderness of Virginia 1671
God shall not be mocked

Lydde shivered suddenly and glanced at Uncle John. He was watching her. He put his hand on her arm. "Let's get a pot of tea."

Beyond the cloister was a self-serve restaurant that opened onto its own walled garden. They carried pots of tea and plates of salmon and cucumber sandwiches to a sunlit table beside a grape arbor. Uncle John looked around as though trying to memorize his surroundings.

"You knew Robert Fallam came from Norchester?" Lydde asked, recalling the print on his study wall.

"Yes," he said.

"And about the one who was lost?"

He shrugged. "Noah. The history books don't mention him. But that's not unusual. They usually only talk about the expedition leader. Sounds like he was something of a family scandal, doesn't he?" He stared at Lydde over his teacup and said, "I wish you'd come home."

Lydde smiled. "Now, there's a change of subject."

But Uncle John looked suddenly as if he were about to cry.

"What's wrong?" she said quickly. "Does this have something to do with why you came over here now, without Aunt Lavinia? Is one of you sick?"

"No," he said. "Nothing except old age pains. But I've got to tell you something and I've been dreading it, because it will do just the opposite of convince you to come back, and because it's so damned . . ." He stared over her head and took a deep breath. "They're destroying the mountains," he said.

Lydde stared at him, uncomprehending. "What do you mean? How do you destroy—"

"The mountains," he repeated. "Mountains that have been there since the beginning of time. Fallam and the two behind it, Droop and Black. They're flattening the entire range."

"But you can't flatten a mountain range!"

"For the coal," he continued as if she hadn't spoken. "They blow up the tops of the mountains and they fill in the hollows and streams all around with the dirt and rock. It makes a flat plain for miles and miles. Three square miles of rock and scrub grass in place of Fallam Mountain. It's gone, Lydde, from the highway up."

She shook her head. "If this was a novel, no one would believe you." But his face told her it was so.

"Robert Fallam," he said. "He wrote, '*a pleasing tho' dreadful sight to see the mountains and Hills as if piled one upon another.*' Not anymore."

Lydde was trying to fathom it. How could a mountain just disappear? How could a mountain range— "But if they took off the top of the mountain and filled in from the highway on up—"

He finished for her. "The house is gone too."

Lydde knew he didn't mean Roundbottom Farm, Uncle John and Aunt Lavinia's house, which was at the foot of the mountain near the River. When they referred to the house, they meant the one that had burned: Carlo and Margaret's house, where Lydde had spent hours digging through a charred ruin with a stick.

"The foundation is gone?"

"All of Montefalco is gone. Climb thirty feet past the Mystery Hole and you come to what they call a valley fill. It's a huge terraced wall of dirt where the hollow used to be. Fallam Point is still there, but you can't get to it. The only way I know it wasn't covered is you can see it from the Overlook across the river on Gauley Mountain."

Lydde couldn't picture what he meant. No mountain, no hollow, no house. He went on to say they'd been blasting and flattening for the five years since her last visit. He'd not breathed a word to her, had wanted her back and knew that would be the end of it.

"That's the truth," Lydde said. "You tell me why anyone would want to go back to that? Why isn't the government stopping it? What kind of crazy—"

"I have to show you," he interrupted. "Now that I've told you about Fallam Mountain, you can't comprehend it, can you? You won't until you see it. But there's more, and it's even more impossible to explain, so you have to come. That's the only way."

Lydde was getting irritated. "You're making this into some kind of weird mystery."

"It *is* a mystery. I can't explain until you come home. All I can say is that we've lost more than a mountain, but not everything, and I need to show you." He took her hand. "It's a physics experiment. I'm getting old. Lavinia and I won't be around much longer. I need to pass on what I know to someone younger."

"But I don't know the first thing about physics!"

"I want to teach you. That's why I need you back."

That night Lydde lay awake and tried to recall what it was like

there, the wild riverbed filled with boulders, the hoary, craggy cliffs
and ragged mountains. Some of them now apparently disappeared.

If she shut out that last terrible image, she could understand Uncle
John's point. Hard to comprehend the intoxication of the stage without standing on the boards, the cathedral without the smell of old
stone and incense, the ancient gorge without the rush of water and
gray ghosts of mist.

BEFORE Uncle John returned to West Virginia, Lydde asked if he
wanted to see the new St. Pancras Church, but he shook his head.
"Wouldn't be the same," he said.

He was just as adamant about the house called Soane's Croft, but
when Lydde was laundering his shirts she found a ticket stub for
admittance to the place in his breast pocket. She said nothing. At
Heathrow she promised him she would come back—home, he
insisted she call it—when her contract with Norchester Rep was done.
Eight months, Lydde said.

It was too long to wait. Three weeks later Aunt Lavinia called. She
had found Uncle John slumped over his desk, dead from a heart
attack.

Chapter 3

Lydde Falling

U NCLE JOHN'S DEATH set Lydde in motion. It was past time, she decided, to return to West Virginia. He had wanted her there to show her something important, and now it was too late. But there was still Aunt Lavinia. And the mystery with which Uncle John had tantalized her might still be able to be discovered. She was done with England anyway. Two years in Norchester had cost her close contact with London friends, and she'd made few new ones in the small town. So she resigned her position, sold her London flat for a tidy sum, and headed home.

Aunt Lavinia met Lydde at the Charleston airport. She seemed little changed, her hair iron-gray and styled the way she'd always had it, parted at the side and worn straight to the bottom of her ears. She had a long nose, high cheekbones, and a broad mouth—more English than the English, Uncle John used to say. She had on a blue cotton knit skirt and striped seersucker blouse, since she never wore pants unless she was working in the garden.

She immediately turned the car over to Lydde, saying driving was beginning to be a strain at her age. It was a bit of a mistake, since Lydde had been driving on the left side of the road so long, but she got them back home with only a few minor scares. Lydde was jet-lagged, but she wanted to see Uncle John's grave before she went to Round-bottom Farm. She was afraid otherwise she would be expecting him to be waiting at the door. He was buried in the community cemetery on the outskirts of Lafayette, although Aunt Lavinia was waiting for Lydde's return before holding a memorial service. Lydde had thought Aunt Lavinia might have had Uncle John cremated. But Aunt Lavinia was uncomfortable with cremation, seeing it as a foreign and somewhat disreputable practice. Besides, she said, there were the terrible memories of fire.

Aunt Lavinia had marked the grave with a bronze plaque provided by the U.S. Army for deceased veterans, rather than a granite headstone. A built-in vase held an arrangement of plastic roses. Beside Uncle John's name and dates—*John Thomas Cabell, born June 6, 1924, died April 17, 2001*—she'd had her own name added—*Lavinia Alice Henley Cabell, born November 14, 1925* and a space for the date of death.

"I'll be beside him when my time comes," said Aunt Lavinia. "And of course your mother is right over here." She gestured to the nearest grave. *Margaret Cabell Falcone, May 10, 1917–December 24, 1948.* "You remember, we used to bring you here on Memorial Day."

"Yes, of course."

"There's plenty of room," Aunt Lavinia said. "You could be here too someday. A regular family plot."

Lydde shuddered visibly.

"Not that it will be anytime soon," Aunt Lavinia hastened to add.

But it wasn't the thought of her own death that had given Lydde a start. At age fifty-five she was acknowledging that she was on the downhill path, that what once seemed unimaginable was now unavoidable though hopefully postponable. No, what she found disquieting was the idea of a family plot with most of the family missing. Her father had, strangely enough, left a will in his motel room in Las Vegas, spelling out his express desire to be cremated and scattered to the desert wind. And her brothers and sisters? Carlo Falcone had steadfastly refused to consider the possibility of their deaths and had dared Uncle John and Aunt Lavinia to put up a memorial stone.

The cemetery left Lydde sad and exhausted. She turned the wheel back over to Aunt Lavinia for the drive to Roundbottom Farm.

"I suppose I should show you what they've done to the mountains," Aunt Lavinia said when they were within a mile of home.

Lydde glanced fearfully out the window, but she couldn't tell what Aunt Lavinia was talking about. Walls of mountain rose on all sides, sporting their late spring green. "It looks the same as always," she said. Except, it occurred to her, they hadn't passed any familiar houses for a while.

"You can't tell from the road," said Aunt Lavinia. "They're real careful about that. What you're looking at is like those fake fronts of western towns they use for cowboy movies. Nothing behind. We could stop and—"

"No," Lydde said quickly. "Not today." They passed the Mystery Hole, which now had a CLOSED sign in the parking lot. Lydde forced herself not to look to the right, where Montefalco had been. She wanted to lie down, turn her face to the wall, and cry herself to sleep.

AT breakfast the next morning, Aunt Lavinia said, "You'll want to see the study. I doubt if you'll notice much different. I tried now and then to talk him into new furniture, or a nice painting for the wall, but he would never let me touch a thing."

Lydde stirred a bowl of granola. "Did he ever talk about his work? Since his retirement, I mean."

"Not much. He was working on a lot of calculations, I know that. But it's all Greek to me."

Calculations. Lydde wouldn't understand them either, no more than Aunt Lavinia. What could they have to do with her?

"When he came to see me," she said, "he hinted that he'd found out something he wanted to show me."

Aunt Lavinia sat down at the table and shook her head. "I wouldn't know about that. To tell the truth, the last few days were very odd. You know I was in Arizona visiting Edith? When I got home he was back from England. But he was acting strange, very strange."

"What do you mean?" Lydde tried to recall Uncle John as she had left him at Heathrow. Subdued, but not strange.

"To be honest," said Aunt Lavinia, "I think he must have suffered a small stroke. You read about that, you know, and I expect it might happen to me too. Old people have them and don't even know it sometimes. Physically he seemed fine, but he didn't talk much. And when he did . . ." She hesitated. "You'll think I'm the strange one," she said.

"No, go on."

"It's just that he talked funny. Sort of halting, and not in complete sentences. Sometimes it sounded like he had an accent. He called me 'thee' and 'thou,' as if he were a Quaker or something. He had a look on his face like he had to concentrate hard to get the words out. And most of the time he'd just communicate with gestures, as though he knew he sounded odd and was hoping I wouldn't notice. Plus he had a hard time understanding me. When I suggested he ought to go to the doctor and have his hearing checked, he just shook his head. But he did tell me he was having some chest pain, so I took him to Lafayette to Dr. Khan.

"Actually, that's something else that was odd. He refused to drive and he seemed terrified in the car. You know he always insisted on driving. Anyway, we found out John's heart was in terrible shape. Dr. Khan couldn't figure it out, it had deteriorated so suddenly. He scheduled surgery, but the next day John was gone. I didn't even have a chance to tell you how sick he was."

"Is Dr. Khan a good doctor? You trust he didn't miss something?"

"Oh yes, he's always been very dependable." Aunt Lavinia started to clear away the dishes, but Lydde beat her to it. After she closed the dishwasher, Aunt Lavinia said, "Something else. Silly to talk about. But when I got back from Arizona he insisted on separate bedrooms. And all he ever wanted to do was watch television. He'd sit there for hours and stare at it." Then she started to cry. "Of course, I shouldn't talk about such things to you. But we had been very happy, in our way. And I felt like—like there was something wrong with me all of a sudden. Did he—did something happen over there in England?"

"You mean— No, of course not! He was looking forward to seeing you again, I'm sure of it."

Aunt Lavinia had barely listened for an answer. "I know I'm old," she sobbed. "But so was he. It never seemed to matter before."

Lydde patted her hand awkwardly. "I'm sure it wasn't that. Nothing happened in England, Aunt Lavinia. But he was very preoccupied, and he kept hinting at some kind of secret. I don't think it had anything to do with you. I think he had something on his mind and I bet he was just wanting some privacy."

"He didn't keep secrets from me," Aunt Lavinia sniffed, dabbing at her nose with a napkin.

Not true, Lydde thought. But she merely said, "He was still working it out when he died. Whatever it was."

LYDDE decided to spend the day in his study looking for "whatever it was." She climbed the stairs with a mug of hot coffee and sat for a long time in his chair, watching dust motes floating in a shaft of light from the window. Trying to recall him, to send a message to him wherever he might be. Uncle John and Lydde used to speak of death when she was a child. He had a telescope he'd bought in Charleston and he would set it up in the lower yard and look at the stars. Lydde often tagged along, but frankly the telescope didn't interest her. She preferred to lie on her back and soak in the starry expanse with her own eyes, to feel as though she were riding the earth through the air, like a captain lashed to the mast of his ship. Sometimes Uncle John would abandon the telescope and join her.

"Is this what it feels like be on a ship in the ocean?" she asked once.

"Yes," he said, "it felt just like this when I crossed to Europe on the troop ship."

"Why are the stars so small?"

"They're not small, just a long ways off."

"Can a spaceship go there?"

"Not yet. But we don't have to wait for a spaceship to be invented. As soon as people die, they take off for the stars. Faster than any spaceship. And they can go anywhere they want, to the stars or across time."

Many people don't approve of bringing up the subject of death to children. One of our culture's hangups, Uncle John said. But he decided, given Lydde's history, to acquaint her with his ideas on the subject. He didn't want her to be afraid of death, he said, he wanted her to wonder and marvel at it.

"Do we go to heaven when we die?" Lydde asked.

He shook his head. "No. Heaven is just what people settled on because they don't have enough imagination to think of anything else. We go to more than heaven. We go everywhere God is, and that means everywhere."

"Is that where my brothers and sisters are? Are they everywhere?"

"I don't know. Maybe." He took her hand and gave it a squeeze. "Don't worry, Lydde. If that's where they are, we'll find them someday."

Sitting in his chair, she could almost imagine him holding her hand again. Is that where you are, Uncle John? she wondered. Are you everywhere? Lydde wished she had seen his body, as Aunt Lavinia had. Then she could know that the real Uncle John was no longer with them, that what was left was not him at all. As it was, he seemed as lost as her brothers and sisters.

Lydde swiveled abruptly in the chair and began going through his drawers. Not much there except the usual odds and ends, envelopes and typing paper, thumbtacks, paper clips, a box of staples and a stapler. In the bottom drawer, though, she found a small red notebook which she removed and laid on the desk.

It was bound with metal rings and filled with closely lined pages, many of them covered with calculations. She flipped through the pages, only half paying attention, until she came to a diagram at the back. Uncle John had superimposed a Chartres labyrinth over a topographic map of the Gorge. He had marked an X at a point on the map where the Mystery Hole stood—which coincided with the entrance of the labyrinth—and labeled it *PORTAL I*. Beneath that he'd added a mathematical formula of some kind.

Whatever, Lydde thought, disappointed there was nothing else on the diagram. Then she turned and studied the wall behind her. The pictures and quotations were still there. But hanging by a nail beneath the Shakespeare quote was something she hadn't seen before—two keys on a chain. One looked perfectly normal, small and coppery and bearing the name U.S. Lock. The other was large, nearly four inches long, and looked very old, like a movie prop. A piece of paper had been rolled like a cigarette and stuck through the handle of the large key. She removed the paper, actually a thick piece of parchment, and unrolled it carefully, for it seemed fragile, the edges somewhat discolored. It was written in a strange hand which was difficult to read, for some of the characters were oddly shaped. It took a while, but she finally deciphered most of it.

Do not forget—secure keys in pocket go through red door past skeleton, GO ON heedless of fear chin down, try not to look over the edge of the cliff

Lydde stared at the note, turned it over in her hands trying to fathom it.

Skeleton? GO ON? And whose was this strange handwriting?

She studied the gallery of frames hanging on the wall. The quotes from Arthur C. Clarke and William Shakespeare. The Dalí print. The litho of St. Pancras Church, Norchester, and Batts and Fallam. The photo of the Hawks Nest Tunnel.

She tried to recall what she knew about the tunnel. A mile downriver from Roundbottom Farm, it had been blasted through lower Fallam Mountain so the New River could be rerouted for hydroelectric power. A strange idea, to take an entire river, an entire, ancient river, and send it tumbling down an artificial channel beneath an equally ancient mountain. It had been called the engineering feat of its time, which was 1931. Hundreds of men died in the drilling of it. That was all she knew. Probably something that upset Uncle John, that he wanted to memorialize.

Back downstairs Lydde asked Aunt Lavinia, "Have you ever seen these keys before?"

She studied them, handed them back. "The smaller one is the key to the Mystery Hole. I don't know what the big one is."

"Did you get back from Arizona earlier than you expected?"

"As a matter of fact, I did," Aunt Lavinia answered. "Edith was getting on my nerves, and I was homesick for John. So I came on back."

LYDDE didn't tell Aunt Lavinia about the note. She wanted to do some exploring herself before she worried her aunt with it. Instead she offered to drive Lavinia into town for Saturday morning altar guild duties at All Saints Episcopal Church.

Aunt Lavinia chatted the whole way, pleased to have Lydde along. "You remember All Saints? Where we took you when you were a girl?" As if decades abroad had wiped clean Lydde's memory of her childhood. Of course I remember, Lydde assured her. She parked the car, and while Aunt Lavinia went inside to her chores—washing and polishing the chalice and paten, arranging the table with fresh altar hangings, setting out flagons of wine and water for the early Sunday service—Lydde walked around the little town, reacquainting herself. Lafayette perched on the rim of the New River Gorge, away from the mining on the other end of the county, still as green and pretty as Lydde remembered. It was an old town with a stone courthouse built in 1844, a square of brick buildings and quiet streets of Victorian gingerbread houses with turrets and bay windows. But much had changed. When Lydde had gone to high school there, the buildings on the square housed a dime store, hardware and clothing and shoe stores, a movie theater. Those were all gone, run out of business by a Wal-Mart and multiplex on the four-lane highway south of town. But few of the storefronts were empty. Now there were outdoor outfitters selling tents and sleeping bags, bicycle and canoe rentals, a combination book and health food store, restaurants and gift shops with handmade wooden signs. Some of the Victorian homes now advertised as bed and breakfasts. The movie theater had become the New River Opry House, home of live music and community theater. All in all, Lydde approved, and thought she might want to look into buying a place in town after she had her bearings.

After a cup of coffee and a bagel (bagels in Lafayette!) Lydde returned to All Saints. The church was three streets from the courthouse square, with only its own back garden and a low stone wall separating it from the edge of the Gorge. Several large poplars hovered over the church, but unlike similar settings in England, there were no graves. Lydde did, however, notice something new, a plaque engraved with the names of people whose ashes had been scattered in the garden. She knew at once that was where Uncle John would have wanted to be, but she resolved not to mention it to Aunt Lavinia for fear of hurting her feelings. She slipped through the front door, painted the traditional bright red of Episcopal churches, and settled in a back pew. The three women who comprised the altar guild were finishing their tasks, arranging flowers and candles, replacing the numbers on the hymn board.

It was a lovely little sanctuary, a copy of English country churches but looking more prosperous than the originals. The roof had richly burnished oak beams, and the stained glass glowed in the morning light from northeast of the Gorge. When Aunt Lavinia joined her at the back, Lydde asked, "Who's the priest now?"

"We're too small to call our own priest," Aunt Lavinia said, "so we'll have a vicar appointed by the diocese. Our last one got married and moved away, so we're in between."

"Where'd he go?" Lydde asked lazily.

"*She* went to Wheeling," Aunt Lavinia replied primly. "Really, Lydde, you're behind the times."

ON the way home Lydde said, "I want to see the mountains now. Or what's left."

Aunt Lavinia pressed her lips together and nodded. When they were close to the Mystery Hole she said, "Take the Old Road down into the gorge and cross to that overlook on Gauley that John used to like so much."

The Old Road had once been the only way to Charleston, before the four-lane highway—still new to Lydde—went in. They wound down hairpin curves to the river, crossed on a new concrete bridge, and climbed the other side of the gorge on Gauley Mountain to the wide shoulder where Uncle John had liked to stop and "rest my eyes."

When they pulled onto the dirt shoulder and stopped, Lydde saw at last what her uncle had been talking about, what had so upset Aunt Lavinia. She opened the car door and stepped out, scarcely able to breathe. Once there had been mountain after mountain, shedding fog in the morning, soaking up light and turning it to purple and gray and green in the evening. Once there had been mountains higher even than the one on which they now stood. Now there was empty sky. Reluctantly Lydde dropped her eyes, lower, lower, to a vast plain of grass and rock. Where the crest of Fallam had been, past where Black had been, and Droop, stretched a flat featureless scape, dotted here and there by a gray pond. At the near edge a few stunted trees clung to life.

"How big is it?" Lydde whispered when she could speak.

"Four square miles for this one," Aunt Lavinia said. "And it goes on farther than you can see. They blew apart the mountains and they filled in the streams and hollows. The blasting was terrible. Enough explosives to blow up Manhattan, John told me. All those trees, and the poor animals too." She shook her head. "They destroyed the groundwater down below, of course, and the people with wells lost those. And the dust—just be glad you weren't here. White silica dust. It coated everything. The trees around us looked like they'd been sprinkled with confectioner's sugar."

"So people left," Lydde said.

"Bought out by the coal company. Everyone except John. He refused to sell. They weren't going to cover us up like some of the other places, he said, because we were near the River. So he was hanging on. Besides, before they bought people out they made everyone sign a deed saying they would never live in this county again, not for the rest of their natural lives. John said no one would ever get him to sign such a thing. You know how stubborn he could be."

"Well, you hung on," Lydde said, trying to see something good in the situation. "And from the farm you can't see this." But you know it's there, she thought, and it eats at you.

"That's not all," said Aunt Lavinia. "I wish it was. But after the blasting was done, after the dust settled, we had an inspector in. The foundation is cracked. Ten, twenty years from now everything will be falling in. I'll never be able to sell. So I'll stay, and I reckon the house will outlast me, but just barely."

Roundbottom Farm. Built in 1840, now on Death Row. With the spring vegetation, it was hidden just then, but Lydde knew where it was, behind a fold of land down and to the left. Farther east, once midway up the mountain and now at the top edge, was the familiar jutting rock of Fallam Point.

"Is Montefalco totally gone?"

"You can walk up there and see," Aunt Lavinia said. "Myself, I don't want to go again. The valley fill starts right there where the house was."

"Valley fill."

"A nice term for taking what's left of the top of the mountain and throwing it over the side and covering up the head of Shades o' Death Creek. The creek floods down below and it never did before. We had water in the house two years ago."

Lydde sighed. "I guess I'll have to go look at it just to get an idea of what they've done."

"Oh, you'll see. If the Devil built a fortress in the middle of your daddy's land, that's what it would look like."

LYDDE didn't believe in the Devil. But when she had climbed the gravel road above the Mystery Hole, hoping against reality that she would find the foundation again, she thought of the book she had devoured three times in her high school years, *The Lord of the Rings*. "The land of Mordor," she said aloud. They were appealing to different literary metaphors, she and Aunt Lavinia, but speaking of the same thing. Blocking her way was a gigantic terrace, a pyramid of obscene size, each level the height of a five-story building. A straight channel lined with rocks cut its way straight down the middle. The new Shades o' Death Creek. Somewhere beneath that massive pile that Lydde had to crane her neck to glimpse the top of, somewhere beneath it Carlo Falcone had tried to raise goats and pigs and grapevines, and Lydde had lived with her family.

She had been carrying a stick, a talisman of hope, to dig with. She dropped it. Fallam Mountain, old as creation, had found its own grave atop the remains of her family's pyre.

·   ·   ·

LYDDE spent a restless night in her old bedroom. The weather was unseasonably cold and she closed her window and piled on the blankets. Still she slept fitfully. At last, when her digital clock glowed 5:30, she gave up and crawled out of bed. Since most of her things were in storage she had little in the way of warm clothes, and after pulling on some jeans she looked around. Aunt Lavinia had kept some of her old things in a chest of drawers, and there she found a gray sweatshirt from her college days emblazoned with the word DUKE in navy blue letters. She pulled it over her head, pleased to find it still fit, though it was no longer fashionably sloppy, and laced up her black Reeboks. She studied herself a moment in the mirror, running her fingers through her short hair, now peppered with gray. Maybe she should get it colored. Her hands looked the oldest part of her, the veins beginning to stand out more than she had noticed before, her knuckles wrinkled and the skin dry.

In Uncle John's study she grabbed the handwritten directions and the keys and stuffed them into her pocket. In the kitchen she found a flashlight. Then she set out, climbing the winding gravel road to the Mystery Hole. Dawn was graying the world around her. Gauley Mountain, still intact across the way, was wreathed in fog. Below, the River was hidden beneath the ethereal mist that flowed above it like a second current. She was sorry to leave the crisp air for a hole in the ground, but dug the smaller key out of her pocket and let herself in, following the beam of the flashlight.

The air was close, for the Mystery Hole had been closed to tourists for several years. Lydde stood for a moment, playing the light over the walls with their goofy posters, hung sideways for effect, the tourists' bench bolted to one side, the ramp for rolling balls uphill. The place was weird enough in the dark, weirder still to see everything turned on end, as though she were standing on a wall looking at the ceiling to her right and the floor to her left.

Above was the red door. She should have recalled that when Uncle John stepped from the door, he appeared to be coming from the wall but was in fact entering from the ceiling. He had built a series of discreet hand- and footholds which he used to keep himself from flying into the laps of the seated tourists. So she would have to find them and haul herself up through the door. It took a while. At last she discovered a light switch and flipped it on. Then she could tuck the flashlight in her waistband and use both hands. She found herself marveling that Uncle John had been able to enter and exit with such seeming little effort. He must have practiced for hours to get it right.

Then she was up and in, and pulled the door shut behind her so she wouldn't fall back down into the main room and break her neck. It took a moment to get her bearings, to relax and let gravity tell her where down was and where to put her feet. The red door had become a trapdoor outlined by the light from the main room below. She flicked on a light switch. A desk and filing cabinet stood in one corner, probably where Uncle John kept his business accounts and props. For some reason Uncle John had tacked a mirror on the wall. There was nothing else except a small passageway opposite. Lydde stepped closer and felt a damp draft that smelled of rock and moss. What had the note said? *Go through red door past skeleton.* She took a deep breath and edged forward, wielding the flashlight in front of her like a weapon.

She had to bend to fit through the passageway and soon found herself on her knees, scrabbling along on a floor of damp stone. From somewhere in the distance came the plunking sound of water dripping into a still pool. She seemed to be inside the clamshell rock outcropping. The knees of her jeans were soaked through and she stopped to wipe her hands on her hips. Then the beam caught a glint of white. Lydde steadied her shaking hands and aimed the light. There was a rib cage, its shadow magnified on the wall behind it. She nearly dropped the light, then rocked back on her heels, lost her balance, and sat down hard.

After a moment she gathered her courage. "It can't hurt you," Lydde whispered to herself. "It's dead. Poor person, poor sad person." She said a quick prayer, and that helped calm her. Then she moved closer and ran the beam of light over the skeleton's length. The skull, backbone, and rib cage were intact, though turned slightly on their side. Other bones—arms and legs, perhaps—lay farther away as though scattered by animals, and the pelvis had disappeared entirely. Decayed strips of cloth hung from a few of the ribs. Lydde reached out and touched the top of the skull, pulled her hand back as though the bone were hot, only it was fear that caused her reaction, then touched the skull again, her fingers resting momentarily on the temple. Poor person.

She could see no sign of injury to the skull, and the face seemed composed, none of the openmouthed screams you see on skeletons in horror movies. Someone who merely got sick or hurt, and then died. Alone, in a lonely place. Lydde sighed, and the movement of the flashlight caught a dull glint of metal near the breastbone. She leaned closer and saw the tangle of a necklace among the ribs. Carefully she tugged on the chain, pulled it up to the light and cradled it in the palm of her hand. It was a tarnished silver cross, a Celtic cross. She placed it back in its bony nest.

So she had found the skeleton. She was to go beyond it, and then? For not far beyond the skeleton was a crack in the rock ledge and beyond it a straight drop through space into the Gorge.

Lydde wished with all her heart that the note had been written in Uncle John's hand. She would have trusted his directions, trusted them with her life. As it was, she should leave, go home to Aunt Lavinia and tell her about the skeleton and call the police, get it a proper burial. Maybe it could be identified, maybe someone had gone missing years ago—

She thought with a shock of her brothers and sisters. No, this didn't fit. But it seemed they weren't the only ones who had vanished in the New River Gorge.

Lydde stared at the insistent words on the scrap of parchment. *GO ON.*

So she did, despite all reason, despite the alarm bells going off in her head as she went on, despite the sudden change in the atmosphere as though all the oxygen had been sucked from the space and all was suddenly colder still and then she felt herself falling. She must have gone too far and hurtled down into the Gorge, only she seemed to be falling *up*. Then she landed with a jolt and all the breath knocked out of her.

Part Two

Chapter 4

The Arrival

F OR A LONG time Lydde lay still, afraid to move, thinking herself on the edge of the cliff and perhaps in danger of pitching over. She was in a dark place, so dark she blinked her eyes hard to convince herself they were open. With one hand she reached out and felt cold damp stone, as before. And yet everything was different. The odor now was close and musty, with not a breath of fresh air, more like the inside of a closet than a cave.

Cautiously she stretched out her arms and legs, moved them around to test that the ground beneath her was solid. She was lying on a ledge whose depth she couldn't fathom, so she edged away and raised herself into a kneeling position, then froze in surprise. Her movements had been easy, extraordinarily so, and a strange surge of energy flowed through her limbs. On the other hand, her jeans seemed larger, for they slid down so that the waistband rested easily on top of her hipbone.

For a while she groped for the flashlight, then gave up, realizing she had lost it somewhere along the way. She could make out the faint outline of a door, and light beyond, so she crawled on hands and knees toward it. She stood and again felt the surge of energy. When she took a deep breath, it seemed that her lungs had also gained strength.

The door proved to be locked. Lydde banged and kicked and cried out, then thought of the large key in her back pocket. Feeling with her fingertips, she found an equally large keyhole and soon enough was pulling the door open with a loud creak. She stepped into a dank stone passageway at the foot of a strange set of stairs. She locked the door behind her and climbed up. There she met another door, this one unlocked, and pushed it open.

She was in a church. The light wasn't good, even though the windows were opaque glass. It seemed either late in the day or especially cloudy, but as she came farther inside she could tell this was a church she had never seen before. She closed her eyes and shook her head. She must have lost her mind, or else she had fallen into a dream, or worse, a coma. But she could pinch herself and feel the pain. She could take deep breaths and smell the church smells of old books and polished wood. When she opened her eyes again she took in what she had only glimpsed before. On all four sides she was surrounded by walls covered with paintings, scenes done in glorious hues, reds, blues, and greens. She turned slowly in a circle. There Mary knelt before a golden angel. Next Jesus pulled a man, part skeleton, still living, from a tomb. Across the way a man on horseback, clad in armor, jousted with a serpent. Above the far doorway Jesus again, enthroned and presiding over two processions of naked people, one group with arms raised in praise, another covering their heads in anguish. A judgment.

Something stirred in Lydde's memory. Her father, back from his travels when he was feeling unusually talkative, telling of the church he'd seen in Italy, in the village of Montefalco. And she'd heard of such churches in Austria and Germany. But not in West Virginia.

And in any case, how on earth had she gotten here, wherever she was, from the Mystery Hole?

What had Uncle John said when he visited her in Norchester?

It's impossible to explain, so you have to come. That's the only way.

And something about a physics experiment. She remembered the quote from *Hamlet* on his wall and whispered it. "'There are more things in heaven and earth, Horatio, than are dreamt of in our philosophy.'"

Yes, indeed.

There was nothing for it but to go to the door and see what lay beyond. Lydde stepped out into a churchyard like the ones she'd seen in England with their gravestones standing close, inscriptions as faint as if they had been written in water with a stick. But these stones were recently chiseled, their inscriptions clearly visible. She knelt beside a grave newly dug, the grass not yet growing upon it—noticing again how easily she knelt, without any aches—and read.

Thomas Lanckford

Born 8 October 1602

Died 23 August 1657

"Impossible," she said, so loudly she startled a robin in a nearby hedgerow. She hurried to another tombstone, then another. Each erected in the 1640s or 1650s, each with inscriptions cut deep as though new. In her panic she didn't wait to search for a gate but clambered easily over the stone wall and found herself in a dusty dirt lane that disappeared into a thick wood. It seemed to be early fall, for there was a bite to the air, and some leaves among the green had turned orange and yellow. She faced in the opposite direction and there in the distance was a walled city. Ambling along the road was an old man herding a small flock of geese.

Lydde froze, not knowing what to do or where to turn. The man, as he drew closer, was eyeing her first with curiosity, then with alarm. He stopped and called to a small brindled dog trailing behind him, which came forward at once, back bristled. Then they stared at one another, Lydde and the old man, each afraid to speak or move. She was noting his clothes, a filthy shirt of rough brown material, a much-patched pair of trousers, and high boots. Then she caught the smell of him.

The gosherd was even more astonished by the outlandish outfit worn by the boy standing in the lane. His pants were of a faded blue fabric such as the man had never seen, his shoes were black and oddly shaped, his formless gray tunic was inscribed with a word in blue letters which the old man could not read, since he was illiterate. He had heard that fairies were garbed most strangely and wondered if he was even now face-to-face with one of the fey folk. Automatically, he crossed himself for protection, then recalled this gesture had been forbidden by the Puritans and looked around guiltily. But the boy, who had an open face with nothing of artifice about it, seemed not to notice, and in truth he appeared to be frightened. The old man gained his composure first, perhaps because, unlike Lydde, he knew where he was. So he addressed her.

"That is a strange manner of dress, lad."

Lad. She looked down at herself—blue jeans, black Reeboks, baggy gray Duke sweatshirt. She was wearing a sports bra, and that, plus the heavy fabric of the sweatshirt, concealed her breasts. She put her hand to her head, felt the short hair.

"It is," she said.

The old man was relieved that the boy's voice, at least, sounded human or thereabouts, though there was a strange flavor to his speech.

"What are the characters on your blouse?" he asked. "Is it a word of some sort?"

Lydde looked down, then back up, her mouth open. "D-Duke," she stammered.

"Duke!" He took a step back. "You're a duke, are you?"

"No, no!" She was winging it, not knowing what best to say. "Not a duke. I—uh, I work for a duke."

"You work for a duke!" He pondered a moment, still puzzled but inclined to be respectful. "There are few dukes in England just now. They've all taken themselves to France with"—he looked around furtively—"you know . . ." His voice dropped to a whisper. "The King. Or at least, son of him that was the King."

England? The King? She tried to recall her history. If it was truly 1657 as the gravestone indicated, then it was after the English civil war. King Charles the First would have been defeated by the armies of Parliament and beheaded at Whitehall. And Charles the Second would be waiting in exile in France to return in 1660.

"Tell me." Lydde took a step toward him and he took a step back. "Who's in charge now?"

He looked at her as though she'd grown another head. "Why, Oliver Cromwell, of course! Unless you know different." This was a strange, perhaps heathenish lad after all. "Who are you? Where do you come from, that you ask such a question? And why does your speech have such an odd sound to it?"

"Oh," Lydde said, thinking fast, "I come from Ireland."

"Ah." He nodded, greatly relieved. "That would account for it."

She hoped he wouldn't remember to ask her name again. But something else had occurred to him and he came back with another sharp question.

"Not papist, are you?"

She had barely enough sense to answer, "Oh, no, no! I've run away from the papists." And to add, "'Tis why I'm here."

"To escape the papists? Good lad, good lad. A right boon for your salvation, as they do say the papists drink the blood of infants at the altar."

"Indeed I have heard the Pope himself is the Antichrist," she said, silently apologizing to her Catholic friends as the old man nodded his approval. "And may I beg your forgiveness? But in Ireland we hear little of the world's doings. Are the Puritans in charge now?"

"They are." He leaned closer and looked around furtively before continuing. "And a sour lot too. No more games, you see, no more sport, no prayer book or music, and no more dancing. They've even banned Christmas, they have."

"Have they indeed? Christmas, of all things."

"Too much fun for 'em," the man said. "The Devil takes you when there's fun about, so they say. I keep clear of 'em Puritans. Afraid of making a mistake, I am. Keep that in mind, lad, never laugh around 'em, and you'll do fine."

"I'm grateful for the advice," Lydde replied, growing alarmed at the prospect before her. "And may I ask what city lies yonder?"

"Norchester," he said, kindly now. "And if that be your destination you are in luck, for the East Gate is yon. You'll just make her before nightfall."

Norchester, she thought, my God, my God.

"And this church?" She waved her hand at the pretty church in its yard, which from this angle was suddenly looking quite familiar.

"St. Pancras-without-the-wall, that be. And if 'tis the prayer book you want, the good vicar Mr. Smythe may yet read it here time to time, though he's been warned he shall be turned out of his living for it."

St. Pancras Church. The print on Uncle John's wall come to life. She bowed her thanks, hoping that was appropriate. He did think it odd, poor man that he was, to be bowed to, but put it down to out- landish Irish ways, waved her off, and was on his malodorous way with his gaggle of geese. With a fine story to tell his wife and grand- children, no doubt.

So, Lydde thought. I am asleep. I am in a coma and dreaming, like Dorothy in Oz. I am insane. Nevertheless, I seem to be in England. In Norchester. During the rule of Cromwell and the Puritans.

She was also hungry, and frightened, and she knew nothing better to do than to go on to Norchester. At least, she thought, I've been there before.

.   .   .

NORCHESTER in Lydde's day (she kept ridiculously thinking of it in the past tense) had been largely Georgian in the city center, and Victorian mixed with modern bungalows in the middle-class neighborhoods outside the wall. Only three Tudor black-and-whites had been saved, including an old pub billed as the Oldest House in Norchester.

The Norchester she now found herself in had few houses outside the wall, and none of them familiar. Inside East Gate the buildings were all black-and-whites, their upstairs hanging out like lopsided cakes decorated with timbered icing. Lydde longed to stop and get her bearings, but she had acquired a trail of curious onlookers, including a gaggle of small boys, who yelled incomprehensible things and threw clods of dirt at her back. She tried to stop and speak to people, but that seemed to make things worse, as they fell back from her in alarm. No one ran away, though, but called out to neighbors so that the crowd grew steadily and came close again.

Lydde decided the safest course possible was to pretend there was nothing odd about herself. She ignored the stares she received and tried not to stare back, but curiosity overcame fear. Everyone was dressed in rough clothing, blouses and coats and breeches and broad-brimmed hats for the men, long dresses and aprons and caps for the women, and not a clean head of hair as far as she could see. She felt as though she'd dropped down on the set of a play, except it was a stage with no wings for an exit, and it stank to high heaven.

She had known the street as Eastgate. She looked in vain for a street sign to confirm this, then narrowly missed stepping in a newly steaming pile of horse shit. Thereafter she dodged piles of several varieties of dung. People stopped to gape at both her strange dress and her manner as she sought to keep her balance while hopping over a cow pile. Then someone called out, "An actor! An actor!" and others took up the cry.

How on earth can they tell? she wondered, and hurried on.

People were pointing at her shoes, her sweatshirt and jeans, and vowing they'd seen no players in such garb, not even in the old days.

They continued to follow Lydde on all sides, pressing so close she was forced to slow down and then stop. Then a hand grasped her arm and she found herself face-to-face with a tall man with thick black eyebrows and cold brown eyes.

"Who are you?" he demanded. "Why are you dressed so oddly? Are you indeed an actor and is this your costume?"

She started to say that she was, but the force of his grip and the threat implied in his question made her cautious.

"Please!" she pleaded, remembering how the old gosherd had grown more friendly. "I am a poor boy come from very far off."

There was a moment of silence at the sound of her voice, then everyone began talking at once. Lydde felt a tug and looked down. A boy of around five had hold of her jeans pocket and was pulling as hard as he could. Then his mother grabbed him up and clutched him to her as though shielding him from great danger.

The crowd suddenly parted to make way for a sturdy man carrying a cudgel and wearing a sword strapped to his waist. He stopped before Lydde with his fists on his hips and said, "I am Constable Baxter. Who are you? What is your business in Norchester?"

"The lad is an actor," said the man with black eyebrows. "A ganymede who appears in plays of the Devil!"

Lydde again had a hard time understanding what was being said, but caught the gist of it. She remembered then that the Puritans had banned the theater throughout the rule of Cromwell. Plays, they believed, were the work of the Devil, and boys playing the part of women with other men was especially offensive.

"I am no actor," she said. "I'm only a poor lad seeking shelter in Norchester after a long journey."

Constable Baxter took a step back and looked askance when he heard her speech.

"Ireland," she said before he could ask. "I'm from Ireland."

"Ah," he said, and an expression of sympathy crossed his broad face. "That will explain it." He turned to the curious crowd. "An Irish lad."

That brought another outburst of alarm.

"Fleeing the papists!" she called out.

This inclined the crowd more to sympathy, though many still stared suspiciously at her, some of the more brazen reaching out to touch the strange fabric she wore, or stooping for a better view of her shoes.

"Why are you clad in such strange garb," demanded the man who still held her by the arm and now shook it roughly, "if not an actor?"

"If I am an actor," Lydde responded, "where is my troupe?"

"Enough, Jacob Woodcock," said Baxter. "You are a blacksmith, not a constable. I ask the questions here. Now, lad." He continued to look kindly at her. "What is this strange manner of dress?"

Nothing to do but brazen her way through. "I was forced to wear this. By the papists."

"And why is the word *Duke* set upon your blouse?"

"And why is there a grinning devil set upon it?" cried Woodcock, who had been examining the fabric at close quarters. This sent the crowd back several paces in a panic. And Lydde realized with horror that set within the *D* was a tiny embroidery of the school mascot, a Blue Devil.

The constable peered closely, his expression turning to alarm.

"Speak up, lad!" he said. "Why do you bear the mark of Satan upon you?"

Just then a voice called out in the halting manner of one with an impediment of speech, "H-hold, Con-stable! I c-can explain!"

A man pushed his way through the crowd, which fell back respectfully. And there, to Lydde's amazement, stood her Uncle John.

Chapter 5

John Soane

AND YET HE was not Uncle John, for Constable Baxter addressed him at once as Mr. John Soane, and he was a man in his forties, not an older man as Uncle John had been.

"Good day to you, Mr. Soane. And what do you know of this lad?"

"Be-before I say," answered the newcomer, in the halting manner of one who has suffered a stroke, "h-how does M-Martin?"

Baxter softened even further. "Well, indeed. Who could imagine the child was so near death only days ago? God be praised for your skill, good doctor."

The man bent his head in acknowledgment, then said, "N-now about this b-boy here. He is kin."

Lydde studied him narrowly. His impediment, real or faked, made it impossible to tell whether he spoke as she did or was one of the townspeople.

"Kin to you?" Baxter said, surprised.

"Indeed." The doctor began to laboriously explain, and it took a good deal of time for him to get his story out in its entirety. But the point of his speech was this: that the lad standing before them was the son of a cousin in Bristol.

"Bristol?" exclaimed Baxter. "He says he comes from Ireland!"

Lydde nodded emphatically and raised her eyebrows at the good doctor. "To escape the papists. 'Tis the story I told."

"Aye, Ireland," said the doctor. He leaned close to her and winked. "But by way of B-Bristol, w-which is the port through which many I-Irish do enter England."

"Is this the same cousin who died and left orphan the child Mary, who now dwells at Soane's Croft?" Baxter asked.

So, Lydde thought. Soane's Croft exists.

"N-not the same, but a relative as well."

"And the devil upon his blouse?" Jacob Woodcock interjected. Lydde took an involuntary step back.

John Soane took his time and managed to spit out the following explanation. That the papists in Ireland had killed the lad's father and pursued him to Bristol along with his mother, who had since died. That, once in Bristol, he had been captured at the docks by a renegade Catholic sect strictly devoted to devil worship. That the unfortunate lad had been abducted and forced to follow papist rituals and wear the shirt with the demonic device, and was told if he removed it he would surely forfeit his soul to Satan that same night. That he had escaped and sent word ahead to his good cousin John Soane that he would seek sanctuary in Norchester, where the prayers of the God-fearing would allow him to safely remove his blouse and live thereafter a sober and righteous life.

"B-but first he must have some rest, and food, for he has been sadly abused. G-go home!" urged the doctor. "Pray for the safety of this lad's soul!"

This seemed to be generally satisfactory and caused the crowd to give way. Then a woman called out, "What is the lad's name, good doctor, that we may pray for him?"

John Soane seemed taken with a spell that made him stammer and chew over his words even more, head bobbing and an eye toward Lydde as if to encourage her.

"Louis," she said quickly, pronouncing it the Italian way as she was used to when speaking of her brother. "My name is Louis, ah . . ."

"Soane," the doctor finished.

"'Tis a French-sounding name," said Jacob Woodcock.

But the doctor had Lydde by the arm and led her south toward the River Pye. Behind them Constable Baxter was urging the crowd to disperse and allow good Mr. Soane to take charge of his new ward.

"Uncle John?" Lydde whispered as they hurried along. "Is it you?"

"It's me," he said. "But what on earth are you doing here?"

"Me? You're supposed to be dead! And how did either one of us end up here? Is this place real or am I in the middle of a Monty Python movie?"

"It's real, all right. It's the seventeenth century—September 1657, to be exact."

They had reached the shelter of a tree-lined path that followed the river. Then they stopped.

"You stink," she said. "Like everyone else."

He laughed. "Wait a week without deodorant or a bath and you'll smell the same. But by then you won't notice." He pointed to a tree beside the riverbank. "Let's sit and rest a minute. We've both got a lot to tell."

THEY sat sheltered from view beneath a large weeping willow.

"Ireland?" he said. "Where'd you get that?"

"I had to think of something. I'll apologize to the Irish later. But what was all that nonsense about me being kidnapped by demonic Catholics?"

"Living here you get lots of experience in thinking fast," he said. "Creatively too. Actually it's a pretty safe explanation for both of us.

Most people here don't know beans about the Irish or Catholics except that they have horns on their heads and long tails. Call somebody a papist here, it's like calling someone back home a Communist in the 1950s."

"Okay. But if you're Uncle John, how come you look so young? You can't be much more than forty."

"I'm not the only one who looks young," he said with a smile. "You don't appear to be more than fourteen, yourself. A fine lad."

She longed for a mirror. "Do I really look like a boy?"

"Didn't you play Prince Hal when you were young?" he reminded her. "You must look the same as then. Remember, people here never see women in pants or with short hair. And women are taught not to look a man in the eye or speak out. So you have to be male just by the way you act. And your voice is high and your skin is smooth, so they just assume you're a boy. I'd guess if you had on a dress, you're really more like twenty or so."

"But how?"

"We've broken the time barrier, Lydde. It's a side effect, because of relativity. Go forward in time, you age; go backward, you grow younger—depending on how fast you travel through the wormhole. By the way, I've got to stop calling you Lydde. It really will be safer, as long as you're here, if you pretend to be a boy. It's that much harder for women. Very little freedom, lots of hard work, and you're not supposed to know anything."

"Oh, God," she moaned. "Am I stuck here?"

"No, no," he reassured her. "We can go back. I'll explain all that later. But first things first. What's this about me being dead? And how is Lavinia?"

"Aunt Lavinia's fine," she said, "everything else is totally nuts. You died of a heart attack. Aunt Lavinia found you, and you're buried in the cemetery at Lafayette. But how could that be?"

He stared a moment, then said, "Oh, my. John. Poor John. I was afraid of something like that."

Lydde jumped up. "Then you aren't Uncle John," she cried. "And he *is*—"

"I *am* your Uncle John," he interrupted. "How would I have known to ask about Lavinia otherwise? Or that you're Lydde? But be quiet or you'll call attention to us."

Lydde sat back down. "Okay. I'll shut up. Now explain."

THE first time, he had come to Norchester accidentally, as she had.

"Though I was more fortunate in my timing," Uncle John told her. "It was nearly dark, so I didn't have a crowd following me. But you can't imagine how confused I was."

"Try me," Lydde said.

"At that time the door to the church crypt was kept unlocked, so I found my way outside, and who should be passing but a man who looked to be my twin? John Soane was returning home from a call to an injured man. He was on horseback, and it was clear from his dress he was from another time. I was wearing a plaid shirt and jeans. We both were terrified, I can tell you. But we were both scientists in our own ways. He was a physician whose generation was the first to be really and truly scientists, who no longer relied on the Church for explanations but instead studied the world around them. Studied it closely, methodically, skeptically.

"He invited me to Soane's Croft with him, and I went, wearing his cloak to cover my odd clothes. We talked the rest of the night. But I began to grow frightened, not of him, but of what effect I might have, a man from the future interfering with the past. So he took me back to St. Pancras, still wearing his cloak, and left me. Probably decided the next day he'd had a hell of a dream. Meanwhile, I found to my great relief that the trip works both ways. Not only that, but objects can be carried both ways. I was back in the New River Gorge with a cloak from seventeenth-century England."

"When was this?"

"In 1950. I built the Mystery Hole later to keep anyone else from stumbling into the wormhole. It took me fifty years to get up the nerve to return. I thought maybe it was a terrible sin, like playing God, to get involved with the past. What if I caused some damage that would alter the future? So I studied, read all the physics I could, worked on the mathematics of it all. For years scientists wouldn't touch this stuff, so it was hard to find material. But that started to change in the 1990s and I grew confident that I could go back in time without harming the present. Our present, I mean. I started to think that consistency will overcome paradox and once events have happened, they have happened and can't be disrupted. And I thought maybe, just maybe, I could do some good for our future."

"But you have changed events here," Lydde said. "What did that constable mean about his child? Did you save it from dying?"

"I stopped it from choking to death."

"Well, then? Whatever that child does from now on will affect the future for good or ill."

"Yes," Uncle John said, "but the child would have lived whether I saved it or not. Someone else would have saved it, or it would have saved itself. It was meant to be."

"Sounds pretty fatalistic," Lydde observed.

Uncle John shrugged. "Physicists talk about something called the instanton. It had four dimensions at the Big Bang and then proceeded to inflate into an infinite universe. Everything existed in the instanton; it determined future time."

"Everything was meant to be?"

"Yes."

"And is our being here meant to be?"

"Yes," Uncle John said. "When I came back the second time I knew I wanted you to come back here with me. That's why I tried to get you to go back home when I came to visit you in England. But you wouldn't come, so I ventured it alone the third time. I thought I'd take advantage of Lavinia still being in Arizona."

"Why didn't you bring her here? Does she even know about a wormhole?"

He shook his head. "No," he admitted. "I know it was wrong of me. But I was going to tell her at the same time I told you and see if either of you wanted to come with me. That you're here and not Lavinia is part of the flow of events."

"So you came back here before you visited me?"

"Yes. I returned better prepared, with the cloak and an outfit of clothes that matched the period. And an understanding of where I was headed. I found John Soane again and we became fast friends. Which was logical, since we appeared identical."

He sighed then, and fought back tears. "When I couldn't get you back to West Virginia, John Soane was so curious I agreed to let him trade places with me. I was expecting him back anytime. He was a good man, I was growing fond of him. It was like having a twin brother. Or more. Now it's like facing my own mortality."

She put her arm around him. "Was he so much like you?"

He turned. "Lydde, more than that. Maybe he *was* me. I'm still sorting all this out myself. But I think we may be in more than just the past. We may be in a parallel universe."

H E continued to talk as they walked along the Pye toward Soane's Croft.

"John Soane hid me away," said Uncle John, smiling at the memory, "as much to study me, I think, as to shield me. I lived in the garret. Not even Mother Bunch was told who I was. Mother Bunch is the widow who cooks at Soane's Croft, and she supplies herbs for the apothecary. The place couldn't run without her. Anyway, she thought that I was a mysterious patient being hid because of a disfiguring illness.

"But after John had heard my story over and over, and asked a thousand or so questions and grew to trust me, he was as convinced I told the truth as I was of his kindness. He would change places with me so I could get out and explore. His main disappointment in life was to be cut off from the new developments in science by living in Norchester. He longed to be in Oxford or London. But he was also devoted to his patients. And he was a good physician for this time and place. As you can guess, however, I knew a lot he didn't know, even though I'm a physicist, not a physician. He'd no idea of bacteria, or sanitation, not even that he should wash his hands before and after examining a patient. So I taught him some things about medicine and he helped me adapt to this place. We made a good team.

"But a bit of doubt remained, and curiosity too. So I let him go back in my place. Lavinia was in Arizona, so he wouldn't need to fool her. It was getting harder and harder to hide from Mother Bunch that there were two Johns in the house. So I tried to prepare him for what he'd find and he wrote out instructions for getting back. I thought he'd be back here and I'd take his place at Roundbottom before anyone noticed."

"Aunt Lavinia came home early," Lydde said, remembering. "She said you were acting strange. No wonder! She said you seemed afraid to drive the car. Poor man, it must have been terrifying to even ride in it."

"I told him about cars, but the reality would have been a shock," Uncle John agreed.

"And he insisted on sleeping in a bedroom by himself. That upset Aunt Lavinia."

"Bless him for that," said Uncle John. "But how did he die?"

"Heart attack. That's another thing. The doctor was puzzled because his heart was in such bad shape."

"He would have aged, just like we've gotten younger coming in this direction. But he was in his forties here, same as me. I didn't think the extra years would hurt him."

"Maybe he wasn't in as good health as you are," Lydde pointed out. "If this is really the seventeenth century, then he didn't grow up with all the nutritional advantages we have. He'd be an older forty than you are."

"That's true," said Uncle John, shaking his head, "and I didn't take it into account. Poor John. He's dead and it's all my fault."

"Maybe not. Dr. Khan said it was amazing he'd not died years earlier. So he might not have lasted much longer here either. Life expectancy here isn't so hot. If what you've been telling me is correct, he was meant to die. And look at it this way. He had some kind of experience before he went."

"It doesn't make me feel any better at this moment."

Uncle John stopped and sighed.

Then Lydde remembered something else Aunt Lavinia had told her. "She said he watched a lot of television. Stared at the set for hours."

Uncle John looked at her. "I wonder what shows," he said.

Then they both started to laugh and were soon hugging each other for comfort.

"And the people here think you're him," Lydde said.

"Yes. We thought it best. Now I wonder if it was a mistake. I should have tried to pass as a long-lost twin or something. It's damn hard to pretend to be someone else. We had to invent a medical condition for John Soane, one that would explain why sometimes he talks normally and other times has a terrible stutter. That covered my accent, since I'm not actor enough to fake it. Plus there were my inevitable lapses of memory, not recognizing people or knowing customs and so forth. All explained by my malady, one that comes and goes. Of course, we could never be seen together. But it hasn't been hard to fool people. These people don't get out much, you know, so they'll believe you're Irish, or have contracted some sort of brain fever from the Indies, and not doubt it."

Then Lydde thought of something that had puzzled her. "But how could you have met John Soane fifty years ago and then come back and he's only in his forties?"

"Relativity again. From here, time there seems hardly to pass, so if I would go back to West Virginia after a few months here, it's the next day. And a year or two there, come back here, maybe a week would have passed. From each perspective, time passes more slowly in the other place. Think of it as mutual *Brigadoon,* if you want to put it in theater terms."

Lydde shook her head. "It's just so hard to wrap my mind around. You could live to be old here and go back home and hardly any time would have passed? It's like living several lifetimes."

He nodded, and a tentative smile returned to his face. "That's exactly what it's like. And very tempting on this end to stay around, rather than face a few short years back home, especially if I can convince Lavinia to join me. Even if we caught the plague and died, we'd probably have more time than we do back home. And I've got work to do, here and back there. I only hope it's not some horrible offense to the way God has set up the universe. But if it was, I don't think we'd be here."

They came to Soane's Croft, which was as lovely as Lydde remembered it from her years in Norchester. If Hawthorne's famous house had seven gables, Soane's Croft had it beat with eleven. And three large chimneys—which meant, Lydde realized with a shudder, that much of the house would be cold in winter. It was a rambling Tudor structure of three stories set in front of a large walled garden. There the house had fronted the paved street, surrounded closely by pleasant Victorian buildings. Here it was in a dirt lane, and its neighbors were more distant thatched cottages. At the smaller of the two doors that fronted the lane, where Lydde recalled a chalkboard posting the hours for the Soane's Croft restaurant and gift shop, a rough hand-painted sign hanging above the entrance read JOHN SOANE, APOTHECARY & PHYSICIAN.

"I'll bet you're hungry," Uncle John said.

"I feel like I haven't eaten for three hundred years," Lydde admitted. She still had a thousand questions but was so hungry and suddenly tired she was willing to wait before asking them.

"Mother Bunch had a mutton stew on the hearth when I left," he said, "and bread in the oven. Plain food, but if you don't let it spoil, it's good. The folks back home into natural foods would love it. One of my projects has been to convince people to avoid spoilage and boil their water," and he went on in this enthusiastic fashion about reforming the health habits of the good folk of Norchester while he led her around the corner to an iron gate which stood open. This, he explained, was the entrance for patients. A very long cord ran into his own bedchamber above, where a bell rang at night in case of emergencies. The house extended back into the garden, and the rooms there, somewhat separate from the rest of the house, served as the physician's waiting room and surgery. There was also a split door between kitchen and garden where people entered to pick up medicines, herbal in nature, prepared fresh each day by Mother Bunch.

"Wait here," he said, "and I'll speak to Mother Bunch. We don't want to give the poor woman a heart attack."

He left Lydde to wander the well-tended garden. The preservationists of her twenty-first-century Norchester had done a good job, for it was much the same, the paths lined with plantings of columbine, roses, and irises. But there was far less grass than Lydde recalled and much more of a barely tamed flowery tangle. A corner of the garden was given over to a plot of herbs: thyme, rosemary, sage, and parsley in neat rows. Mother Bunch had an outsized green thumb, it seemed. Lydde was admiring her work when Uncle John returned.

"The food's almost ready," he said. "While we're waiting I'll show you the surgery."

Inside, Soane's Croft was all dark wood paneling, as Lydde remembered, but like the people she'd met, it smelled. Not so offensive though, Lydde thought, just pungent. The predominant odor was smoke, wood smoke and something else—candles? herbs?—and food, the smell of stewing meat coming from the nearby kitchen.

"Look here." Uncle John took her on a quick tour. The waiting room was small and lined with rough benches. The next room held two tables, a small one for examinations, Uncle John explained, and a larger one where surgery was performed.

"You don't actually cut people open? Not without anesthetic?" Lydde shuddered.

"Not unless there's nothing else for it," Uncle John replied. "I've already done an amputation. Not much to that, actually, I could teach you in half an hour. The poor fellow whose leg I took was pretty well soused by the time I got the saw out, and I don't mind telling you I'd had a nip or two myself."

"Uncle John!"

He shrugged. "John Soane himself would tell you he did the same. Easier to handle the screams and to saw away with abandon. Beyond that, it takes four strong men to hold, a good tight tourniquet, a hot poker for afterward."

"But can you really pass yourself off as a doctor?"

He put his finger to his lips and said, "I'll show you my secret weapon."

The next room was at the front of the house, and Lydde remembered it as holding the restaurant where she'd often lunched. Here it was the doctor's study, with several shelves of leather-bound volumes that Lydde guessed was quite a library for its day. Uncle John went to a cabinet in the corner, unlocked it, and took out two books. *The Good Housekeeping Family Health and Medical Guide* and *The American Medical Association Handbook of First Aid and Emergency Care.*

"Brought them from home. John loved them. And I treat them like holy scripture. Surreptitiously, of course. We never let the patients see them." He patted the books. "In fact, I blame these for John's curiosity about where I came from. I think he wanted to learn more about medicine. The funny thing is, I'm just as interested in the concoctions Mother Bunch puts together. I've seen them work too many times. Put them to good use myself. I'd hate to suffer through a cold again without chamomile, and willow bark tea works well on a headache." He clapped his hands. "Speaking of Mother Bunch and her concoctions, let's eat."

.   .   .

HE had prepared her well, for when Mother Bunch saw Lydde and her strange outfit, she raised an eyebrow and said, "They do dress outlandish in Ireland, do they not?" then turned to ladle stew into bowls.

It was mutton and root vegetables, Uncle John said. "Parsnips, carrots, potatoes, leeks, whatever's available. Typical fall meal."

Lydde chewed appreciatively. "Is that spiced with sage?" she asked.

"It sure is. Mother Bunch is the best with herbs."

He was talking freely, without trying to fake an impediment, and Mother Bunch ignored them as she tended to the hearth. She was a short, stout old woman with a round red face that looked as though it had been scrubbed too hard. Throughout the meal she made appropriate clucking noises over Lydde: Oh, the poor lad, to have been so mistreated by those dreadful papists! So Lydde was officially male, though she and Uncle John agreed it better to be good English Lewis than Louis.

Lydde tried awkwardly to manage the large chunks of mutton with her spoon, then looked around. "Where are the forks?"

"No forks," said Uncle John. "That's a French affectation that only the rich have adopted so far. Good solid Norchester folk use their fingers."

"Which explains," Lydde said, "why so many good solid Norchester folk walk around with grease stains on their clothes."

"You'll learn to lick your fingers well," Uncle John said. "But don't look so dainty when you're doing it."

Lydde propped her elbows on the table and dug in.

"Where's Mary?" Uncle John asked.

"She went on her rounds delivering medicines," said Mother Bunch, "and planned to end up at Carter's inside West Gate to visit little Gwen. She'll have her supper with them."

Uncle John nodded. "I know Lyd—er—Lewis will want to meet Mary. They should be great friends."

"Indeed," said Mother Bunch with a twinkle, "they may be more than friends."

"Now, Mother Bunch!" Uncle John wagged his finger at her. "You must let the young people alone."

Lydde tried to ignore this and plunged her fingers into the stew.

SHE was shown to an upstairs bedroom that overlooked the garden, though she could only see it in a haze through the milky glazed windows. There was a rope bed that held a feather mattress, a wooden chest for clothes, a chair, and a stand for washbowl and pitcher.

She felt worse than jet-lagged—time-lagged—and sank gratefully into the feather bed for a nap. There she dreamed of falling, and that Mother Bunch was in the kitchen at Roundbottom Farm engaged in a hair-pulling match with Aunt Lavinia. She woke to an insistent tugging at her arm. When she opened her eyes, she found herself staring at a face from her photographs of her sisters.

"Oh, my God!" she exclaimed, still groggy.

The girl stepped back in alarm and put her hand to her neck. "Please, sir, have I offended or has God?"

"No, no." Lydde sat up. "I was having a nightmare, that's all. Please, what is your name?"

But she already knew. The girl was about thirteen, with long dark hair parted in the middle and pulled back from her face, her eyes wide-set and her mouth dainty.

The girl dropped a curtsy. "I am Mary. I'm your cousin."

"So you are." Lydde could barely speak. "And what is your last name? I mean—what is it called?—your Christian name?"

"Soane, sir. Same as the good doctor."

"Well, Mary, I see the resemblance."

In fact, Lydde had always thought Mary's face, so grave and intelligent in the black-and-white photo, most resembled the pictures of her mother Margaret, who had also looked much like her brother, Uncle John. And here was the girl in the flesh. Overcome, Lydde fell back against the pillow and began to sob.

"Oh, sir, I didn't mean to frighten you. I only came from Mother Bunch with your clothes. They are all in an upset downstairs, for there is a disturbance at St. Pancras Church." She held out a pair of breeches, stockings, a shirt, and boots.

Lydde covered her face with her hands for a moment and regained control of her emotions. When she looked up she said, "Will you send the doctor to me at once?"

Mary curtsied. "I will. Are you ill, sir?"

"No, Mary, not ill. Just very tired. And please. Call me Lewis, and no more curtsies. We must be friends."

"If you say so," Mary said, obviously pleased. She went to the door, then turned. "Will you be my brother? It will be so nice to have a brother again. All my brothers and sisters died of the scarlet fever."

Then she disappeared. Lydde said to the empty door, "And mine died of a fire."

Chapter 6

St. Pancras Church

C ONSTABLE BAXTER AND Jacob Woodcock ran a tight race to see who could first carry news of the strange arrival to Lieutenant Major-General Noah Fallam. Woodcock the blacksmith wound his way through the warren of little streets between East Gate and South Gate, calling out to those he recognized that he was on a mission to inform the lieutenant major-general of "some devilish mischief come among us." Baxter was more deliberate but, like the tortoise, more purposeful, and he avoided the curious to make his steady way to the Pye, then along its bank past Soane's Croft, unencumbered except to dodge the occasional swan. So he reached his object first, and in less of a lather than Woodcock, who came along the gravel walk of the cathedral close in an agitated state just as the constable was lifting Fallam's door knocker.

The lieutenant major-general was comfortably established in the former Bishop's Palace at the cathedral, now closed, since Puritans held cathedrals to be un-Christian dens of iniquity, the "gaudy whores of the Antichrist's Church of England," as Jacob Woodcock was fond of saying. Woodcock chafed to see Pastor Fallam set up housekeeping in the shadow of such a monstrosity, yet had to admit as he waited with Baxter that it was indeed a handsome residence, all mellow brick with large windows, and therefore fitting for Cromwell's representative. Let this former habitation of sinners be thus redeemed by the presence of a godly man, he told visitors to his smithy. Though he also wondered at the isolation of Pastor Fallam. The deserted cathedral and its grounds presented a silent and indeed eerie atmosphere that frighted even good Christian men certain of their place among the elect. Fallam must be assured of the unassailable state of his soul.

Baxter, for his part, was wondering how he might be rid of Woodcock, who, though the constable shared his Puritan sentiments, was so shrill and meddlesome in urging Baxter to root out iniquity that he often longed to pitch Woodcock into the Pye. Baxter kept his hand on the doorknob as he waited, to make it plain to whoever answered that he, Constable Baxter, was the true bearer of news.

The door was soon opened by Pastor Fallam's secretary Cleyes, a scrawny lad of around twenty. Cleyes seldom had much to say, Baxter had noted, so he was not surprised when he and Woodcock were ushered through the house in silence. Baxter kept his own counsel while Woodcock nattered on about visits from the Devil, and was gratified when, before opening the door to Fallam's office, Cleyes turned to Woodcock and said, "Please wait here, sir," while indicating the small reception room. Then, "You may go in, Constable." So Woodcock was left to cool his heels and grumble about the impertinence of youth, even as Cleyes ignored his glowering looks and departed.

Noah Fallam heard Baxter's report with the appropriate amount of interest and only faint alarm. As should be, Baxter thought, for though others may be as stirred up as any boiling pot, yet the lieutenant major-general must remain calm. And calm he was, Noah Fallam, young still at thirty-two, but a Cambridge man from Emmanuel College, a man of the cloth and a hero of the wars. Such a one would not be excitable, Baxter thought admiringly. He would know all the world had to offer and fear only God.

Fallam leaned back in his chair and did not offer a seat to Baxter, as was proper. He heard the constable carefully, asked for a full description of the boy's strange outfit, then said, "Did you see them on to Soane's Croft?"

"No, sir, for I came straightway to inform you. But I have no reason to doubt the good doctor did escort the lad there, being an honorable man."

"And a useful one," Fallam noted. "He snatched your child from the jaws of death, did he not?"

"Indeed," Baxter agreed, suddenly nervous that Fallam might think him easy in his perceptions because of services rendered, "yet I believe I might judge him of good character even if he had not been useful to me."

"Tell me, Constable, for I have not heard the details of that miracle. How did it occur?"

Baxter was glad to recount again the recent dramatic event. How Martin, a feisty lad of four, had been left in the garden to amuse himself and had been seen by Baxter's wife to fall suddenly down as if in a fit, jerking and unable to speak. How all had thought the Devil possessed the boy. How the oldest girl had run fast to Soane's Croft while all despaired of Martin, who was turning red, then blue, and passing from a fit to a swoon. How Mr. Soane had arrived quickly, since the Baxter cottage was fortunate in being well less than a quarter mile from Soane's Croft. How the good doctor had raised the unconscious child to face his frantic parents while the doctor stood behind, wrapped his arms about the boy's small chest, and squeezed with all his might as though he might crush the very life from him. Indeed, said Baxter, John Soane had treated the boy as if he were a rag doll so that his good wife screamed and rushed forward in protest. Just then a round object popped from her son's mouth and landed on the ground. At that the boy began to breathe easily and, the color soon restored to his cheeks, he began to speak.

Mr. Soane meantime was searching the ground and held up a crabapple, still whole save for a single tooth mark.

It seems the boy was hungry for that which he would not have enjoyed once he bit it, Soane had said in his halting manner.

"For the lad had swallowed the crabapple whole, and it became lodged in his throat," Baxter explained further, "which we did not know, and if we had would have turned him upside down but likely to no avail. Yet the good doctor restored him."

"With God's help," Fallam reminded him narrowly.

"No doubt," Baxter agreed.

Just then came a banging on the door, which burst open to reveal an agitated Jacob Woodcock. Fallam stood, angry to be thus interrupted, but Woodcock cried, "Pardon, sir, but a messenger has arrived from without East Gate." Behind him stood said messenger, a boy white with fear and glad for Woodcock to make the dreadful announcement.

"St. Pancras Church!" Woodcock cried. "'Tis blasphemous again!"

Baxter felt a chill run through him, and noted that even Fallam blanched.

"We shall see at once," declared the lieutenant major-general. "Cleyes!" he called. "Saddle my horse!"

A crowd had gathered in the usually quiet churchyard at St. Pancras. Some were angry, others frightened, women cried hysterically, men shooed away curious children and forbade them to set foot inside the church. The vicar of St. Pancras, the Reverend Smythe, stood in the midst of his parishioners, who gathered around him in a tight knot as though for protection.

The Reverend Smythe was an old man who had seen much—the persecution of papists under Elizabeth, the liturgical innovations of the Stuart kings, and now censure and proscription by the Puritans. He counted himself fortunate to be possessed of a living in his old age, yet he could not turn his back entirely on his beloved *Book of Common Prayer*. Nor could his parish. And so they had continued, whenever they felt the stern eye of Cromwell and his minions looking the other way, to secretly pray together the good old words in which the bread became flesh and the wine blood—*Holy holy holy, Lord God of Hosts, heaven and earth are full of thy glory*—without advertising to their neighbors that they still subscribed to such heresy. Until the previous curse—as some deemed it; or miracle—as others whispered—had come upon them. And now had come again.

So the Reverend Smythe and his flock waited nervously for the arrival of Lieutenant Major-General Fallam and his constables, who were soon enough upon them in a thunder of hooves, the constables with hands on their cudgels to discourage any from pressing too close.

"At least," said the Reverend Smythe quietly to his frightened people, "the mob will not set on us now in blame, if they are so inclined. For Pastor Fallam will keep order, come what may."

Fallam dismounted with a grim look on his face. The frantic crowd fell silent. Noah Fallam had been a boy among them, yet not well recalled except as the quiet and studious son of a local squire, and gone to Emmanuel College Cambridge while still a lad. He had returned in authority a year past, and was stern beyond his years, with a handsome face and dark eyes which led many a Norchester wife to push a daughter or two in his way, so far to no avail. He satisfied himself, looking around, that the crowd was in no danger of a riot, then gestured his constables to follow and entered St. Pancras Church.

But though the constables entered bravely enough, they stopped dead, and Baxter, following behind Fallam, was so stunned that he cried, "God preserve us!" and bumped into his superior.

For the walls of St. Pancras were decorated as in old, papist days, with paintings, colorful images of angels, demons, serpents, the Virgin Mary, and even the Lord himself.

"This place belongs to the Devil," hissed Woodcock, who had entered uninvited with the constables.

"Silence!" Fallam commanded. He was not looking at the walls, as though to do so would cloud his thinking. Then he turned on his heel and left abruptly, causing the others to scurry after him.

Outside he made straight for the Reverend Smythe. "Who discovered this?" he demanded.

"W-why," Smythe stammered, "two women come to prepare the church—"

"For a forbidden service!" Fallam interrupted.

"No, indeed," Smythe protested, but further words died in his mouth.

Fallam spun around. "Who applied the whitewash to this church on the previous occasion?"

Woodcock stepped forward. "I did myself," he said, "and proud to serve God in that way."

"When?"

"While this post was vacant, barely a month before you arrived, sir."

"And you do swear you made a thorough job of it?"

"Of course," said Woodcock. "Those paintings were well concealed as whitewash could make them, and I used a specially thick mixture, to stand up to the Devil."

Fallam had been searching faces in the crowd, even as he listened. He saw fear, and wonder, but none who betrayed any guilty knowledge, only puzzlement. He had heard the stories when he arrived in Norchester, of the church beyond East Gate, its medieval images covered with whitewash in the purifying reign of the boy King Edward the Sixth, before the living memory of anyone in Norchester. Memory, in fact, had failed to remind that such wall paintings had even existed. Yet the congregation of St. Pancras had arrived one Sunday morning to find them exposed as if newly painted. The scandal was enormous and they had been quickly covered again. But because all this happened before Fallam's arrival, it had seemed a fairy tale to him, the working of overwrought minds. Yet here were the paintings clear to be seen.

Fallam turned to the Reverend Smythe. "If not for your advanced years," he said loud enough for all to hear, "I would clap you in irons and put you to trial for this. Yet . . ." he added as Smythe stepped back as though struck, "I shall for that consideration tell you to go to your home and stay there. Woodcock!" he called.

Woodcock came eagerly forward. "Sir?"

"You shall once more whitewash these walls. They are an affront to God."

"Amen!" came a few scattered cries from the crowd.

"Gather some others to help you," Fallam continued, "and start at once. For I would have the job done by Sunday morning, when I shall preach in this church, purified as it shall be. I command the members of this parish to be present, but you should expect others to join you. Be assured many of the elect shall attend, those who reject idolatry and such"—he paused for the proper word—"trickery."

Then he sent the people buzzing away to their homes, and the constables to escort them so there would be no disturbances. He kept Baxter, however, and set him to stand outside the church door.

"I'm going back in," he explained, "to look for any clues to this mystery I might find. For I believe it is not sorcery but in fact a crime of some fashion which may be solved."

Baxter nodded, though he was uneasy to remain alone outside the church while the late afternoon shadows passed over the graves. He glanced at the sun from time to time as it made its way down toward the tops of the trees, then disappeared behind them.

Inside St. Pancras, Noah Fallam walked slowly down the aisle, around the perimeter, into the transepts, up to what had been the altar in Anglican days and still was if Smythe was dissembling. He went with his head tilted back until his neck ached, mouth slightly open and hands clenched in fists, studying the paintings.

When he finally emerged, he said to Baxter, "Come with me to Soane's Croft."

Chapter 7

The Interrogation

W HEN UNCLE JOHN knocked on the door, Lydde threw it open, then turned her back on him. "When were you going to tell me?"

"Tell you what?"

"Damn it, Uncle John! About Mary!"

He came in and shut the door behind him. "Soon," he said. "Soon. I didn't know Mary was back and I thought Mother Bunch was bringing the clothes."

"It's my sister!" Lydde collapsed on the bed. "My sister came through the Mystery Hole too!"

"No." Uncle John sat beside her. "Mary didn't come through the Mystery Hole. She came from Bristol. Did she tell you about her family?"

"Yes." Lydde turned her head away. "She said her brothers and sisters died of a fever."

"And her father Charles," said Uncle John. "Her mother died years earlier in childbirth. That's why Mary came here. John Soane was her nearest kin."

"Who were the children who died? Were they Louis and Grace and Dominic and Jane?"

Uncle John hesitated, aware of a growing commotion in the street. "They were Lewis and Grace and Nicholas and Jane. And Lydde."

She sat up and stared. "I died?"

"Maybe you. But not you." He put his hand on her shoulders. "I'll explain it as soon as I can. As much as I know, anyway, which isn't much. Right now, there's trouble brewing. You need to get into these boy's clothes. But first empty your pockets."

She rubbed her face and stood up, then fished out the keys and laid them on an oak chest.

"Here." Uncle John held up the breeches. "They're not complicated, the pants button instead of zip."

"What about underpants?"

"Don't wear them here."

"My God," Lydde said, rolling her eyes.

Uncle John turned his back while she dressed. When she was done she turned in a circle for his inspection.

"It needs a waistcoat," he said. "I can just see your bust."

He called for Mary, who soon returned with a spare waistcoat from his closet.

"Is Lewis all right?" Mary whispered as she handed it through the door without looking.

"Yes," Uncle John reassured her. "Now go to Mother Bunch."

When Lydde had put on the waistcoat, he nodded. "Kind of large, but it does the job."

"Why the rush?" Lydde said. "What's happened?"

He pulled up a chair while she sat on the edge of the bed.

"We're going to have visitors soon. There's a big to-do outside town, at St. Pancras Church."

"What's wrong at St. Pancras? I just came through there, and I didn't notice anything."

"No paintings on the wall?"

"Sure. Religious scenes. Looked like they'd been there for a long time."

"They had," he said. "And then disappeared for over a hundred years. Covered over with whitewash in Edward the Sixth's reign."

"Then how—" Lydde stopped. "Uh-oh."

"That's right," said Uncle John with a twinkle in his eye. "It causes big trouble here, but it's incredibly exciting for my research. Every time someone comes back here from the future, the paintings uncover themselves. This is the fourth time, actually. The first two times I came through, the Reverend Smythe discovered what had happened before anyone else and managed to have them covered back up secretly. In fact, John Soane was a member of St. Pancras and helped with the whitewash. The Reverend Smythe was terrified he'd get the blame, and of course he was mystified about why it had happened. But I had an idea." He winked. "John was sad to see the paintings disappear again. He thought they were wonderful. I told him not to worry, they'd be back.

"The third time a couple of church women found them first. Word got out then, and you'd think Lucifer had strolled right through Norchester in his underwear. That was before Noah Fallam came on the scene. There was talk of witches, of burning. I was afraid they'd pick on some poor old woman and carry through on their threats. But Jacob Woodcock took it on himself as a holy mission to cover the paintings, so things quieted down. Now here we go again. I have no idea how Fallam will react. He's an enigma."

"And this is the Noah Fallam who came to the New River in 1671?"

"His brother definitely did. Robert, the one in the history books."

"The one in the print in your office?"

"Right. He's already in Virginia, as we speak. He was a Royalist, a supporter of King Charles the First. Noah is a Puritan, and fought for the parliamentary forces that brought Charles down. The English Civil War was like our own in that way, brother against brother. But it sure looks like Noah will travel with his brother in America later. You remember the inscription in Norchester Cathedral? Noah will be lost in the Virginia wilderness."

"So is Noah Fallam one of the bad guys?"

"I don't know. There are some terrible things going on in some parts of the country right now, people being tortured and murdered for their religious beliefs, women being lynched by mobs under suspicion of witchcraft, sometimes having their breasts cut off first. But nothing like that has happened here. Fallam's been here less than a year, although he's not a total stranger. His father had an estate just six miles away that Robert inherited, but the younger brother has charge of it now. Like I said, Noah's a cipher. People here seem to respect him, even though most of them aren't Puritans, because he hasn't allowed chaos to break out. But he's strict, and Cromwell trusts him or he wouldn't have been appointed."

"What's a lieutenant major-general, anyway?" Lydde asked. "I don't remember hearing about them."

"That's because they won't last long," Uncle John said. "Cromwell just appointed the major-generals and their lieutenants last year, and three years from now the Puritans will be kicked out and the monarchy will be restored under Charles the Second. Of course, nobody here knows that."

Just then came a knock on the door. "Will you have some hot cider?" asked Mother Bunch.

Uncle John opened the door and ushered her in. "Now, Mother Bunch, what do think of our young lad?"

She set down a tray holding two cups and a steaming bowl. "A handsome boy," she said. "He'll do, indeed."

"He was just asking," said Uncle John, "what a major-general does."

"Whoosht!" Mother Bunch cried. "What do they not do?" Then she hesitated. "Is it safe to speak?"

"Yes, indeed, Mother Bunch. Lewis is family and of a like mind."

"Well, lad, you would not have heard way over in Ireland. But our Cromwell and his gray followers think we are not glum enough, nor sufficiently Christian. So they have sent us a major-general to Bristol, and his lieutenant here to Norchester, to make us holy. They will keep us from celebrations, no Morris dances or maypoles, no sports or plays. They have even forbidden Christmas! For they think Christmas is based on pagan superstition and far too jolly. The major-general and his lieutenant Pastor Fallam are sent to save us from happiness."

"We're under martial law here," Uncle John explained further. "There are eleven major-generals in England and they are like God the Father. Whatever they say the law is, that's the law."

"And what does that make the lieutenant major-generals?" Lydde asked. "Jesus Christ and the Holy Spirit?"

"Close enough. In Norchester district, Noah Fallam is sheriff, judge, and jury, and no one can overrule him except Elisha Sitwell in Bristol and Cromwell himself."

Mother Bunch pointed to the clothes and shoes Lydde had arrived in. "I must go back to my kitchen. What is to be done with these strange garments?"

"I think," said Uncle John, "we'd best burn them in the kitchen hearth."

"Do we have to burn the Reeboks?" Lydde asked. Mother Bunch looked at her oddly. "My Irish shoes," she explained. "They're very comfortable."

"Sorry," said Uncle John. "You can buy another pair when you get home."

"Mr. Soane," said Mother Bunch with a laugh, "your speech is more and more like the lad's."

"Yes." Uncle John trusted her to believe anything he said. "I am falling into the habit of mimicking those I hear. It is becoming a pastime of mine."

Mother Bunch was shaking her head good-naturedly at his oddness, Lydde's jeans and sweatshirt bundled to her chest, when there came a banging at the front door. She froze and looked at Uncle John.

"That will be the authorities, come to question Lewis," he said, trying to sound calm. "You will let them in, Mother Bunch, and tell them to wait in my study. But before you answer the door, take those clothes to the kitchen."

When she'd gone, Lydde said, "Won't she be wondering what's going on?"

"She's an old woman, and loyal to John Soane as the day is long. Besides, she worships at St. Pancras too and she doesn't care for the Puritans, as you could tell."

But the visitors had let themselves in and intercepted Mother Bunch, for there was a clatter of boots on the stairs. Noah Fallam entered the room, carrying Lydde's clothes in a bundle under his arm, followed by a sheepish Constable Baxter.

"Is this the Irish boy?" Fallam demanded.

"It is," said Uncle John, once again feigning his speech impediment. "And are you accustomed to entering a man's home without asking entrance?"

Lydde and Fallam were staring at one another. A damned attractive man, she had to admit. His was an unusual combination of light brown hair and dark eyes, with a slight flush to his cheeks and a dimpled chin. Lydde felt a nervous tickle in her stomach.

"If I believe it warranted," Fallam replied, never taking his eyes from Lydde's. "Norchester suffers two uproars in the space of a few hours. A lad arrives in strange garb bearing the insignia of the Devil, and a church is bewitched. Could there be a connection? If the answer be 'yea,' then indeed, there is reason to force entry before these"—he held up the clothes—"are lost."

"This boy is a cousin."

"So I am told. And I would know what else he may be. First remind me, Mr. Soane. Are you not a member of St. Pancras parish?"

"I am."

"As I thought. I shall preach there tomorrow morning. You, sir, will be there with your household."

It was clearly an order, not a request. "We shall attend as usual," Uncle John said mildly.

Fallam turned back to Lydde. "These clothes which your servant was so anxious to do away with, are they the ones you arrived in?"

Lydde looked at Uncle John and he nodded again.

"Yes," she said. "My cousin has only just convinced me it was safe to remove them, and we thought it best to burn them."

"Boy," said Fallam, "you speak as strangely as was reported. You shall come with us."

"But he is tired from his journey," Uncle John protested.

"All the better. Perhaps we'll get the truth more easily."

Then Lydde wailed, "Please, sir, may I not wait until after you preach tomorrow morning? For I am greatly in need of the word of God. Please, sir, it would be such a comfort to hear you first."

Fallam, she was pleased to see, had been taken off guard. Uncle John had put his hand on her shoulder. "There, there, Lewis. You are safe now."

Fallam looked from one to the other with narrowed eyes. Then he said, "Your certainty of receiving spiritual comfort from me is touching. Still I would ask you some questions. Since you claim to be weary, we shall go downstairs and proceed there. Mr. Soane, which room would be most appropriate?"

It was clear he would not be denied. "The study would be best," Uncle John said, and threw a helpless glance at Lydde.

"It will do. Constable Baxter, you shall attend the good doctor to ensure we are not disturbed." Fallam turned and clattered back downstairs, followed by Baxter.

"What am I supposed to do?" Lydde said in a sudden panic.

"Act," said Uncle John.

.   .   .

FALLAM sat at Uncle John's desk, laid his hat beside the bundle of clothes, then leaned back. Lydde pulled up a chair.

"You will stand," Fallam said sharply.

She straightened and stood up slowly, looking over his head.

"Look at me," Fallam commanded.

She did, and held his gaze steadily.

"How old are you?"

"I'm not certain, for we didn't pay attention to such things. But I believe myself to be around fourteen."

"Your voice has not yet broke."

"No."

"And you are Irish."

"Yes."

He leaned forward abruptly and smiled, but his eyes were hard. "I have been to Ireland. You sound nothing like an Irishman."

She swallowed, then said, "I am from a remote part of Ireland. In the far, far west. We spoke differently there."

"Where?"

"Um—Gloccamorra." It was from an old Broadway musical, the first thing that came to her. Figure that out, she thought.

"Gloccamorra. A distant place indeed, for I have never heard of it."

"We used to joke, sir, that neither had the leprechauns."

She forced a smile, but he continued to stare at her in stony silence. Then he picked up her jeans and said, "What fabric is this? I have seen it neither in England nor Ireland."

"I—I do not know the name of it. It was said in my village that it came from the indigo plant."

"The what?"

She fell silent, confused, trying to recall where indigo came from and remembering it was a dye, not a fabric. He held up the jeans and discovered the label.

"What is the purpose of this . . ."—he tugged on the label—"this small piece of writing?"

"In the west of Ireland they trade with strange places. I do not pretend to understand all their customs."

"'Eddie Bauer. De-*nim*.'" He pronounced *denim* with the accent on the second syllable, as though it were French. "Who is this Eddie Bauer?"

"Ah. A Frenchman, we were told. From a town called De-*nim*. These breeches came aboard with a shipwrecked cargo."

"'Eddie Bauer,'" he read. "'Since 1920.'"

He waited with arms folded.

Lydde took a deep breath. "I don't know what it means," she said.

"You don't know what it means?"

"No." She smiled brightly. "Do you?"

"Do I?" He reared back indignantly. "Don't be impertinent, boy." Then he noticed the zipper. She watched the growing amazement on his face as he cautiously tugged on the tab and it slid along, locking the row of tiny metal teeth. "What is this?" he asked wonderingly.

"It's called a zipper," she said. "It's in place of buttons."

He ran it back and forth, zipping and unzipping more quickly.

"You have to be careful," she said, "not to catch your hair in it. That is, I mean, if you're not wearing any underpants. Which people here—um—seem not to do." He was glaring at her and her voice trailed off uncertainly.

He dropped the jeans and took up the sweatshirt. "And this. This is made of strange stuff as well, odd to the touch. 'Duke,' it says. With a devil embossed."

"The doctor suggested," she said quickly, "that it means the old dukes who supported the late King were all in league with the Devil."

"Indeed?" He raised his eyebrows. "And that is supposed to please me, is it?" Yet he didn't seem pleased. He resumed his scrutiny of the label in the sweatshirt. "And this—Jansport?"

"*Yan*-sport," she corrected his pronunciation. "Scandinavian. A port in Greenland which sent ships to our part of Ireland."

"I thought the devil blouse came from papists who kidnapped you."

"Yes," she volleyed back. "The papists were also from the west of Ireland. They added the devil themselves, I believe."

He threw down the sweatshirt and seized the shoes, waved them at her.

Lydde crossed her fingers. "The man who made them was told leprechauns were thus shod. He tried to copy leprechaun shoes."

"What is this emblem on the side?" He pointed to the little British flag near the laces. "And what sort of cow produces leather of this type?"

Lydde was exhausted and out of explanations. "A Reebok?" she said helplessly.

He stared at her a moment, then threw back his head and laughed. When he was done, he smiled at her a moment as though fond of her, then stood abruptly, came around the desk, and seized her roughly by the arm.

"You are lying, boy," he said, his face close to hers, "and I shall get to the bottom of this. Do you understand?"

"But I—"

He shook her into silence. Then he froze, as though just noticing something. He studied her face, while she held her breath. Then he just as suddenly let her go with a final shake, threw open the study door and called, "Baxter! We are going!"

He turned and watched her as he waited for the constable.

"Perhaps," he said, "I should have you stripped and examined for marks of the Devil."

Her head came up then, and she stepped back.

"No," he said with a smile. "I thought not."

Just then Baxter appeared from the direction of the kitchen with Uncle John, calling back his thanks to Mother Bunch for the delicious apple tart.

"You have had your tart," Fallam said, "and I have had an experience of another sort. The boy yonder." He pointed at Lydde. "Keep an eye on him. And put these clothes in the sack. I shall take them with me for further examination."

When the door closed behind them, Uncle John said, "How'd it go?"

Lydde shook her head. "I don't think I got the part."

Chapter 8

The Sermon

Noah Fallam had chosen the former Bishop's Palace as his seat of government for several reasons. It was large, and though he did not himself require so much space, he thought his endeavors did. The palace itself had been remodeled by a bishop sympathetic to Protestants during the reign of Bloody Mary and so there were numerous hiding places, false walls, and secret staircases. From the tower at the southwest corner one could survey all the cathedral precinct, much of the town, and even the estuary beyond the walls. And the closing of the cathedral meant there were no visitors except those on official business for the lieutenant major-general. Simon Cleyes, ever watchful, had little trouble keeping an eye out.

Here Fallam returned from his visit to Soane's Croft and, after sending Baxter on his way home to supper, went straight to his office. He turned the sack of strange clothes upside down over his desk, picked up the gray blouse with the embossed devil. A strange fabric indeed, smooth on one side but without the consolation of velvet, and a nubby white on the other like the stunted fleece of a fairy-struck lamb. He rubbed it thoughtfully. Then he took up the breeches and marveled at the impossible closeness and uniformity of the stitching. On an impulse he buried his face in the crotch and took a deep breath. He came out of his chair and threw the breeches from him, as stung as he had been when he seized and shook the boy. He trusted himself in this as in other ways. Just then Cleyes appeared at the door.

"A letter," he said. "From Elisha Sitwell."

The major-general. Sitwell had only been at his post in Bristol for a month, having replaced the previous major-general, who had died suddenly of a fit. Fallam knew Sitwell of old and was not pleased with the change. He groaned.

"Throw it on the desk," he said. "It shall keep good company with these odd garments."

Cleyes stared at the pile of clothes. He picked up a shoe and turned it this way and that. "Is it some sort of player's costume?"

"Of a sort," Fallam said, "though I have not yet determined what sort of play it is. You have not seen this boy, have you?"

"No," Cleyes said.

"When you do, I would like your opinion. Study him closely."

When Cleyes had gone, he opened the letter.

Now that I am a month in my new post, wrote Sitwell,

I am pleased to note that the works of the Devil have been suppressed in Norchester as well or better than any place in the Commonwealth. I commend you for the thoroughness with which you enforce your ban of plays, of games, of music, and of other such frivolous tools of Satan. I do however notice the rise of another sort of lawlessness. Smuggling thrives in your district as nowhere else in my jurisdiction. Your situation in a more remote area of the coast has something to do with this of course. Yet I hear from men of property, especially from those industrious and pious members of Parliament of the sort who have set England on its present godly course, that the situation grows steadily worse and is cause for unrest among those inclined to rebellion. You have yourself reported that a brigand styling himself the Raven has organized a gang of smugglers which even now trouble your district and disrupt government revenue. I hope to hear soon of steps you have taken to bring this blackguard to the scaffold. If this proves beyond you, I shall leave Bristol to lend you assistance.

Fallam sighed and leaned back. He had been expecting this letter ever since he heard of Sitwell's appointment. What he had not counted on was to receive it in the midst of a mystery. He picked up a black shoe and put his hand inside. Noah Fallam had a long hand with slender fingers, and the shoe's strange binding gripped him tightly. He easily touched the inside toe. A dainty foot despite the shoe's bulky shape.

So. The new arrival might prove to be a costly distraction. Or—and he allowed himself a smile—an interesting diversion.

THE next morning Lydde sat at the breakfast table with Mary and Uncle John while Mother Bunch prepared fried bread and thick-cut bacon. Lydde watched in horrified fascination while she dropped a great dollop of butter into a simmering pot of beer, then poured the buttery beer mixture into a pot of raw eggs. She stirred this mess a moment, then emptied it into tankards and handed them around.

"Here, lad," the old woman said kindly. "Take the chill off."

Lydde leaned over and whispered to Uncle John, "While you're improving the health habits of the population, shouldn't you do something about this?"

"What would you suggest?" he whispered back. "Fresh-squeezed orange juice?"

Later they tottered along the road toward St. Pancras, Lydde enjoying a pleasant buzz that warmed her to the tip of her toes, and feeling less inclined to complain. Mary walked ahead, then slowed, came alongside Lydde, and put her arm through hers. They had been observing each other all morning. At daybreak Mary had greeted Lydde with a pitcher of water for her washing up, and soon after, looking out the bedroom window, Lydde had seen her returning from the henhouse with an apron filled with eggs. Mother Bunch was obviously fond of her, and the reason was obvious. Mary was a pleasant, useful girl.

As for Mary, she was fascinated by her new cousin. Lewis was a strange mixture of awkwardness and assurance. When Mother Bunch had called for help with the fire, he had stared at a common bellows, turning it this way and that as though he had never seen one before. Then he handled it so awkwardly that Mother Bunch had to take it from him and fan the flames herself. Mary generously put this down to his deprived Irish raising. And yet he spoke to good Mr. Soane with a confidence beyond his years, and Mr. Soane returned the respect.

Inside the crowded church, people turned to stare when the Soanes entered, to whisper behind their hands. Mary clutched Lydde's arm even more tightly, as though to protect her cousin. As for Lydde, she first noticed the smell of a hundred unwashed bodies. This despite the fact that Saturday night was bath night for many, including everyone at Soane's Croft. She herself had a go of it, rubbing her skin gingerly with a rough evil-smelling bar of soap while crouched in a tub of tepid water in the washroom between kitchen and doctor's office.

Uncle John looked around calmly, ignoring the whispers and stares, and led Lydde to the back pew beside the aisle, while Mary and Mother Bunch went to sit on the other side with the women. Lydde stared at the freshly whitewashed walls, trying to recall which painting had been where.

"Don't stare at the walls," Uncle John whispered. "People are watching you."

So Lydde dropped her eyes to her lap. Then a door at the front of the church opened. Noah Fallam stepped through, severe in a black robe with white tabs at the collar.

The service was pointedly not from the prayer book. There was no music, since the Puritans had taken ax and flame to the organ along with other "frivolous" items such as candlesticks. There was merely a prayer, several lengthy readings from scripture: Jeremiah, Revelation, and the Gospel of Mark. Then Noah Fallam stepped to the pulpit. He had no notes, only a Bible, which he laid before him with the gravity of an offering. He surveyed the congregation with a stern look on his face. Then he began.

"We are gathered this morning in a building set aside for the worship of God which has been stained by idolatrous and illegal practices." He here cast a severe eye on the Reverend Smythe, who instead of standing in his own pulpit was slumped in the front pew. Then Fallam continued.

"And there is more. For this is a church bewitched."

He got no further, for Jacob Woodcock stood and pointed a trembling finger at the women in the back of the church.

"And yonder sits the witch!" he cried. "For we had none of this upset before that girl came among us from Bristol. And my wife, who died, as you will recall, four months past, believed that girl was trying to poison her!"

A general tumult then, while Mary sat with a stricken look on her face. Mother Bunch put her arm protectively around the girl while fighting back angry tears.

"Why would they single her out?" Lydde whispered angrily to Uncle John. "I thought they would pick on me, if anyone."

"But you're a boy," Uncle John answered. "They rarely charge a man with witchcraft unless he's thought to be homosexual. They think the Devil uses seduction to win his converts, and only women and homosexuals would yield to him."

Mary had buried her head on Mother Bunch's shoulder while Jacob Woodcock shouted above the others, "She delivers the doctor's medicines, that one does. And the doctor may mean well, but the girl serves another master, who is Satan!"

Then Noah Fallam brought his Bible down upon the pulpit with a crash and cried, "Silence!"

And amazingly the din ceased.

Then he said, "You are not here to accuse this girl, or anyone else, of witchcraft. You are here to listen to the word of God. Sit down, all of you."

And they sat, Uncle John with a relieved sigh and a whispered, "Thank God for that, at least."

"As I said," Fallam continued, biting off his words as though lecturing unruly children, "a church bewitched. Not by a poor girl in league with the Devil. That is fantasy, as much so as belief in fairies and such. Satan has no such power. But by these fantasies does the Fiend truly tempt us, for they close our eyes to the true sources of evil. I speak of disobedience. The bewitchment of this church was brought about by those who mock God with their *Book of Common Prayer,* their clandestine games and revels, their morris dances, their plays." Like Woodcock he was pointing his finger, ranging across the congregation and beyond, in the direction of the Norchester walls. "Oh, yes. A play was performed in Norchester just before my arrival, while God's servants slept. Adultery and gaming continue. And in this church, idolatry is practiced, with a pagan worshiping of a piece of bread as the supposed body of Christ, with the debauched prayer book. Here is the evil. It must end, once and for all."

He went on with a slew of Bible verses which seemed to Lydde to have little to do with his point. But she was grateful attention had been deflected from Mary, who was still trembling and sobbing silently.

"Here is what the sinner believes," Fallam continued. "The sinner hears beautiful music and is moved. Because the sinner is moved, he mistakenly believes God loves him. Nothing could be further from the truth. God hates the sinner and loves only the elect. And the elect are known by their obedience to the word of God."

The heads of all the Puritans in attendance were bobbing in agreement. They were the elect, all of them were certain, not one of them or any member of their families a hated sinner.

"The sinner," said Fallam "straps bells on his legs and goes morris dancing at Michaelmas, and taunts God at Christmas with trees and candles and Yule logs, worshiping the pagan deities of light and trees rather than the one true God. The sinner attends a play where so-called actors pretend to be someone other than who they are, and where chastity is mocked, where demons are conjured and a love of violence tempted, where young boys in the guise of actors are lured into lewdness. The sinner's mind is on the play he sees, not on God. He believes what he sees is true, not a mockery of truth. Then there are the women among us who sin, who *think* not at all, but only *feel,* which is a woman's nature. Vain women gossip and spread the knowledge of evil. Women are as weak and giddy as children, and that is how Satan captures them."

Here Lydde sat up straight and looked around. No one seemed outraged, so she bit her lip and ducked her head. "Jerk," she muttered under her breath.

"I have heard rumors," Fallam continued, "that another play may be performed in Norchester. I assure you, it will not. Michaelmas is only days away, and I have heard morris men are ready to dance. I assure you, they will not. Nor when so-called Christ-mass comes will there be pagan or papist celebration, for the godly constables of Norchester shall go from house to house if necessary and root out all such evil. Christmas is but another form of playacting, and I forbid the mention even of its name. The risen Christ would not condone a papish mass nor have his name linked with one."

Lydde stole a glance at Mother Bunch, who was seething. Then they all gave a great start, many crying out in fear, for the doors at the back of the church were just then violently thrown open. A man stood outlined by the sunlight, and when he stepped forward he was seen to be roughly dressed and wearing a black hood over his face. He pointed a long arm—people here do point a lot, Lydde thought—at the pulpit.

"Noah Fallam!" the man cried. "I have a message for you from the Raven."

And even as a dozen men rose to go and throttle the man, he dropped a dagger on the stone floor with a clatter and was gone. He was pursued, but because his horse was waiting and ready, he was easily away, as his pursuers later reported.

In the meantime Fallam had involuntarily flinched at the man's entrance but now gathered his composure. He came forward from the pulpit and strode down the aisle, holding out his hand. Lydde sat nearest to the dagger and Fallam looked at her as though he expected her to hand it to him. She picked it up gingerly and turned its hilt toward him.

"There is a paper attached," she said.

"So I see." His voice was cold. He grasped the hilt so forcefully that Lydde failed to let go soon enough and the sharp edge of the knife cut her finger. She winced. Fallam reached out and grasped her wrist tightly, held up her hand to examine the wound. A thin line of blood rose from the tip of her forefinger. Then he just as abruptly dropped her hand, turned on his heel, and was back at the front of the church, unwrapping the parchment as he went. He read the message silently, then aloud.

"'Brother Fallam,'" he read, "'you set yourself above all before God. The Raven shall bring you down. Call not your Elisha Sitwell from Bristol to harass poor men, or I shall hang you myself from a limb in Oxgodby Forest. The Raven.'"

Fallam held the note out between thumb and forefinger as though it were infected. "Here is what I think of such crude threats," he said in a clear voice. He crumpled the parchment into a ball, dropped it, and placed a booted foot firmly upon it. "This Raven and his men are brigands who do not care for the souls of poor men, for they do tempt them to sin unto hell. Major-General Sitwell will not be deterred. As for myself, I assure you, I shall not cease to protect property or souls in my jurisdiction. In Norchester, I am the law."

With that, he bowed his head, prayed for a length of time, and dismissed the congregation, who left hastily, noisily, and with great relief. But while most were distracted with loudly discussing the strange events piled one upon another in the last two days, Uncle John and his little band were caught up short when Noah Fallam, accompanied by a flustered-looking Constable Baxter, appeared in front of them. He spoke to Uncle John but was looking at Lydde.

"Send the boy to me tomorrow," he said. "As near to noon as possible."

"B-but why must—" Uncle John was slowly replying, but he spoke to the air, for Noah Fallam was away toward his horse, the constable in tow.

SOANE'S Croft was quiet the rest of the day. John Soane did not see patients on Sundays, as all observed the Sabbath, but there was sometimes an emergency which called him out. No such event troubled him today. Mother Bunch and Mary did no Sabbath work in the garden; the flowers and herbs were left to fend for themselves, and Mother Bunch served a cold dinner of old bread, cheese, and cold bacon. Uncle John stood up when this frugal meal was done and said, "Pardon, Mary, Mother Bunch, but I must speak now with the boy. He will face a trial tomorrow." So Mary went off to study her letters, which Uncle John insisted upon, since she had never learned them before. Mother Bunch sat in a rocking chair outside the kitchen door, casting her thoughts here and there and silently offering encouragement to her herbs.

Uncle John led Lydde to a stone enclosure at the back of the garden. Empty niches two feet high were chiseled into the wall. Uncle John sat on a bench.

"Used to be a chapel to the Virgin," he explained. "And when that became forbidden, the statues were removed. So it just became a quiet place."

"A good place for making out," Lydde observed.

"That too, I bet," Uncle John agreed with a grin. Then he sighed. "God, I miss Lavinia."

"At least you know she's alive. That's more than she can say."

He shrugged and only said, "That won't last long," then looked away.

"I'm waiting for more explanation," Lydde said. "And I want it now. Especially if I've got to go before the Inquisition tomorrow."

"I know. So here it is. Not that you can tell any of this to Fallam, but you should know. I'd rather have told you back home, but you wouldn't have believed it anyway. Now"—he waved his arm to encompass the grounds of Soane's Croft—"you will."

"You bet," Lydde said. "And I remember things you used to tell me when I was a kid. You may have forgotten, but they were important to me. You said when people die they can go anywhere they want to, even across time. Is that what you want to tell me about?"

He took her hand.

"That's it," he said. "But now you don't have to die."

Chapter 9

Thin Places

UNCLE JOHN EXPLAINED about thin places. A thin place, he said, is located at the boundary between heaven and earth. A place where you can ever so briefly glimpse what lies beyond, perhaps even talk to God. When Moses met Yahweh in the burning bush he was standing on a thin place. The Celtic monks who came from Ireland to pagan England identified thin places, like the island of Iona, for their monasteries.

Thin places were like any other at first glance. If one goes into such a place heedless, nothing may appear out of the ordinary. But in these places only the most delicate of membranes separates mundane reality from the Infinite. Go in with eyes and heart open and you can sense this.

"Diaphanous," Uncle John said. "I love that word. That's how to describe the membrane between dimensions. You could call the altar rail of a church a thin place, where people kneel and meet the divine as though God stretched an invisible hand through a curtain. Or the New River cutting its old, old way through ancient mountains, God's finger tracing a jagged path. And the thinnest of all places, where the jagged crests of those old mountains touch the sky. Stand on such a place and you're close to true reality. Destroy it and you rip a hole in the fabric of creation."

"Hold on!" Lydde held up her hand. "You're talking like a mystic or something."

"You're here and confused," he said. "That should be enough to make you listen to me."

"Yeah. Well, I'm tired of the weirdness. You're a scientist. I want a scientific explanation."

He smiled. "Okay. You don't want thin places. How about a combination of relativity and quantum theory that posits ten or more dimensions including more than one dimension of time? Each dimension separated from the other by the thinnest of membranes pierced by wormholes too small to be detected. How about space-time so elastic that you can't even get an agreed-upon sequence of events? Time not as a straight line but like—like a handful of shaving cream. How about universes that continually split off one from another into an infinite number of universes that proceed in infinite parallels?"

She sat back against the bench. "You're not making any sense!"

"You of all people should understand," he said. "What's a well-told story but a parallel universe? When you step onto a stage and become another person, you pass into another dimension. The book, the play, that's the wormhole."

"That's not real."

"Yes, it is. You certainly believe it at the time, or you wouldn't read the book or play the part." He rubbed his head in an old familiar gesture. "Look. There's not a physicist in the world who understands how this works. I can barely begin to grasp it. All I understand really is what I'm working with here, and that mostly because I'm living it."

"Then start with that," Lydde said.

"All I know," Uncle John repeated, "is the math I'm working with to plot the dimensions of the New River Gorge. Because the Gorge is a place where the membrane between universes has been ruptured. We've known about wormholes for a while, but the technology doesn't exist to pass through them. Now, back home in the Gorge, you don't need any kind of futuristic technology. At least one of the wormholes has been enlarged."

"The one you and I passed through?"

THE one Uncle John inadvertently discovered back in 1950. He explained to Lydde how he'd been looking for runes in caves and fallen into the seventeenth century by mistake.

"Same as you," he reminded Lydde.

"Okay," she said. "So how did the wormhole become large enough to pass through?"

Instead of answering, he asked, "Have you ever been to a battlefield? One time Lavinia and I were on vacation up in the Eastern Panhandle at Shepherdstown and we decided to drive across the river to Antietam. It was October, a cold blustery day, and there weren't any other tourists around. We got out of the car and I took a few steps and stopped. I saw that Lavinia had stopped too. And she said, 'Do you feel something?' And I said, 'Yeah, I sure do. Want to go back?' And we got back in the car and drove back to Shepherdstown."

"What was it you felt?"

"A heaviness. A dread. The atmosphere trying to bear the weight of thousands dying in agony, was how I thought of it later. The departure of all those souls at once, even if you don't believe in an afterlife, even if they were just extinguished, it would have to scratch the thin membrane between dimensions. Though not tear it completely. And if you went in summer in the heat with cars and buses and people everywhere yakking about this and that, taking pictures just to say they were there, wondering where to buy souvenirs, kids crying— you'd feel nothing then. Do you understand? It takes silence to sense the closeness of another dimension. And a battle may not be enough to tear the fabric in a place that was ordinary otherwise, but a battle in a thin place might do it."

"What's happened in the Gorge that could do that?"

"I don't know for certain. But I think it may have started with the blasting of the tunnel under Gauley Mountain back in 1931."

"You think the blasting shook something loose?"

"Maybe. The unprecedented blasting combined with something else. The inhumanity. What you had was a company sending hundreds of poor men, mostly black men, to their deaths. Knowingly. They were blasting through pure silica without protection, going in and breathing ground glass every day."

"It's not the only place people have been treated inhumanely."

"No. But thin places are by their nature recognized as special, even holy. They're usually protected, a focus of pilgrimage, not atrocities. It's so seldom that terrible evil is committed in a thin place. You know how special the Gorge is. You know you can stand and look down along the river and it's like a force that tries to draw you in. The entire Gorge seems to exist in another dimension. A thin place. Yet we've killed people there, and since then there's the strip-mining nearby, blowing apart the mountains. So much blasted earth you can see it from outer space. And all this in a place already thin, with the divine already pressing in like an aneurysm ready to burst."

"In which case you end up here."

"Or somewhere. Where you end depends on who you are, I think, and who you're connected to."

The light was fading so she could no longer see his face. "Are you trying to find my brothers and sisters? Do you think they ended up here?"

He shook his head. "Not here. I don't think they would have found that particular wormhole. It's too far down the hollow from Montefalco. But I think there might be other wormholes. That's what I've been trying to calculate. I've done a lot of the math already. I've superimposed a Chartres labyrinth on the Gorge and tried to plot out my calculations."

"So that's what the red notebook in your desk is all about. Why a labyrinth?"

"It's a geometrical figure," he said, "but with spiritual implications. I've tried other things, squares, trapezoids, rectangles, but didn't see much of a pattern. With a labyrinth, with its entrance superimposed over the Mystery Hole, some interesting things show up."

"Like what?"

"It doesn't totally work yet. But how about a potential wormhole across the river on Gauley Mountain where there are other cliffs? Or in the town of Lafayette? And near Montefalco, although that one is covered by a valley fill now."

Lydde leaned back. "My God," she whispered. Then she looked at Uncle John. "But we've found Mary. Except you say it isn't really Mary."

"Not the Mary Falcone who lived at Montefalco in the 1940s. And yet she is the same Mary. I knew her, remember. This is Mary, same face, same voice, same personality. She's just had different experiences and she has different memories."

"And the Noah Fallam who's interrogating me is the same Noah Fallam who's going to go to colonial Virginia and disappear somewhere in the mountains?"

"The same, but he may not have the same experiences."

"You said we may be in a parallel universe, not the same one we left?"

"Anytime you travel through time you also travel through dimensions," he said.

"Explain that," Lydde said.

He shook his head. "I can't. The only way to explain is to follow the story and see what happens to this Noah Fallam and Mary. And John and Lavinia and Lydde. Then maybe we'll start to see how things connect. That's the key to the puzzle—the connections."

Lydde was laughing softly to hide her bewilderment. Uncle John put his hand on hers. "Relax. It's a fancy way of saying God is in charge."

Lydde stood up. "No, Uncle John, don't give me that fatalistic stuff you were talking about before. If God's in charge, He's doing a lousy job of it, because all kinds of bad things happen."

"If people have free will, then bad things are going to happen."

"But if everything is plotted out like you say, then people don't have free will and we're just a bunch of automatons."

"Not so. I don't mean the same thing Fallam and these Puritans think, with predestination and all that. Yes, bad things happen and maybe they're built into the fabric of reality, maybe set in motion since the Big Bang. But what's important isn't what happens to us. What's important is how we respond. We've still got free will to make decisions. But sooner or later we'll see the connections too."

"Connections," she said. "You keep using that word. So why did the wormhole send us here? Why England in 1657? What's the connection?"

"I have no idea. It may seem like pure chance. But it's not totally random, you know. You lived in Norchester once. And Noah Fallam went with his brother to the mountains of western Virginia. Maybe that's part of some divine plan."

"That's crazy," Lydde said.

He spread his hands. "And the rest of this isn't?"

Several decades in England had insulated her from the religious language of America, and to her ears Uncle John was sounding like a tent preacher. The idea of wormholes and dimensions was fascinating, but she decided to dispense with the connection part, especially if Noah Fallam was involved.

Night was falling and Mary appeared with a lantern, dispatched by the ever-watchful Mother Bunch, to lead them to the house.

"What about tomorrow?" Lydde asked.

"I think," said Uncle John, "that you and Noah Fallam will be very interested in one another. Because somehow he's part of all this."

"Too bad, because he's such an asshole. Although it's interesting that I'm going to be threatened and bullied by a man who, if I wanted to, I could inform of the year he's going to vanish."

"Which of course you won't do. Because none of us should bear the burden of that kind of knowledge."

"No. But it's weird to have that power. So what if things go bad? What if I'm in danger?"

"If worse comes to worst, you can go back to West Virginia anytime you want. As long as the passage stays clear."

"Meaning what?"

"Meaning we have to be able to get to the crypt of St. Pancras Church and drop into the cistern. The cistern room is locked and you brought back the key that John Soane took with him. The Reverend Smythe lets me keep charge of it. He thinks I do medical experiments down there."

Lydde felt a thrill of alarm. "Didn't you tell me once that St. Pancras burned down?"

"Yes, the authorities will burn it and that will probably close off the wormhole. But not until after the New Year. Hindsight is pretty damn helpful, isn't it?"

Thank God, she thought. She doubted she could stand more than a short time in the seventeenth century. Although, as she followed Uncle John and Mary into the house and up the stairs, a spring in her step even though she was tired, she pondered the delicious possibilities of possessing a fifty-five-year-old mind in the body of a twenty-year-old.

When she undressed for bed she felt further proof of her rejuvenation, a shiver of desire as she imagined the invisible hand of a man running the length of her naked body. Then the man materialized briefly in her mind's eye—Noah Fallam as he had stood close at the end of her interrogation.

"God, no!" she cried aloud, and with a shudder of disgust, threw herself into bed and pulled the quilt over her head.

Chapter 10

Virginia Copperheads

AFTER THE QUIET of the Sabbath, Monday in Norchester was a bustle of activity. The town was famous for its oysters, and the first fruits of the day's harvest were already arriving in the estuary, where women and men waited with brine and barrels for pickling. Alongside the fishermen, small boats in from France, Sicily, and Virginia were being relieved of an array of goods, from pelts to tobacco to spices, cheese, wine, and lace. Some of the merchandise would go straight to the market set up outside the cathedral precincts. Most would end up in the warehouses of the local gentry who would send it on to Bristol and especially London, at great profit to themselves.

But some of the money would find its way into the pockets of the poor people of Norchester and vicinity, thanks to the Raven and his gang of "roguers," as Mother Bunch called them. It was a term she used without approbation, for she claimed that if not for the Raven and his band of thieves and smugglers, many a poor child would go without and many a poor woman turn to selling her body for food.

"Hanged they'll be," she said. "Or at the least transported to the Colonies. The Raven himself is a dead man and must know it, for he will be hanged for certain if he be caught. And he will be someday caught, as they all are. Yet he'll go straight to his reward in heaven. For who is the greater thief, when poor folk are dying, than the rich man? Isn't it so, good doctor?"

Uncle John had nodded over his morning libation of hot beer and said, "Mother Bunch, I do believe you are a Leveler."

"Call me whatever you like. But you know yourself how hard it is on the poor folk hereabouts."

"Don't I treat the poor every day?" he agreed.

"And so kind of you," she said, "to take nothing save what they can spare. And sometimes sending along an egg or two for those who have none. Mary knows, don't you?"

Mary gave Uncle John an affectionate pat on her way to the hen-house to feed the chickens. "Lewis, you must come with me some-times when I deliver medicines," she said. "You shall see how sad the people are. And how well they speak of the Raven. There's a price on his head, but they'd rather die than turn him in."

Mary had turned out to be a storyteller, holding forth in the evenings before the hearth at Soane's Croft. As they sat in front of the fire, she told tales of the Raven and his gang she'd heard around Norchester—how a widow with small children had waked one morning to find a milk cow thrusting its head through her cottage window, how a poor girl on her way to Bristol to turn prostitute had been showered with gold coins and returned to her family. Mary sat close to the hearth, her face golden in the reflected light, and spoke in a voice that seemed strangely familiar to Lydde, as though she had heard it before, telling her stories when she was a small child. As Mary recounted the Raven's exploits, Lydde imagined a handsome man cloaked in black galloping through the night on his horse like Robin

Hood or Zorro come to life, risking his life to defend the poor and the weak. And perhaps, she imagined, to sweep a woman off her feet.

"How long has the Raven's gang been operating?" she asked.

"They put in their first appearance last Christmas," Uncle John said. "Sacks of grain and purses of coins started turning up on the doorsteps of poor families. There were three landlords hereabouts ready to turn out their tenants, and glad to do it to clear and enclose the land. But they had to hold off when the rent money showed up unexpectedly. They were pretty upset! Mother Bunch is right. It's a dangerous undertaking and the Raven won't last long, I'm afraid. They say Major-General Sitwell may come from Bristol to direct the pursuit personally."

"I'm surprised our excellent Pastor Fallam hasn't caught him by now," Lydde said. "He seems as tenacious as a terrier."

"Don't think he hasn't tried," Mother Bunch said. "But the Raven is too smart for him. Isn't he, Mr. Soane?"

"He's a sharp one," Uncle John agreed.

On Monday morning, Lydde was set to run errands for Mother Bunch. She carried a basket and a list of items to obtain: cheese, oysters, potatoes, carrots, onions, turnips, flour. They would be treated to oyster stew for supper. Then there were needles and thread to be purchased, along with a new paring knife, writing parchment, and ink. It would be all she could carry as she headed to her interrogation.

"And you tell that Noah Fallam," said Mother Bunch, "you must be home soon with those oysters before they go off, or I shall send him a bill to replace them."

"Mother Bunch commands," Uncle John said, and winked. He was packing a saddlebag for a day-long trip to visit the sick in the surrounding villages. Lydde walked with him to the stable.

"Something I haven't told you," he said. "The Raven knows he has friends here at Soane's Croft. Sometimes I'm wakened in the middle of the night and called out to treat one of his men who suffered an injury during some skirmish or other. So don't be surprised if it happens again. I've always been discreet, so I've earned the fellow's gratitude."

"Good Lord," Lydde said, "are you up to that kind of risk?"

"Hey," he said. "I took risks in World War II. Anyhow, lots of people here give the Raven's men secret aid. And what do you want me to do? Go back to Roundbottom Farm and watch TV every night?"

"Sorry. I can see your point. So, what's the Raven like? Is he cute?"

"Is he cute! What kind of question is that?"

"It's a twenty-year-old's question," Lydde said. "I can look out for cute guys, can't I? I want to meet this Raven."

"Cute!" Uncle John said again with a snort. "I hate to disappoint you, but he goes around in a black hood, and even his own men don't know who he is. It's how he survives. So if he's cute, nobody knows it."

"Who could he be?"

"My guess is he's a former soldier who got bored. Probably not from around here, a rootless sort who got addicted to adventure. There are lots of thieves in England just now."

"Yes," Lydde said, "who keep their plunder for themselves. But this one is different."

"He is," Uncle John admitted. Then a mischievous look crossed his face. "Tell you what. Next time the gang is in touch with me, I'll set up a blind date."

She punched him in the arm. "Stop making fun of me," she said, and headed down the garden walk with her basket.

"Lewis!" Uncle John called after her.

She stopped without looking back.

"Walk like a guy."

She took a deep breath, shook herself as though loosening her limbs, and began to stride.

At the market she went from vendor to vendor, buying the items on Mother Bunch's list. She liked purchasing vegetables from the stalls country people had set up, pressing coins into the palms of hands still dirty, their fingernails cracked and broken from the labor of harvesting. Most of them were tenants, Uncle John had explained, like the sharecroppers in the American South, eking out a pittance after paying tribute to their masters. These poor would be the ones who most benefited from the Raven's activities.

Lydde saved the perishable oysters for last, making her purchase from a thin girl about Mary's age who cast an obvious longing eye on the boy Lewis.

"What's your name?" Lydde asked, not wanting to lead the girl on but anxious to show some human kindness.

"Gen," said the girl with a slight curtsy. "And thank you for buying from us. 'Tis a scrimpy harvest this year and ten hungry young ones at home."

The girl leaned toward Lydde as though trying to impart some hidden meaning. Lydde backed away and wandered on, aware the sun would soon be overhead and she must present herself to Noah Fallam. She was about to turn reluctantly toward the cathedral when the word *Virginia* caused her to pause near a crowd standing outside an alehouse.

"Ha'penny to see the snake!" a sailor was crying. "Straight from the wilds of Vir-gin-i-a! Poisonous snake! Look but don't touch! Ha'penny a look!"

When someone handed over a coin, the sailor looked it over and thrust it in his pocket, then said with a grand manner, "Step back, now, all but the gent that paid. Step back."

The small crowd fell back and the paying customer leaned over while the sailor lifted the lid of the barrel and poked inside it with a stick. A moment of quiet, then the lid was clapped back on and the sailor was back to his chanting, "Ha'penny to see the Virginia snake."

Lydde pushed her way forward, holding up a coin. Mother Bunch, she knew, would not be pleased, and she would not be able to explain why she felt so compelled to view the creature. She did not like snakes, had unpleasant childhood memories of cowering in terror while Aunt

Lavinia killed a copperhead that had invaded her potato patch. Yet this snake was from home.

"A brave lad!" the sailor said. And he lifted the lid with a flourish.

Lydde leaned forward. A copperhead rested in a bed of bran. It was lethargic, head barely moving. The sailor prodded the snake with a stick and it flinched and fell back, tongue flicking, unable even to coil. Lydde knew then that the snake was dying, that it had come captive across an ocean without sustenance.

"It needs food and water," she said.

The sailor shrugged and clapped the lid back on the barrel.

She turned away, suddenly and sharply ill with sadness, more homesick than she had ever been during her years away from the New River. She wondered where the snake had been captured, how close to the mountains it had lived. She fought back tears as she headed toward the cathedral. Over thirty years she had stayed away from home, decades of living alone, of failed relationships, shutting down memories of blue mountain evenings beside the roiling river by refusing to miss anything or anyone, even Uncle John and Aunt Lavinia. Not thinking of her family, like everything else too easily lost.

She paused as tears slipped down her face, and wiped her cheeks with the heel of her hand. Poor snake. Poor Lydde. She was outside the cathedral, now deserted since no one was allowed to worship there, the same cathedral where she had made a tentative rapprochement to God in the twenty-first century. Now she had been flung up here in the seventeenth, the cathedral door padlocked to forbid entrance. Was that her answer? When she had mastered her tears, she trudged on across the close with her basket and presented herself at the door of Noah Fallam's fortresslike residence. A thin young man opened the door and ushered her into a waiting room just off the entrance, said, "I'll tell Pastor Fallam you are here," and left her alone.

She waited in the silence. Then she heard a sound that caused her to lift her head in amazement, for it was not at all what she expected to hear. Farther down the hallway, in the gloom of the old building, someone was laughing. It was the clear, relaxed laugh of a man who was at that moment relishing life. And though it did not fit, she was certain that the laughter belonged to Noah Fallam.

THE servant, if such he was, reappeared soon after and ushered Lydde farther along the corridor to a small room, bare except for a table and chair. A large flat cross hung on one wall was the only decoration. Noah Fallam stood leaning against the table, arms folded across his chest.

"Well, well," he said with a smirk. "The Irish boy."

She longed to give him a swift kick to the groin. She made up her mind then. She would take no bullying from this odious man, and if he pressed too hard she would say good-bye to Uncle John and go straight back to West Virginia.

"Mother Bunch says you should not keep me long," she informed him coldly, "or the oysters will go off and you must repay her."

He threw his head back and laughed at that, and was at once confirmed as the source of earlier merriment.

"You are having a jolly day," she said.

"Indeed," he answered. Then he came forward and grasped her by the wrist so suddenly she nearly dropped her basket. But he had anticipated that and took it from her, placing it on the table in one easy motion. He continued to grip her wrist tightly.

"You're hurting me," she protested.

He ignored this and pulled her hand closer.

"And how is your finger?" He made a show of examining it. "I should not want you to suffer because of my clumsiness yesterday. But it seems to be healing nicely. Good Mr. Soane will have seen to that."

She glared at him for answer.

He dropped her hand then and sat himself behind the desk.

"You are unhappy with me," he said. "Perhaps it was my sermon. I noted yesterday that you did not seem pleased by it. I wonder why."

She thought he was simply baiting her, but he waited as though expecting an answer, so remembering her earlier resolve she said, "Your so-called sermon was nothing but narrow-minded fanaticism."

"Ah!" He seemed not at all put out. "People do not speak such truths as I did in . . . Where did you say you were from?"

"Gloccamorra." It sounded foolish now even to her, and she had to fight not to look away.

He nodded. "Gloccamorra. And what in particular did you find objectionable?"

"Your views of women, for one thing."

He waited with eyebrows raised.

"Women are not weak," she said in a rush. "They are not foolish, they think as well as feel, their minds are every bit as fine as a man's, and they can do anything they set their minds to."

He stared as though he found her fascinating. After an excruciating—to Lydde—silence, he said, "And why would a boy defend women in such a manner? Would you subvert nature by placing yourself under their command?"

"I would acknowledge them to be my equal," Lydde replied hotly.

"Do you know the work *Malleus Maleficarum*?"

At her look of confusion, he added, *"The Witches' Hammer*. Since they obviously don't teach Latin in—um—Gloccamorra. A classic which I commend to you. The author sets forth all the wiles of women and explains how every woman is a potential witch. Like your Cousin Mary."

Lydde came forward and leaned over the desk, right hand clenched and finger pointed at his face. "How dare you! If any harm comes to Mary because of you, I shall make you pay for it!"

"You forget yourself. *Sir*." Fallam stood and shoved Lydde so hard she lost her balance and fell. She blinked back angry tears and willed herself not to look away as she stood slowly, rubbing her bruised elbow.

"Mary is not a witch," she said in a voice that barely seemed to work.

"Cleyes!" Fallam called so suddenly that Lydde flinched.

When the young man came to the door, Fallam said, "How warm is it outside?"

"The day has turned quite pleasant," Cleyes answered. "Autumn can be no more lovely."

"Then I shall continue this interrogation in the rose garden." He walked to the door, then turned to the startled Lydde. "You. Follow me."

She looked at Cleyes, who shrugged as if to say, You heard what he said. Then she followed Fallam down the hall and out a small door at the back of the house that led to a walled garden. It was indeed a crisp sunny day—Indian summer, they would have called it back in West Virginia. Fallam headed for a bench, where he sat, propping his long legs on a table in front of him. He gestured toward a chair.

"Sit," he said.

Lydde took an uncertain step forward.

"Go on," he said. "Sit."

She sat, feeling more uncomfortable than when she was on her feet. At least then I could run, she thought. In her nervousness she started to cross her legs but caught herself just in time and sprawled in the chair instead. She hoped her confusion didn't show in her face, and knew that it did. Fallam's attitude had changed to that of a solicitous uncle.

"You really are a boy who needs to be taken in hand," he said. "Wherever you are from, you have not been properly educated. And John Soane is a good man, but I would not say he is known as a disciplinarian."

Lydde sat up, growing angry again. "I continue to be concerned about Mary," she said, "and your charges against her, and I will not be distracted by your criticism of me until you retract those charges."

He studied her a moment, then said, "Whatever your deficiencies, your spirit and loyalty are to be admired. As to Mary, they are not my charges. Since you failed to notice, I defended her in church."

At last Lydde felt free to look down at her lap. "You did," she admitted.

"Yet the man who accused her, Jacob Woodcock, is not alone. Though he is the one I would judge who is most intent on causing her trouble. She is a fanciful girl, from what I am told, and likes to tell stories."

"She does," Lydde agreed again. "She tells stories before the hearth at Soane's Croft. There is no harm in that."

"Stories of enchantment, of fairies and goblins and sorcerers and other enchanted creatures."

Lydde looked up and said nothing.

"They have noted that she is left-handed."

"My God, what are you—"

"She also is seen talking to animals."

"She loves animals!" Lydde protested. "What is wrong with that? She has a tender heart, that is all! Who dare accuse her of witchcraft on such grounds?"

"Jacob Woodcock," Fallam answered calmly. "And others he has stirred with suspicion."

"Then it is him you should deal with."

He sighed. "If you would not come here with your claws out ready to scratch, you might notice I am trying to help Mary. I have a proposal for you. No, not a proposal, an order. John Soane should have dealt with this, but he has not. As lieutenant major-general I am responsible for the well-being of the people of Norchester. If he will not manage his own household and thus inadvertently places its members in peril, I must intervene. Mary is no longer to be allowed to deliver medicines. It is not proper for an unattended girl of her age to be traipsing all over the district in any event."

"But she enjoys it. She loves to visit people. And why should she be kept home because of someone else's ignorance? Women should not be kept in prison when the transgressors are others."

"Ah." He leaned back. "Defending women again."

Lydde looked away.

"You shall take over the deliveries yourself," Fallam said.

She stared at him.

"You are a lad. Soon you shall be a man." He smiled slightly as though something amused him. "It is proper that you, not Mary, deliver the medicines. If she wishes to accompany you from time to time, I shall not forbid it. But no more than once a week."

"But—"

He shook his head. "This is an order. A boy should do a boy's job."

There was nothing for it but to agree. "Very well," she said.

He clapped his hands in dismissal. "Good. Now, Mother Bunch will be wanting her oysters."

He stood and began to remove his coat, for the day had indeed turned warm. And as he did, a silver chain caught in his waistcoat fell forward. It was a necklace, a small Celtic cross, identical to the one she had found with the skeleton in the cave. Lydde gasped.

It was Fallam's turn to be startled. "What?" he said.

She stared at him, trying to gather her wits. You cannot say to a man, I know where your dead bones lie. Nor, as Uncle John said, should anyone be told such a thing, not even a man as insufferable as Noah Fallam. Though she was a little pleased to see how uneasily he watched her. It was the first moment of doubt she'd seen in him.

"Nothing," she managed to say. "That cross you wear. I have seen such crosses on tombstones in Ireland."

"Oh." He looked relieved, took out the cross, and held it up a moment. "I got this in Ireland, as a matter of fact. It seemed to me a symbol of an earlier, purer form of Christianity." He smiled and let the cross fall back inside his shirt.

He stood there in that unguarded moment and she suddenly saw him as akin to the Virginia copperhead, dangerous for certain yet doomed to someday lie, a skeleton alone, beneath a cliff in the New River Gorge. *Lost in the wilderness of Virginia,* the memorial plaque had read, and something about God being mocked. She must tell

Uncle John and ask if he recalled the date on the memorial. Not so close to 1657, surely, and yet not far either. Poor lonely person.

WHEN Cleyes had fetched the boy's basket and sent him on his way, he went back to the rose garden, where Noah Fallam paced back and forth. He sat and waited. Eventually Fallam stopped and absently tucked behind his ear the shock of hair that fell onto his forehead. He was remembering the delicate hand whose wrist he so easily encircled between thumb and forefinger. And the changeability of the face.

"That's no boy," he said.

"No?" Cleyes asked, surprised. "Surely he is too bold to be otherwise?"

Fallam waved his hand dismissively. "At least I have got Mary out of the way. She should be in less peril now."

"Good," Cleyes said. It was he who had begged Fallam to do something to quash the rumors about the girl.

"And this one . . ." Fallam shook his head. "This one I shall watch like a hawk."

Chapter 11

The Raven

A T SOANE'S CROFT, Uncle John listened with concern to Lydde's story.

"Maybe Fallam's right about Mary," he said. "I've got to remember how differently people think here. It's just that John Soane before he left also let her do most of the deliveries, and Mother Bunch hasn't objected either."

"I think Noah Fallam is behind this," Lydde fumed, "not Jacob Woodcock."

"Now, now. He did Mary a good turn in church, the way he deflected attention away from her. On the other hand, he may be keeping an eye on us. Mary says she keeps running into Fallam's servant, a young fellow named Simon Cleyes."

"Is he a thin young man? He was there today when I was being bullied. What do you mean, she keeps running into him?"

"Well, she actually seems quite pleased about it. She's told me on at least three different occasions over the past few weeks that Cleyes has spoken to her, or offered to carry her basket for her. And once he walked the entire route with her."

"That's terrible!" Lydde said. "Mary's only thirteen!"

"Thirteen here is a lot older than thirteen back home. Here, Mary is only a year or two away from marriage."

Lydde flexed her aching elbow, rolled up her sleeve, and held up her arm.

"A nasty bruise," Uncle John observed.

"And Noah Fallam gave it to me," Lydde answered. "I think he's setting some kind of trap. You should have seen the way he treated me, threatening one minute, pretending to be kind the next. He was trying to catch me off guard. And that fellow Cleyes is spying for him, I know it."

But their fear for Mary, who was on a delivery even as they spoke, forestalled any defiance. For when the girl returned she was breathless and clutching a black puppy, and was followed soon after by an angry Jacob Woodcock. Woodcock, a blacksmith by trade, was still wearing his apron, and holding a hammer, which he waved menacingly. Mary, meanwhile, darted behind Lydde, pressing the whimpering pup to her breast.

"Here, here," Uncle John said as he stepped in front of Woodcock. "What does this mean?"

"You are harboring a witch!" Woodcock cried.

"Don't be absurd!" Lydde said, putting her arm around Mary. "There are no such things as witches."

"No such—no witches!" Woodcock sputtered. He gave Lydde a close look. "You do tempt Satan, foolish boy. The hand of the Devil lies heavy upon this household."

"Calm down, Jacob," Uncle John said. "Mary and the boy here are still learning our ways. They are young and a bit foolish, perhaps. But surely it is no more than that. What has the girl done to rile you so?"

"She has taken that dog." Woodcock pointed at the puppy.

Uncle John turned and said, "Mary? What have you to say for yourself?"

Mary took a step back and held the dog tighter still. "Mossup at the stable gave it to me. When he"—she pointed at Woodcock—"saw me with it, he said he was going to drown it. So I ran home."

"'Deed I was," Woodcock said. "It bears the mark of Satan. And this is an impertinent girl to disobey me."

"Why should she obey you?" Lydde said sharply. "You are nothing to her."

Woodcock stared at Lydde, his dark eyes looking her up and down. "I am a man," he said, "and one of the elect. That is the only authority I need to deal with a wretched girl. Why do you think otherwise, boy?"

Uncle John shot a warning glance at Lydde as she opened her mouth to reply. "Mary," he said, anxious to draw attention away from Lydde. "Let me see the pup."

Reluctantly Mary loosened her grip and allowed Uncle John to take the whimpering animal. He held it up. The dog was a bitch, black, with a blaze of white on its chest, and it had no tail.

"I see nothing demonic," Uncle John said.

"A female black dog born with a stunted cross on its chest but without a tail! That dog shall make a witch's familiar," Woodcock said. "Its master will be Satan and it will carry messages from its master to seduce this girl. Best to kill it now."

They were interrupted just then by the arrival of Constable Baxter, summoned by alarmed townspeople who had witnessed the spectacle of Jacob Woodcock chasing young Mary Soane through the streets with a hammer. And hot on the heels of the constable came Simon Cleyes.

Baxter, a burly man, struggled to catch his breath. "Mr. Soane. Mr. Woodcock. What sort of disturbance is this?"

Woodcock would of course be heard first, and when he was done, Uncle John held up the pup and said mildly, "The girl has a tender heart. She meant no harm except to save the poor creature."

Mary burst into tears. "Please," she begged, turning to Simon Cleyes, "please don't let Jacob Woodcock kill it."

Lydde glared at Cleyes. He pressed his lips together and looked grimly back but said nothing.

Baxter had taken the dog from Uncle John and was turning her this way and that. "Poor bitch has no tail," he commented.

"A cursed dog," said Woodcock.

"Now, now, Jacob," Baxter said mildly. "I knew of a tailless dog when I was a boy, and it was harmless. Nor would the good doctor harbor a creature of the Devil."

"You, Elijah Baxter, do enforce the law with partiality," Woodcock fumed. "Since the doctor did save your child from choking, you will hear nothing against him or his household. It is not fair and I shall complain to Pastor Fallam."

Baxter turned to Simon Cleyes. "What think you, Simon?" he asked. "Is this charge worthy of enforcement?"

"I think," Cleyes said, "Pastor Fallam shall not wish to be bothered with it. If the Devil puts in an appearance, then Noah Fallam shall lead the fight against him. But lacking the Devil and beholding only a pup . . ." He shrugged. "He would take the same course as Constable Baxter."

"Thank you," Uncle John said with relief.

"Do not thank me," Cleyes continued, "for the lieutenant major-general has also expressed his strong disapproval of the way you conduct this household. The girl Mary is no longer to be allowed such unsupervised freedom. This boy here is to take over her deliveries. If these orders are not followed, Pastor Fallam shall have you up on charges before him, respected in Norchester though you may be. Is that clear?"

Uncle John glanced at Lydde. "It is," he said.

"Will that satisfy you, Mr. Woodcock?" Cleyes asked.

Woodcock shrugged ill-naturedly. "It shall have to," he said.

Cleyes nodded. Then he doffed his hat. "Mary," he said with a slight bow.

Through her tears, Mary smiled and blushed.

Oh, Lord, Lydde thought.

DESPITE her anger at Noah Fallam's order, Lydde found she enjoyed the delivery of Mother Bunch's herbal concoctions. It was a change to leave Soane's Croft—poor Mary, who no longer had such a diversion. It was good exercise and Lydde loved the feeling of striding along on her newly young legs. Some of the people she met were regular customers and soon became familiar, hailing her if they saw her in the street (though she sometimes forgot to respond to a call of "Lewis!"), and seemed to look forward to her visits. With new customers she must ask directions and often found herself exploring a different part of the countryside, to her great enjoyment.

But some of those needing medicines lived several miles outside Norchester. Uncle John sent these by a man on horseback from the livery stable, or sometimes went himself. He had learned to ride horses when he was a boy. Lydde did not ride. That should change, she decided. A young man in the seventeenth century who could not ride was at a severe disadvantage, and only the poorest men would be in such a position. Women, she noted, were forced to ride sidesaddle, yet even these were more proficient than she was. She put the matter to Uncle John.

"I could teach you," he said, and began to give her lessons on the mare, Lady, who was the only horse living at Soane's Croft. For several days thereafter she made her rounds with a rump sore from the unaccustomed bouncing. But gradually her body became used to the pounding. Another day or two with supervision, Uncle John said, and he would send her out on her own.

Lacking a horse, her longest trek was to Mother Brown, who had just begun to receive Mother Bunch's tonic for rheumatism. Mother Brown lived in a cottage in Oxgodby Forest two miles beyond St. Pancras Church. She was a widow whose children had all died or left home, and she was lonely and loved to talk. Sometimes Lydde had difficulty getting away from her.

On her last visit without a horse she found herself outside the city walls as darkness was falling. She was alarmed to realize, as a blue twilight came on and she hurried along, that she could hear the sound of horses following her. She stopped to listen and could just make out the forms of two men on horseback who paused when she did. They seemed to be wearing cloaks of some sort but were too far away to see clearly. She turned and walked on as though she were not concerned. Travelers on their way to Norchester, most likely, and meaning no harm. Besides, she must pretend not to feel the fear that any woman of any time knows when alone on a road with no protection against a rape. As a boy she should not possess, nor show, such fear. She forced herself to keep a steady pace as the clop-clopping of horses' hooves came closer.

She was just about to emerge from the forest and into the clearing of St. Pancras churchyard when the horses quickened their pace and drew abreast of her. One pulled in front and stopped, while the other behind her stopped as well. Alarmed, she turned around to see the rider of the rear horse dismounting. Beneath his hat he wore a black hood that covered his head save for slits for his eyes and mouth.

He came forward with hand raised. "Don't be alarmed. We mean no harm," he said in an odd guttural delivery which Lydde assumed was meant to disguise his normal speaking voice.

Lydde spun around to run, but the other horse and rider continued to block her path. The second man was also hooded.

The man spoke again. "Don't be afraid. You are the doctor's lad, Lewis, are you not?"

"Yes," she said. "Who are you? Why are you disguised?"

He took a step closer and she retreated.

"I am the Raven," he said. "You have heard of me?"

"Yes," she whispered, her heart beating quicker. He was an extraordinary figure with his cloak wrapped around him and a sword strapped around his hips.

"Then you know I go disguised for the sake of my life. You know also I count John Soane as my friend."

She nodded, feeling less afraid. "Yes," she said. "He says he has helped you."

"Good. Then you will not mind to come with me? I need your help as well. You have nothing to fear from me, only you must fear Noah Fallam if you are caught with me. The decision is yours. If you say no, I shall disappear and trouble you no more."

Lydde felt a thrill of excitement. "I'm not afraid," she said. "I'll come with you."

"Good." He mounted his horse, then leaned down and held out a gloved hand. "Put your foot to the stirrup and climb up behind me."

She did as she was told and he hauled her easily onto the horse's back. He turned his head and said, "Hold on," then pulled her arms so tightly around his chest that she was pressed close against his back and forced to rest her cheek against his shoulder. Then they were away, soon leaving the road and plunging into the blackness of the forest. By the time they emerged, Lydde saw they were headed toward the coast southeast of Norchester. Beneath a wedge of moon they crossed a dark heath and followed a windswept headland until they reached their destination. It was the ruined abbey of Joseph of Arimathea that overlooked the Channel, which Lydde had not seen since she left Norchester in the twenty-first century.

They pulled up beneath the shelter of a wall. The Raven handed Lydde down with a flourish, then dismounted. In the back of her mind a warning sounded. He was treating her too chivalrously, not at all the way a boy should be treated. She needed to reassert herself, to be masculine. When he nodded toward his companion and said, "This is the Crow," she strode over and shook the man's hand as vigorously as she could.

"The Crow shall serve as lookout while we talk," the Raven continued. "I trust him with my life, and you should trust him as well. Now come this way."

They passed beneath a Gothic arch, once a large doorway within a wall, now freestanding. It was dark and they carried no lantern, but there was just enough moonlight to show they were walking upon grass that had taken over from occasional patches of paving stones. Then they entered a roofless cloister, carefully picked their way down a ragged staircase, and entered a small underground room. It had been made comfortable with straw pallets, a table, and a bench. The Raven found a candle hidden beneath the table and lit it. Their shadows flickered over the walls.

"We find this place useful," he said. "From the watch tower where the Crow waits, a great stretch of heath is visible, so we cannot be taken unawares. Behind us is the sea, and the ships we meet often come to us on the shingle below."

"Still," Lydde said, "aren't you afraid of being seen?"

"Always, of course. But few people come here. The place is haunted, they say, and bewitched by fairies who will steal the soul of anyone found here at night." Behind the mask his mouth curved in a smile. "So they say."

"You don't believe in fairies?"

"Not of that sort," he replied. "I imagine fairies appear in more workaday forms. Like yours."

"I don't know what you mean," she said. She was growing alarmed again. What had possessed her to come away so easily with a masked man to this remote place where no one could possibly find her?

"I have been watching you," he said.

She waited.

"I saw you arrive in Norchester. You were oddly attired. I have noted you since on your errands."

"How do you manage that?" she said, trying to sound nonchalant.

"I live in town. I see you in the market and now and then I glimpse you on your delivery rounds."

She wracked her brain, trying to recall who she saw on market days, who might catch sight of her as she walked around Norchester.

A constable, perhaps? A merchant at the market? Jacob Woodcock the smith?

"I think," the Raven continued, "you are a bold and spirited boy. And yet"—he stepped closer—"I think you are no boy."

Lydde's throat went dry. "You mock me," she managed to say, "because my voice has not yet broken."

He slipped a hand so suddenly inside her coat she had no time to dodge, and beneath the fabric of her waistcoat he cupped her breast.

"As I thought," he said.

She struck out at him, but he was too quick and grasped her arm to fend her off.

"Peace!" he said, and through his mask she saw him grinning. "I mean you no harm."

She pulled away and ran for the door. He followed and caught her again.

"Where shall you run?"

She began to beat her fists against his chest and he wrapped his arms around her and held her tightly against him so she could not move.

"I say, peace," he repeated. "Your secret is safe with me and I swear before God I shall not touch you again. Do you hear me?"

His words at last penetrated and she began to understand that she was being held firmly yet without further rude treatment.

"Come sit upon the ground," he said in her ear, "and I shall sit across from you. And you may tell me as much of your story as you wish to tell. Will you do so, calmly?"

After a moment she nodded and allowed him to lead her to a pallet, then watched warily as he seated himself opposite her.

"What is your name?" he asked.

"Lydde."

"A pretty name. Why do you pretend to be a boy, Lydde?"

"So I can be free," she said.

"Free?" He seemed surprised.

"To move about as I like, to do as I like. As I am used to."

"Who are you? Where do you come from?"

She hesitated. He was sitting quite calmly across from her, and now that he had satisfied his curiosity as to her sex, he made no move toward her. But could she trust him?

"You would not believe me," she finally said.

He said in his guttural voice, "I have told you fairy stories do not fright me."

"This is stranger still."

She covered her face with her hands for a moment and thought of Uncle John. What would he advise her to do? Then she recalled that he had shared in his own hour of need with John Soane, who had believed him. And the longing she had felt, barely noticed yet now prevailing, to find a friend here, someone to confide in, overwhelmed her. The man across from her was fearsome, with his black mask and vivid dark eyes, but he had fondled her in a manner that brought a blush to her cheeks as she recalled it. Her breast still seemed to burn from his touch and then she wished for that hand to be pressing against her once again, and that decided her.

"Oh, God," she whispered, "I wish you had not touched me, for now I cannot forget it."

He stirred at this and she thought he might rise, but instead he leaned forward and said, "Tell me everything."

So she did. She told him that she had come from the future through the cistern in the crypt of St. Pancras Church, and that she had come unprepared. She described what she knew of the paintings. She told him Uncle John's story, and what had happened to John Soane, and why her uncle now affected a manner of speaking as though he'd suffered a stroke. She told him of her life, of losing her family to the fire, of her father's quest, of how she had gone as a child to search through charred ruins with a stick. How she had been an actor in England and ended in Norchester. How the mountains back home were being blown apart and the burned foundation of her family's home had been covered and her Uncle John had gone searching for the children down the wormhole. About Mary.

Now and then he shifted his position. But he never took his eyes from her face. In the candlelight she could see him watching her, almost unblinking. He asked no questions. Sometimes she would stop and explain something he might not understand—Oh, a telephone, that's a thing that lets you talk to someone far away—and still he didn't stir. Yet he watched her. She had never been listened to so intently in her life.

When she was done, she burst into tears. She did not sense his approach, but then he was wrapping her in his arms and held her against his chest, sobbing as she had never allowed herself before, while he stroked her hair and said nothing.

When she was finally able to speak, she said, "Do you believe me?"

She felt the rise and fall of his chest against her cheek.

"Much of what you say," he replied, "is fantastical, not to be believed. And some of what you say is, I think, as sad as anything I have ever heard."

He held her face to the candlelight as though studying it, rubbed her tear-stained cheek with a fingertip. She tried to see his eyes, but they were hidden in shadow. Then he was kissing her, gently at first, then more insistently. He slipped his hand beneath her waistcoat and once again caressed her breast, then stopped and wrapped her in his arms.

"Who are you?" she whispered.

He leaned back, staring at the ceiling.

"I am a man caught in his own trap," he said.

"What do you mean?"

"I have brought you here to satisfy my curiosity. I wanted to know that I was correct in my judgment that you were a woman. I wanted to know about your circumstances. And so I tricked you into coming here by telling you I needed your help. Yet your story is more than I expected."

She sat up straight and pulled away from him. "So you don't believe me after all."

"I didn't say that. I can scarce imagine that anyone could make up such a tale. Besides, I have seen enough to know there is something extraordinary about you. But it is a lot to take in on top of the doubts I already had. I shall be as honest with you as I can. I did not want to bring you here, because of the danger you will be in by associating with me."

"But you *did* bring me here and you have kissed me and caressed me so that now I want you badly."

He shifted uncomfortably. "My God, you speak plainly," he whispered.

"It is how you have made me feel by the way you have treated me. How dare you say now it was a mistake?"

"Lydde, I have admired your courage. And since I guessed you to be a woman, I must confess, I have lain awake at night with longing for you. At last my desire for you overcame my judgment."

"You are not the only one who feels such desire, or such doubt," she said.

He drew her close again, took her hand, and traced a pattern in her palm with the tip of his finger.

"To understand my reluctance you must know the precariousness of my situation," he said. "If I am caught, I shall be killed. And most likely I shall be caught."

She remembered the words of Mother Bunch—The Raven is a dead man and must know it—and shivered. "Is there no hope?"

He shook his head. "Very little. Perhaps I shall have enough warning to take ship away from England. That will be my only chance."

She sat up suddenly. "But it's 1657. That means in just—" Then she stopped. Should she tell him what the future would hold? Would it cause more harm than good?

"What?"

"Maybe I shouldn't tell you. But in a year, Cromwell will die and his son will take over. But people will be sick of the Puritans by then."

"You know this!" he marveled.

"Yes, and don't look at me as though I were some sort of fortune-teller. Where I come from it's all in the past, and I studied history in school. In 1660 the King will return. Charles the Second. So Noah Fallam and the major-generals will be out of power."

He shook his head. "That won't help me. The King will be as set against me as Cromwell. I have made men of property my enemy. And men of property do not forgive. No, my future is limited to two possibilities. By the time you speak of, either I shall be in America or I shall be dead."

"If it is so hopeless, why are you doing this?"

"Because I must be true to myself. I fought for the revolution. The revolution has been betrayed, but I will not desert it."

"There will be a number of revolutions through the centuries after yours," Lydde said. "Most revolutions are betrayed, sooner or later."

"That is not what I need to hear just now," he said with a sigh.

"I'm sorry," she said.

"No, no, I am not so naive as to be surprised by what you say. And yet I have a propensity for lost causes, and find myself drawn to stand with those who are suffering and are bound to lose. It will be the death of me, I know. But if I tried to live any other way, I would truly be dead. Do you understand?"

"Not yet," she said.

"England now," he said, "is as it was when I was a boy. It is a place where a poor man is hanged for killing a rich man's deer to feed his family. It is a place where a child is hanged for stealing food to put in his belly. I had hoped that would end when the monarchy ended. But it was a false hope. And I hoped England might become a place where each man and each woman could believe what they will and say what they will and worship as they see fit. And that too was a false hope. But if I accept the way things are and do nothing, I will be less of a man. You are a strong woman. Would you have me be a weak man? If so, then nothing more must pass between us."

"I wouldn't have you be less than you are," she said. "But I'm afraid I am not so strong as you think. I have never done anything particularly brave."

"You came here tonight. You offered to help me. When you feared me, you did not scream and faint, you fought me."

"Where I come from, many women would do the same. And would do so here if given a chance. Only the men here will not listen to women, or allow them to be educated, or encourage them to stand up for themselves. Like that Noah Fallam. He is a bully and fool."

The Raven laughed then. "Do you think so? I have found him so myself."

"Well," Lydde confided, "he is the one who shall have to run for America someday. At least, that's where he'll end up."

"Indeed?" This seemed to give him pause.

"Yes. I know because he and his brother will be among the first Englishmen to see my mountains. The mountain I grew up on, the one that has been blown up, was named for them. Fallam Mountain."

The Raven was quiet for a time. "Well," he said. "That is something to think about."

He stood then, and helped her to her feet.

"Forgive me," he said, "for drawing you into such danger."

"I have no reason to forgive you," she answered, "unless you turn away from me, for with every word you speak I am falling in love with you."

"Lydde, I have every reason to take you back to Soane's Croft and try to put you out of my mind. For both our sakes. And yet, God help me, I cannot do it. If you are a witch of some sort, you have already cast your spell on me, for I do love you as well."

"Kiss me again."

He took her in his arms and kissed her mouth as he unbuttoned her shirt and pulled it off her left shoulder. Then his lips followed the curve of her neck and ended on her bare breast. She pressed against him, felt the proof of his desire.

"As I thought," she said.

"And God help us both," he replied, breathing hard. He let her go and stepped back. "I must talk to your uncle."

"Uncle John! Why? I don't need his permission to make love to you."

"No?"

"Certainly not! In the future women make such decisions for themselves."

"But still I must speak to him. Because I will not love you while wearing a mask. I will not make love to you while you cannot see my face or hear my true voice. Yet I am not ready to show myself, not until I have spoken with John. You may not think I need his permission to take you into my bed, but once you see my face, your peril will be great, and mine will be greater, for no one knows who I am except the Crow. It is how I have kept my head on my shoulders. Yet it is a risk I shall accept if there is no other course."

He doused the lantern and led her back outside, where the Crow joined them with the horses. "All clear," the Crow said.

The Raven nodded, and mounted his horse. He handed Lydde up again, but this time to sit sidesaddle in front of him so he might hold her in his arms. The Crow cocked his head to one side.

"Crow," said the Raven, "meet Lydde."

The Crow bowed in his saddle.

THE Crow rode several lengths ahead, both to scout the ground before them and to allow the couple privacy, for they seemed unable to keep their hands off one another. The Raven had unbuttoned Lydde's shirt again so he might rest one hand against her warm skin. They spoke little, though now and then they whispered together.

"How did you guess I was a woman?" Lydde asked. "I have so prided myself on my acting and that no one could tell."

"Oh," he said, "do not fault your acting. It was the smell of you that told me."

"The smell of me!" She put her hands to his chest and leaned back, trying to see his eyes. "When have you been close enough to smell me?"

He smiled and at first didn't answer, then said, "I have jostled you in a crowd."

"And by that you could tell?"

"I have a keen nose for women. It is because I love them."

"You're teasing me."

"No," he said, "I am simply proud of my nose."

And she could get no more out of him on the subject save for a playful sniff and nibble at her earlobe, which ended in another kiss.

THEY arrived too soon for Lydde at the outskirts of Norchester and there parted. The Raven handed her down from the horse, then said, "You must go on foot from here. But don't be afraid. The Crow shall follow you from a distance and make sure you arrive safe at Soane's Croft."

"Will I see you again?"

"Yes," he said. "I can't say when. Not for a few days. But you have my word, I shall see you again, if you want."

Then he vanished into the forest. She walked on toward East Gate, now and then hearing the distant sound of the Crow's horse. She could not tell that the Crow had removed his mask so as not to call attention to himself if seen by a constable. For a constable who saw him masked would be alarmed, but without his garb he would be recognized and accepted. He watched Lydde to the gate of Soane's Croft, where lanterns still burned despite the late hour, then went on to a last meeting with his friend, now unmasked as well and removing the saddle from his weary horse.

"She's safe," said the Crow. He waited a moment, then added impatiently, "So I was right. You wanted to seduce her."

The Raven answered with a sigh, "Yes. Though I have not yet. I cannot take this one lightly."

"It is not your way," said the Crow, "to lightly seduce a woman. You will want to be certain of marrying her."

"Yes," said the Raven. He lifted the saddle across a rail and let it drop. "But there is more to Lydde than meets the eye. In my head I know there are no such things as witches, yet I could think myself bewitched, for she has told me a tale so strange I cannot accept it. And yet something about her urges me to believe her."

"What sort of tale?"

"Do not ask me that yet. I must investigate further. Then I shall tell you what I have learned."

"And if she is proven false?"

The Raven shook his head. "I don't know. I care about this woman very much and I cannot think ill of her, even if she is dissembling. She has courage, and a sorrow within her that calls me to protect her." He put his hand on the Crow's shoulder. "My friend, what have I done? To all of us? I have forced things into the open which might have been safest kept secret. I have put her in danger, and myself, and you, all for desire of her."

His voice cracked as he spoke, for he had never talked so much in his false voice and the strain of it had burned his throat.

The Crow shook his head. "We could be in no more danger than before. It might even be a help, because I know you, my friend. You will hold on until the end and the noose is around your neck. Unless you have a reason to leave before it is too late. And now you do."

"Do I? Do I dare put a woman's life in jeopardy for loving me?"

"If she loves you, she will not want you to spare her."

"She doesn't yet understand what a life with me would mean. Most women are not comfortable with a man who goes his own way as I do. They want a man who will sit by the hearth and talk with them and smoke his pipe in peace."

"She seems to know her own mind."

The Raven reached out and tousled his friend's hair. "Do you play Cupid now?"

"I do not understand this mystery you hint at, but I like her. I think she is just what you need."

"So. You would have me kill another woman with my love?"

The Crow looked grave. "You should not say that. You could not help that your wife died in childbirth. Besides, the danger for a woman, any woman, is to love a man. For even the wife of the most cowardly man can die in that fashion, so what more danger to love a man who takes risks?"

The Raven walked to the door of the stable and looked around to see if they were observed. "We are perilous to them in every way, you say?"

"We are," the Crow said with all the solemnity a very young man could muster. "It is their burden since the Fall."

The Raven said, "Do not tell that to Lydde. She will scratch your eyes out."

The Crow smiled at the note of pride in his friend's voice.

Chapter 12

Mossup, Bounder, and Rose

Inside Soane's Croft a pandemonium broke out when Lydde appeared, Uncle John, Mother Bunch, and Mary all talking at once. Where had Lewis been? They had been beside themselves with worry, had thought again and again to call out the constables to search for him. Except that the good doctor continued to hold back, afraid this might do more harm than good. Whyever could it hurt? Mother Bunch had asked. Yet he waved her off with "Wait a bit longer, Mother Bunch." And at last here came the wayward boy, looking unaccountably pleased with himself.

Mary and Mother Bunch were determined to make a fuss over Lewis, but Uncle John took a firm grip on the boy's shoulder and said, "Now to bed with you women. I shall deal with the boy myself." He shook Lydde. "You shall come to my study and explain yourself," he said sternly. And Lydde followed him into the study while Mother Bunch led a reluctant Mary upstairs.

Uncle John had scarcely shut the door when Lydde began, "Oh, Uncle John you won't believe! I am in love, I am madly in love . . ." and proceeded to pour out the story of her adventure, though omitting most details of the frequent kisses and horseback gropings.

Uncle John sat wearily at his desk with his chin resting on his hand. It was hours past his bedtime and he had been truly worried, but had felt nothing like the alarm he felt at this new Lydde gushing on with no seeming sense of the danger of her situation. He thought that next time he was called out to assist the Raven's gang he would find their leader and thrash him within an inch of his life. When at last Lydde fell silent he said mildly, "This is sudden, Lydde," in hopes that a calm response might subdue her spirits.

"Sudden!" She stared at him. "Uncle John, you forget how old I am. I look like a girl now, but I am fifty-five years old. I have fallen in love before, usually with idiots. I have been cheated on, I have been stood up. I have been used as a shield by gay men passing as straight. I have been told how marvelous I am by men who lied about being married. I have been with weak men who expected me to fight their battles for them." She stopped, out of breath. Then she said, "I know I have only just met this man—"

"And not even seen his face," put in Uncle John.

"And not even seen his face," she agreed. "And yet I feel I have been waiting for him all my life. Tonight he came for me. And I went and I will go back if he will have me. I don't care about consequences."

When he continued to shake his head, she said, "I'm disappointed in you. You're the one who is always talking about connections. Why did I end up here, of all places, in Norchester, England, in the year 1657? If not for this, then what?"

"Lydde." Uncle John put his hand on hers. "I'm concerned about your safety, that's all. Did he level with you about the danger?"

"He did. He was everything he should be: honest, considerate, worried about me—" She stopped and smiled. "Well, he was a bit forward. But in a good way."

Uncle John groaned. "Here's what I think. I think you're in love with the idea of an outlaw. And I think you're horny."

"Uncle John!"

"Well, it's natural. You're in a twenty-year-old body now and you just got carried off by a masked highwayman. But Lydde, this isn't a movie."

"You're not being fair! I think he's lonely, like I am, and he needs love as much as I do."

"Did he tell you what he's facing?"

She sobered up then. "Yes. He said he'd be caught and killed."

"More than killed," Uncle John said. "Drawn and quartered. Do you know what that is?"

She stared at him, not wanting to know.

"This fellow has the district so stirred up he'll get the worst sentence the seventeenth century can devise. Can you face up to that?"

"If Noah Fallam hurts him, I'll kill him myself."

"It isn't just Noah Fallam. You don't do what the Raven's doing in seventeenth century England. Not without consequences."

"He's going to escape to America."

"Lydde, Lydde."

She stood then, in tears. "What am I supposed to do? Turn my back on the most extraordinary man I've ever met? He said he loves me!"

He doesn't even know you well, Uncle John started to say. But the words died without being spoken. He wondered if that was true. He hadn't known Lavinia at all when he walked into her classroom at West Virginia Tech. Then she read to them from *Henry V,* her voice an odd mix of patrician American and West Virginia twang, proclaiming *He who sheds his blood with me this day shall be my brother, be he ne'er so vile, this day shall gentle his condition.* John had been enthralled as the heroic words poured from the tiny young woman in a green sweater and gray skirt, nose in her book as she waved her arm before an audience of battle-toughened GIs just returned from Europe and the South Pacific. Hadn't he known then?

Lydde stood before him, the niece he had raised as a daughter and worried over from afar. She'd often had her heart broken and called him from across the ocean to cry, and she had run from men who, to Uncle John, sounded perfectly suitable. I don't know, she'd tried to explain. I don't feel a thing for this one. She was shy, he'd reckoned. She was heartbreakingly independent. She was afraid of more loss.

What he said now was, "You must be exhausted. Go to bed. We'll talk more in the morning."

LYDDE stumbled wearily up the stairs to her room, where she began to undress. When she stood naked, she started to blow out her candle but hesitated. She looked down the length of her body, trying to imagine what he would think of her. Would he like the shape of her legs? Where might he touch her first? She placed her own hand on the breast he had fondled.

Her reverie was broken by a sound behind her. She turned and there stood Mary, cradling her puppy in her arms, a look of astonishment on her face.

LYDDE slept little that night. If she was not recalling the kisses and caresses of the Raven, then she was listening to the even breathing of Mary and the puppy, who had been named Bounder, beside her in the bed. Mary had been upset at Lydde's deception, but Lydde had managed after a few incoherent attempts at explanation to assure her that Uncle John knew and approved.

"But why are you doing it?" Mary had asked. "It is sinful, isn't it, to pretend to be a boy?"

"You must understand where I am from in Ireland," Lydde

pleaded. "It is a place where women do the things men do. That's what I'm used to and I don't think I could pretend otherwise. I would have to go back there instead of staying here."

"Oh," Mary said. "Don't do that. I'm too fond of you."

They had hugged then, sitting on the edge of Lydde's bed. "And I'm very fond of you," Lydde replied. "I love you like a sister."

They agreed that Uncle John would be told that Mary knew, but that Mother Bunch would continue to think that Lydde was Lewis.

"But what is your real name?" Mary asked.

"I don't think I should tell you yet. Someday I will. But for now you must keep calling me Lewis. It's for my safety, do you understand? If Jacob Woodcock or Noah Fallam knew I'm only pretending to be a boy, they might do something horrible to me."

"They would burn you at the stake," Mary said solemnly.

Lydde started to reassure her, then realized she was right. "Well," she said, "I know I can trust you to keep my secret."

"I shall never tell." But Mary could never stay solemn for long. She turned and threw herself full-length across the feather bed so that Bounder, true to her name, jumped up after her, thinking it time to play. "And now we can be like sisters. We can share a bed when it is cold. That shall be ever so nice as winter comes on. And we can talk about things."

Lydde smiled, for she recalled from her teenage years what those things would be. Boys. And sure enough, they had scarcely settled beneath the goose-down comforter, with Bounder curled up at their feet, when Mary said, "Don't you think Simon Cleyes is the most handsome man in Norchester?"

Lydde groaned to herself, then said, "I know nothing but good of Mr. Cleyes, but the man he works for is odious."

"Noah Fallam? Oh, he is strict, but Simon—I mean, Mr. Cleyes— says he owes everything to him. Simon was from a poor family and his father died. But Pastor Fallam sent Simon away to school, and gave money to his mother so she could feed her children. And Simon did so well that now he is Pastor Fallam's secretary, and that is a very important position." Mary edged closer to Lydde and then whispered, as though someone might overhear them, "Can I tell you something? Once I let him hold my hand. All the way from St. Pancras crossing to East Gate. It was lovely."

"Mary, you must be careful," Lydde said sternly.

"Oh, it was nothing more. Sim—Mr. Cleyes acts like a gentleman, even if he is from a poor family."

Lydde relented and gave the girl's hand a squeeze. "And you might as well call him Simon when you speak about him to me. He has obviously invited you to call him that."

"He has," Mary said, and Lydde thought she could feel the heat of her blush in the dark.

And who am I to caution the girl? Lydde thought. I am far more rash than she. Then a thought struck her. Simon Cleyes was watching out for Mary and knew the workings of Noah Fallam's government. He had also been a poor man and might have sympathy for others who were poor. Might he be the Raven? But she dismissed that at once. Cleyes was not so tall as the Raven, nor could she imagine the man who had kissed her being false enough to lead Mary on. (I am becoming more trusting of men, she noticed, and smiled in the dark.) But the Crow had been about the size of Cleyes. It was an intriguing thought—Simon Cleyes by day the loyal secretary to Noah Fallam and at night passing on what he knew to the Raven. She was still playing with this idea when she at last drifted off to sleep.

DAYS passed with no word from the Raven. A restless Lydde helped Mary and Mother Bunch dig a straw-lined pit in the garden, where they would bury the cabbages and potatoes to last the winter. It was hard work even for Lydde's young body, though she was glad for the distraction. She was grateful that Uncle John hired a pair of sisters, poor widows before he employed them, to come to Soane's Croft to do the laundry, the heavy cleaning of pots and pans, the hauling of water from the pump in the street. Lydde guiltily doubted she could live a woman's life in this place without such help, and that thought gave her uneasy moments that interrupted her daydreams about the Raven. She wondered if he was a man who could afford servants.

After a meal of mincemeat pie (and fighting back a craving for a slice of pepperoni pizza), she took a nap. When she woke, Mother Bunch had a basket of herbal remedies ready for delivery. So Lydde walked along the Pye to the livery stable outside East Gate to see about a horse.

She had visited the stable twice with Uncle John so she could have a horse to ride alongside Lady. Now she was ready to go out on her own. She found Mossup, the proprietor of the stable, mucking out the stalls. Mossup was a short, grizzled, greasy-headed old man of sixty-some years who looked as though he could fill a similar role on a television western.

"Come for your mount?" he said amiably when he saw her.

"Yes," she said. "And this time Mr. Soane says I can go out on my own."

He nodded and walked her along the stalls to where a gentle gray mare waited. Rose, the horse was called, and she had never given Lydde a moment's trouble.

"Ye'll be wanting Rose regular, then?" Mossup said.

"Every day in the afternoons. The doctor says he'll pay you by the week."

Mossup nodded. "That'll do. But before you go out today, a word with ye, if ye will."

He had the look of a conspirator about him.

"What do you mean?" Lydde asked cautiously.

Mossup leaned closer so she could smell his stale breath. "I've been talking about ye, young lad. With a mutual friend of ours."

She waited. He obviously enjoyed keeping her in suspense. He looked around, then leaned closer still.

"The Raven," he said.

An invisible finger ran down her spine.

"I don't know what you mean," she said.

"Sure ye do," said Mossup with a grin. "Though you're wise to take care how ye answer. Our friend tells me you've been an actor. He says you've done Shakespeare."

"Yes," Lydde whispered, and knew Mossup could not be making this up. "I've done Shakespeare."

"A ganymede, are ye?"

Ganymede was the pejorative term Jacob Woodcock had hurled at her upon her arrival in Norchester. It was, Lydde knew from her college days, the term for boys who played women's roles on the seventeenth century stage.

"Yes," she said.

Mossup nodded approvingly. "I too am an actor. Or was before the infernal Puritans closed the theaters and I fled London to fetch up here and live as I can. In Will Shakespeare's troupe, I was, in my own ganymede days, and trod the boards at the Globe. When that good old stage burned, I went with the Red Bull Company. That was after my voice changed. I was never a leading man, you'll understand. I've been Caliban and Pistol, Dromio and Dogberry and Sir Toby Belch and the Porter in *Macbeth*. You're too young to have known the London days. But the Raven says you've been underground in Bristol, though I'm to mention it to no one here. I understand well enough the reason for that. Who have ye played?"

Thank you, Raven, Lydde thought silently. She felt like crying with joy to be talking of theater again. "Violà," she said. "Beatrice, Audrey, Lady Macbeth, Gonoril and Regan both."

Mossup nodded. "Would you like to act again, lad?"

"Yes! But how?"

"There are a pair of my fellow actors in the district. Guill and Sharpe, they are named, young fellows who fled London as I did. Now they keep a hostelry together at Little Gallops, which is but two miles from here. We meet on a regular basis to keep our hand in, just for the fun of it. Rehearsing, it would be like, with no audience in mind, since it is illegal and Noah Fallam keeps a close watch. But we all do miss it, and this suffices for the present. We need someone to play the female parts, for Guill does them badly. Will you agree?"

"Gladly!"

Mossup clapped his hands. "Good," he said. "We gather here in the back room of the stable some days, and other days you and I shall ride to Little Gallops."

"But how do you know the Raven? Are you in his gang?"

"Not properly speaking. No stomach for that sort of thing, don't care for the idea of dangling from a gallows. But"—Mossup put a finger to his lips—"he does use my horses when he goes out at night. A different one each time so he won't be recognized by his mount. And pays me well for the privilege."

Then Mossup saddled Rose and watched while Lydde hauled herself up onto the horse's back. "A good enough seat," he said approvingly. "You'll make a horseman someday. But don't let her into a fast trot yet, else you'll be on the ground with a broken crown."

So Lydde squeezed the mare's flanks with her knees and set off through Norchester at a slow pace, now and then leaning over Rose's neck to praise the horse with soft words. Though the marketplace was less crowded than usual, she went cautiously for fear of Rose starting at some unusual noise. Mossup had assured her that Rose was not one to bolt, so she finally relaxed. But at the main intersection of the town, where a medieval stone cross marked the meeting of East, North, West, and South Gate Streets, she was startled by an incursion of horsemen, more than a dozen of them, moving along at a pace that scattered all before them, women tugging on the arms of their children, skinny dogs dodging the horses' hooves. Noah Fallam and his constables. Lydde was barely able to urge Rose to the side before they passed. Fallam, in front, noted her struggle with her mount, met her eyes with a cold, unsmiling countenance, then was gone. Lydde muttered curses under her breath, calling him every foul twenty-first-century name that came to mind. Then Rose calmed herself with a shake of the head, and Lydde rode on about her errands.

LYDDE was consumed with curiosity over the Raven's identity, and the long wait without hearing from him only made her more desperate, though she consoled herself with the encounter with Mossup, a kind gift, it seemed to her. Most likely, she decided, if he unmasked himself she would not recognize him, for there were hundreds of Norchester men with dark eyes and above-average height who might have jostled her in the marketplace. Even the crowd that had surrounded her on her arrival held a number of such men. But one stood out in her mind for the intensity of his stare, one who might have been secretly undressing her in his mind's eye while pretending other interest.

Jacob Woodcock.

At first she dismissed the idea. The man was a fanatic. And he had tried to turn the congregation against Mary at St. Pancras. Nor could she imagine the Raven drowning a pup, though she supposed seventeenth century men of all stripes would be less squeamish about animals than she would like.

But as she thought further, she considered with what elaborate care the Raven might present himself as someone totally different than who he was. How better to fool Noah Fallam than to hide behind a cloak of religious fanaticism? How better to examine Lydde at close quarters than to chase after Mary on a pretext and pretend to berate her? The Raven liked her boldness; Jacob Woodcock had aroused it.

One of Mother Bunch's regular customers was an old man who lived near Woodcock's smithy in Catte Street. She saved him for last, and after leaving him a mixture for a poultice, she entered the smithy. The interior was smoky, and Woodcock stood shirtless over his open fire, holding a red-hot length of iron in a gloved hand while waiting to take his hammer to it. His arms and shoulders were well muscled, she noted, and a mass of black curls covered his chest. When he noticed her, he looked startled, then motioned she should wait. She stepped back and watched as he expertly shaped the length of iron into a horseshoe with a few deft raps of his hammer, then dropped the shoe into a tub of water, where it sizzled as though charged with electricity, then subsided just as suddenly.

"What do you want?" Woodcock said.

"I want to apologize," she answered.

He looked surprised, then nodded. "I accept. Your manners need improving, but it is a small sign of grace to admit that. Though I have some advice for you."

He stepped closer and she stared into his eyes, trying to see in them some signal that would say, Yes, here I am, the man who kissed you behind my mask, beneath the moon, the man who caressed your naked breast and once leaned close to taste it. All this she tried to read in his eyes.

"What advice?" she asked, afraid to breathe, hoping he would say, Take care of riding alone with masked men, or something equally significant.

"You should attend church at Trinity, here in town," Woodcock said. "It is where most of the elect worship. I was at St. Pancras once because of the upset there, but Trinity is where I am usually found on a Sabbath. On the chance you are one of the elect, though so far I see no sign of it, it were better for your soul to be at Trinity."

She nodded, disappointed. "I shall consider it," she said carefully, "though I doubt the doctor would approve."

Back in the street, she stopped and looked back a moment, then wandered away. If Jacob Woodcock was the Raven, he was not yet ready to reveal himself to her.

THE Reverend Smythe, vicar of St. Pancras Church, was an uneasy sleeper. He suffered in his old age from intestinal ailments that forced him to sleep sitting upright, else he regurgitate his food while insensible, and that from time to time caused his stomach and innards to burn as though on fire. He was also forced at such times into the indignity of relieving himself rather quickly, and kept a chamber pot handy for such purposes. Yet he avoided this necessity when possible. If the weather was decent and he had advance warning, he made his way to the privy outside the vicarage instead. He was making such a return trip on a crisp October night when he was startled by the sound of a horse's hooves, and before he could gain the safety of his door found himself face-to-face with a masked man. The Reverend Smythe quailed, but he did not run, being too old for such exertion, and besides, not a man inclined to be craven.

"Do you know me?" the masked man asked with a raspy voice.

"You must be the Raven," the Reverend Smythe replied in a small yet firm voice.

"I have a request," said the Raven. "I am alone now. If what passes here tonight is broadcast abroad, it shall go hard with you. Am I clear?"

The Reverend Smythe bowed his head in acquiescence. He knew of the Raven's exploits and, though a Church of England man of the old school, he had little quarrel with the outlaw. Some of his own flock—widows, mainly—had found supplies of unlooked-for coin on their doorsteps, which had purchased chickens and milk cows and put much-needed food in their larders. They would come all in a dither to the Reverend Smythe and ask in quavering voices if it was un-Christian to accept such bounty. He had assured them that the Lord provides in mysterious ways. The Reverend Smythe listened now to the Raven's request.

"The crypt of St. Pancras," said the Raven. "It is under lock and key?"

"It is," the Reverend Smythe acknowledged.

"Why is that?"

"Mr. Soane, the town physician, asked that the door be locked. He is conducting experiments of some sort there and does not wish the space to be disturbed."

"And you accept this without questioning it?"

"I admit to being curious," said the Reverend Smythe. "And I was certainly anxious that the experiment, whatever it is, would not be something offensive to God. There are reports these days of indecent activities by those pursuing this new knowledge, of horrors such as dissecting the dead, which is said to occur in Oxford. But Mr. Soane assured me no such thing was transpiring in the crypt. Indeed there is no more trusted man in Norchester than Mr. Soane, and besides, it would make no sense to conduct such an undertaking there, since the light is not sufficient."

"Then what is he doing there?"

"As I've said, I don't know. As vicar of the church I asked to be shown the space as an assurance, and he was glad to take me there. I could see nothing that had been disturbed. Yet Mr. Soane seems to feel people should not be often allowed to wander there. I have been under the impression he thinks some sort of pestilence might be contracted which he is anxious to shield people from. Though he assures me," the Reverend Smythe hastened to add, "that there is no danger if we continue to worship at St. Pancras."

The Raven listened to this explanation and said nothing for a moment, as though considering what he had heard. Then he asked, "Does John Soane possess the only key?"

"No. As vicar I felt it my responsibility to keep a key as well. Though I promised the good doctor I would not let it out of my possession."

"I require that key," said the Raven.

"Then you ask me to break my word to Mr. Soane?"

"No. You have in good faith kept the key. Now I forcibly take it from you."

It was the turn of the Reverend Smythe to hesitate, then the Raven said, "I give you no choice. I am taking the key. But I promise you I shall disturb nothing, and I shall not tell John Soane you have done anything wrong. If I encounter some misfortune, then the fault is upon me. Is the key in the vicarage?"

"It is."

"Then bring it to me at once. If you refuse, I shall go in the house with you. You understand me?"

Again the Reverend Smythe nodded, and went inside to fetch the key. He considered that John Soane could not much object. At his advanced age he was no match for the Raven and could not deny him if he wished. And though he was mystified as to why the Raven should want to visit the crypt, there seemed to be nothing that would alert the physician that his quarantine had been breached. When he returned with the key, the Raven took it, then said, "Go inside and go to bed. Today is Wednesday. You've no need to enter the church until Sunday, so I advise you to stay away from it, else you are blamed for another uproar."

For the first time, the Reverend Smythe felt true fear. "You mean the paintings?" he said.

The Raven shrugged. "Perhaps," he said. "We shall see."

"Noah Fallam shall persecute us!"

"The Devil take Noah Fallam," said the Raven. Then he laughed, a raw sound that caused the blood of the Reverend Smythe to run cold.

THE Raven moved slowly, for he carried no torch. Sounds were magnified in the dark—the rasp of the key seemed a screech loud enough to summon devils, the ring of his boots on the flagstones were like blows on an anvil no matter how softly he tried to tread. He closed the crypt door behind him. The air was close. He removed his mask and dropped it in front of the door. Then he inched cautiously forward until he found the edge of the cistern. Carefully he sat on the edge, feet dangling into space. He took from his pocket the stone he had placed there, held it out, and opened his hand. The stone dropped, but there was no sound after. He listened and heard only silence. So. He was about to plunge into an abyss because the woman who haunted his daydreams claimed it was a way to the future, to the world she had come from. And what was almost certain was that he would break his neck at the bottom of a well and that would be the end of him. A strange end for an outlaw.

He stood up, determined to leave. Then he saw Lydde's face in the dark of the old monastery, heard her voice as she told her tale of wonder and woe, felt her body pressed against him, and tasted the spices of her mouth. He remembered her strange courage, her fiery defense of Mary. Might she not stand by him as well, were he so fortunate as to gain her love? And could he not risk as well as she?

Perhaps she was not a woman, but a witch. Then he was already lost; he would learn the truth, or he would die. He cleared his mind, as he did whenever he put himself in danger, then crouched and took a deep breath, hoisting himself over the edge of the cistern and letting go.

Part Three

Chapter 13

Aunt Lavinia's Visitor

H E PASSED OUT, but then his eyes opened. He was lying on his back, arms akimbo, and for a moment his head spun and he thought he might be sick to his stomach. He had felt this way as a child when he had tried to turn in a circle as fast and long as possible but instead collapsed on the ground—always the first to fall, it seemed back then. He shut his eyes and took deep breaths. He soon felt steadier and opened his eyes again, sat up slowly, and looked around. He was in a cave. To his left the light of day was a jagged brown crack like a flaw in amber. He crawled carefully toward the light, realized he was heading for the edge of a precipice, and drew back, disoriented by the place and by the heaviness he felt in his body. He could not seem to move as easily as he was used to. Cautiously he made his way along the ledge, his knees paining him. Then, as his eyes continued to adjust to the gloom, he saw a skeleton.

This stopped him. A disagreeable surprise, for Lydde had said nothing about it. He considered retreating but decided to press on toward another light source, though giving the bones a wide berth.

Lydde had neglected to lock doors, since she'd had no reason to expect she wouldn't return, and she had left the light burning in Uncle John's office. A good thing, for a visitor from the past would not have known to press the light switch. A strange orb burned above the Raven's head, and as he studied it his eyes began to burn and he was forced to look away. His eyesight was so suddenly blasted he clapped his hands over his face in despair of going blind. But this passed as quickly as the vertigo, and again he examined his surroundings, careful this time to avoid looking up. An ugly desk, and equally hideous case of some sort of metal stood in one corner, and a mirror hung on the wall.

He stepped closer and peered into the mirror, then jumped back in alarm. He had seen a much older man. But that matched his sluggishness, and the ache in his knees when he had struggled to stand up. Lydde had said she was fifty-five in the future. He gathered his courage and looked again. Mid-sixties? His hair had receded—his full head of hair, he realized now, had been one of his vanities—and when he placed his hand on his head he felt a large bald spot on the crown. He seemed to have become a scrawny old man, but his stomach protruded and he had burst the first two buttons on his breeches. He sighed and thought, It is only temporary. Besides, I will likely come to the scaffold long before I reach this age.

Gradually he made his way out of the Mystery Hole and into blinding sunlight. It was full day in the future, and when his eyes had adjusted once again he gaped at the striking mountainscape across the way, the spring-green trees interspersed with bursts of white pink colors and edged with cliffs. Far below was a twist of wild river. Then he looked behind him. There was the blasted landscape Lydde had lamented, the wall of rock and spoil that filled the nearby cove and would have loomed high over the spires of Norchester Cathedral, the flat wasteland barely glimpsed beyond. A sign with oddly uniform letters read:

NO TRESPASSING
PROPERTY OF AMERICAN COAL CORP.

The Raven lacked patience with warnings of no trespass, which recalled the strictures at home of the wealthy who kept the poor from hunting on their vast estates. He walked toward the sign thinking he might tear it down, but stopped, confused by the strange dark path that ran like a border between the Mystery Hole and the desert land. It was smoother than any road he had ever seen and two yellow stripes bright as egg yolks ran down the center. He had just knelt at the edge to examine the sticky black surface when he heard a distant whine like a concentrated wind that grew steadily louder, and then a bright object large as a wagon came hurtling, screaming toward him. He dove for cover, pressing himself in terror against the wall of the Mystery Hole. Before he could take a breath, the terrifying phantasm was gone.

It was quite a while before he could be calm, and he was embarrassed to find he had wet himself. Not even in the closest calls in his smuggling operations had this ever happened. He retreated into the Mystery Hole where after much poking around he found an odd white ceramic bowl which held water, though he could not imagine how a man could drink from it without standing on his head, it was so low on the ground. He removed his pants and plunged them into the smooth bowl, swishing them around and then trying to wring them out as best he could. The pants clung to him like a clammy second skin when he put them back on. When he encountered someone, he would just have to make up an explanation.

Back outside, he walked around the road, careful to stay as far as possible from the sticky black path. Soon he saw a small hand-painted sign pointing down over the hill. ROUNDBOTTOM FARM, it said. The road it indicated was smooth dirt like the tracks at home in the dry season. With a sigh of relief, he turned into the more rustic way.

·   ·   ·

AUNT Lavinia made tuna sandwiches for lunch, but Lydde never appeared. She had gone off to explore, Lavinia supposed, though she'd assumed Lydde would call if she was going to be away all day. But her niece was a grown woman (middle-aged, Lavinia reminded herself) and was used to being on her own. Perhaps she wouldn't consider that her aunt might be worried about her.

Aunt Lavinia turned her attention to what to do for supper. She had a craving for pasta, but John had always cooked the Italian dishes. Carbonara, white and red clam sauces, spaghetti and meatballs. Thinking of the food reminded her how much she missed him and she shook her head as though trying to empty it of painful memories. She would do one of her roasts instead. She placed a piece of sirloin tip in a pot with potatoes, carrots, celery, cabbage, and tomatoes, and left them to cook all afternoon. Perhaps Lydde would make pasta tomorrow night.

When the pot roast was done, she turned it off to await Lydde's arrival. Now and then she cast an anxious glance out the front door. A cold morning had given way to a warm spring evening, and she kept the door open with the screen door latched. All was quiet save for the occasional whine of a car engine on the highway above.

She had just turned on the television to catch the evening news when she heard footsteps on the porch. She flicked the TV off and went to the door, saying, "It's about time," when she stopped short. A man stood on the porch, framed by the door.

Had he been younger, she would have been alarmed. Roundbottom Farm was out of the way and no one came there without a purpose; even Jehovah's Witnesses and Mormons missed it. But this was an older man, in his sixties, Aunt Lavinia guessed. A handsome man, with a deeply lined face and an air of quiet dignity. But he was dressed oddly, in old-fashioned clothes that appeared to have been made by hand, and his trousers were dripping wet. A tramp, perhaps. She became frightened again, but noted the screen door was securely latched.

The man spoke first. "You are Lavinia?" he said.

She stared at him in surprise. "How do you know my name?"

"I am a friend of Lydde's," he said in an odd, thick accent.

"Oh. Well, I'm afraid she isn't here. She left this morning before I got up and I haven't heard a word from her since. Although I expect her anytime."

"No," the man said. "She won't be coming back yet. I have come to see you, not her."

"Me?" She began to wonder at his accent, which, though odd, was somehow familiar.

"You are John Soane's wife?"

"John who?" Aunt Lavinia was alarmed now.

"Wait. I misspoke his name because that is how I know him. I mean John Cabell. I don't mean to upset you. But I think you deserve to know that your husband is alive."

"My—my husband." Aunt Lavinia took a step back. "Who are you? What do you want? Go away! I'll call the police if you don't go away."

"Please believe me. He is not dead. I don't know how much he has told you of what is going on, I am only just coming to believe it myself." He put his hand on the door handle. "If you let me in, I can explain more easily."

"I most certainly will not let you in!" Aunt Lavinia said angrily. "You say what you have to say and then leave."

The Raven stepped back and held up his hands. "Very well. I won't trouble you long. I hope you will believe me, though I know it is difficult. John has gone to the past, and Lydde is with him. The man who died was not your husband. His name was John Soane and he came from the past to visit your time. Only he died before he could return and switch places with your husband."

"This is not funny!" Aunt Lavinia managed to say, and slammed the oak door.

She went to the telephone to call 911. But the man had moved to a window and called out, "Wait! Lydde is my friend and so is John. Lydde lost her brothers and sisters in a fire. Didn't she? You and John raised her. When you returned from your trip, John was different. He talked oddly like I do. Didn't he? That's because he lived in the year of our Lord 1657. And that's where John and Lydde are now."

Aunt Lavinia stood frozen inside the door, the phone in her hand, listening to him.

"How would I know all this if Lydde hadn't told me?" the man continued, his voice muffled by the window glass. "I love Lydde. I want to marry her. I was hoping to receive your blessing."

Cautiously Lavinia set down the phone and moved closer to the window. "Prove you know Lydde," she said. "Tell me something about her no one would know except a close friend."

The man turned his head away, thinking, then said, "When she was a child she often went to the ruins of the burned house with a stick and searched for clues. All she found was an object I don't understand except it is used to light tobacco. We do have Virginia tobacco in England in my time."

Aunt Lavinia felt her throat tighten. The man's eyes met hers through the window glass.

"Upstairs on the wall," he said, "you have a picture of St. Pancras Church, Norchester. I am from Norchester, and Lydde and John are there now." His voice was lower, more gentle as her face began to collapse with weeping.

"You're trying to tell me they're dead."

"No, no. They are as alive as you and I are," he said. "You'll see them soon. I promise."

She dabbed at her eyes with the sleeve of her blouse, then went to the oak door and opened it. The man came to stand in front of the screen. She looked him up and down.

"And how did you get so wet?" she said.

He opened his mouth to lie but found himself telling the embarrassing truth. "A strange conveyance passed me on the road above, like the thing that sits still beside your house." He gestured cautiously at her car, as though pointing at it might cause it to roar to life. "It passed so quickly it nearly struck me and I am ashamed to say"—he blushed—"I had to wash my breeches."

She nodded her head sympathetically. "When you get to our age," she said, "it doesn't take much." She lifted the latch on the screen door. "Are you hungry?" she asked.

"I'm starved," he answered.

"Won't you have supper with me? If Lydde isn't coming home this evening, someone has to help me eat it."

She stepped aside and he came into the living room. When she offered her hand, he bowed over it.

"Oh, my," she said, "Lydde has found herself a gentleman."

THE visitor obviously knew John and Lydde, but Aunt Lavinia remained skeptical about his story of being from the past. She found him a pair of John's old jeans and threw his pants in the washing machine, pausing first to examine the rough fabric and uneven stitching, obviously done by hand, the row of buttons on the fly that appeared to be carved from some sort of bone. If he was lying about where he came from, he certainly had dressed the part. She decided to test him.

"Would you turn on the light over the kitchen table?" she said as she ladled the vegetables into a bowl.

He looked around, bewildered. "I don't know how," he said sheepishly.

She switched on the overhead light and he stared at it.

"This one does not hurt my eyes so badly as the first one I saw," he said. "It has some sort of cover, yet it doesn't catch fire. How does it work?"

"Electricity. You don't know what that is?"

He shook his head. "No."

She pulled an electric knife from a drawer and plugged it into a wall socket. "You want to carve the roast?"

Just as he took it from her, she turned it on. He started violently and dropped the knife, which clattered along the counter. She grabbed it up and turned it off.

"My God!" he exclaimed. "You could kill someone with that!"

She regarded him a moment. "You're telling the truth about being from the past," she said.

"Of course I am," he said, slightly offended.

Aunt Lavinia opened the drawer again and took out a carving knife. "Here," she said as she handed it to him. "I bet you'll do a fine job with this one."

Then she sat him down at the kitchen table. He ate with obvious relish, taking three helpings of pot roast and wiping his plate clean with a piece of bread. He had started by using his fingers but when he saw Lavinia wielding her fork, he had switched, an embarrassed look on his face, and awkwardly jabbed at his food. Aunt Lavinia was glad she hadn't attempted the pasta; it would have been too much for him. He was in a state of bewilderment as it was, sitting at the kitchen table and staring around him while Aunt Lavinia explained each appliance and how it worked. It was a bit like being trapped in an episode of *The Beverly Hillbillies,* she thought, except her guest was a man of such obvious dignity she wouldn't have dared laugh at him.

He told her everything Lydde had told him. He explained that Lydde and he both were younger where he had come from. And he told her again that he was in love.

"Though I haven't done anything about it," he said. "Each time I start to take the final step, I hold back. I was reluctant to believe Lydde's story at first, I have to admit. Besides that, I don't want Lydde hurt, not after she's lost so much."

"But if she loses you because you're afraid of that, she'll have lost you anyway," Aunt Lavinia said sensibly.

"There's something I haven't told you. I'm a smuggler and a thief."

Then, fearing she might think him a complete rogue, he told her more about himself and added, "I keep nothing. I'm only trying to help the poor people of Norchester. But there's a very good chance I'll be caught and hanged. Is it fair to put Lydde through that?"

"Oh, dear," said Aunt Lavinia. "That is a tough one." She thought a moment. "Does Lydde know the danger you're in?"

"Yes."

"Then you've been honest with her. And I'd say it's up to her. Lydde's tough and she doesn't back down. Takes after her father that way. She was a loyal child and she didn't like to see other people picked on." Aunt Lavinia got up to pour two cups of coffee. He stared at the cup she set before him. "You may not like this," she said, "but it will be all the rage in England in the eighteenth century."

He took a cautious sip and she could tell he didn't care for it but was too polite to say so. She liked him more and more. Amazing, she thought, how people were still people, even after several hundred years.

"I can give you one other piece of advice," she said. "There's an old story here in the mountains. A long time ago there was a boy who was afraid to go out hunting because a panther had been seen hereabouts. The boy was scared the cat would get him. Finally an old man took him aside and said, 'Son, you go on out there, because if you're born to drown, you'll never hang. So let the big cat jump.'" She reached over and took back his cup. "Now, you don't have to drink that. And do you understand what I'm saying to you?"

He smiled. "I do," he said.

"They say we're fatalistic here in the mountains, and maybe we are. But I think we cope better. And I can tell you're tough too. Don't try to protect Lydde from life. She may have lived a long time in London, but she's from these hills."

He seemed disinclined to help her with the dishes, but she let him know it was expected. So he set about scrubbing the pots with a grudging grace, though he was so awkward about it she could tell he'd never done it before. If he marries Lydde, she thought, that will be the first fight.

Then she took him on a tour of the house, stopping every place there were pictures of Lydde. She had to explain what photographs were. He looked a long time at a recent one before setting it back down with a smile. "She will age well," he said, pleased. He lingered especially over a snapshot of Lydde at seventeen, when her hair was so long it covered her breasts and she wore a tank top and short-shorts. Aunt Lavinia removed it from its frame and gave it to him. "You keep that," she said. She picked up another frame, this one showing Lydde at her college graduation. "I never thought of her as my niece, you know. She was my girl, my daughter. I could never have children of my own—woman problems. But Lydde was mine. If she stays back in the past with you, I won't see her again, will I?"

"You will," he said. "I'll bring her for a visit."

"When?"

"It shouldn't be long. Lydde has been there for weeks and yet she only left here this morning, you say. How very strange this all is."

"Amen," Aunt Lavinia agreed.

Then it was time for him to leave. She offered to take him for a drive. "You really should ride in a car while you're here, especially since one scared you so bad. I'll take you across the gorge and back, and then I'll drop you off at the Mystery Hole. Save you a hike."

She drove him down into the gorge, across the bridge, and back up to the overlook on Gauley Mountain. The devastation of what had once been Fallam Mountain spread below them. "Used to be the most lovely view you could want," she told him.

He shook his head. "I would like to think people had learned some things over the centuries. But it seems people can still be foolish, only they have more to be foolish with."

"Some things don't change," Lavinia agreed.

They went back the way they had come, and stopped at the Mystery Hole. Lavinia turned off the engine and they both got out, the visitor seeming a bit shaky in the legs from even the short jaunt in the car. Then Lavinia said, "Lord almighty!"

"What?"

She pointed at the cove across the road. "The house that burned used to be up there, at the head of that cove under the valley fill. Only the valley fill came almost to the road. Now you can just barely see it at the edge of the turn up there."

"When I arrived," he said, "it wasn't close to the road."

She grabbed his arm. "You tell John. When you get back, you tell John the valley fill has retreated. It's in a different place. Don't forget."

"I won't."

Then she loosed her grip on his arm and patted it instead. "And you tell that Lydde if she doesn't marry you, her Aunt Lavinia thinks she's a darned fool."

He smiled, and bowed over her hand once more. "I will. And I hope we will meet again, Lavinia Cabell."

Then he disappeared inside the Mystery Hole.

Chapter 14

The Hanging

T HE NEXT NIGHT Uncle John was roused from sleep by the tin-
kling of the emergency bell in his room. Some poor soul was
standing outside the back gate in need of aid. He rubbed his eyes,
dressed, and threw on his wool overcoat, for the nights were now cold.
Outside, he opened the gate, and at first saw no one. Then a masked
figure emerged from the shadows and slipped inside the garden.

"The Raven requires you," said the masked man. "There has been
an accident."

"What sort of accident? What should I expect?"

"We were bringing in a shipment at Dalkey Cove. A man has gone
over a ledge."

"Very well. Wait while I dress."

.   .   .

HE had never before been to Dalkey Cove and was relieved it was not far, only two miles or so to the southwest. There he found, to his surprise, only the Raven and the Crow. The Crow walked over to Uncle John. "It is no good," he said. "The man fell too far. He is dead."

Uncle John bowed his head a moment. "I'm sorry."

The Raven still stood some way apart, staring out to sea.

"He is upset," said the Crow. "It is the first time he has lost a man."

"What happened?"

"We thought to meet a ship at a new place, to give ourselves more choices in future, but we were not quite so familiar with this terrain. The man slipped there and fell over the edge. We all removed our shirts and made a rope, and the man's brother went down after him. But there was nothing to do except bring up his body. The brother took away the body and the Raven has sent the others on with the cargo. He waits only to apologize to you, because you were called out without need."

At that the Raven seemed to rouse himself and walked over to them. "You," he said to the man who had brought the doctor on his horse. "Go on home. And you," he said to the Crow, "go ahead as well. I will escort Mr. Soane back to Norchester."

"But—" the Crow began to protest.

"Go!" the Raven said angrily, and waved his arm.

The two men reluctantly mounted their horses and rode away through the gorse, leaving Uncle John to stand shivering in his coat beside the Raven.

"How will a man's unexpected death be explained to Noah Fallam?" Uncle John asked.

The Raven shrugged. "The widow will tell how he lost his balance while storing hay and fell from the loft of his barn."

They stood for a while and watched their breath turn white in the cold air.

"I had decided," said Uncle John, "to tell you, next time I saw you, what a scoundrel you are. But I suppose now is not the time."

"You have spoken to Lydde," the Raven replied. "And I have spoken to Lavinia."

Uncle John stared at him.

"Lydde told me enough about how to go to your time that I was able to do it last night," the Raven continued. "I had to know for certain she was telling the truth. I wanted to trust her, but I had to know I was not bewitched."

Uncle John pushed his hat back from his forehead. "Now you know," he said.

"Yes. And you should be thrashed for leaving your wife to think you dead."

"You should be thrashed for drawing Lydde into all this danger. And for trying to seduce her when you scarcely know her."

The two men faced off as though they might indeed come to blows. Then the Raven said, "I did something foolish tonight."

"What do you mean?"

"I took off my shirt to add it to our makeshift rope. I forgot that I have a distinctive birthmark on my shoulder and in this moonlight I'm sure it was seen. If any of my men prove turncoat, I shall be easily identified."

"All the more reason not to involve Lydde."

The Raven seemed to slump, his posture conveying despair more clearly than any facial expression could.

"Is it? Lavinia said otherwise. She said it must be Lydde's decision."

"She would," Uncle John said. Then he relented, despite his own misgivings. "Why did you tell me about the birthmark? Now I'm one more potential betrayer."

"Yes. And if Lydde sees me without my mask, she shall be another. But I cannot bear to continue living a life of such isolation. You are Lydde's family." He shrugged and left the rest unspoken.

Uncle John put his hand on the younger man's shoulder.

"The man who died," said the Raven, "left five children. Tonight's take was small, only a few cases of Flemish lace. The proceeds shall go to his widow." After a moment he added, "The men who rule us are more concerned with the purity of their faith than with the well-being of the people. There is already starvation in Somerset and Devon. It will be a difficult winter. That means I have more to do and a long lonely road ahead. Without Lydde, that is."

He offered his horse to Uncle John and walked alongside. After a time Uncle John dismounted and walked with him. "How is Lavinia?" he asked.

"She is well. An admirable woman. She misses you greatly, but I convinced her you are still alive. I had supper with her. Roast beef."

"Ah. Lavinia does a great roast."

The Raven reached into the pocket of his coat and took out a square of paper. "She gave me this."

Uncle John studied the photo of Lydde in the moonlight, handed it back. "Amazing," he said.

The Raven told him how the valley fill over Montefalco had moved. He was surprised at how excited Uncle John became. "I have to go back and see that. I should measure the distance."

"What does it mean?"

"It may be like the church restoring its paintings whenever a living thing breaches the time barrier in this direction. Maybe it works the other way too; maybe when someone living from this time goes forward, a thing of beauty destroyed there is restored."

"But most of the destruction remained. I saw it with my own eyes, though I would not have believed it otherwise. To flatten an entire range of mountains . . ." He shook his head. "It is an affront to God. Your leaders are as foolish as ours. Perhaps it will take more than one person going forward to undo such damage."

Uncle John stopped and stared at him. "You may be right," he said. "You certainly have given me a lot to consider when I do the math."

"I have an idea," said the Raven. "St. Pancras is closed and will be until Sunday, Mr. Smythe promises me, so no one has seen the new paintings. Why not go back before then? You can visit Lavinia yourself, and study the valley fill, and when you return there will be no more upset than there already will be because of my visit."

"I think I'll do just that. And why don't I send Mary along with Mother Bunch to visit Mother Bunch's widowed sister in Bradway village until Monday? It would be a good idea to have Mary out of the way when the paintings are discovered on Sunday." Uncle John hesitated. "Then Lydde will be by herself. I could tell her to expect you Friday evening."

The Raven said nothing. Then he removed his hat, put his hand on top of his head, and took off his mask.

On Friday morning Mother Bunch and Mary set off for Bradway in the company of Mossup and a hired carriage. Mother Bunch had fretted for the two days before that "the men shall have nothing to eat," so she wrung the necks of two chickens and roasted them, baked several loaves of fresh bread, took a ham from the smokehouse (as though Lewis and the good doctor could not find their way there), and stocked the larder with cheeses, potatoes, and a sack of dried apples.

When he had seen them off, Uncle John took his own leave. He had done his calculations and determined he could have a couple of months with Lavinia and still be back in plenty of time to deal with the upset Sunday morning would bring. Lydde kissed him on the cheek and waved good-bye. Then she went inside and headed for the attic, Bounder following happily behind.

Mother Bunch had once told her that poor Mr. Soane, after the death of his wife many years before, had placed her clothes in a trunk and had it sent to the attic, never to be opened again. Lydde located the trunk after much sneezing. When she opened it she expected must and mold, but was surprised to be met with a pleasing scent of lilac. One of Mother Bunch's sachets, she supposed, and after rummaging around among the staid wool and linen frocks she found a silk dressing gown in a lovely rose color that she had always thought to be her best, and a low-cut green velvet dress. The doctor's wife had been shorter than Lydde and a bit wider, but the clothes fit reasonably well, even if they were moth-eaten. I will look pretty for him, she thought, and shivered so that she was propelled back down the stairs with a burst of energy that left Bounder scrabbling to keep up with her.

She had just set kettles of water to boil so she might wash her hair and have a bath when she heard a distant commotion. She hastily pulled on her boy's clothes. When she went to the gate to look out, a gang of boys ran along Sheep Street. They spied her and called, "Lewis! There's to be a hanging! Come along!"

"Oh, God, no!" she cried. The boys paid her no mind and ran on ahead. She followed them, terrified at what she might find, joining the growing crowd that made its way toward the jail, praying over and over, Dear God, don't let it be him, please God. All around her people pressed close, talking and calling out to one another, some of them laughing, as though they were about to witness a game of some kind, a festive performance. She looked at their dirt-streaked faces and suddenly hated them all with a passion she'd never before felt, hated them for their filth and narrowness and stupidity. In her mind she heard the Raven's voice, speaking of his care for the sufferings of ordinary folk, and she asked him in turn, How can you risk your life for these horrid people?

Ahead of her she saw Jacob Woodcock, fresh from his forge and still wearing his apron. Pray God he is the Raven after all, she thought, for he is here in the crowd, safe.

A permanent scaffold of wood flanked the jail. Lydde had always avoided looking at it when she walked by, grateful that so far in her time in Norchester there had been no hangings. The gibbet was now draped with a length of knotted rope, like an obscene decoration. Then a cry went up and the crowd parted as a procession of the constables of Norchester passed on their way past the market cross. Behind all, stiffly arrogant and stern on horseback, rode Noah Fallam.

She screwed up her courage and asked the woman standing beside her, "Who will be hung?"

"One of the Raven's men, a tenant of Lord Radford. He was taken last night and his sentence is already pronounced by Pastor Fallam."

Lydde felt ill, not just for what awaited the condemned man, but for the threat this must mean to the man she loved. Perhaps Fallam had had the captive beaten, perhaps tortured, to extract such a quick confession. What if the man knew something of the Raven's identity and had divulged it to his captors? Perhaps her lover would be too frightened to come to her that night; certainly he would be upset. Her eyes filled with tears, most unbecoming for a boy, and she pressed the back of her hand against her mouth to steel herself. She edged toward the fringes of the crowd, thinking to bolt before she became sick, but as she reached a less crowded place, the doors of the jail were thrown open and the poor wretch emerged, supported by a pair of constables, one of them Baxter. The prisoner was a short, sturdy man—not the Raven himself, thank God—who was barely able to stand upright. His hands were bound in front of him, and he had been gagged.

"Never seen a man gagged at a hanging," a man in front of her said. "Do they fear he will utter some curse?"

Noah Fallam had dismounted and climbed the scaffold, waiting with arms folded as the condemned man was dragged up the steps. He surveyed the crowd as he waited and his gaze alighted on Lydde. She glared at him, her expression filled with as much contempt as she could muster, and he stared back, his face never changing expression but his eyes hard. So, she thought, he knows how much I hate him.

Fallam was the first to look away. Then he stepped forward and said in a loud voice, "Here is a man condemned to die, out of favor with God and the Commonwealth, for he is a thief and a brigand who disturbs the peace and threatens prosperity."

A low murmur of protest ran through a portion of the crowd, then died.

"Jonas Bent has been taken while serving the so-called Raven, himself a lawless bandit who will one day stand in this place. Therefore I have found said Jonas Bent guilty and pronounced a sentence of death upon him."

Lydde couldn't take her eyes off the condemned man, who was shaking his head vigorously and uttering muffled cries behind his gag. Fallam turned suddenly, raised one hand, and nodded at the hangman, who wore a black mask much like the Raven's. The hangman placed the noose around the man's head and tightened it. Fallam dropped his arm abruptly and the hangman shoved the man off the edge of the scaffold to twist in a deadly silence with only the creak of the rope for a sound. Lydde slipped into an alley and was sick to her stomach.

Chapter 15

The World Turned Upside Down

LYDDE RETREATED TO her room and wept. She could not clear her mind of the hanged man swinging from his rope, the front of his breeches darkening with piss. She understood now what Uncle John meant by danger. It was one thing to imagine, another thing to see a man dragged onto a scaffold and horribly killed. Whoever the Raven was, he faced the same fate. She wondered what he might be thinking. Perhaps he would be frightened enough to stay away, or perhaps he would need her desperately. She stood up and straightened the bedclothes, tucking sprigs of Mother Bunch's dried lavender between the sheets. Everything must be as lovely as possible for him.

Back in the kitchen she rebuilt the fire and heated the water—feeling some pride that she was able to accomplish the task alone—took her bath, and washed her hair. Then she rubbed another handful of Mother Bunch's dried lavender against the wet skin of her neck, shoulders, and breasts and into her hair. She had searched for a woman's shift in the attic trunk and, finding none, decided to do without. The velvet dress slipped easily over her naked skin. She stood for a moment with her eyes closed, and imagined what might soon come. Perhaps he would think her wanton when he found nothing beneath her dress. Her body twitched as though invisible feathers teased her from the back of her neck to the insides of her thighs. She felt hot, then cold, and her feet were like ice, so she forced herself to climb the stairs to her bedroom, where she had built another fire and brought up a pile of logs to keep it going. She found a pair of Mary's fur slippers and pulled them on, then sat on the edge of the bed for a moment. Was she ready for this?

Her body most certainly was. She couldn't recall wanting a man so badly. And yet she had no idea what he would look like when he removed his mask. Nor could she fathom what it would mean to love a man from another century, especially one in such dangerous circumstances. When Uncle John had told her to expect the Raven's visit, she had been surprised. "Have you changed your mind?" she asked. "Do you approve now?"

"I'm just as afraid for you as ever," he said. "But I have spoken with him. I think you're right. This was meant to be."

Meant to be. She clenched her fists and took a deep breath, then went downstairs to the study, where another fire was blazing, to wait.

DARKNESS fell and Lydde lit two candles, one for the hall, the other for the door at the back of the house that opened onto the garden. She had left the gate unlocked and now listened for the sound of its opening, but heard nothing. She feared the day's events had indeed frightened him enough to stay away. Then Bounder barked in the garden, followed by silence.

She stood nervously, rubbing the palms of her hands against the nap of the velvet dress. She could not see the garden door but heard it swing open with a creak, heard a man speaking softly to the dog. Then the door closed. She waited.

Slow footsteps sounded in the hall then he stood in the doorway. He was wearing his black mask.

"That is no watchdog," he said.

"No," Lydde managed to say. "She likes people too much."

"You look lovely." His voice was almost a whisper.

"Thank you."

He stepped into the room. "I entered masked," he said, not with a false rasping voice but with one that sounded familiar, "so as not to give you such a start." He took off his hat, laid it on a chair, and put his hand to the black hood. "I'm afraid you will not be pleased with what you see when I remove it."

She waited, unable to speak. He lifted the hood.

Noah Fallam stood before her.

"You!" she cried. She stumbled back toward the hearth and grabbed a poker, held it before her for protection.

He came toward her, but she drove him back.

"Stay away from me!" she cried, flailing at him with the poker. "You murderer! What have you done with him? If you've hurt him, I'll kill you, I swear to God I will!"

"Lydde," he said, and tried to approach her again. She swung the poker wildly, catching him a glancing blow across the arm that caused him to wince.

"Stay away!" she cried again, then began to sob. "Where is he?"

"Lydde, he is here. I am the Raven."

"No!" She shook her head. "No, you aren't. You can't be."

"How did I know your name otherwise?"

This gave her pause. He came a cautious step closer and she retreated until her back was pressed against the stone wall of the hearth, the poker held straight in front of her. She was so upset she couldn't catch a breath. He backed up then and sat on a chair, said, "See, I won't approach you."

"Stand up!" she commanded.

At his look of surprise, she jabbed at him with the poker. "Stand up, damn you! You made me stand when you bullied me."

He stood, hands held out from his body, and watched her warily.

"Where—is—he?" she repeated.

"Here!" said Noah Fallam. "And I have placed my very life in your hands by telling you so. Does that mean nothing to you?"

When she didn't answer, he let his arms drop. A look of pain crossed his face. "I have watched you all these weeks," he said in a low voice, "and I have grown to love you. But I forget you have watched me these same weeks and grown to hate me."

"I saw you on the scaffold," she said coldly, "and you saw me. If you are the Raven, how could you hang your own man? And how dare you come here tonight with blood on your hands?"

He spoke in a flat voice that held little hope. "I hanged that man because he and others saw me without a shirt the other night, and noticed a birthmark I have on my right shoulder. A red patch shaped like a leaf." He unbuttoned his shirt and pulled coat and shirt off his right shoulder, turned his back to her so she could see the vivid red mark. "Your Uncle John was there that night. Ask him what sort of danger this places me in."

He turned back to face her. "And that man came to me, Noah Fallam, and told me he had seen the mark and that he would collect the bounty placed on the Raven's head. All that would be needed is to find a man in Norchester who bears this mark, and the Raven is identified. As the Raven, I knew he had betrayed me and would betray others if given a chance. As Noah Fallam, I knew I must offer the authorities in Bristol some assurance I was making headway against the Raven and his gang. So I hanged the man. Do you think I took pleasure in it?"

He came a step closer.

"Please, Lydde, try to understand. When the Raven flourishes, then Noah Fallam's situation grows more precarious. The major-general in Bristol, Elisha Sitwell, threatens to come here himself to catch the Raven, since Noah Fallam seems unequal to the task. But if Noah Fallam is relieved of his duties, the Raven has no protection. I am both men, and both men are in mortal danger."

She shook her head, tears blurring her eyes. "I don't know which man is the real one."

"Do you think I would risk my life and the lives of others to play games?" he said softly. "Lydde, I saw the hatred in your face today. I very nearly stayed away from you because of it, and I should have. I see now that while you may love the Raven, who is no more substantial than this black hood, you have nothing but contempt for Noah Fallam. So be it. I shall leave you alone. I only beg you to tell no one what you have learned tonight, for if I am caught I shall be tortured. Do you know how it will be done? I shall be taken upon that same scaffold and hanged, but not pushed over the edge for a quick death. Rather, I shall be hauled up by the neck with a burning brazier before me, and while yet living disemboweled and my entrails burnt in front of me. Only then will I be beheaded, and afterward my body hacked to pieces like a butchered animal. And I pray you do not want me to suffer that fate no matter how much you may despise me."

He had come so close he was able to take the poker from her hand and drop it with a dull clang.

"Do you?" he asked. She remembered the shadow of the Raven's eyes, dark behind their mask, and knew she looked into the same eyes. She shook her head, too stunned to speak. He reached into his coat pocket and held up his hand, palm out. Lydde found herself staring at her long-haired mirror image.

"If looking could wear out such a marvelous thing as this," he said, "it would already be faded." He replaced the photo, then touched Lydde, his fingers caressing her cheek, tracing a gentle line down her neck to her breast.

"My God," he said, "I wanted you, and meant no harm."

He turned and left the room.

The world seemed to depart with him. Lydde ran after him, caught him in the garden.

"Raven!" was all she could think to say. He kept going. Then, "Noah, wait!"

Just when he was about to disappear into the shadows, he paused. Without looking at her, he said, "You speak my name and this time I hear no contempt."

She followed him into the darkness. "Noah," she said again softly. Then, "Noah Fallam. Your name is the name of my mountain."

The name of the skeleton that lies beneath it, she thought. I should have known.

She stood close and placed her hands on his arm. He leaned toward her, a finger lifting her chin. His mouth covered hers. Then he stepped back.

"Is it not the same kiss?" he asked.

"It is," she whispered.

She took his hand and led him back inside the warmth of Soane's Croft. The garden door closed behind them and he leaned against it as though afraid to move. Lydde stood still at the foot of the stairs, waiting.

"I must be sure of you," he said. "Can you truly love me tonight when you have seen me do a man to death this morning?"

"It was terrible, what you did," she said. "And it frightens and horrifies me." She thought a moment. "Yet it must be done. And I love you for taking it upon yourself. You seem to bear so much of other peoples' burdens."

Noah closed his eyes. "When my soul is sick," he said, "I believe you may be the healing of it."

He held out his hand, and when she grasped it, he pulled her to him. She stood a moment, her hands resting on his chest, and looked up into his face, trying to understand how she found herself in the arms of the man she had so recently feared and despised. What she saw dispelled the last of her doubts. It was not the studied mask of a scheming manipulator, as the Raven might have been, nor the guilty face of a religious fanatic succumbing to temptation. He was regarding her with a guileless mixture of uncertainty and tenderness.

He kissed her gently, his lips barely brushing hers, then again, and teasingly again, until her mouth parted ever so slightly and she tasted the sweetness of his tongue. She moaned as he kissed her more deeply. He stopped.

"I should not do this," he said, "I should not for your sake, and yet I have no strength to turn away."

She took his hand and led him up the stairs to her bedroom. He waited while she closed the door behind them to keep out the cold. Then his arm went around her waist, and while he kissed her neck, his fingers found the buttons on the front of her dress and one by one he loosened them. He pulled the dress from her shoulders down to her waist. Her skin seemed to melt in the firelight.

"No shift," he said appreciatively, and covered one breast with his right hand.

"I couldn't find any," she said.

He laughed then, the same vibrant laugh she had heard the day of her interrogation in the Bishop's Palace.

"Laugh if you will." She pressed against him and he held her close. "I wanted to dress like a woman for you. Like a lady. Now you shall think I am a wanton. I know the ladies here are more modest than where I am from. And you find me without a shift and"—she pressed harder against his groin—"wanting you desperately."

He began to kiss a bare breast. "Indeed you are bold. In every way."

"Is that bad or good?"

"It is very, very good!" His hands moved over her body. "You look me in the eye. You speak out, and sometimes out of turn."

"I don't speak out of turn! I simply say what's on my mind. Why shouldn't I?"

He kissed her neck. "I have been dreaming of a woman like you."

"How can you be sure what sort of woman I am?"

"I have observed you, as you know, and I consider myself a good judge of women."

"Are you indeed?"

"I am. I watched you fight for Mary, and I thought if I were so fortunate that you loved me, you might stand by me the same way."

"I would fight for you," she agreed.

"Your Uncle John thinks so. And how do you suppose I came by my little portrait of you?"

"Uncle John."

"Oh, no!" he said with an air of triumph. "I have been to your time and your house and met your Aunt Lavinia."

This surprised her so much she stepped away from him. And the sudden movement caused her gown, too large for her, to slip over her hips and fall to the floor.

"Oh," she said, and stood naked before him, unsure of what to do.

Noah retreated to a chair and sat down, a broad smile on his face. "Let me watch you a moment," he said. He began to pull off his boots, never taking his eyes off her.

She folded her arms self-consciously across her breasts and ducked her head, which increased his amusement. "Why don't you turn around?" he suggested.

She did so, stealing a look back over her shoulder at him. Then her embarrassment overwhelmed her and she did the only thing she could think to do to extricate herself. She went to him and pulled him close to press his head against her belly. He dropped the boot he was holding and nuzzled her ribs with the tip of his nose, teased a nipple with his tongue.

Then she gasped and pulled away, backed up toward the bed, and held on to one of the bedposts.

"What?" he asked.

"I have just thought of something." She took a deep breath. "Those awful things you said in your sermon. About women. Did you mean them?"

"My sermon? Of all things—"

"You said women were weak and silly. Did you mean it?"

He leaned back, and a look she had seen before crossed his face, a look she had once interpreted as an arrogant smirk at her expense. Only now she saw it for what it truly was, amusement mixed with admiration, and charged with the sheer vitality of Noah Fallam.

"Do you know the teachings of the Quakers?" he asked. "They hold with the equality of men and women before God, and that is one reason many consider them so scandalous. They even place women in positions of authority. Where women are concerned, I am of that persuasion."

"Oh," Lydde said in a small voice.

He stood up. "Indeed, there are weak and silly women in the world. But if that was what I wanted, I would not do what I am about to do."

With that, he pulled his shirt over his head and tossed it in a corner. The Celtic cross glittered in the firelight. He went to her and pulled her close with one hand, while with the other he unbuttoned his breeches. Together they looked down at an erection Lydde judged more than pleasingly adequate. She touched him with the tips of two fingers.

"At home we have several names for it," she said. "What do you call it here?"

"A cock," he said, studying her face.

"You have a lovely cock," she said. She held it like a quivering bird in the warm palm of her hand, then began to stroke him.

He closed his eyes and leaned against her. His hand moved from her breasts to between her thighs. Her head went back.

"Now," she said urgently, "please, now."

He pushed her back on the bed, kicking his breeches away with one motion, and climbed atop her. She gasped when he entered her, then eagerly answered his thrusts. His left arm supported her shoulders, but he pressed his right hand hard against her groin and kept it in place as they rocked so she thought she would go mad with pleasure. She cried his name over and over, and when she came he moaned in turn as she gripped him harder. Then he wrapped his right arm around her thighs and pushed himself even deeper into her. They thrashed and rocked, he pounding her so that the creaking of the rope bed mingled with their moans. When he gave a final cry, he collapsed so completely she thought she had killed him.

He lay without moving, his face turned away from her and his hair a wild tangle on the pillow. The beating of his heart reassured her. After a time he raised his head and pressed his face against her damp neck, the bristles on his chin scratching her soft skin.

"Stay inside me a little longer," she whispered.

He kissed her cheek for answer and lay still, his breathing slower and more even.

"Am I crushing you?" he asked.

"Yes. And it's wonderful."

He laughed and so did she, and their sudden movement caused him to slip out of her, leaving a wet trail along the inside of her thigh. She sighed and he rolled off her, pulled her close. They were quiet for a time, hands exploring, pausing now and then for a gentle kiss. Amazing, Lydde thought, everything works the same way it does in the future. Then she started to laugh.

"What?" he said.

"This is so odd," she said. "It is so very, very odd. I'm not even born yet. My great-great-great-great-grandmother isn't even born yet. And here you have made love to me."

"While in your time," he said, "I will have made old bones."

She stopped laughing and pulled him closer, squeezing her eyes tightly shut against the image of the tumbled skeleton. No, it was not the same as in the future, not the same as anything she had ever felt before. His back was soft and warm and she caressed it with her palms and fingertips, burrowed her nose into the flesh of his neck and felt the pulse of his lifeblood.

"You must not ever be dead," she said fiercely. "You must not ever be."

He placed his hand on her forehead. "You will keep me alive," he said. Then his stomach rumbled loudly.

"Are you hungry?" she asked.

"Starving," he admitted.

"I almost forgot. There's supper in the kitchen."

They left the bed's warmth and pulled on clothes, Lydde wrapping herself in the rose silk gown instead of the dress. They ran down the stairs, laughing like a pair of children. Bounder heard the commotion and scratched to be let in, jumped up to each in turn to have her head patted. The kitchen was too cold for lingering, so Noah found a knife and a pitcher of ale, while Lydde took a cold roast chicken, bread, and cheese from the larder. Back in the study, they set the food on the floor. Noah grabbed a pillow from a bench and tossed it in front of the hearth, then sank down onto the fur rug, drawing Lydde to his side.

He cut a drumstick from the chicken and handed it to Lydde. They sat cross-legged and ate, tearing the chicken with their fingers and teeth and taking turns sucking the grease from each other's fingers. The bird was soon picked clean and they turned their attention to Mother Bunch's good black bread and cheddar.

"I doubt I have ever enjoyed food more," Noah said as he popped a yellow sliver of cheese into his mouth. He put his arm around Lydde and pulled her close, fed her a piece of cheese. She breathed in the good earthy smell of him as she chewed. Sated at last, they sank back onto the pillow, legs entwined. Noah pushed Lydde onto her back, pulled open her robe, and watched the firelight play across her skin.

"Now we must talk," he said.

She felt a cold chill pass over her despite the fire's heat. In her experience that line would be followed by a neat speech about not taking things too seriously, followed by her lover's quick exit. She couldn't tell Noah that, afraid to mention she had been with other men, had been deserted by other men. His next words caused her to sit up in alarm.

"I can't make love to you again unless you promise me something," he said.

"You—" She was unable to look at him. "You don't want a relationship?"

"A relationship? What's that?" He sat up. "Lydde, I want to marry you. I must marry you or I cannot make love to you."

"Marry me!" She felt dizzy. "That's an awfully big step. My God, I've spent my life running from marriage."

"That's because you hadn't met me," he said.

A glance confirmed that he was not teasing her.

"You're asking me to forsake my own time and be with you," she said.

"I am asking you to be with me," he said, "for as long as you decide to stay in this time. Though there are risks you must consider. If I am in trouble, we might both decide it best for you to go. But I think"— here he pulled her back to the pillow, ran one hand over her body— "you want to live life as fully as you can while you possess it. I know I do. And that means joining our lives one to another. It could be a grand adventure. What do you say?"

"But you can't make love to me again unless I marry you?"

"No. I spoke at length with your Aunt Lavinia. She told me much about you and about the way things are in your time."

Gee, thanks, Aunt Lavinia, she thought, and closed her eyes. So he would know about her failed relationships anyway.

"Lydde, I know that in your time people make love without being married and think nothing of it. But I am a man of my time. And although I am an admitted fraud as a lieutenant major-general, I hope I remain a true pastor. In this time, if a man and woman make love and are not betrothed or married, we call it fornication. I have committed that sin before, I must confess, but I would not want to commit it with you. I don't want that between us. So I should not make love to you again unless you agree to marry me."

"You made love to me just now without us being betrothed or married."

It was Noah's turn to look embarrassed. "Yes," he said. "I meant only to visit with you tonight. Well, I do not regret any of this, far from it. But I believe it is a sin, though sins of loving pale before others, I hope. I shall have to go down on my knees and ask forgiveness for it. Unless, that is, you agree to marry me."

"I don't want you to marry me just because you don't want to sin," she said.

He stared at her. "Do you really think that is why I want to marry you?"

"No," she admitted, and felt ashamed. Damned twenty-first-century cynicism. She touched his cheek. "No. Forgive me."

"You must trust me," he said.

"I want to trust you," she said. "But I don't know you yet, only the parts you've been playing." She took a deep breath as though preparing to plunge into deep water. "But I will tell you this. Whatever impression you may have gotten about women in my time, I don't take lightly what just passed between us. I would never have done that unless I loved you, or at least loved who I think you are."

He leaned over to kiss her and the cross on its chain slipped from beneath his shirt and lodged between her breasts. She gasped as the image came again of the skeleton in the cave, the chain tangled in its rib cage.

"I'm sorry," he said, and started to lift the chain over his head, but she stopped him.

"No," she said, "leave it on. The moment I saw it was the moment I knew our lives were entwined."

He smiled. "Then it is my most precious possession."

He lay back on the pillow. "I must go soon," he said, "else I shall not be able to resist loving you again, and I am thinking it best if you do not give me an answer tonight. It is not fair to expect it as we are now. You should give your answer in the clear light of day, without the influence of my caresses. And you're quite right, you must know more of me before you decide. What are your plans tomorrow?"

"I have none. Mother Bunch and Mary won't be back until Monday and Uncle John will return tomorrow night."

"We could ride out to Coombe Manor tomorrow. That is my ancestral home. Would you ride with me? You can see where I come from and I can tell you about my life. Then you can give me your answer."

As he was gathering up his coat and hat, Noah said, "One thing I'm curious about. You must have been trying to guess who the Raven might be. Who had you thought?"

"Jacob Woodcock," she said.

Noah gave a yelp of laughter.

As he was about to go out the door, she called him back. "Noah. I'm glad it turned out to be you."

He smiled for answer and held her close. "You," he said, "are becoming very precious to me. And you are a difficult woman to leave. But I must."

He went out, closing the door behind him.

Back in her room, she huddled beneath her comforter in the now-cold bed, trying to pick up his scent in the bedclothes, listening to the last crackling of the fire. This was what life would be like without him. She imagined Noah moving alone in the dark along the path that followed the River Pye to the Bishop's Palace. She imagined four centuries separating them. Then she could not imagine it.

Chapter 16

Coombe Manor

THE NEXT MORNING was cold with a bright blue sky. Lydde dressed in her boy's clothes and warm coat, then pulled on a wide-brimmed hat and saddled Uncle John's horse Lady. The Saturday market was stirring behind the jail in Priory Park, though it had grown smaller as the year waned. No longer did lines of farmers' carts piled with produce wait to unload their goods. Butter and milk were still available, and rounds of yellow cheese, but most of the market was given over to herds of geese and pigs, squawking and squealing through piles of offal while ragged dogs nipped at their heels. The cold air had chapped the cheeks of men and women as ruddy as any painting by Brueghel, and they blew on their hands and beat their arms across their chests to keep warm. They were the same folk, Lydde considered, who had yesterday viewed a hanging as sport, though she remembered the undercurrent of protest when Noah had denounced the condemned man. Perhaps it had not been a game for them at all but a way of being alive while facing their own fearful deaths. Some men gossiped with their neighbors while they watched another neighbor killed. Noah Fallam hanged a man and then sought out a woman's bed.

Lady kept her head as Lydde guided her into North Gate Street and on through North Gate. Noah was waiting on horseback and with him was Constable Baxter.

"See here, Constable," Noah said at her approach. "Is this not a promising lad?"

"Indeed," Baxter agreed. "The good doctor has done wonders for the boy. He has less and less of that frightened look about him."

"And I shall do more," Noah said. "For I propose to take this boy under my wing and educate him as I did Simon Cleyes. What do you think of that, Lewis?"

Lydde bowed her head, hoping the brim of her hat hid her face. "As you will, sir," she said.

"So, Lewis, will you live at the Bishop's Palace?" Constable Baxter said kindly.

"As Pastor Fallam wishes," she answered, and shot Noah a glance that said, Don't push it. His dark eyes were gleaming with mischief.

"I am taking the lad with me to Coombe Manor today," he told Baxter. "I want him to see what a rich estate may be guaranteed to the elect. And as I have observed Lewis, I believe he may be indeed one of us. For not many may be so directly attacked by the minions of Satan and yet escape unscathed."

"A fortunate lad," Constable Baxter agreed, and waved them on their way with a sweep of his hat.

They went on, their horses at a walk, until clear of the town, before Lydde dared steal a glance at Noah.

"What was that all about?" she said.

"I've thought of a way for us to marry. I'll pretend to take over your guardianship from John Soane. I'll be your benefactor, as I was to Simon. That way you can live at the Bishop's Palace with me."

"If I agree to marry you."

He nodded and said nothing, but the expression on his face told her he had little doubt of her answer. She felt a twinge of irritation. It seemed the self-regard she'd seen in Noah Fallam before was not part of his disguise.

"So," she said, more sharply than she meant, "do you believe that nonsense about the elect?"

"No. I used to." The tone of her voice had caused him to glance at her. "Are you aware," he said, "that women here are supposed to wait to be spoken to?"

"What! If you think—"

He raised a hand. "Put down your back, my lady cat. I only want to point out how much I tolerate in you, so that you might try to be equally patient with me."

She looked away.

"Now," he said. "Have I done something to anger you?"

"No. It's just that in the cold light of day, last night seems a bit of a dream and this place seems too real."

"Last night seems real enough to me," he replied. He was watching her carefully, as though afraid he had misunderstood something. "Do you have regrets?"

"No." She shook her head. "No. I would like to relive it. It's sad that we can't revisit such moments over and over and instead they are fled and we are left with something else. Where do they go, do you think, such happy moments?"

"That is a question for John," Noah said. "Perhaps somewhere we are again loving one another for the first time. Only I would prefer to dwell on what might be again, not what is past. I would like to think our love continues."

Just then Lady took a step that caught Lydde wrong. She winced.

"What's wrong?" Noah asked.

"Nothing serious," Lydde said, and readjusted her seat. "I'm a bit tender, that's all." She glanced at him. "Someone seems to have been having his way with me last night."

He actually blushed and had the grace to look sheepish, but when he spoke he sounded not the least contrite. "I must confess, I wanted you badly. And everything that happened between us answered and elevated all my expectations. Being with you last night was a revelation."

She felt it suddenly hard to breathe. "Was it?" she whispered.

He nodded. "I have imagined loving a woman that way."

"Last night you said you had some experience of women. Was this so different?"

"It was. It's true, I am not inexperienced. My brother Robert and I came often to whores in Norchester, and they taught me much."

"That's terrible!"

"Is it? You sound like a Puritan."

She opened her mouth to reply but could think of nothing to say. Noah looked amused.

"At that time it was what young gentlemen did," he continued. "My father encouraged it. Part of my education. There was a certain house on Wood Street before the war that was famous for procuring fresh girls from the country, so there was much less danger of acquiring the pox. All of the gentlemen of the district sent their sons there. But after a time I came to understand the poor lasses were selling themselves because they had no other means of survival. When they had aged a few years—say, become sixteen or seventeen—and carried more danger of infection, they were sent on to the stews of Bristol or London to make way for new girls. I learned this from my favorite whore, a redheaded lass named Kate. Once I understood, I befriended her and paid her for conversation. I went to her more and more often, and ever after that was all I paid for. Often I bought an entire night with her to spare her the company of other men, and we curled up together upon her bed and talked and slept." He smiled. "Though now and then, I admit, we still made love from affection. We both knew it would come to naught, but Kate was generous and I loved her in a boy's way. She taught me much. Poor country girls know more of these matters than ladies do. Before she could be sent away I secretly supplied her with a small dowry, and she was able to wed a local farmer. They live outside Bradway. She has five children and her husband is a Raven's man."

"Does her husband know of your tie to her?"

"Of course not."

"If you have been to whores," Lydde said, "then why was last night a revelation? You cannot think me particularly forward compared to a whore."

"Oh, you are much more so!"

"Noah!"

He grinned. "Without doubt, you are. You mustn't think whores are amorous. With them it is all business, and an onerous one at that. Some of them are good at pretending otherwise unless you look into their eyes. But you!" He shook his head. "Last night was pure joy for you. Your face, my God! And every move I made, you answered. I dreamed it would be so when I carried you back from the monastery on my horse."

"It was because I was with you."

"I know," he said, with such assurance (or bravado, she later suspected) she wanted to smack him. Then he added, "I was not lying when I said I smelled you. The first time I was close to you at Soane's Croft, the hairs on the back of my neck stood up."

"I used to dream of you at night, though I tried not to."

"When I shoved you too hard in my office it was all I could do to keep from taking you in my arms."

"It was all I could do to keep from hitting you," she said.

He laughed. "In your defense of women, how could you have hit a man who loves women so?"

And she knew in her heart that some men did fear and hate women, but Noah Fallam was not one of them. Still, he was looking and sounding far too satisfied with himself. So she asked, "If you love women so, why are you not married?"

She regretted her light tone at once, for his face turned to stone.

"I am a widower," he said.

So there had been a wife. She chastised herself for not guessing. A man in his early thirties would likely have been married before. But the fact that she knew nothing of a wife was a reminder of how little she actually knew about him.

"I'm sorry," she said.

"Her name was Margaret. She died a year ago this past spring, in childbirth."

They rode on in silence, Lydde waiting, sensing he would tell her in his own time. Then he said, "It was horrible. She'd had two miscarriages and two stillbirths. The last was a breech birth and the midwives couldn't turn the baby. She screamed for hours upstairs while I sat below and listened to her torment. Then she died, and the baby with her."

Lydde rode closer and linked her arm with his, but he gently disengaged from her. "Someone might see us," he reminded her.

"I'm sorry," she said. And afraid, she thought, though she kept her fear to herself.

"I blamed myself," he said. "I felt I had killed her. Though I know it is the way of the world."

"You must have loved her."

"Everyone loved Margaret," he said. "How could I not? She was kind and gentle, and loyal as the day was long. But it was not a passionate marriage. We'd known each other since childhood, you see. Our parents were friends and had promised us to one another when we were small. It was simply assumed we would wed, and when I was eighteen and she fifteen, we did. But she was more like a beloved sister in many ways. She was never comfortable with lovemaking. I tried to please her, but she was always . . . I don't know . . . afraid. Perhaps it was because ladies here are taught to be modest. Or, perhaps with someone else . . ." His voice trailed away and he shrugged. "She would never allow me to see her naked, and she wouldn't look upon me. She wouldn't move during lovemaking, would make not a sound except to whimper now and then as though I hurt her. Which I probably did. Nor would she touch me intimately or allow me to touch her."

Then he turned toward Lydde, a stricken look on his face. "I do not belittle her, please believe that," he said. "Margaret stood by me when the rest of my family turned away, and at great cost to her happiness. It was no more her fault than mine that our love was more kindred than anything."

"I believe you," Lydde said. "I hear nothing but affection and respect in your voice."

"Good," he said with relief. "I only wanted you to know why you are so different to me. And to tell you I was faithful to Margaret while we were married. I take the marriage vow quite seriously. After her death, I went to whores again, for a few months. But since I came here and became the Raven, that has been too dangerous, nor should Noah Fallam be seen in a brothel."

"No wonder you were ready for me," Lydde said.

"I have burned," he agreed, "as St. Paul so aptly put it."

"Sorry, but I just can't believe what we did was a sin."

Noah smiled then. "If God loves sinners," he said, "He must be especially fond of that sin."

THE landscape north of Norchester turned rugged, long swells of downs cut here and there by hidden hollows—as Lydde would have called them—or coombes, as Noah did. The way rose steadily, then Noah led them through a stone gateway that stood beside the road. Here the path narrowed and disappeared into a dense wood, a track that seemed faded and old as time. A hundred yards or so along stood a thatched cottage. They drew up in front of it and Noah dismounted.

"Wait here," he said. But before he could approach, the cottage door opened and a bent old man emerged, a scowl twisting his deeply lined face.

"Symms," Noah said. "How are you and your wife?"

Symms was oddly shaped, his upper body that of a substantial man, his legs wizened and bowed. He took his time answering, as though he hoped to make Noah uncomfortable, then said, "The wife does tolerable."

Noah nodded, seeming to ignore Symms's hostility. "I require the keys," he said. "I want to show Coombe Manor to this lad."

Symms turned his malevolent stare on Lydde. "Why?" he said.

The question seemed rude even to Lydde's twenty-first-century ears. But Noah refused to be riled.

"I have taken the boy under my wing as I did Simon Cleyes," he said coolly. "You will remember Simon."

Symms didn't reply, and instead turned and went inside, returning with a group of keys hanging on a ring.

"Thank you," Noah said. "We shall be back later today."

But his words were lost on Symms, who had retreated inside once more and slammed the door.

"What was that all about?" Lydde asked when they were on their way again.

"I should have warned you," Noah said. "Symms despises me. He has been the caretaker at Coombe Manor for thirty years. Symms it was who caught Simon's father poaching and turned him over to be hanged. He took it as a personal insult when I befriended Mother Cleyes and her family. And to Symms, I am the renegade son of his beloved late master and the usurper of my older brother's estate. It is family history I shall soon explain. For now, Symms is angry because I do not collect rent from my tenants. My brother's tenants, Symms would say. And it's true, Robert doesn't like it. We correspond twice a year, Robert and I. But since he fought for the losing side in the war and has now fled to America, he has no authority here. I am the younger brother, but for the immediate future I am master of Coombe Manor. And I will not keep our tenants in poverty."

"Does it make such a difference to forgive their rent?"

"It does to them. For the first time in their lives they can put away money. Some have been able to leave the land and strike out on their own. The Bland family has moved to London and set up a business trafficking in hides from Virginia. The Wood family—and this especially infuriated Robert—has gone to Virginia and purchased a farm near my brother's estate there. The poor tenants, suddenly neighbors on an equal footing." Noah smiled. "Robert's wife Elizabeth was especially put out. It seems she encounters Mother Wood on a regular basis and the woman has the gall to bid her good day without curtsying."

"Horrors," Lydde said. "But what about your brother? Are you making it difficult for him to survive?"

"Robert made his escape with a goodly portion of our father's gold. He has purchased an estate on the James River." He shook his head. "No, my brother and his family lack for nothing that America can provide."

"And you?"

"I am not a wealthy man. I have set aside a sum to take to America if need be, enough to establish myself. I live on part of the stipend I receive as lieutenant major-general and save the rest. When my brother returns, as he hopes to do when Cromwell's government falls, he shall have all and I shall have nothing. It is the lot of younger brothers. So, dear Lydde, if you decide to marry me, it should not be for my money."

The house materialized before them, or, more accurately, below them, for Coombe Manor was named for its situation in the bottom of a bowl of land so deep that the chimney pots were on a level with the upper road. It was a pretty house of red brick, built by Noah's grandfather in 1576, a jumble of towers and diamond-glazed windows with lacy iron casements. They stopped on the grassy expanse that fronted the house.

"Is anyone around?" Lydde asked.

Noah shook his head. "The house is closed and there have been no servants for seven years now."

They sat on their horses for a moment looking at one another. Then

Noah dismounted and reached up to Lydde, let her slide off Lady into his arms. He held her close, knocking her hat off as he did, and cradled the back of her head with his right hand.

"I have not wanted to come here," he said, "or go back into that house. But I will, with you beside me."

He removed his own hat and stuffed it in his saddlebag, then turned the horses out to graze in the tall grass. As he unlocked the front door and led her into the great hall, he continued to hold her close, as though she were a shield. His face betrayed no emotion, as though he willed himself to feel nothing. They stood before a rank of portraits that ran the length of the hall.

"Five generations of Fallams," said Noah, "and these last are my father and mother and brother."

Noah and his brother took after different parents. Robert Fallam was sturdy like his father, William, with dark hair and a beard. He seemed also—could a formal portrait reveal this?—duller than his younger brother. Catherine, the mother, was a pretty woman, with the light brown hair and dark eyes that were so striking in Noah.

They stood gazing up at the larger-than-life faces, Noah's fingers pressing too hard against her ribs.

"You are not there," Lydde observed.

"No," he said. "I am not there."

Then he began to tell her of his life.

NOAH adored his older brother Robert when they were boys. Robert could run faster, sat a horse better, was the superior shot. When they fought, Robert always won. But something changed as they grew older. When a gang of boys gathered for an adventure, it was Noah they looked to for leadership. Robert seemed not to notice or care. He could still beat Noah at wrestling or a foot race, and that was what counted.

As they grew older, their differences became even more apparent.

Robert loved company, and enjoyed the rounds of social visits the country gentry made throughout the year, moving from great house to great house for balls, masquerades, hunts, festive dinners. His conversations were all of horses and dogs and neighborhood gossip. Noah could hardly bear these social gatherings and found them more and more onerous as he grew older. He was bored by the empty formality and bland conversation at parties, but when the subject turned to politics he must keep his mouth shut or risk angering his conservative neighbors. He often slipped out as soon as was polite to walk the grounds of whatever estate they might be visiting, and in summer when the light lingered and the air was warm, he carried a book and fishing pole with him. The other young people joked about him behind his back.

William Fallam let it be known he was disappointed in his younger son. He was a supporter of the absolute monarchy and he ruled his own family on the principle of the divine right of fathers. His punishments were harsh enough that Robert and Noah, different though they were and much as they wrangled, learned to hide one another's misdeeds for the sake of brotherly affection. Noah had at an early age ceased to share his thoughts with his father, who then came to see his youngest as an awkward, shy lad with little to recommend him. Too bookish, William Fallam thought, a future cleric of the more tedious sort.

At age fifteen, Noah was expected to attend Oxford with Robert, as had Fallams before them. Noah decided on Cambridge instead. At first his father refused to send him, but Noah stood his ground despite a series of beatings. In the end, William Fallam relented at Robert's urging and reluctantly saw his stubborn son off to what was in his mind a second-rate haven for the discontented (though perhaps, he admitted, therefore adequate enough for a younger son). While Robert Fallam lived the life of a gentleman and leisurely sometime scholar at Oxford, Noah immersed himself in politics, theology, and the new learning at Emmanuel College. He pondered the radical notions of Copernicus and Galileo while studying the night sky with a telescope, despite warnings from some of his fellows that the instrument might be designed and manipulated by Satan to lead man to perdition. He pored over mathematical formulas, disputed late into the night over predestination (which he came at last to reject, though most, not only Puritans but also many Anglicans like his father, held to it), the true interpretation of scripture, and the claims of conscience. He took holy orders, though he was not certain if he would be able to obtain a living in a parish due to his radical leanings. Then he returned home to wed his childhood friend Margaret Exton. It was a marriage her father and mother would soon come to bitterly regret.

An anonymous pamphlet appeared in London, to great scandal. *The Kingdom of God Glimpsed In Albion,* it was boldly titled. It had been appropriately banned, but was circulating nonetheless, copies churned out in their hundreds by the underground printing presses. A copy of the pamphlet had reached even into Norchester and must be moving throughout the kingdom, stirring up anarchy in its wake.

"The rogue who wrote this piece of filth," William Fallam proclaimed over dinner, "will be clapped in jail when he is caught, and a good thing if he should rot there. We are too lenient with these troublemakers."

The dinner was a festive occasion, the third anniversary of Robert's wedding to his wife Elizabeth, in attendance with Noah and Margaret and both sets of in-laws. Robert and the two young women looked bored at the serious turn the conversation had taken, while Noah studiously cut the slice of boiled beef on his plate.

"What does this dreadful pamphlet contain?" asked Henry Exton, Noah's father-in-law. "Is it against the King? Have you seen it?"

"I have," said William Fallam. "A copy came into my hands this morning. It is worse than against the King, it is heretical and treasonous. I read it, and then I set it afire."

"Oh, dear," said Catherine Fallam, hoping her husband would not go off on a tirade. "Must we hear of it over dinner?"

"I do hesitate to pollute young ears with such foulness," he replied. "But the young people should know what sort of threat we face. The pamphlet calls the King a tyrant, but claims Parliament is equally tyrannical. The only just government, it declares, is one in which all participate. Not only men of property, mind you, but all men. All should be educated, as if one could imagine the butcher and the shepherd together spouting Latin. Oh, and there should be a sharing of goods from rich to poor. The tract goes on to rail against the supposed mistreatment of Red Indians and African heathens, and calls them equal in the eyes of God to an Englishman."

"Good Lord," Robert murmured, and Elizabeth looked faint.

"Indeed," William assented, pleased to see he had roused his eldest son's interest. "And"—he leaned forward to spear a roast pigeon from a plate proffered by a servant—"it proclaims universal salvation."

They sat in silence for a time, considering the enormity of such an idea, the very threat to the security of *this* world in the notion that all would gain entrance to the next.

Then Noah looked up. "I wrote the pamphlet," he said.

None at the table could trust their ears. Had he indeed spoken? They stared at him. He laid down his knife.

"I wrote the pamphlet," he repeated. "I used my own funds for the initial printing and it is indeed gone out across the land, for other printers have reproduced it."

William Fallam stood, and Noah, frightened at his father's expression, stood as well.

"Get out," said his father. "Get out of this house. You are no son of mine, nor shall you see a penny of my money."

The women all cried out at this, except for Elizabeth, who had turned toward her husband Robert as though for protection from Noah.

"William, please," Catherine begged her husband. "Where shall he go?"

"You are right, my dear," William Fallam replied. "Freedom to roam is not a proper punishment for this . . . this despicable reprobate who I will not lower myself to call son."

Margaret clutched Noah's hand and began to sob.

"Higgins!" William Fallam called his butler. "Fetch two of the footmen and bind this man so he cannot escape."

"Bind Master Noah?" asked an astonished Higgins.

"That won't be necessary," Noah said. "I don't intend to flee."

"As you will," said William Fallam. "Then, Higgins, send to Norchester for a constable. Tell them we have here a fresh inmate for Norchester jail."

"William." Catherine Fallam clutched her husband's sleeve. "Must you be so hasty?"

"I condemned this villain out of my own mouth before I knew his identity," William Fallam answered her. "Would you have me now show undeserved mercy and bring more shame on this family?"

Then he left the dining room. Noah still stood, so stricken he could not move. Robert rose and said, "Good God, Brother, whatever possessed you?"

"And what have you done to my daughter?" demanded an angry Henry Exton.

Margaret then fled the room, sobbing, to be followed by the other women.

Noah faced his brother and father-in-law. "I cannot renounce what I have written," he said. "I believe it. I did publish anonymously for my protection. But I could not bear to hear my ideas so scorned by my own father without defending them. I did think I might convince him to at least listen."

"Your ideas!" cried Henry Exton. "You call such rantings ideas? You are ruined. I shall counsel my daughter to return to her home despite her marriage to you."

"If I am lodged in jail," Noah said miserably, "that would be best."

It was the last time Noah Fallam, then eighteen years old, set eyes on his father. He was held in Norchester jail for a year. He might have suffered longer, but war had broken out and he was helped to escape by young Constable Baxter, who was sympathetic to the cause of rebellion. Noah tried to return to Coombe Manor to speak to his mother and father. His father was away and his mother agreed to see him. When Catherine entered the anteroom where he waited, she did not go to him and kiss him, but stood at a distance in front of him, back straight.

"Your brother has taken up arms with the King," she said in a cold voice. "You will only please me if you say you are joining him."

"Though my father no longer considers me his son," Noah replied, "I still do bear my parents and brother love and affection. But though it must grieve you, I am going to join the rebellion."

His mother regarded him an unblinking moment. Then she said, "I pray to God above, if only one of my sons survives this war, it is not you."

NOAH led Lydde through the empty corridors of Coombe Manor. Now and then he stopped—here was the dining room where the disastrous meal had taken place and he had last seen his father. There was his father's study, rich with paintings of hunting scenes but woefully bereft of books, which Noah had only had access to in great numbers when he reached Cambridge. Upstairs was the nursery where a wet nurse had held the infant Noah to her breast, the schoolroom where he had learned his letters from a bored tutor.

Noah's bedchamber.

Like all the other rooms the bedchamber was closed, but unlike the others, which held furnishings covered by sheets, Noah's room was bare.

"My father had every trace of me removed," Noah said. "Bed, chairs, the rug I had trod upon, clothes, books, my boy's collection of rocks and insects. All burnt upon a bonfire."

He lingered a moment staring across to the dusty window. Then he closed the door. They stood alone in the long hall.

"But Margaret supported you?" Lydde asked.

"She did. I went to see her before I joined Cromwell. She was distraught, to say the least. Her entire family was Royalist and threatened her with the same isolation I faced. Though her mother later relented, and I thank her for it. But they would not turn her out while I was off fighting, for then she seemed to belong to them and not to me. She stayed with her family and we wrote to one another. She didn't receive many of my letters; her father intercepted most of them. But we eventually managed to keep in touch through a servant."

"So you fought on the parliamentary side in the Civil War?"

"Yes."

"Was it horrible?"

He hesitated, then said, "Yes. And nothing I want to talk about."

She did learn that he had distinguished himself at the decisive battle of Naseby when, as a captain serving under Lord Thomas Fairfax he had rallied his men to stand firm against the main Royalist charge which threatened to end all, a stand which allowed Cromwell to gather his storied cavalry and countercharge, thus breaking the back of the Royalist army. Noah would only add, "Fairfax noticed. And Cromwell noticed."

IN 1648 the King's army was at last defeated and in the new year King Charles himself was executed. Noah Fallam became a penniless exsoldier like many another. The difference was he had impressed men who now found themselves in high places. At first he ignored this, uncomfortable with the idea of trading military glory for advancement. Too many people had suffered and died for what they considered other, more important reasons.

He tried to return to Coombe Manor to effect a reconciliation, though he vowed to accept none of his father's fortune even if he were to be taken back into the family fold. But he found both his mother and father a year dead and buried from an attack of contagious fever, and Robert, under interdiction for his close dealings with the King, fled to France and then Virginia with Elizabeth.

Noah could have taken over the estate and its income. Instead he closed the house, paid the servants a generous severance save for Symms, who was retained to keep an eye on the house, forgave the rents, and went to London. He took with him the boy Simon Cleyes, whose father had been hanged for poaching during the war. Noah found places for them both in a print shop, to learn the trade. His dream was to own a shop with Simon as his assistant, to write and publish broadly about politics and theology, perhaps to found a weekly newspaper or journal. Now was the time, with a new republican government, unprecedented freedom of the press and ideas never before allowed openly to be written about, and scientific exploration on the rise. It was clear there would be a struggle for the heart and mind of the revolution, with men of property ready to carry on as usual, only without the meddling of a king, while men of intellect craved exploration and the mass of people still struggled, were turned off the land, and were denied their voice. Noah Fallam would throw his weight on the side of the latter. But first he must learn the printer's trade and establish himself.

When they were settled in a position and rough lodgings near Lincoln's Inn Fields, he sent for Margaret, not knowing if she would come to him. She did, bearing with her a small purse provided by her grieving mother, who feared her daughter might starve to death due to the neglect of her derelict husband.

The purse did keep hunger away, since Noah and Simon were paid but a pittance. Margaret was soon pregnant. She longed for a child, in part because of a general desire for children, but also because she believed a grandchild would restore her, along with her husband, to her family's favor. Vain hope, for the baby, a girl, was stillborn. Again she became pregnant, and this time miscarried in the fourth month. Her health failed. Noah decided not to make love to her again until time had allowed her recovery. And, he determined, she must be made more comfortable.

He was older than the other apprentices, but his keen mind allowed him to learn the trade quickly and he chafed at long hours setting type with no say in what was printed. It was time to strike out on his own, for Margaret's sake as well as his. Margaret begged him to restore himself to Coombe Manor, but he could not bear the thought of it. Instead he would set out on the only other course he knew. He needed a loan. He swallowed his pride and went to Oliver Cromwell.

AFTER leading Lydde through the house, Noah took her outside, locking the door behind him. He stood a moment looking up at the brick and glass facade, then turned to her.

"It is likely," he said, "I shall never set foot inside again."

She held out a hand and he took it. He nodded at a track that cut through the nearby woods. "The family church is half a mile yonder. Margaret is buried there among the Fallams. I would like to visit her grave."

"I would as well," Lydde said.

They retrieved the horses and led them by their bridles as they walked. Noah continued his story.

CROMWELL, he said, had not only noticed Noah Fallam's service, he had remembered. He knew men who, at a word from the Lord Protector, would back Noah's printing venture someday. But first there was a more pressing matter to tend to. In Ireland, Royalists escaped from England had banded with Irish Catholics to foment rebellion, and Cromwell would lead an army to put them down. He wanted Noah Fallam near his right hand.

At first Noah refused. He was sick of war and unwilling to leave

Margaret, who remained in frail health. But he was desperate for money. On a day when he and Simon returned home at night to find the cupboard held only a handful of flour, a single wedge of cheese, and three carrots, Noah made up his mind to go. He would be paid well, enough to keep Margaret comfortably and still set money aside for his printing press.

The cause might be just, Noah convinced himself. He had no love for Catholicism. In 1641 when he was at Cambridge he had been sickened to hear of the massacre of thousands of Protestant men, women, and children by Irish Catholics. The Catholic Church was the worst enemy of dissent, he thought, with its inquisitions and burning of heretics, its murderous treatment of Protestants in France and the Low Countries, and its elevation of papal authority above conscience and intellectual pursuit. Cromwell wrote Noah would be appointed a major and placed in charge of troops under the command of Colonel Elisha Sitwell, who was charged with clearing towns in the east of Ireland of their Catholic and Royalist garrisons. Noah accepted the commission.

By the time he arrived in Ireland, Cromwell's campaign was well under way and the enemy divided, for the Irish Catholics were as distrustful of their English Royalist allies as they were of Cromwell. Soon the Protestant army had taken the town of Drogheda. What Noah found there sickened him. Upon storming the town, Cromwell's army had slaughtered the entire garrison, some four thousand Irish Catholics and English Royalists. (Noah was thankful Robert had gone to Virginia instead of making a last stand in Ireland.) This was horrific enough, though still within the accepted bounds of warfare. But every priest taken in the town was also killed, along with hundreds of women and children. A Catholic church was burned to the ground along with all those who had taken sanctuary in it. When Noah arrived, Drogheda still stank of smoke and blood. He was glad to leave it and join the siege already laid outside the coastal town of Wexford.

At Wexford a spy within the town had arranged to open the gates to the Protestants. On the night before the attack Noah met his troops and spoke to them of his expectations. He was appalled, he told them, by the massacre in Drogheda and the general lack of discipline displayed by the Protestant army. In Major Noah Fallam's command, discipline would be maintained, and any soldier caught mistreating a noncombatant would be severely punished. Any man who killed a noncombatant would be hanged. His soldiers received these orders silently, but spoke sullenly among themselves after they had been dismissed.

Noah could not sleep, and so he was already awake when summoned to Colonel Sitwell's quarters at four in the morning. Sitwell, a stocky man with dark gray hair, was seated behind a camp table reading last-minute instructions from Cromwell, whose aide-de-camp stood nearby. He laid down his papers to look Noah up and down.

"Major Fallam. I've received some complaints from your men."

"Sir?" Noah said, startled.

"You were not at Drogheda," Sitwell said, "I realize that. Still I do not appreciate your condemnation of what took place there. Nor did the men, nor would General Cromwell."

"Sir, it is clear that at Drogheda discipline broke down. When soldiers run rampant through a town—"

"Silence!" Sitwell said sharply. "I did not ask for your opinion. As with any assault, there were moments of chaos. But overall discipline was maintained and orders were followed."

"Orders, sir? To kill noncombatants?"

"Orders to kill *Catholics*. They are all combatants."

Noah took a step forward. "Orders from whom?"

"My orders, Major. Approved by General Cromwell."

Noah stared at Cromwell's aide, who stood silent and refused to meet his eye. "I do not believe it," Noah said.

"Ask him yourself," said Sitwell. "Except there is no time now, for we are set to attack upon the opening of the gates at six, and the general is preoccupied."

Noah drew himself up straight. "With respect, sir, I cannot issue such an order to my men, nor can I rescind my previous one. I will not command my men to kill women and children and old men, however wrong-headed their religious views."

"Fallam!" Sitwell stood, came around the table and stood in front of Noah, his face red with rage. "You will give that order to your men and you will lead them in their duty. Or if you do not I will relieve you of your command now and hang you from the nearest tree. Is that clear?"

Noah fought back a wave of nausea. "It is," he said.

"Then get out of my sight and get you to your duty."

Again he stood before his troops at the birth of an October morning while a flight of wild geese passed overhead and urged his men to fight bravely, to stay together as much as possible, and when all was done to regroup at the market cross in the center of Wexford.

"You are further ordered," he said, his own words threatening to gag him, "to kill any soldier of the garrison you encounter, whether or not he seeks to surrender, and to likewise k—" he faltered momentarily. "To kill any inhabitant of the town you deem to be a threat."

The gates of Wexford swung open in the gray dawn and Noah led his men through. He fought bravely, slashing with his sword in close quarters as the town garrison counterattacked. He was cut on the arm, then suffered a deep slash across his thigh. Another sword swipe knocked off his helmet and split open his scalp just above his ear. He fought on, the superior numbers of the army with him gradually overwhelming the defenders, who died or fell back. His memories from then on were tinged in a bright red that made them burn as though he were looking straight into a blinding sunlight. Women spread-eagled in alleys or dragged screaming from their houses by the hair and spitted with swords. Noah seemed to be constantly running now, first away from the madness, but there was no escape, so back into the heart of it. Soldiers rushed past him, throwing open the doors of houses and rushing in. Noah went ahead to a corner house and looked inside. A terrified woman with three children cowered before the hearth, all of them shrieking at the sight of him. He slammed the door shut and stood outside. Three soldiers rushed up.

"There is no one there," Noah said.

They pushed past him toward the house.

"I tell you, there is no one there!" He was screaming so loudly his throat seemed to catch fire. He struggled with the closest Englishman, dragged him to the ground. The man pulled a knife and Noah hit him hard in the face, twice, breaking his nose and knocking him senseless. He staggered up in time to see the other two soldiers inside the house cutting the woman and her children to pieces.

He could not say how he got there, but he found himself back at the market cross, unconsciously following his own orders to reconnoiter. The market was a mass of screaming women and children, pressed together seeking sanctuary, many of them kneeling, praying loudly in Latin, crossing themselves, holding out hands clutching rosaries in entreaty. The worst things they could do. The slaughter had already begun. Noah rushed forward. Somewhere he had lost his sword. He slipped and sprawled headlong in a pool of blood, got up, and nearly fell again, for the cobblestones were slick in all directions. Blood drenched his clothes and covered his hands and face and filled his mouth. He retched and threw himself at the back of a knot of men who were methodically chopping at the writhing mass of women like gardeners clearing weeds. Then he felt a blow to the head and he lost consciousness.

He had been knocked down and come close to being run through by a Protestant swordsman, who only spared him because he had stood in the ranks that previous night and morning and now recognized his commanding officer. Though he did not much like him, he had followed him into battle and seen him fight well enough. Nor did this soldier relish killing his superior and the trouble it might land him in. So he dragged Major Fallam aside and propped him against the wall of an alehouse.

Noah awoke in a tent, lying on the ground, still covered in dried blood that clotted his nose and glommed his eyelids nearly shut. Sitwell stood over him, speaking as from a great distance. "You fought bravely, Fallam. Lucky for you. If not for that, I'd hang you now, and happy to do it. But it would displease General Cromwell. He's sent for you."

THE next day, Noah, wearing clean clothes and with his wounds dressed, sat across from Oliver Cromwell in Wexford Castle.

"Sitwell doesn't care for you," Cromwell said.

"Nor I, him," Noah said curtly.

"You were insubordinate. Yet your men report you fought bravely. Your troops were the first through the gate and you carried the fight deep into the town. The enemy never recovered."

Noah said nothing.

"On the other hand, you attacked and severely beat one of your own men without provocation. There were witnesses. And you tried to impede progress in the market."

"Progress," Noah said contemptuously.

Cromwell regarded him, not unkindly, for a time. "Sitwell wonders why I don't punish you for your insubordination. He doesn't have my memories, Fallam. He didn't see you at Naseby as I did, standing in the breach when all seemed lost and holding your men there, buying me time to countercharge. Had you fallen back then, neither of us would be sitting here now."

A nice irony, Noah thought.

Cromwell stood and looked out the window. "I know you are bothered by the slaughter. Well you might be; I hate it myself. But these people are themselves barbarous murderers of God's chosen people, and this bloodshed in Wexford may prevent more down the road and save Protestant lives. Still, I have misused you. You are a leader, not a butcher. This was work for Sitwell and his sort, not you. I still need you here in Ireland, but I'm taking you off the front lines. I will give you a chance to make amends to the people of Wexford if your conscience is troubling you, as their governor. I'm leaving a military governor to guard Wexford and its harbor. It's an important port, England to the east, America to the west, France and Spain to the south, nothing but open sea between all. Wexford will play a major part in English dominance of shipping over the coming years. Good Christian men like you are the backbone of the revolution. I want you in this post."

THEY had reached the churchyard and Noah leaned against the stone wall. He had not looked at Lydde the entire time he spoke and she noticed his hands shook as they rested on the wall. She could think of nothing to say, nothing that would either comfort or absolve. Finally she said, "Is that why you take all these risks? Some sort of penance?"

"Penance," he replied bitterly. "A Catholic concept, and therefore quite appropriate, is it not? No, I have no need of penance." His voice rose as his tone of self-mockery deepened. "I'm one of the elect, am I not?"

After a moment, she said, "You tried to stop it."

He shook his head dismissively. "I gave an order that will likely send me to hell."

"I thought you believed in universal salvation."

He surveyed the slices of gray stone in the churchyard.

"I do," he said. "For everyone but myself."

NOAH accepted the appointment in Wexford, he told her. He knew already what he was going to do, knew it would set him on the road to his own likely death.

"I understood the presbyterians and the prayer book men and the papists will fight wars with each other over how to parse a Bible verse. But they will act together to hang an old woman for picking mushrooms on a rich man's land, or each will kill the innocent of the other faith. A plague on all three houses, I decided." He laughed mirth-lessly. "There, a paraphrase from Shakespeare just for you. I held the post in Wexford for four years. Margaret and Simon joined me the second year. Then Parliament was dissolved for good and Oliver Cromwell was made Lord Protector."

"He's a dictator now," Lydde said.

"Yes. He called me to London for three years as one of his top aides. When he created the major-generals, it was believed he would appoint me to Bristol. Instead he sent me to this out-of-the way spot as a lieutenant. It's because Cromwell has begun to sense my estrange-ment, though he has nothing solid against me. What he does not know, Lydde, would hang me many times over.

"Starting in Wexford I went about establishing my smuggling con-tacts. I gave secret aid to roving Irish gangs who stole grain to feed the poor. In London I had secret contacts among dissenters of all stripes. I have even, through Robert, made contact with the King's party in France. Not because the restoration of a king would change anything, but because the Royalists have from time to time sent cargoes of con-traband my way, which furthers their cause and mine, and in return I have passed along secret correspondence for them. I have come to know some of them as individuals and even admire them, as I love my brother though I don't agree with him. When one of the King's men I respected was about to be arrested as a spy, I got word to him and he escaped to France. I search for goodness in whatever quarter I can find it, for it is a precious commodity."

Lydde said, "And you look out for unfortunate women and girls who might be accused of witchcraft and in need of protection, such as Mary and myself."

"That too," he said, and tried to force a smile but failed. "Do not try to comfort me, Lydde. I set out this morning certain I was riding with my future wife. I meant to show you Coombe Manor and tell you of my family, but I had resolved not to speak of Ireland. I never told Margaret, for fear of losing her love, and I meant to hide it from you as well, to carry it secret in my soul until I stand face-to-face with God. Yet against all reason I have felt compelled to tell you. And now that you have heard this story I know my sins have killed my own chances for happiness with you." He turned to her. "I see it in your face. You know the true Noah Fallam rather than the parts, as you said, that I have been playing. You will not want me."

"What you see in my face," Lydde said, "is fear for you. And sorrow for you, that you must suffer so." She reached down and took his hand. "Show me Margaret's grave."

He led her among the tombstones, pointing out one ancestor after another. She noted the graves of his parents, and that he did not stop there. Then they reached a headstone set apart in the far corner.

> **Margaret Anne Exton Fallam**
> **1628–1656**
> **Beloved wife of Noah Fallam**
> **Fidelis ad urnam**

"What is the Latin?" Lydde asked.

"'Faithful unto death,'" Noah said. "When we were established in Wexford she again wanted to bear a child. The result was another miscarriage and then the fatal stillbirth in London. I had her buried here, for her father would not allow her in the Exton plot. Poor Margaret. In a just world she would have been my sister and a dear companion of yours. Yet here she lies alone, killed for her loyalty to me."

A tear slipped down Lydde's cheek and she wiped it away with the back of her hand. "I love her because she stood by you," she said.

"I would have brought a flower for her grave," said Noah, "but there are none so late in the season."

"We could honor her another way," Lydde said. "Jews find small rocks and lay them on top of the tombs of their loved ones. We could do the same."

They looked around. Noah found a smooth gray stone and Lydde a brown rock rippled with gold. These they placed atop the edge of the gravestone.

Lydde said, "Uncle John believes when you die you can go any- where. Perhaps Margaret has found my brothers and sisters and they are as connected as you and I are."

It seemed a silly thing to say, for what connection could there pos- sibly be? And yet Lydde felt it in her bones, the drawing up of odds and ends of colored thread to weave into a magical tapestry. Noah was watching her, and the despair in his face was giving way to something like hope.

"You speak as though we have some future together," he said, his voice barely above a whisper.

"Noah," she replied, "I doubt we can be severed."

"I must warn you, I still have nightmares about Ireland. Sometimes I wake and know I have been crying out in my sleep. And I fear now, when you look on me, you will see me covered in blood."

"No," she said. "I'm glad you told me. You shouldn't face such memories alone."

"I am ever reckless," he continued, "and doomed, I fear, to make a hard life for those I love."

"Yes," Lydde agreed. "You are a strange, strange man. I adore you."

He leaned close. "Do I dare hope you might marry me?"

She studied his face a moment, a cacophony of voices shrieking warnings inside her head, then tailing away to nothing.

"Yes, I will marry you."

He kissed her then, and of all the kisses he had bestowed on her, this one seemed the most tender.

"Take me back to Norchester," she said, "and make me your wife."

WHEN he returned to the Bishop's Palace, Noah Fallam was met by an exultant Simon Cleyes.

"The messenger you sent to Bristol yesterday morning has

returned," Simon announced. "Major-General Sitwell is pleased that you hanged a Raven's man and make progress against the outlaws. He is himself beset by the Quakers and must put them down or he fears they may overwhelm the city."

"Indeed," Noah said, "the Quakers threaten to fairly melt Bristol with love."

"In any event, the major-general has postponed indefinitely his visit to Norchester to inquire into the Raven's activities. You must manage on your own for a while longer."

"Oh, I shall," Noah said with a broad grin. "And the way is now clear for our happiest endeavors."

LYDDE had just finished building fires in several hearths when Uncle John returned, lugging a large box with him. He caught Lydde up in a great hug, then let her go.

"Well," he said. "How was it?"

"How was what?" she said innocently.

Uncle John shook his head. "You don't fool me a bit. I can see it in your face. Have you made your peace with Noah Fallam?"

"Peace! There is no such thing as peace where that man is concerned. And the first time we have a fight it will probably make all Norchester shake." Then she hugged him again. "Oh, Uncle John, I am so happy. I'm going to marry him."

"Marry him! Lydde, my girl, you're moving awfully fast."

"I know. But please don't try to make me think about it. I already know it's insane."

"Lydde—"

She turned away from him, her hands over her ears, and kept talking. "After all, he's been dead for almost four hundred years. Or is that *will* be dead for four hundred years? And do you know what I did, there in the cave under the Mystery Hole? I found the necklace he wears tangled in his rib cage, and I touched his skull. And if I think about that very much, I will truly go mad. So I won't think about it. And I will marry him. Because I love him, and he has made love to me. He needs me, and his family turned on him, and I won't do that to him, I won't. So don't you dare try and talk me out of this."

Uncle John put his hands on her shoulders and shook her gently. "Lydde, hush. I won't try to talk you out of it."

She stared at him doubtfully. "You won't?"

"No. For one thing, Lavinia would kill me if I did. I just meant it was sudden."

"It has to be sudden," Lydde said. "He won't make love to me again otherwise, and that would drive me mad too. By the way, we want you to perform the ceremony."

"Me?"

"Actually, there's no one else except Simon, and we need him to be witness. We can't let anyone know we're married because I'm still a boy. It all has to be done in secret. Then Mary and I are going to live at the Bishop's Palace and pretend to be his wards."

"Sounds like a plan," Uncle John said. "And I agree with him that Mary should join you when she returns. There's going to be a fine to-do tomorrow morning when they find out St. Pancras is painted again."

"The paintings are back?"

"Oh, yes. The colors seem more vivid than before, if possible. And that's not all. When Noah went to visit your Aunt Lavinia, the valley fill moved."

"What?"

"It's true. You know how it covered the entire hollow of Monte-falco? Now the cove is almost uncovered and looks like it always did. The foundation of the house is still underneath the pile. But if something else living goes from here to there, I think it will come clear again."

Lydde took his hand. "It really is all connected, isn't it?"

He shook his head. "It's still too much to comprehend. But I'm making headway. I've done a lot of math since I've been away. But there are still problems to work out." Then he smiled. "I'm not doing so bad in the romance department myself. Lavinia and I had two wonderful months. I think you have inspired us, my girl. Old as we are in the twenty-first century, the spark is still there."

"You should have brought her back with you," Lydde said.

"We talked about it. But we both agreed that someone new showing up from the future would be too dangerous for all of us. Especially for Noah. Lavinia doesn't want that. She was quite taken with him, you know." He nudged the box at his feet. "I brought some things back. Including this." He reached in and extracted a package wrapped in silver paper. "From Lavinia."

"What is it?"

"I have no idea. She wouldn't tell me."

Lydde carried the package to her room, sat on the bed, and pulled off the shiny paper. She gasped. The box was from Victoria's Secret. In a nest of fluffy white paper nestled a black lace push-up bra and panties, and a sheer nightie. When she lifted them, a piece of paper fell out.

Don't ask me how I got these, Aunt Lavinia had written. *I'm afraid I have corrupted the medical profession.*

Underneath the underwear she found stacks of plastic packets that held a three-year supply of birth control pills.

Chapter 17

"I Thee Worship"

T HE ALARM SOUNDED throughout Norchester even before Lydde and Uncle John could set out for church. Constables fanned out to each quarter of the town, pounding on doors. St. Pancras Church was bewitched once more, and Constable Baxter would this time apply the whitewash. Lieutenant Major-General Fallam would preach on the crisis at Sabbath service in Trinity Church, the town's bastion of Puritanism. Because Trinity would not hold all of Norchester, only heads of households and older males would gather there. Women and children would repair to their own parishes. Failure to attend church, except for those who were ill, would result in imprisonment.

Lydde, as an "older male," slipped into Trinity Church with Uncle John. As they found a seat, she noticed Jacob Woodcock turned around in his seat as though he had been watching for them. He glared with a malevolence that caused her to look away and pretend she had not seen him. The gathering was unusually quiet as they awaited Pastor Fallam. Lydde listened to the heavy breathing of the congregation, keenly aware she was the only representative, however covert, of her sex. She longed to take Uncle John's hand for comfort, but was afraid to touch him for fear of being noticed.

Then Noah Fallam swept into the chancel, his black robe billowing behind him. The Raven, she thought, and was amazed no one had made the connection. He climbed into the pulpit, which towered above the sanctuary, a symbol of the absolute authority of the preacher.

He bent his head a moment in silent prayer. Then he looked up, his face stern.

"Satan is abroad in Norchester," he proclaimed.

No one spoke, but a fearful sigh swept through the church like a gust of wind. Noah raised his hand.

"St. Pancras once more bears the marks of the Devil upon its walls. Why would Satan choose St. Pancras Church to threaten us? Not because of witches among us, but because of the apostasy of that congregation, which continues in the unlawful use of the prayer book. I therefore decree that St. Pancras Church be locked indefinitely, its minister Smythe deposed, and its congregation required to worship here at Trinity Church. I doubt many are of the elect, yet they might examine their souls before facing final judgment.

"Let us understand what Satan is," Noah continued. "Satan is watchful as a hawk. He preys on those who are pure of heart. For none poses a greater threat to the realm of darkness than those who are innocent. Satan plots against the good, to bring about their ruin. That is why Satan would wish us to seek after so-called witches in the hope we might mistakenly destroy one of the elect.

"For Satan preys on the elect. Yet never forget, he has already been defeated by Christ Jesus. Christ has crushed the head of the serpent beneath His heel. Therefore, when Satan attacks the elect, he becomes, for us, a figure to be ridiculed, a laughingstock. The elect cannot be defeated, since God has already guaranteed them through Christ's sacrifice a place at His right hand. The elect are children of God and nothing can change that, not even the wiles of the Serpent who tempted Eve to perdition."

He surveyed the upturned faces of his audience. "We have, over the past few months, welcomed strangers into our midst. I speak of the girl, Mary, who fled the loss of her family in Bristol to seek refuge in Norchester with her kinsman, John Soane. And I speak of her cousin, the boy Lewis, who only recently arrived after nearly losing his life to the agents of the Antichrist."

It seemed the entire congregation turned to stare at Lydde and Uncle John.

"You all know the reputation of John Soane, who has brought God's healing to you and your kin in times of sickness and adversity. You know his kindness and good service. You can understand why two young orphans, two cousins, would seek him out in time of need. You will therefore not be surprised that Satan would seek to destroy such a good and decent man. And what better way than to pursue these pure, innocent ones who sought his aid, themselves among the elect—for yes, I have examined them closely and they stand fast in the face of attacks by the Devil—what better way to attack God's servant John Soane than through these little ones? But Satan's plan has failed, as it must."

Here Noah paused to cast a benevolent gaze on Uncle John and Lydde. A murmur of sympathy rose from the congregation.

"Brilliant," Uncle John whispered.

"While St. Pancras is closed," Noah said, "I can think of no better guardian than John Soane. I therefore decree that none shall approach St. Pancras, not even to set foot in its churchyard, save for Mr. Soane." Noah pointed at Uncle John. "He shall be the caretaker of St. Pancras while I undertake to study that building overwhelmed by demons, in order to learn how Satan works his wiles. Thus we shall between us hope to prevent further attacks. John Soane I trust to withstand the temptations of the Devil while performing this service. Any other caught at St. Pancras shall be thrown into Norchester jail.

"Further, I am greatly concerned for the safety of the boy Lewis Soane and the girl Mary Soane. They are being targeted by Satan, who would have them blamed for his own misdeeds, and therefore they are deserving of protection. So I will take them into my custody. They shall live with me until this danger has passed, protected by my constables and by my own position as God's representative in Norchester. All the might of the Commonwealth, of the Lord Protector Oliver Cromwell, of Major-General Elisha Sitwell, and of my own vigilance shall ensure that their souls remain undefiled."

Noah went on to preach at length on the myriad ways Satan attacks the faithful. When he finished at last, the congregation filed out, talking loudly, and most of those present sought Lydde out to shake her hand, or wish her good health, or clap Uncle John on the shoulder and offer prayers for his safety as he undertook his perilous responsibility. But Jacob Woodcock rushed past them to confront Noah when he came out of the church.

"Take care, Pastor Fallam," he cried, "lest you be yourself fooled by the Devil! For the doctor belongs to St. Pancras and if their worship has been unlawful, he has been a part of it!"

Noah glanced at Uncle John, then leaned toward Woodcock and said in a low, conspiratorial voice, "And how do you think, Master Woodcock, I have been so well informed about the transgressions of St. Pancras?"

Woodcock sputtered a moment, not knowing how to answer. He finally contented himself by muttering, "You were not present when the boy entered Norchester and did not see him as some of us did."

"I have his odd clothing in my possession," Noah answered coldly, "and I do see the boy now. Never fear, Jacob, I shall keep an eye on him. If I find any fault in him, it shall be addressed."

Then he turned away in clear dismissal of Jacob Woodcock, and said to Uncle John, "Bring the boy to me this evening."

It didn't take long to gather up Lydde's few belongings. Everything went into a basket—the green dress and rose wrapper with Aunt Lavinia's present in the bottom, topped by Lydde's single change of boy's clothes, her three pairs of stockings and boy's undershirts. She had nothing of her own, really, and the realization caused her to sit on the edge of the bed a moment and fight off a surge of panic. There Uncle John found her a few moments later, her knees drawn up to her chin, eyes shut.

"What's wrong?" he asked.

She opened her eyes. "Uncle John. What on earth am I doing?"

He sat beside her and took her hand. "You don't have to, you know. We can walk to St. Pancras instead and leave. You can have your old life back."

She shook her head. "I couldn't do that to him. Or to myself, because I couldn't bear to be back home knowing he was dead."

"We could try to talk Noah into going with us."

"He wouldn't just leave what he's doing here. And he'd be so much older if he did. How could you ask anyone to skip the prime of their life?"

"You could stay longer, but not marry him."

"What is this, a buffet? I get to pick and choose?"

"I'm just reminding you of your options. There are always options."

She turned and clutched his arm. "What do you really think of him?"

"Does it matter what I think of him?"

"Yes."

"I think he's a good man. I think he's a dangerous man."

"Dangerous? But not to me, surely."

"To your happiness. Of course he would never harm you. Just the opposite. But it's hard enough, Lydde, to marry. Harder still for someone who has been independent as long as you have."

"It's not just that," she said. "He's a hard man. He's endured things I can't imagine, and for all I know he may be capable of things I couldn't abide."

He squeezed her hand and gave her a wry smile. "To my knowledge, marrying a man from the past hasn't been done before. And you *would* choose a man who is likely to be caught and executed."

"But he won't be, will he? His body lies in the New River Gorge. Horrible as that is to think about, it gives me hope right now. He'll escape to America and live for years, won't he?"

Uncle John put his arm around her. "Lydde, I was afraid you were counting on that. You can't. I just don't know yet what is going on. Are we in the past, or are we in a parallel universe?"

"What do you mean?"

"Remember when I tried to explain wormholes to you? The Mary you met here isn't your sister Mary who disappeared in your time and place. I don't know yet what that means. The Greeks, like Plato, believed in the Eternal Recurrence. People coming back over and over, kind of like reincarnation except in the same body, not a different one. Is that what happens? Is the Mary who disappeared in a fire a recurrence of this Mary? Or are we in a parallel universe with parallel Marys, but with different fates?"

"You're saying the Noah I love here may not be the Noah who goes to America and dies along the New River? You're saying it's just as possible he could be caught and killed here because this is a parallel universe but with different outcomes?"

"That's exactly what I'm saying. And there's no way to know except to see what happens."

"Oh, God," she whispered.

"Lydde, there are some things that don't change about life, as far as I can tell. There may be some sort of plan or connection, but we still don't know when we're going to die, or how. Going backward or forward in time doesn't change that. Our ultimate fate remains hidden from us."

"I can't bear to think of them catching him."

"It may happen. And if you can't face it, you should go back to West Virginia now, before you become more attached to him."

"I already love him too much," she said. "I couldn't abandon him."

"Then that's the way it is. Lavinia and I talked about it. You're our daughter. And we'll be proud to have Noah Fallam for a son."

THEY entered the cathedral precinct in the growing dusk, passing through the medieval gate and along the cobbled alley that had changed hardly at all over the centuries. The cathedral loomed in shadow on their right, and straight ahead the Bishop's Palace glowed with candlelight in several windows.

They stopped before the heavy oak door and Uncle John pounded with his fist. The door opened at once and a smiling Simon Cleyes ushered them in.

"Come in, come in! Noah is just—"

"Here," called Noah as he clattered down the stairs. He was wearing a stiff black coat and his collar-length brown hair was neatly combed and tucked behind his ears. He kissed Lydde on the forehead, pumped Uncle John's hand. "All the servants live off the premises and are dismissed on the Sabbath, so we are alone and"—he grasped Lydde's hand—"free."

She took the basket from Uncle John. "I would like to change clothes. I want to marry you in a dress."

"Let me show you upstairs. Simon, offer John some sherry."

Noah held a candle high and led her up the stairs, fingers twined with hers, his face so radiant with joy it nearly broke her heart. At the top of the stairs he drew her to him and kissed her. Then he led her along the hall while pointing out rooms.

"This is Simon's room, and this shall be Mary's. At that far corner is the library, and I have a goodly collection of books which I hope you will enjoy. It is a pleasant room, and when you are here during the day, that is where you will be most comfortable. Here"—he pushed open a door to reveal a blazing fire and a canopied bed—"is my bedchamber. Yours, at night. But you must put your things in the room next to it and pretend that is yours. You must roll in the bed regularly so Nan the chambermaid will think it slept in."

"I understand," she said. They went to that room, smaller and cold, for no fire had been laid. She dropped the basket on the bed and suddenly found it hard to look at him.

"Lydde," he said. "Are you having doubts?"

"Doubts? Why do you ask?"

"Something in your face." He held the candle close and laid the back of his hand against her cheek.

"Some people think if you have doubts about something, you shouldn't do it," she said.

"I believe it is human to have doubts," he replied.

She turned her head slightly and brushed his fingers with her lips. "I have been thinking of reasons not to marry you," she said. "None of them is good enough. Still, I am afraid."

"So am I," he said. "And yet I am so very happy."

She rested her head against his chest a moment. Then she stepped away and said, "I'll be down soon."

He smiled and set the candle on the table beside the bed before leaving.

THE men waited in Noah's office in nervous silence. Then Uncle John said, "Noah, there's something I've been worrying about, and I must ask you by way of a warning. Would you ever hit Lydde?"

Noah looked surprised. "Why," he said, "I doubt that will be necessary."

"I was afraid you'd put it that way," Uncle John said.

"I don't understand."

"Let me explain it like this. From your point of view, what is the worst thing a wife here could do to her husband?"

"To be unfaithful," Noah replied.

"And that's something you don't have to worry about," Uncle John said. "Lydde is loyal as the day is long. Well, where we come from the worst thing a husband can do to a wife is hit her. We don't look on it the way you do here. Back there, it's against the law, first of all. And women like Lydde won't put up with a man hitting them. They'll leave and never come back. So, for God's sake, even if it does become 'necessary' in your eyes, don't ever raise a hand to her. Even though it may be acceptable here. It would do to her what unfaithfulness would do to you."

Noah had been listening carefully. He inclined his head. "I understand," he said. "Thank you."

Uncle John held out his hand and Noah grasped it. "Just love her, son. It will work out."

LYDDE changed clothes, then realized she had no women's shoes. There was nothing for it but to put on her boy's stockings and boots. Back downstairs, she found the men standing before the hearth in Noah's office, sipping from small glasses of sherry. Noah held out his hand.

"And where has my boy gone?" he asked.

"Fled," she replied, "but he has left his feet behind." She held up one booted foot.

They laughed.

"I need some warm slippers, like Mary's," she said.

"I shall see to it tomorrow," said Simon Cleyes. "You do make a handsome woman despite your feet." He was looking at her admiringly, and she caught a glimpse of his own longing.

Noah handed her a glass of sherry, and Uncle John proposed a toast to the couple soon to be wed. They clinked glasses, Noah and Lydde exchanging glances as they sipped. Noah leaned forward and whispered, "Doubts?"

"Forgotten," she whispered back.

"Shall we perform the ceremony first?" asked Uncle John. "And then eat supper?"

"Indeed," Noah said. "I would dine with my wife tonight."

Uncle John set down his glass and reached into his coat pocket. "I have brought this, though I know it is against the law. Do you object? I don't know what else to use."

He held up the *Book of Common Prayer*.

"Why not?" Noah said. "It is a lovely wedding service."

"Only don't tell Jacob Woodcock," Simon said.

"Woodcock," Noah scoffed. "If I had not turned from the Puritans on my own, he would have turned me."

Lydde took Noah's arm. "If we can use the prayer book, then may I make another unlawful request? May we be married in the cathedral?"

Noah looked at Simon, then shrugged. "Why not?" he said. "It seems I do nothing these days that is lawful. The cathedral it is."

They carried lanterns with them and crossed the courtyard to the cathedral's massive door. Simon fumbled with the huge key but soon it turned in the lock and he pulled the heavy oak door open with a creak. Inside, they walked slowly, their boots ringing on the cold stone. The air was heavy, with a musty but slightly sweet smell, as though centuries of incense still infused the air. Uncle John was looking down. Then he stopped.

"Of course!" he cried, so loud his voice bounced along the vault. The others started. Uncle John pointed down. "The labyrinth! It's a Cretan pattern instead of Chartres, and its dimensions are different from the one I've been working with. I saw this one when I visited Lydde in Norchester in the twenty-first century, but I didn't remember it exactly. That's why my calculations have been off. I should have been using this one!"

He looked around. Noah and Simon were staring at him as though he were raving, and even Lydde looked confused. He waved his hand. "It's a long explanation and it involves mathematics. But I'm looking for other wormholes back home and I'm plotting on the geometrical form of a labyrinth. This may make a huge difference. Could I come back here sometime in daylight and copy this one?"

"As you will," Noah said. "Simon will see to it."

Simon nodded, though he looked doubtful. Noah laughed and clapped him on the back. "Never fear, Simon. I have been through the wormhole myself. It is a great mystery, but it is not madness nor witchcraft."

They continued on, while shadows danced across the vaulted ceiling above their passing lanterns. On either side, effigies with folded hands lay atop tombs like recumbent witnesses who might rise at any moment and pronounce a blessing. They traversed the cathedral's length, climbing higher and higher as they passed through the choir and approached the altar. There they halted. Uncle John opened the prayer book, while Simon held the lantern so he could see. Lydde and Noah stood close together, holding hands. Uncle John studied their faces, so luminous and full of hope in the lantern light, and for a moment was unable to speak.

Then he read, "Noah, will you have this woman as your wedded wife, to live together after God's ordinance in the holy estate of Matrimony? Will you love her, comfort her, honor, and keep her, in sickness and in health; and, forsaking all others, keep you only unto her, so long as you both shall live?"

"I will," Noah answered.

Lydde repeated the second vow while smiling up at Noah.

"I, Lydde, take you, Noah, to my wedded husband, to have and to hold from this day forward, for better for worse, for richer for poorer, in sickness and in health, to love, cherish, and to obey, till death us do part."

Uncle John turned to Simon, who dug into his pocket and placed a gold ring on the pages of the open prayer book.

"Noah!" Lydde said. Her eyes filled with tears.

He smiled. "It was a difficult purchase to explain," he said. "But I was determined you should have it."

He picked up the ring, held up her left hand, and slid it onto her finger. Then, with his hand over hers, he said, "With this ring I thee wed, with my body I thee worship . . ." Here he paused, teased the palm of her hand with a fingertip, and gave her such a look that Uncle John cleared his throat. "And with all my worldly goods I thee endow."

Uncle John placed his hand over theirs. "Those whom God hath joined together let no man put asunder. I pronounce that you be man and wife together, in the Name of the Father, and of the Son, and of the Holy Ghost. Amen."

They stood a moment in absolute silence as though unable to believe what they had just done. Then Uncle John said softly, "Son, where we come from, you're supposed to kiss her now."

Noah kissed her gently. Then Uncle John and Simon were clapping them on the back, exchanging handshakes and laughing. Lydde held up her hand. The ring glinted in the lantern light.

"You'll have to take it off after tonight," Noah said.

"I shall sew it to the inside of my breeches pocket," Lydde said, "and then I can slip my finger into it whenever I want."

Back at the Bishop's Palace, they dined on slices of cold mutton pie left by the cook on Saturday. Then Simon stood and said, "I shall escort the good doctor to Soane's Croft and spend the night. It shall be easier to fetch Mary from there. Can you two manage?"

.   .   .

THEY carried armloads of firewood upstairs and piled it beside the hearth in Noah's room. The fire had dwindled, but they soon had it blazing again. Noah pulled the curtains around the bed so that only the side exposed to the hearth was open.

"Now," he said, "you shall be warm as can be."

Lydde stood near the hearth and raised her hand to the firelight. She had felt, when he slipped the ring onto her finger, the same thrill as when he first entered her—to be cherished, to be possessed.

"But I am not a possession, am I?" she murmured.

He came close. "What did you say?"

She looked up. "What does this ring mean to you?" she asked.

Noah took her hand and kissed it. "It means you are mine. And I would die for you if need be." He pulled her close and unbuttoned her dress. Then he saw her bra.

"A wedding present from Aunt Lavinia," she said, and let the dress drop to the floor to reveal the lace panties.

"God bless Aunt Lavinia," Noah said in a strangled voice.

She went to him and took off his coat and shirt, unbuttoned his breeches while he slid the bra straps from her shoulders and kissed her neck. He stood naked before her. Then he drew her onto the bed, where they knelt side by side, touching, kissing, exploring.

"How does this come off?" he asked as he tugged at the bra.

She showed him the front closure snap and he soon freed her breasts for fondling.

"With my body, I thee worship," he whispered as his other hand pulled down her panties and moved between her thighs.

She stroked his cock, leaned close, and pleasured it with her mouth.

"I love doing this for you," she said. "Is that a gift from God?"

"It is." He pushed her back gently and entered her, moving slowly, then ceasing. "This is as close as we can come to God in this world." He moved again, more insistent, then stopped, like one who, walking ahead, pauses and waits for the other to catch up. To slow himself he whispered, "Do you know the words of John Donne? 'Batter my heart three person'd God . . . o'erthrow me, and bend your force, to break, blow, burn and make me new.'"

He spoke against her mouth as she moaned softly.

"'Take me to you, imprison me, for I except you enthrall me, never shall be free, nor ever chaste, except you ravish me.'"

Then he moved inside her again, now fast, now slow, listening for her cries, pausing, waiting for the desperate scrabbling of her fingers on his back as she urged him on before he once more resumed his thrusts, until she wept for pleasure and they rocked together like two angels wrapped in one another's wings.

In a cold bedchamber off Sheep Street, Jacob Woodcock, squinting beside his candle, dipped his quill in an ink pot.

In addition to making light of the further outbreaks of witchcraft in the town, he wrote,

> *I am become aware of other lapses in security. Although the district continues to be plagued by this band of smugglers, the constabulary is scarcely to be found at night. I came to know this by screwing up my courage to venture out several times after midnight, braving the possible assault of brigands or, worse, an emissary of the Devil. Nowhere did I find a constable and, from an offhand question to Constable Baxter, a dull and credulous fellow, I learned that Pastor Fallam has assured them only a single constable was needed after dark and he is allowed to stay inside the jail. The rest might tend to their families. Thus are we protected in Norchester.*

Jacob Woodcock paused for more ink, thought a moment, and finished.

My skepticism about Fallam has grown as time has passed, and I now share your reservations. It was disturbing to hear of your experience of him in Ireland. I know not whether or no he is merely negligent or if more is involved. But I question the trust the Lord Protector places in him, whatever good service he may have done in the past.

Your servant,

W.

He read through the letter once more, then sealed it with a drop of hot wax and addressed it to Major-General Elisha Sitwell in Bristol.

Chapter 18

The Tempest

T HEY FELL INTO a comfortable routine. At breakfast, Mary—
who had arrived at the Bishop's Palace in a state of high excitement—chattered with Simon as they ate their porridge and the maid
Nan watched over the budding romance with a kindly eye. Nan was,
like many servants, a widow, and since she had raised only boys, she
took to the girl at once. Mary, for her part, could not get used to having servants around all day and kept trying to help with dishes or
sweeping, and insisted upon making her own bed. She was quickly
installed as the servants' favorite and, when they were at their chores
in the kitchen, was often called on to tell one of her stories of fairies
and goblins. At their gossip the servants wondered if stern Pastor Fallam would tolerate such wild tales if he knew of them, but were too
taken with Mary and her stories to give her away.

At table, Lydde and Noah must be circumspect. They sat quietly,
now and then speaking formally for Nan's benefit about the state of

Lewis's soul. Noah brought a Bible with him to the table and would read a set of verses, then challenge Lydde to parse them. As she struggled to explain what they meant, he would question her sharply, his face solemn except for his eyes, which seemed to her always full of mischief. When Nan left, they relaxed, but found it hard to pick up a thread of normal conversation lest she suddenly return. They contented themselves with smiling at one another. Smiling was something they could not help doing. Once, when Nan had closed the door behind her, Lydde whispered, "I suppose a day will come when we no longer smile each time our eyes meet and we shall begin to take one another for granted."

"I suppose," Noah said.

"Someday we will have a huge fight."

"Will we?" he said, surprised. Then, sounding doubtful, "I suppose we will."

They pondered this, their eyes met, and they smiled again.

Then Lydde would take Mary off to Soane's Croft, where they helped Uncle John and Mother Bunch with the chores and ate their dinner, while Noah worked in his office and took his food at his desk. He dealt with his usual tasks—paperwork for London, disputes over this neighbor's pig and that village's well, correspondence with the local gentry, road maintenance, and tax collection. Boring stuff, and not how he would like to spend his time. But he was a competent administrator, as he must be to preserve his cover.

After dinner Lydde and Mary together delivered Mother Bunch's medicines. If there was a meeting of the players they stopped by Mossup's livery stable for an hour or so, Mary serving as audience. More and more often they played scenes from *The Tempest,* for Mossup was determined to master Prospero's speeches. Sometimes they drew Mary in, and Lydde loved to watch the girl deliver her lines, her dainty features alive with the joy of living a story. When they did *The Tempest,* she played Miranda to Guill's Caliban, and brought tears to Lydde's eyes with her care and disgust for the hapless wild creature. In another time and place, Lydde thought, she would have been a wonderful actress. Were it not for the fire—Lydde turned abruptly from the thought.

The rest of the afternoon and early evening were spent in the upstairs library at the Bishop's Palace, where Lydde gave Mary lessons in reading, writing, and arithmetic. After supper the servants retired to their homes. Mary and Simon were allowed to sit downstairs or walk about the grounds on Simon's solemn pledge he would do nothing to compromise Mary's honor. Then Lydde and Noah were on their own.

Usually they went back up to the library, where by hearth and lantern light they explored Noah's books. He was inordinately proud of his collection of some forty volumes which would have given scandal to Jacob Woodcock and his ilk. It included the 1632 First Folio of *Mr. William Shakespeares Comedies, Histories, & Tragedies* (when Lydde asked, "Isn't this illegal?" he had smiled and said, "Performances are banned, but I read what I like"), the poetry of Anglicans John Donne and George Herbert, medieval theologians Thomas Aquinas and William of Occam, St. Augustine's *City of God* and *Confessions,* and Milton's *Areopagitica,* with its defense of a free press. There were volumes of Plato's *Dialogues* and Aristotle's *Ethics, Physics, and Metaphysics,* and books on the new learning—anatomy, astronomy, botany, mathematics.

Noah liked to read aloud to Lydde and she was content to listen, for she had not yet adjusted to the closely set Gothic typeface and—to her—archaic spellings of the printed volumes. They sat on pillows with their backs to the hearth, Noah's arms around Lydde, who held the book in her lap while he turned the pages. He paused now and then and they talked about what he had read. One night, after a discussion of what constituted matter, she said, "I wish you could spend more time with Uncle John."

"I would love to spend more time with him," Noah said wistfully. "I want to know what he knows."

"I don't mean just that," Lydde said. "I think you will come to love each other because you both are seekers."

Noah smiled. "We are already on our way to loving one another," he said, "for we have you between us."

Then he kissed her in a way that promised they would make love that night.

LYDDE was exploring him like a foreign country, a new continent. Her past experience of relationships was that they were fleeting, a drive across barren ground in a fast car. Best not to get to know the other too well, safer to spend more time noticing if the end was coming so as to be prepared. To study one's partner in a leisurely way was a luxury for those unfamiliar with abandonment, and that had never been Lydde Falcone.

Being married to Noah was like traveling on foot with plenty of time to survey the lush landscape, and she took him inch by inch. She noted the differing textures of his skin depending upon which part of his body she caressed, the various consistencies of the brown hair on his chest and groin and the nape of his neck, the shape of his toenails and the size of the dimple on his chin, the red birthmark on his shoulder and the black mole on his buttock, the taste of his fingertips as compared to his nipples and cock, the varying calibration of his kisses.

She loved to press her face against his underarm and take a deep breath, preferred his natural odor to the chemical tang of deodorant. He kept himself scrupulously clean in the places most desirable; the rest of him had a rich Noah Fallam smell. His essence was changeable. When he went out once or twice a week on the Raven's nighttime duties, she fancied she could tell by the smell of him when he climbed into bed whether he was too tired for love or desperately craving it.

On her first Sunday at the Bishop's Palace she started to crawl from the bed at the cock's crow, reluctant as always to move to the other bedchamber. But he put his hand on her arm and pulled her to him.

"It's the Sabbath," he said. "No servants about, and no church for hours. You don't have to go."

Later she lay bundled in the feather comforter and watched while he stood in his breeches before the cloudy mirror and shaved, his only equipment a bowl of cold water, rough soap that produced little lather, and a long sharp razor. He stood still except for the small quick movements of the blade, with an air of one whose mind is preoccupied.

"You are so quiet," she said. "You look as though you are praying."

"I am," he replied. "While I shave, I look inside myself, and then I look beyond. When I cut myself, I am reminded of my mortality. When I look into my own eyes, which front my soul, I pray I continue."

She was afraid to say anything more, not wishing to disturb him, but after a moment he said, "Come here. Stand behind me and wrap your arms around my waist while I finish."

She did as he asked and saw her own gray eyes staring from the mirror behind his shoulder. Twenty-first-century eyes.

Noah smiled. "We continue," he said.

LYDDE had not spoken with Noah about her time spent at the livery stable with Mossup, Guill, and Sharpe, but she assumed he recalled that he had himself, as the Raven, told Mossup of her acting. It was not the only thing she hadn't talked over with him; she had never explained about the birth control pills. Nor had he mentioned whether they should try and avoid a pregnancy, which—given his personal history—bothered her somewhat when she thought about it. She decided not to think about it.

Noah came to the library one afternoon when Lydde and Mary were happily chattering about the scene from *The Tempest* rehearsed earlier with Mossup. Ariel the fairy had passed the years as faithful servant to Prospero the magician. Ariel was not human but longed for human feeling. When Prospero commanded a further service, Ariel replied with a fairy rhyme,

"'Each one tripping on his toe Will be here with mop and mow.'" Then a pause, as Lydde acted it, a turn to Mary, who was standing in as Prospero, and a stroke of the girl's arm. "'Do you love me, master? No?'"

At this Mary, melted by the yearning in Lydde's voice, forgot her line, which was to be "Dearly my delicate Ariel, do not approach," and instead cried, "Oh, poor fairy!" and held her arms wide to Lydde.

They fell laughing into one another's arms.

From the doorway, Noah said sharply, "What's this?"

Mary immediately stepped back and ducked her head.

"Mary is helping me with my lines," Lydde said.

"Lines?"

"For *The Tempest*. It is what I practice most with Mossup and his fellows, though we have also tried *Macbeth* and *Richard III*."

"You are acting?" He frowned.

"Of course," she said, growing irritated at his tone. "Remember? *You-know-who* told Mossup I played women's parts, and I have been going to the livery stable since to rehearse."

"Well," he said as he turned away. "You must stop."

"What?"

He stopped and turned back. "I said, you must stop. Indeed I had forgotten, you must forgive me for that. But it was one thing when you were simply a woman who intrigued me. It is quite another when you are my wife."

"Why?" she demanded.

He stared at her, taken aback at her defiance. Then a hard glance at Mary that clearly said, Go along. Mary curtsied and fled the room. Noah stepped inside and closed the door.

"Because," he said, "you are living under my roof and if you are noticed it will cause trouble. But also because it is not seemly."

"'Not seemly'?" Lydde struggled to control her temper. "How dare you say such a thing to me? You know I am an actor."

"It is one thing to imagine and another to see with my own eyes," he said. "I did not like the way you cajoled Mary just then. It is not a way I am comfortable seeing my wife behave, and I forbid it."

"You—" Lydde felt as though the breath had been knocked from her. "You forbid it!"

"Yes."

"You can't *forbid* me to do something!" Her voice rose. "Do you understand? You sound as ignorant as Jacob Woodcock!"

He stepped close and seized her arm. "Will you be reminded," he said in a low angry voice, "that there are servants in this house?"

She pulled away from him. "And will you be reminded that I am not a servant and I am not a child? I do not take orders."

He gripped her arm again. "You vowed before God," he said, "to obey me."

"How dare you bully me!" Lydde pushed him away and flung open the door, not even pausing to look for a coat. She ran out of the house and along the River Pye to Soane's Croft.

She lay across her old bed, weeping so hard it was a while before she was able to explain to Uncle John. Bounder leaped onto the bed and tried to comfort her, pressing her muzzle against Lydde's neck, licking her ear. After Uncle John heard her out, he shook his head and said, "I was afraid something like this would happen."

"How could he turn into such a tyrant all of a sudden?" Lydde sobbed. "He swore to me he wanted a strong woman."

Uncle John sighed. "What he means by that and what you mean may be two different things."

"He said he agreed with the Quakers that men and women are equal."

"Lydde, I'm not sure even the Quakers here see that the way you do."

"What have I done? How could I go and marry a Neanderthal? What was I thinking?" She sat up, rubbing her face. "Was it just the sex? Did I want him so badly I wasn't thinking clearly?"

"Maybe," Uncle John said. "For a while there you could have chewed through leather."

"Oh, God," she wailed. "Now what do I do?"

"You take a deep breath," Uncle John replied, "and you remind yourself of all the things you love about him. Unless you're ready now to go to the future."

They heard the door at the foot of the stairs open and close, and heavy footsteps on the stairs. Uncle John had his back to the door. Lydde raised a tear-stained face when Noah entered, but Uncle John continued as if there had been no interruption, his words clearly meant for Noah to hear.

"Let me tell you something. He's a good man. He's a better man than a lot of the ones back home who talk a good game but treat women like dirt. He's human, though. You can't make him over into someone from our time. That means this will take a lot of work by both of you. Think about how he felt. You probably damn near gave him a heart attack when you left the way you did. And I'll tell you another thing. I asked Lavinia once if she'd ever thought about leaving me. She said, 'I've thought about killing you. But not leaving you.' Hell, there've been plenty of times when Lavinia and I could have killed each other. Let anybody come after either one of us, though, and they'd have a hell of a fight on their hands. From both of us. That's what marriage is—at least the ones that work."

Lydde and Noah were staring at one another. "The first time you came here to harass me, you didn't knock," Lydde said, "and you didn't this time."

Noah ignored this. "I was stopped five times on the way here by people wanting to know why young Lewis was so upset," he said.

"What did you tell them?"

He went to a bench by the fire and sat. "I told them you were upset because I'd had to discipline you."

Lydde smacked the bed with her fist. "Damn it, Noah, that's just what I'm talking about. You don't discipline me."

"I was talking about the character you're playing," he said. "Not you. You are an actor, are you not?"

Uncle John looked back and forth between them as though watching a tennis match. "Something I should point out," he said. "In the twenty-first century a lot of women don't vow to 'obey' anymore. Lydde forgot that would be in the prayer book here, and so did I. She didn't mean to mislead you, Noah."

"And what is to bind us together, if not obedience?" Noah said to Lydde.

"Love," she said. "Respect."

"I doubted a moment ago that you love me."

"I doubted that you respect me."

Noah raised his hands and looked helplessly at Uncle John.

"Do you want her to go back to West Virginia?" Uncle John asked Noah.

"Of course not!"

"Lydde?"

Tears welled in her eyes again. She glanced at Noah and shook her head.

"Then here's what I suggest," said Uncle John. "Lydde, you can't run away every time there's a problem. You've been running away all your life. Stay and work things out. Noah, don't order her to do things. Ask her. And if she doesn't agree, talk to her. I know this woman and you can't force her. It just won't work, and it shouldn't work. And now I'm going down to eat my supper. Mother Bunch has a chicken stew. Want to join me?"

They ate in near silence, Noah and Lydde still stung by the angry words they had hurled at one another. After supper Noah escorted her back to the Bishop's Palace. It was not quite dark and people were about, so they walked discreetly, Noah nodding at passersby. One man stopped and said, "Well, Pastor Fallam, is the lad penitent?"

"He is," Noah said curtly. When they had safely passed beneath the cathedral gateway, Noah said, "Margaret and I never argued."

"I'm not Margaret," Lydde said. "And I'm not like a sister to you."

He stopped and she wondered if he was angry again. Instead he held out his hand and drew her close.

"No," he said, "you are not." Then, "I suppose I cannot ask you to stop acting any more than you can ask me to stop being the Raven. Keep on with Mossup if you must. But it must be a secret. If you are seen, you will have to stop for the safety of all of us. And I shall have to make a public show of punishing you."

She kissed him for an answer.

CHRISTMAS was approaching, but not to be celebrated. With less than two weeks before the day, Noah repeated his previous threats from the pulpit. Anyone caught observing Christmas Day or the twelve days of Christmas would be thrown into jail. He went on to rail against those who were not among the elect.

"The unsaved walk among us," he proclaimed to the congregation of Trinity Church, severe in his black robe. "They already burn in hell, though they appear outwardly to be living. They are as a walking carapace filled with maggots ready to burst through at any moment to reveal their corruption. They play at cards and dice, they dance, they sing, they fornicate, they plot sedition against God's appointed government, they listen to the prattle of women, who are neither elect nor unelect but unworthy of any consideration by God. They are the ones who will try to infect society with the frivolity of a so-called Christ-mass. But Almighty God shall not be mocked by idolatrous Yule logs and trees, nor by pagan carols and dance."

He closed with a vivid description of the Last Days as depicted in

Revelation, when the elect would be carried off to heaven while the damned remained to suffer trials and tribulations during the reign of the Antichrist.

After church, Noah led Simon, Lydde, and Mary back through the streets in silence, for he had decreed that his household must set a sober example for the town. It was a bitterly cold day. The remains of an old snow had frozen to a crust, what once had been puddles of mud were now cracked ice, and roofs and windows were patterned with frost.

Once they had passed inside the gate and reached the cathedral precinct, Mary's spirits burst forth. She ran ahead, gathered up a crusted snowball, and heaved it at Simon, who immediately gave chase. Lydde stepped closer to Noah and linked her arm to his.

"That was the worst sermon I ever heard in my life," she said.

He laughed, though tentatively, for he was still wary of her mood.

"Someday," he said, "I will preach you a true sermon from the heart. Then you will not think so ill of me."

Mary and Simon went down in a jumbled heap on a patch of ice and lay laughing helplessly.

"Mother Bunch will be at Soane's Croft just now railing against you," Lydde said. "She will be begging Uncle John to rescue us from your clutches."

"Oh, dear," he sighed. "And I was hoping she would invite us for supper tonight. Cook has left us cold mutton pie again and I am heartily sick of it."

"Why do they hate Christmas so, the Puritans?"

"They hate mystery," Noah said, "and wonder and beauty. They hate the Holy Ghost, which moves where it will and they cannot control it."

"Must you ban Christmas? Can you not look the other way as you do with other things?"

"No. It's precisely because of those 'other things' that I must stand firm on this. I must do nothing that will call more attention either to

St. Pancras Church or the Raven. So you and Mother Bunch and the rest of Norchester will have to do without your carols and Yule logs and Christmas puddings for the sake of my safety. Am I not selfish?"

For an answer she scooped up her own snowball and hurled it.

DARKNESS like a curtain fell over England and a sharp wind blew down from the north, so strong it rattled the shutters and panes of the Bishop's Palace and howled through the cracks and eaves like a troupe of pennywhistlers. Noah and Simon retired to their rooms to rest, for they were going out that night to meet a shipment. Noah would say little, despite Lydde's curiosity. If things went wrong, the less she knew, the better, he said. But she gathered from overheard snatches of conversation between the two men that it was the most desperately awaited shipment of the winter. She feared that meant it would also be the most dangerous to achieve, and the bitter gale outside did nothing to reassure her. After supper she watched as Noah put on extra clothes.

"Can you at least tell me if there is more danger than usual tonight?" she asked.

"It will not be pleasant in the surf," he said as he laced his boots over two pairs of wool stockings. "But if there is no one sent on purpose to intercept us, the weather should discourage anyone from discovering us by accident. The men aboard ship will face the most peril."

Clearly he was worried, but perhaps it was simply care for the safety of the ship's crew. Mary sensed the mood as well. When the men had gone, she huddled with Lydde for warmth in the library. They wrapped themselves beneath a comforter before the fire.

"They're with the Raven, aren't they?" Mary asked.

"You mustn't ask that," Lydde said.

Mary started to cry. "I'm frightened," she said, "that something will happen to Simon before I'm allowed to marry him. I don't know what I would do."

"Oh, Mary." Lydde held her and rocked her back and forth as though the girl were a baby she was quieting. "I don't know what to tell you."

"They will be so cold tonight," Mary said. "But at least Pastor Fallam will be warmed when he comes back to bed. Simon will have no one. Do you think I might at least prepare a warming pan for him so his bed will not be so cold?"

"Of course you can. In fact, we can both stay up, and have a hot drink waiting for them as well."

They fetched two metal warming pans with long handles, filled them with hot coals, and heaped more coals atop them to keep them warm beneath the hearth fire in the library. Then they built fires in the men's rooms. Mary showed Lydde how to mix eggs, cream, sherry, and spices for a hot posset. Then they took turns sleeping in the comforter or stirring the posset and tending the fires.

Still the men did not return. On previous outings Noah had come home after a few hours. Unable to sleep, Lydde joined Mary beneath the comforter but lay listening for the creak of the front door. When she heard them at last, she shook Mary awake to run and place the warming pan between the covers of Simon's bed. Then she went downstairs.

The men moved slowly as though underwater, stamping their boots on the stone floor.

"My God," Simon said, "I can't feel my feet. Is there a fire?"

"In your room," Lydde said. "Mary is there. And we have hot posset in the library."

"God bless you both," he replied, and made his way stiffly upstairs.

Noah hadn't spoken, still stood at the foot of the stairs as though stunned.

"What's happened?" Lydde asked.

He shook his head as though clearing it, then placed a gloved hand on her shoulder. "The ship never made it," he said.

"It wrecked?"

"Not that we know, thank God. But we waited all night and never caught sight of it. The wind must have blown it off course. It could be a hundred miles away by now. And the goods we would have received will go someplace else."

He climbed the stairs slowly, still leaning against her, as though the night had somehow aged him.

"The cold was terrible," he continued, his voice a rasping lame version of the Raven's, "and nothing to show for it."

"What was on the ship?"

"Cases of sherry from Spain, which would have fetched enough to feed the district through the winter. But now our hopes for winter are blasted. There will be starvation, children will die. The men were so overcome they could not speak."

"What will you do?"

"I've called a meeting of my captains tomorrow night at the old abbey. We'll have to figure out another way to bring in some revenue."

She stood him before the fire in the bedchamber and began stripping off his layers of clothes. Then she sat him on a chair, wrapped in the comforter, while she pulled off his boots and stockings and began to massage his frozen feet. He closed his eyes and leaned back.

"I don't feel well," he said. His face was flushed. She placed her hand on his forehead. It was hot to the touch. He began to shiver.

"Get in bed," she commanded, all her maternal instincts roused. "I'll pile the bedclothes on you and bring you a posset."

She sat with him while he sipped the posset and continued to massage his feet, was relieved when a bit of color returned.

"Wiggle your toes," she commanded.

He did so successfully, then leaned back on his pillow and was soon asleep, snoring softly. Lydde pulled a pair of stockings over his feet, replaced the comforter, and climbed into bed beside him, pressing herself close. She felt the heat of his body through her nightshirt and yet still he shivered. She realized with growing alarm that every remedy she could think of to restore him to health was unavailable. No aspirin, no Vitamin C tablets or orange juice, no IVs, no antibiotics. And hadn't Noah's parents both died of a fever?

She stayed awake listening for the arrival of the servants. At the first sound she crept downstairs and, finding Nan about to take off her cloak, sent her back out into the cold to fetch the doctor.

"Tell him to come at once," she urged, "and bring whatever remedy Mother Bunch has for a fever. Tell him Pastor Fallam is very ill."

By the time Uncle John arrived, Simon Cleyes was up and about, as was Mary. They all hovered anxiously outside Noah's room. Lydde set Mary as lookout so she could be warned at the approach of a servant. Then she went into the room to find Noah with a thermometer in his mouth. He gave Lydde a weak smile.

"Where did that come from?" Lydde asked.

"I brought it back last time in that box I was carrying," said Uncle John, "along with some other things I thought you'd need if you stayed around here. But I wish I was a real doctor, with a real lab behind me. I don't have any way to figure out if I'm dealing with a virus or a bacteria." He took the thermometer from Noah's mouth and held it up to the light. "A hundred and four," he said.

"Oh, God," Lydde whispered.

"May I see?" Noah asked, his curiosity undimmed. "What is the principle behind this rod?"

Lydde showed him the numbers on the thermometer and the black line of mercury.

"Throat hurt?" Uncle John asked.

Noah nodded. "It's hard to swallow."

"Okay. I don't know if it's flu or if it's strep throat. And there's always pneumonia to worry about. So here we go." Uncle John held up two plastic bottles. "Aspirin, to help with the fever and aches if it's the flu virus. And erythromycin in case it's strep throat, and to prevent bacterial pneumonia from developing. Oh, and Mother Bunch sent along some willow bark for tea. It's actually got an ingredient that's in aspirin."

Lydde hugged him. "You are a treasure."

Uncle John popped open the bottles and handed Noah two pills. "Swallow these quick or you'll have a bitter taste in your mouth."

Noah did as he was told. "What is a hundred and four?" he asked.

"It's how hot your body is inside," Uncle John explained. "Your body temperature is very high, which means that until it goes down, you stay in bed, drink lots of tea, and get lots of sleep."

"What about my meeting?"

Lydde dipped a cloth in a bowl of hot water from the hearth and laid it across his forehead. "You know you couldn't go to the old abbey tonight even if you wanted to. Send Simon instead."

And in fact he was falling asleep even as she spoke. She watched him a moment, then turned to Uncle John, who said before she could ask, "We just have to wait and see."

"And what else did you bring back in that wonder box of yours?"

"Pepper spray." At her look of disbelief, he added, "No, really."

"Why?"

He shrugged. "Just in case."

NOAH slept most of the day—waking only to sip cups of willow bark tea and swallow more pills—and into the night, while Simon went as planned to the meeting at the old abbey. Lydde tried to stay awake, though she was exhausted, and when she checked by candlelight Noah's temperature had climbed to 105. He tossed and turned, plucking fretfully at the covers and muttering to himself, then fell into a deep sleep that frightened Lydde. But despite her resolve to stay awake, she slept at last. When she woke, their bedclothes were drenched with sweat. She took Noah's temperature again and checked it by candlelight. It had dropped below 100. The fever had broken.

He was still asleep the next morning, but clearly the danger had passed. Lydde went down to breakfast and saw Mary off to Soane's

Croft to help Mother Bunch. Then she returned to Noah's room, where Nan found her reading by the hearth.

"So, young master," Nan said, "you will have earned Pastor Fallam's gratitude when he is well."

"I hope so," Lydde replied. "He has been kind to me and I am glad to return the favor."

"He has been kind to me as well, and so I have told everyone I see to pray he may be healed."

"That is good of you," Lydde said.

"Cook wants me to go to market so she can make him a nice broth," Nan said. "There is no one else to ask save you."

"I'm sure that is fine," Lydde said.

She read for a while longer in *The Canterbury Tales,* but laid the book down when she heard the creak of the front door. Perhaps Simon had returned, though she had thought he said he would be out on Noah's business. She began to read again, but some uneasiness caused her to lay the book aside and creep softly down the stairs in her fur slippers.

The door to Noah's office was closed except for a crack. That was odd, for the door usually stood open. She held her breath and pushed it slowly open. The door creaked just as a man came into her sight, hovering over Noah's desk. Jacob Woodcock slammed a drawer shut and stepped back.

"What are you doing here?" Lydde demanded.

She had frightened him, but when he realized she was alone, a look of cunning stole over his face.

"Pardon, boy," he said. "I have come to see Pastor Fallam, but he is not here."

"He is not," she said coldly. "He is ill."

"Is he? I am sorry to hear it."

She was surprised he did not know it, since Nan seemed certain the news was around town. "What are you doing behind his desk?" she said sharply.

"Ah." He came toward her and she noticed for the first time he was holding a book. "I was bringing the lieutenant major-general a present." He held out the brown volume. "It is a book I have written myself, with God's help, and just arrived from the printer in Bristol. Pastor Fallam should find it profitable, and indeed, it might also be a boon to your soul, boy, since you are in such peril."

She was forced to take the book from him and open it to its title page. She read:

A SURVEY OF THE THREATS AND PUNISHMENTS
RECORDED IN THE SCRIPTURES,
ALPHABETICALLY COMPOSED
By Jacob Woodcock

"Every sin committed in the Bible may be found in that book," Woodcock said proudly, "from 'adultery' to 'worship of God neglected.' Over six hundred of them. There are, unfortunately, no sins beginning with *x, y,* or *z.* But most important, I have described in detail the terrible punishments visited by God upon the sinner. This reading I do commend to you, boy, and to your new master."

He walked past her and left the room. She stood still until she heard the front door close behind him, and followed to open the door a crack to make certain he had truly gone. Then she ran upstairs, clutching the book.

Noah was sleeping lightly, so she shook him awake. He smiled wanly at her.

"Do I not mend?" he said.

"Yes." She placed her hand on his forehead. "Your fever is much reduced."

"Then why do you look so worried?"

She sat on the bed and took his hand. "I went down to your office," she said, "to find Jacob Woodcock standing over your desk."

"What?" He struggled to sit up.

"Nothing you can do now," she said. "He's gone. When I challenged him, he claimed he had come to bring you this." She held out the book. "He wrote it himself and claims it has just come from the printer. He especially wanted you to have a copy, and made it clear he thinks you are in need of the book's message."

Noah studied the title page, then tossed the book aside. "Indeed he is the wizened sort of man who would give himself up to such an enterprise. He has the soul of a prune."

"I'm worried. He obviously suspects something. And you should have seen his face when he spoke of you. I believe he hates you. He pretended he didn't know you were ill, but Nan has put it out all over Norchester. How could he not know?"

"People know I am ill?"

"I'm certain of it. The servants will all have talked of it."

His face was so pale she thought he might faint. Then he said, "Where is Simon?"

"He went to the quay to see what ships have come in. I think he still had hopes of your lost cargo."

"Go after him. Tell him to come here at once."

"Noah, what is it? You're frightening me."

"Just do as I say. Then get you off to Soane's Croft for your chores there."

She stood. "And you won't tell me what is going on?"

"No."

"But you'll tell Simon."

"Simon is my trusted lieutenant."

"And I am not to be trusted. You continue to treat me like a child, keeping things from me and ordering me about."

"And you continue to act like a child."

She went out, slamming the door behind her.

Noah lay still a moment, a sick feeling in his stomach that had nothing to do with his fever, then stood up on still-wobbly legs and began to search for his clothes. When Simon returned, he found

Noah dressed and sitting at his office desk, searching through the drawers.

"You shouldn't be here in the cold," Simon said. "There's no fire."

"Jacob Woodcock was here."

"I know. Lydde told me. Has anything been disturbed?"

"I don't know. Lydde may have discovered him soon after he arrived."

Simon knelt by the hearth and made a pile of kindling. "Lydde's angry."

"Is she?" Noah said curtly.

"Or perhaps I should say she's hurt. She feels you are keeping things from her."

Noah continued to sort through piles of parchment. "I have more serious matters to tend to just now than Lydde's need to prove herself my equal."

Simon didn't answer and set about lighting the kindling, sensing from Noah's mood that anything he said would only make matters worse.

"One thing is certain," Noah continued. "We have, the three of us, been equals in our foolishness. Did you go to the meeting last night?"

"I did. And we came up with an idea for bringing in more revenue. I was just waiting for you to wake up to share it with you."

"Do you not understand?" Noah said. "The Raven was absent from last night's meeting and now it is talked all over Norchester by the servants that Pastor Fallam is ill. It would be a stupid man among my captains not to connect the two."

"Oh." Simon considered this. "I had not realized your illness had been talked about."

"No." Noah slammed the drawer shut and looked at him. "You did not, nor did I."

"You think we are in danger?"

"I do. My God, what was I thinking?"

"You were ill," Simon said.

"Yes, but I should have realized, I should have called off the meeting."

"That would have been noticed as well, wouldn't it?"

"We should have hid my illness from the servants."

"The captains, surely," Simon said, "will be loyal."

"There is the bounty," Noah pointed out. "And men gossip as well as women."

The kindling had refused to catch fire. The two men sat and watched their breath turn to fog in the cold.

Simon spoke first. "No one could carry this off indefinitely. We knew it would come to this."

"We did."

"Then it is time to go."

Noah nodded. "If it is not already too late. I want you to leave at once for Southampton. Go to our friend there and explain how things stand, see if he can send a ship as soon as possible."

Simon nodded. "Is the shingle below the abbey still the safest place to meet?"

"I think so. But first we must come up with a reason to explain your sudden disappearance."

"There is a very good reason, and one that everyone, even Jacob Woodcock, will find plausible. I plan to run away and elope with Mary Soane against her family's wishes."

Noah smiled bleakly. "Yes. Yes, that will work. And it will get her on board ship so the two of you, at least, will be saved. But we must speak to John about it. And about more than Mary, for Lydde will have her own decision to make."

Simon was surprised. "Do you doubt what it will be?"

Noah looked away. "Yes," he said.

Chapter 19

Decisions

LYDDE TRUDGED THROUGH the cold past East Gate to Mossup's stable. He was surprised to see her.

"You're early, lad," he said. Then he noted the misery that showed plain upon her face. "What ails ye?"

"Nothing I can talk about," she said.

"Ah. I can guess the way of it." He winked. "You've taken a fancy to someone and it's not going as it should."

"Something like that."

"Well. I've some news to cheer you a bit. We've an engagement."

"What do you mean?"

"Come here, sit you down." He pulled a pair of stools to the edge of an empty stall. "Not a regular play, but still a chance to perform. At last." He leaned close so as not to be overheard. "There's to be a party at Lord Radford's estate. A Christmas party."

"Isn't that forbidden?"

"It is. And don't you dare breathe a word of it to that Noah Fallam what took you in, or there'll be trouble. You'll not give us away, will you?"

"Of course not!" Lydde said indignantly. "I've nothing much to say to Noah Fallam just now anyway."

"Well, then, a Christmas party, as I say. The gentry and their wives from all over the district will be at Rosewood. And they want a mumming."

"A mumming?" She vaguely remembered holiday mummings from her other life in England as corny affairs, the sort of thing the local civic club endured after a mediocre meal of roast chicken with potatoes and peas at the town's only hotel. She had avoided mummings like the plague.

"Oh, lad! You're so young and we have been under the thumb of these Puritans so long you've never seen a mumming? 'Tis great fun! The mummers—that's us—wear costumes with masks and we act a play. We may dance a morris dance as well. And when it is over we pretend to rob the audience, and in so doing we collect a bit of remuneration for ourselves. It's a great silliness. And we might even work in a scene from *The Tempest*."

It would be wonderful, Lydde thought, to perform again. Though she could imagine Noah's reaction when she told him. Perhaps she wouldn't tell. Why should she ask his permission like a teenager asking her father if she could go to the mall? If he wouldn't tell her what was going on, she decided, she was under no obligation to share her activities with him.

"I'm riding to Little Gallops to tell Guill and Sharpe. Will you go in with us?"

She thought about the chores at Soane's Croft. But with winter set in there was little to do outside and she decided Mary and Mother Bunch could handle the inside work for one day.

"I will," she said.

.   .   .

AT Soane's Croft, Noah and Simon sat with Uncle John in the study.

"I thought she'd be here," Noah said.

"Haven't seen her," Uncle John said. "I thought she must still be at your place."

"Noah sent her to fetch me," Simon said, "and then she headed toward the river. I don't know where she was going." He glanced at Noah and fell silent.

"We should look for her," said Uncle John. "Wouldn't it be best if you all leave with Simon and Mary?"

Noah shook his head. "No, I can divert a search for these two, but if it is known I have fled, I fear we would all be looked for and apprehended on the road. Besides, one thing remains here for me to do."

"Where Mary is concerned, I would like to have Lydde's support," Uncle John said, "but she isn't here, so that's that. I'll make the decision myself." He turned to Simon. "If there were no danger, no need to flee, what would have been your intentions toward Mary?"

"I love her," Simon said. "She is young for marriage, I do know that. I would have asked for her hand in a year or two. But we do not have the luxury of waiting. I must flee to America, and if she does not go with me it will be all over for us. She has no dowry and no other prospects here. She will be better off as my wife. I will take care of her, and I promise you I will take heed of her age. I will be in all things gentle."

"I vouch for Simon," Noah added. "He will care for her above himself. She could do no better for a husband."

Uncle John looked from one to the other and nodded. "I agree," he said. "And if the situation here is unraveling, as you say, then I myself will be gone soon as well and unable to protect her. There's no better place for Mary than with Simon."

"And," Noah said, "if she leaves with him today, she will be well out of the danger here."

"Unlike Lydde," said Uncle John.

Noah gave him such a look of despair that Uncle John had to fight back the impulse to put a consoling arm around the younger man's shoulder.

"I think," Noah said, "Lydde will want to leave too."

NOAH had brought with him most of the gold he had kept in a strongbox at the Bishop's Palace, which he now handed over to Simon.

"I've kept a bit for the servants," he said, "to ease them until they find other positions. Here is the rest. If I don't make it, you can use it to buy some land. Robert writes that land in Virginia is more dear than you might think."

"I'll give you most of what is left from John Soane as well," Uncle John said. "I've no more use for it, except to settle a nice amount on Mother Bunch."

"Where will she go?" Noah asked.

"I've spoken to the Reverend Smythe. He will see she arrives safe at her sister's cottage in Bradway, and the amount I am sending with her will keep them both."

Mary was ecstatic to learn Simon had asked for, and been given, her hand in marriage. Nor was she daunted at the prospect of a sudden departure followed by a voyage across the ocean. The optimism and energy of youth, Uncle John thought. While Mary went off to pack her few belongings, he gathered up those items most helpful for the voyage and placed them in an oilskin pouch. In went his supply of antibiotics, the aspirin and Vitamin C tablets, the thermometer, the books on health and first aid. After a moment's thought he added the boxes of birth control pills, most of them left behind by Lydde for safe-keeping. On a piece of parchment he wrote down instructions for each item, then explained them to Noah and Simon, cautioning them the bag must be kept dry.

When he showed them the birth control pills, Noah said, "Lydde has been taking these?"

"Yes," Uncle John said.

"She didn't tell me."

"You two don't seem to be talking much."

Noah turned away and walked to the window, staring out as though he could actually see through the milky glass pane.

"Where is she?" he said.

JACOB Woodcock sat at his kitchen table composing another letter for Bristol.

I have taken to frequenting taverns, an occupation noted by my neighbors with much gossip, for they have known me as one who shuns the Devil's spirits. Yet for the sake of God's work I imbibe a small amount as I listen to those whose tongues have been loosened. And I have at last learnt something of worth at a hostelry in Little Gallops. Two rustics in their cups were gossiping about the Raven. One of them, it seems, has a brother in the gang. And the brother spoke of seeing the Raven without a shirt, and possessing upon his upper back a red birthmark. It was, these two decided after some discussion, a distinguishing mark that set the Raven apart as a man of greatness. Cain's mark upon him more like, I longed to cry. But of course I kept my peace, for I know as you must this is the opposite of the mark of Cain placed by God upon that murderer for protection, and rather a brand seared upon the flesh of this outlaw so he may be finally purged from among us.

I will tell you as well, though I as yet have no proof of it, that if you come to Norchester in search of the man with the red mark, I will not be surprised if he is found to be known to Noah Fallam. Indeed, perhaps known so well to Noah Fallam as to be indistinguishable from him. I state this with respect for the judgment of the Lord Protector and if I am wrong I beg pardon. But even now there are rumors in town to this effect, though people are afraid of both Fallam and the Raven enough not to openly accuse.

I recommend you arrive on Sunday. Then you will find most of Norchester together in one of three churches and may quickly examine the men of the various congregations for the bearer of the mark. Pastor Fallam preaches at Trinity and I suggest you begin there.

Your servant,

W.

THE afternoon light was waning when Lydde arrived at Soane's Croft. She'd felt some guilt about leaving Mary with the chores, so she paid tuppence for a length of ribbon at a shop in Sheep Street. Inside the door she was met by Bounder and, after greeting the dog, called out, "Mary! I've a present for you!"

She was startled when Uncle John appeared in the hall outside the study and beckoned to her, a grave expression on his face. When she entered the study, Noah was standing by the hearth. He turned away abruptly and stared at the fire.

"Where were you?" he said. "I've been waiting here all afternoon."

"I was with Mossup. We went to Little Gallops to rehearse." She had expected him to chastise her, and that made her more irritable. "Do you trust me so little you must check up on my every move?"

Lydde knew as soon as she spoke it was the worst thing she could have said, though she didn't know why. She stepped closer to Noah, but he moved away from her.

"She doesn't know what's happened," Uncle John said to Noah. Then, to Lydde, "Mary and Simon are gone. They are married and on their way to Southampton."

"What? Has no one tried to stop them?"

"We wanted you here, but we didn't know where you had gone,"

Uncle John continued, his voice a warning. "Noah performed the ceremony, and Mother Bunch and I stood as witnesses."

"Uncle John!" she protested. "How could you let—"

"For God's sake!" Noah cried. "Tell her and let us be done with it!"

"She's your wife," Uncle John said. "You need to tell her."

Lydde looked from one to the other.

"She thinks her own thoughts and goes her own way as though nothing else matters," Noah said, his back still turned to them.

"Noah, I'm standing here," Lydde said. "If you have something to say, say it to me."

"She does think her own thoughts," Uncle John said. "It's one reason you said you love her."

"It was," Noah said. "Only just now I am too frightened to consider that."

Uncle John urged her toward Noah with a nod of his head. Lydde went to him then and wrapped her arms around his chest as she had when they looked in the mirror together. She felt him stiffen, but she didn't let go.

"Tell me," she said.

"All is lost here." He stood with head bowed. "It is rumored about that I am the Raven. It may be a week or more before I am arrested, or it may be at any moment."

"Oh, God!" Lydde whispered.

"There is a man in Southampton," Noah continued, "who has sent more cargo our way than any other. His brother was the Royalist whose life I saved two years ago, so he owes me a debt and has given a standing offer to pick me up when the time comes. Simon and Mary have gone to Southampton to arrange for one of his ships to stop for . . ."—he hesitated—"for us, or for me if you choose not to come with me."

Lydde stepped back and ducked her head, ashamed. "No wonder you're angry at me," she said. "If you had needed to get away quickly, I might have been the death of you."

"No," he said. He turned then and faced her. "You would never have been that to me, but only life."

For Lydde time stood as still as it did for Aunt Lavinia while she and Uncle John had their adventures in Norchester. Before her eyes images of her own century passed like flickers of light—rooms always warm in winter, lamps that flared at the flick of a finger, flushing toilets and shampoo and hot running water, television and movies. All a dream, as insubstantial as that pageant conjured, then dissolved, by Prospero in *The Tempest*. Noah, though, was flesh and blood.

"When will the ship come for *us*?" she asked.

He studied her face. "It will be a hard crossing in winter," he said in a voice so low she could barely hear him.

Uncle John cleared his throat. "Lydde, we've been talking while we waited for you. You have to be realistic. If you get on a ship for America, you lose all contact with the future. I'll go back to the Gorge and I may be able to find another wormhole, but God knows if I will, or if it would bring us together again. If you go with Noah, you are facing a hard life, more difficult even than here, and with no escape close at hand. You risk all the diseases of the seventeenth century—smallpox, malaria, typhoid. You risk dying in childbirth. And that's not all. What if something happens to Noah?"

To Lydde's mind, all unbidden, came images of the skeleton in the cave, of the plaque in Norchester Cathedral, Noah Fallam lost in the wilderness of Virginia with the date suddenly remembered, 1671, and that was less than fourteen years away.

"What if something happens to Noah," Uncle John continued, "and you are left a widow? It's not the same as at home, where women have their own lives and the means to support themselves. You would have to marry again or prostitute yourself or starve, unless Simon and Mary were able to take you in."

Lydde still looked at Noah. "Is that what you think?" she said. "Do you want to leave without me?"

Noah shook his head. "No," he said. "I am just prideful enough to think that my wife's place is by my side, and that I am as able to take care of my wife as is any man."

He said this last with a defiant glance at Uncle John, who, to Noah's surprise, smiled and nodded.

Lydde thrust her hand into the pocket where she had sewn her wedding band with three strands of thread, slipped her finger into the ring, and pulled it loose with a snap. She held up her hand.

"I didn't intend to vow to obey you," she said, "but I meant the rest. Wherever you go, I am going. Husband."

She was astonished to see a tear slip down Noah's cheek. He took her in his arms. Out of the corner of her eye she saw Uncle John leave the room and close the door behind him.

"We have been angry with one another and will be again," Noah said.

"Yes."

"My anger does not mean I have ceased to love you."

"Nor does mine."

"Please understand why I have been so secretive," he said. "I have only wanted to shield you from both danger and worry."

"I don't want or need that kind of protection. Don't ever leave me behind, not ever. That sort of separation I couldn't bear. I want to share your fate, whatever it is."

"You don't know what you're saying."

"I do know. I can face anything you can. Now I want you to take me home."

"Home. Where is home now?"

"Noah, *you* are home."

Lydde placed the palm of her hand against his, wove their fingers together. At the front door Noah said, "In Virginia we will walk down the street arm in arm and everyone will know you are my wife. But now you are a boy who has been chastised, for your cousin has scandalously absconded with my secretary."

And they composed themselves to face Norchester, stern Noah Fallam and the penitent boy who straggled alongside him, hand in his pocket to hide the gold ring he had decided not to remove.

They passed by the jail, which was housed in the former priory along the north wall of the town. There Noah dispatched two constables to try and catch up to the eloping couple.

"I believe they will head toward Bristol, since the girl hails from there," he told them.

The two constables galloped on their way, even as Simon and Mary were well along the road east toward Southampton. Outside the jail, Lydde and Noah met Constable Baxter returned from his rounds. The constable fixed a speculative eye on Noah, then said, "May I speak with you a moment, sir?"

"Of course," Noah agreed. They went back inside. Lydde waited in the small foyer. After a time she walked idly to a door with a small sliding panel at eye level that opened to the inside. No one seemed to be around. Curious, she slid the panel open and peered inside at the cell block. A constable who had heard the panel slide open stepped into the inner hall from a room on the left. His broad face filled the opening.

"What's this?" he demanded as she panicked and slid the panel shut.

He came through the door into the foyer, then recognized her as the lieutenant major-general's ward.

"What do you want?"

"I am waiting for Pastor Fallam," she said meekly. "He is speaking with Constable Baxter. I meant no harm."

"Very well. Don't touch anything else."

"No, sir."

In the room where Noah had closeted himself with Constable Baxter the two men stood close so they would not be overheard when they spoke.

"Ye'll be away yourself soon, won't ye?" Baxter said.

"What makes you say that, Baxter?"

"I'm hearing talk, sir. Others are hearing it as well. And if the wrong one hears it, things will be all up with you."

Noah waited.

"I wish you godspeed," Baxter said. "I've known you since you were a lad and I've fought beside you in the war, and never a better man could I want at my side. I have no quarrel with what you've done here. I thought, if you find yourself in trouble, you might want to know that."

"Thank you," Noah said. "But I would not want you to do anything that would endanger you or your family."

Baxter inclined his head.

"There is one favor I might ask," Noah said, "though it is not for myself. On Saturday night, God willing, I will send you and a party of constables out to search for an illegal Christmas party and mumming. I will send you to the wrong place and I want you to take your time getting there. Your slowness will mean a great deal to the district's poor this winter."

Baxter's eyes gleamed. "I shall be a perfect tortoise," he said.

At the Bishop's Palace they encountered Nan carrying a bundle of bedclothes down the hall.

"Go fetch the other servants," Noah told her, "and bring them to my office."

Soon they were gathered there, the two maids, the cook, the groundskeeper. Lydde stood to one side.

"It appears," Noah said, "that Mr. Cleyes has run away with young Mary."

Nan let out a cry and Cook clapped a hand over her mouth.

"Mary left behind a note for Mr. Soane at Soane's Croft. It seems they have been planning this for some time and are on their way to Bristol. I have sent a pair of constables to fetch them back, but I doubt if we shall see them again. It is, as you can gather, most upsetting. If people in town ask, you shall tell them the simple truth, but please, no more. I do not approve of gossip.

"The boy who remains"—a nod to Lydde—"continues as my ward. I am greatly concerned for the state of his soul, since his cousin has set him so poor an example. I intend to spend this afternoon in the library with Lewis, praying. We shall pray for Mary and Mr. Cleyes, for the salvation of their souls. I do not wish to be disturbed for any reason. Is that clear?"

It was, and the servants took themselves to the kitchen and the market to gossip among themselves as eagerly as Noah had expected they would. Upstairs, when the library door had closed behind them, Noah drew Lydde close.

"Let us pray," he said, and kissed her.

AFTER a session of lovemaking made more frantic by their situation, they lay on the floor beside the hearth, their heads resting on a cushion taken from a bench.

"John told me of the pills you take to keep away pregnancy," he said. "I didn't know."

"I was going to tell you," she said. "I should have. But then we started arguing. And to tell the truth, I was a little hurt because you didn't seem to care if I became pregnant."

"Of course I care. How could I not, when Margaret died as she did? But I know no way to prevent it save to withdraw during lovemaking, and that is counted a sin. Perhaps it is not, but I have never felt comfortable with it. So I saw nothing to talk about, only that we would accept how God dealt with us."

"Of course you wouldn't know. These pills were—or will be—invented in the 1960s. If I take one a day, I won't get pregnant."

"And if you change your mind?"

"I just stop taking the pills. I only have enough pills for three years. But I thought at least I should take them until things are settled here.

Until after we are safe." She combed the hair on his chest with her fingers. "Do you want children?"

"I would like children," he said, "but not at the cost of losing you. I'm just as glad you have the pills right now."

"I'm glad you aren't angry at me about it."

"No," he said. "But John is right. We both must talk more. You must tell me what you are thinking."

"And you will tell me what is happening from now on?"

"I will. Actually, I have something to tell you that will interest you greatly. One reason I did not go with Simon is to take a final opportunity to help the poor this winter. Simon learned of illegal Christmas festivities at Lord Radford's estate, Rosewood. We heard there would be a mumming and I am guessing your group of players will be involved. Isn't it so?"

"Yes. Are you angry with me again?"

"Not this time. Do you know of Rosewood?"

"Mossup says it's on the way to Coombe Manor."

"Yes. When we went to Coombe Manor we passed the gate to Rosewood just before we headed up onto the downs. Lord Radford is the wealthiest man in the district and counts his wealth to be a blessing from God, as though it is proof he is more virtuous than the poor."

"We've got people like that in America," Lydde said.

"More than any other of the men of property he pressures me to catch the Raven. Indeed, I have this past year cost him a sizable portion of what he believes God intended for him alone. But, though he fought for Parliament in the war, he is not a fanatical Puritan like Woodcock or Sitwell. He is one of those men who wanted to replace the King to increase his own power. So he hosts a Christmas Eve party and mumming on Saturday night, and no doubt a Christ-mass on Sabbath morn. A number of the gentry and their families will stay at Rosewood, according to the intelligence Simon had, and with the wives will come their jewelry. Besides that, each man will bring a pouch of gold to be placed in Lord Radford's strongbox. This gold will be sent to London after the New Year to buy influence with Cromwell. While children starve, those who rule us sell themselves to the highest bidder."

Lydde sighed. "We've got that in America too. So what are you going to do?"

"On Saturday night I intend to send all my constables under Baxter's command to a manor four miles in the other direction while I plead I must stay behind to continue recovering from my illness. Then I will take a handful of my men, most likely my four captains and no more, and attend your mumming. At the moment the mummers play at robbing their audience, I shall do so in earnest."

"Noah!" Lydde pushed him onto his back and pretended to pin him down. "You're terrible!"

"I am," he agreed, and laughed. "Well, it serves them right. By celebrating Christmas they are breaking the law, are they not?"

"A robbery on Christmas Eve!"

"It will more than make up for the lost ship," he said, "and it will be the Raven's parting gift to Norchester."

Lydde was laughing, but stopped suddenly. "It sounds dangerous," she said. "There will be a lot more of them than you."

"We will be armed with flintlock pistols," he said, "and by then the men at Rosewood will be in their cups. I know the layout of the house and grounds, for I went there often as a boy, and I know where the strongbox is kept as well. We do, however, need someone on the inside, someone who can make certain a door is unlocked and who can give us some sort of signal when it is best to enter."

"Mossup?"

"Mossup has been good about sending intelligence my way and providing horses," Noah said. "He can be trusted with a secret, but not to keep a cool head in an emergency."

He sat up and pulled her up beside him. "I'd thought of you," he said.

She stared at him in astonishment. "Me? Noah, truly?"

He nodded. "Not gladly, you understand, because of the risk. I'm afraid you might be recognized."

"I don't think the country gentry have seen much of me. They don't even come to church in Norchester. They may have heard of me, but nothing more. Besides, Mossup says it's bad luck to recognize a mummer, so I think they won't be trying to figure out who we are. But if I do this properly they won't notice me, will they?"

"I hope not."

She kissed his cheek. "Thank you for saying you trust me."

They lapsed each into private thoughts while absentmindedly stroking one another. Then Lydde said, "If you go in with pistols, does that mean you would shoot those people if necessary?"

Noah didn't answer for a long time. "I would not," he said at last. "If we were challenged, I would flee. And I must ensure that my captains do the same. I would not have this be blood money."

"Will they agree?"

He stared at the ceiling. "I think they will agree," he said, "if I tell them beforehand who I am and speak to them as a pastor."

THEY lived in such a state of dread and hope—waiting to see if Simon or Elisha Sitwell would reach them first—that the days seemed to creep by. And yet they were happy as well. Noah had decided there was no longer any reason to spend time at his desk engaged in the tedium of governing, since there was no project he might set in motion that he would be present to complete. So he spent his days with Lydde, aided by a break in the weather. In the mornings they went to Soane's Croft, where Noah helped with chores to the amazement of Mother Bunch, who was distrustful of this new, domestic Noah Fallam.

"What is he doing here?" she whispered to Uncle John. "Was it not enough to kidnap poor Lewis? Must he spy on us?"

"Now, now," Uncle John said. "I think Pastor Fallam sincerely cares about the lad's welfare, and he knows how you miss Mary. He has taken a liking to us. To you."

She reared back indignantly. "To me? And why would Noah Fallam like an old woman who longs to see the back of him so we might have our dear King once more? And our Christmas! Sunday is Christmas Day and he will deprive us of it. I have the makings of a pudding hidden in the kitchen, and if he finds my currants I shall scratch his eyes out, I will!"

"He will not find your currants, Mother Bunch. They are too well hidden. And do you know what I think? I think the Reverend Smythe would be very glad to come share pudding with you."

Her face was cracked by a grin. "Do you think so? Poor man, he has not eaten well since his wife died, I would wager."

"Then you are the woman to provide for him. Lewis says even Noah Fallam's cook is no match for you."

Mother Bunch smacked him on the arm. "Go on," she said.

Lydde and Noah, oblivious to this conversation, scattered grain for the chickens, collected eggs, and mucked out Lady's stall in the small barn. When chores were done, they went off to Mossup's stable, where they engaged the two fastest horses. Noah insisted that Lydde get in as much riding practice as she could in case they must flee suddenly.

"I doubt you could sit a galloping horse," he pointed out.

"So do I," she admitted. "We'd better pray it doesn't come to that."

On Friday Noah was digging up a cabbage for Mother Bunch to turn into stew as Lydde sorted dried herbs into bundles when a letter arrived at Soane's Croft. Uncle John was out on his rounds, so Mother Bunch came back through the house to fetch them.

"There's a man here from Southampton who says he must be paid for a letter he bears," she said. "A rude fellow who—"

Noah was up and running through the house before she could finish. Mother Bunch shook her head.

"The world is a strange place," she said. "Pastor Fallam orders us about, then digs in my garden, then rushes to meet a scoundrel. These must be the end times."

Noah returned soon with the unopened letter in his hand. He motioned for Lydde to come in the house, and led her to the study. They stood near the milky light of the thick-paned window, Noah's arms around Lydde so they could read together when he tore the letter open.

Dearest Friends, they read:

I pray this does not reach you too late. Our ship departs at dawn on Saturday and we expect a joyful reunion on Sunday, I hope before dark. Mary will stay on board and I will accompany some of the crew in the shallop to the shingle below the abbey where we will wait for you. The crew assures me they will stay until sunrise on Monday as long as we do not come under attack, but I doubt I can hold them longer, so pray God there is no delay in your departure, and may He bring us safe together again.

They stood, Lydde leaning back against Noah, without speaking. Then Noah dropped the letter on the dying fire in the hearth. It flared a blue light and burned.

"Now, Lydde," Noah said, "we can do nothing but wait and pray."

THEY walked back to the Bishop's Palace in the growing dusk. They had nearly arrived when Jacob Woodcock appeared as from nowhere and fell in beside them.

"Pastor Fallam!" Woodcock exclaimed with false joviality. "I wonder, do you have a birthmark?"

Noah never broke stride, though he refused to look at Woodcock.

"Why do you ask?" he said. "Do you plan to write a book that catalogs birthmarks as thoroughly as you did sins?"

Woodcock's face turned red with fury. "Oh, yes," he said, "you mock now. But those who mock God will suffer the fate of Jezebel, whose blood was lapped by dogs."

Then he disappeared into a dark alley.

They continued on through the gateway to the door of the cathedral, where Lydde drew Noah into the shadow.

"My God!" she cried. "He knows."

"Yes." Noah looked around. The close was empty and silent save for a pair of ravens nattering to one another on a tree limb outside the Bishop's Palace. "I suspect he has all along been Sitwell's eyes and ears in Norchester. Well, he can do nothing until Sitwell arrives, for I still control the local constables. Baxter is loyal to me."

"What if Sitwell arrives tonight or tomorrow? Shouldn't we run now?"

"Where to, Lydde? There is no place to run until the ship arrives."

"We could go through the wormhole."

"I cannot. My task here is not done. And if I go there, I will have lost the best part of my life."

"We wouldn't have to stay. We could come back."

"How would we know when to come back? We might step back into a trap. Or we might miss the ship entirely."

She couldn't answer. Perhaps Uncle John would know, but she doubted he could predict with such accuracy.

A brisk wind swirled dead leaves, promising the return of cold weather.

"If he has been spying on you," she said, "then your protection of me is one of the things that has drawn his attention."

"Lydde, you mustn't think like that," Noah said. "I would not do anything differently where you are concerned. Now come inside. The servants will be gone by now."

They ate a supper of roast beef and black bread and went straight to bed, pulling the curtains on all four sides to keep out the cold.

Lydde lay close to Noah, stroking him, but after a while he turned on his back and said, "It is no use. I cannot love you tonight. My mind is elsewhere."

"All right," she said, and ordered him to lie on his stomach while she massaged his back to give him some ease.

When they were lying side by side once more, neither able to sleep, he said, "I am not afraid of death, Lydde. But I am terrified of dying."

She pressed against him, unable to reply.

"Promise me something," he whispered. "If I am taken, I do not want you there when I am executed. I cannot bear the thought of you being there when they—" His voice broke. Lydde buried her face against his shoulder, trying to block out images of his evisceration. Then he continued, his voice strong again. "I could not bear for you to be there. Promise me if I am taken you will go back to your time before I am killed. And know when you are there that you have been loved for hundreds of years. For I will continue to love you and I will find you again."

"Noah—"

He raised up and leaned over her.

"Promise," he repeated.

She pressed his hand to her cheek.

"I promise," she said.

Chapter 20

The Mumming

L ATE SATURDAY AFTERNOON, Lydde rode with Mossup to the Red Rooster Inn, the hostelry at Little Gallops where the players would meet and wait for a conveyance from Rosewood to take them to the party. Guill and Sharpe had costumes stitched by Guill's old mother, who lived at the inn and did the cooking. They tried these on in an upstairs bedroom, strange garments made of colorful strips of linen worn over their clothes, which Lydde thought made them look like motley abominable snowmen. Over all was a type of shawl of the same material which covered their heads and faces, with only slits for eyes, nose, and mouth. Last they strapped bells to their legs.

Mossup surveyed the lot.

"We will do," he proclaimed. "We will do indeed. Now, lads, shall we practice while we wait?"

"Open your door and let us in," they chanted, "for we would your favor gladly win."

They bounced up and down, bells jangling. Lydde had trouble concentrating on the words, terrified as she was that Noah might be taken while she was gone.

But Noah was by then on his way to the ruined abbey on the coast to meet his captains. They would not arrive until dark, but he felt uneasy in Norchester, so he departed early. At the headland he stood and surveyed the sea as though willing the ship to speed on close to shore. But the gray horizon remained empty.

At dusk the captains arrived one by one and stood before him.

Noah said, "Now, gentlemen, I would not startle you, but I am going to reveal myself. For this is the last time we shall meet. I want you to understand why we have been successful so far in our smuggling venture, and why you cannot continue in safety from here on. In any event, you will have guessed who I am."

He removed his hat and pulled the mask over his head, looking from one to another.

"Sir," said the tallest captain, Ingles, "we did indeed guess your identity when the Raven failed to attend that meeting and we learned later you were ill. But we all knew you from boyhood. We served with you in the New Model Army. Though we only just realized who the Raven might be, I think I can say none of us is surprised. Will you go to America?"

"I will," Noah said.

"Then perhaps we will meet again someday. For many poor men do look across the ocean now."

"Indeed. I can no longer remain here safely, and so I will leave soon. If you continue the smuggling operation, you must understand you will face a much greater risk. Elisha Sitwell will keep a close watch here. That is why I believe it so important to carry out this robbery. I had hoped the cargo we missed would sustain our people through a hard winter; now we must find another way. One thing I must beg you, as your pastor rather than as your leader. We will enter Rosewood armed in order to intimidate, but I would not have us use our weapons save in extreme self-defense. I would not have us murder to secure this money, for then there will be a curse upon us rather than a blessing. Do you understand? If you stay calm and follow my directions, I believe we can be in and out quickly with no harm to ourselves or to those attending the party. Do you agree? If not, then you should leave now."

They nodded. Then one by one they shook his hand. They walked to their horses and Noah took a last look out to sea.

"Well, then," Noah said, "we have half an hour's ride to Rosewood. Let's be off."

Rosewood, a gabled stone house, was lit with candles in every mullioned window. "A surfeit of tallow," said Guill with a shake of his head.

"But it is lovely," Lydde said. She supposed she should not admire the extravagance of the wealthy. But for the first time she felt the presence of the season, of Christmas, with its lights and decorations and treats.

The coach carried them around to the back of the house, where they entered the basement kitchen, ablaze with light and smelling of spices. The servants stopped their bustling about to cry out with delight at the multihued hulks in their midst, to giggle and make japes that caused the mummers to prance about and jingle their bells. One serving girl pretended to guess who each mummer might be.

"Bad luck, bad luck!" Mossup cried with a waggle of his finger. "We are spirits come to restore light and receive gifts, no more!"

They were led to a table in the corner and plied with all the treats that would be served upstairs, sweetmeats and saucers of beef pudding with mustard, gingerbread and spice cake, and hot spiced cider to wash it down. Lydde sipped judiciously at her cup, fearful of growing tipsy when she must be most alert. From upstairs came sounds of the party, a distant jangle of voices like discordant chimes punctuated now and then by a high-pitched laugh, and above all the lilt of music, violin and harp and drum. It had been so long since she'd heard music that it brought tears to her eyes.

When she mentioned this to Mossup, he said, " 'Tis why Noah Fallam and his ilk shall soon be gone from us. People can only be good for so long. At last, we must sing and dance."

At the sound of Noah's name spoken so disparagingly, a chill ran the length of her spine. She missed him terribly, wished he could be there in a normal time and enjoy the music, perhaps squire her around the dance floor. She wanted to act for him, not a mumming but a serious play, and afterward have him come to her dressing room with flowers and tell her how wonderful her performance had been.

She shook her head to clear it. Such thoughts would not be helpful tonight, she told herself, not helpful at all. She must be cold and clear and mechanical.

They were ushered upstairs and huddled together in the central hall, the noise of the guests' merrymaking close by in the ballroom. Noah had gone over the layout of the house with her. The front door in the hall must be unlocked, and the study with the strongbox was at the top of the central hall's staircase. The ballroom was at the back of the house overlooking the formal gardens. Lydde glanced around. The mummers were alone, awaiting their cue to enter. She went quickly to the front door and turned the handle. The door was locked, as Noah had guessed, for at that late hour he supposed no more guests would be expected.

A footman with black hair sculpted into a wing at the back of his head stepped into the hall from the next room. "What is it?" he said.

She started at the sight of him, then said, "I only wanted a breath of fresh air. I feel a bit nervous."

He opened the door solemnly and held it while she stepped out and took a deep breath. Then she nodded at the footman and went back inside, watching carefully to see how he worked the lock. It seemed simple enough, for he only turned a single brass knob. But then he said, as though to himself, "Perhaps I'd best leave it unlocked. Greevey may be still on his way with Lord Shepperson," and turned the lock back. He looked up and saw Lydde watching him. "Don't want to miss the mumming for answering the door, do I?" he said, and grinned at her.

"Certainly not," she replied.

"You're a young 'un, by the sound of it." He ran a hand quickly over his sleek hair.

"I'm only a boy," she replied, "but I am the best actor of all."

"Well, well," the footman said slyly, and gave her rump a pinch as he passed on his way to the ballroom, "we shall see about that."

So her first job was done, for the door was unlocked and would remain so unless a Lord Shepperson arrived. She took a deep breath and joined the others.

"I saw that Woodley give you the pinch," Guill said archly. "Have a care, Lewis. He was once after Sharpe, he was."

"I never gave him the time of day," Sharpe protested.

Lydde laughed and started to reply, but just then there came a cheer from the ballroom and a cry of, "The mummers! The mummers!"

"That's us!" Mossup said. "Look lively, lads!"

The musicians who had been playing for the dance struck up a tune, for Mossup had told them ahead of time what the troupe would be singing. So the mummers danced in, bells jingling in morris style, to a lively rendition of "Here We Come A-Wassailing," followed by a traditional opening chant.

> "Open your door and let us in,
> for we would your favor win.
> Whether we rise or whether fall,
> we'll do our best to please you all.
> Active youth and active age
> the like was never acted on any stage."

Lydde had time to survey the room quickly. It was long and elegant, painted a light green, with a row of chandeliers suspended from the ceiling, each holding a dozen gigantic candles. More waste of tallow, she supposed. The guttering of the candles made the shadows dance in the room like a slow-motion strobe light at a disco. A bank of floor-to-ceiling windows took up much of the outside wall. These were the pride of Lord Radford, newly imported from France as a sign of his wealth. The garden was beyond, and somewhere in the shadows, she hoped, stood the Raven and his men, waiting. With the ballroom lit, Noah explained, he would be able to gauge the size of the crowd and its disposition. And, she thought, he'll see me perform.

Lydde was playing St. George and at her cue she strode forward waving a wooden sword, pantomiming a fight.

"I am St. George," she proclaimed, "a noble champion bold,/ 'Twas I who fought and won three crowns in gold,/ 'Twas I who fought the fiery dragon and brought it to its slaughter,/ And by this means I won the Queen of Egypt's daughter."

She bowed with a flourish before a trio of bejeweled young women in the audience, who giggled and prodded one another. The mumming continued with Mossup, Guill, and Sharpe variously playing the Turkish Knight, the Doctor, and a Horse, each pretending to kill another, who was then brought miraculously back to life. Lydde had taught them a few new bits, such as one ripped off from an old *Pink Panther* film. When Sharpe with a fake horses' head approached, Lydde asked Guill the doctor in her best fake French accent, "Does your 'orse bi-ite?" Guill replied, "Oh, no, sir." When Sharpe clamped down on her hand, Lydde screeched and cried, "Ah thought you sayd your 'orse did not bi-te?"

"'E is not my 'orse," Guill replied, to a storm of laughter. Lydde rolled her eyes at the success of the joke.

To finish, the actors launched into a scene from *The Tempest,* which was not a traditional part of a mumming, but Mossup was determined to have it. When he began his Prospero soliloquy, "Our revels now are ended . . ." Lydde felt a nervous rumbling in her stomach. As he continued, "We are such stuff as dreams are made on, and our little life is rounded with a sleep," she edged closer to the windows. When Mossup was done, she faced outside and made a deep bow to signal Noah the fake robbery had begun. Mossup glanced quizzically at her, but she rushed forward to pick up her cue.

"I am a poor man dressed in rags." She waved her sword. "And my pockets do grow thin. I'll take some of your Christmas coins to line them well within."

Then she cried, "Back against the wall, all of you," and the crowd pressed closer together into the corner, laughing, as she swung her sword wildly. Some broke into song: "Christmas is coming the goose is getting fat, please put a shilling in the old man's hat." There were fifty or sixty people there, Lydde judged, and many were indeed flushed with drink, a few of the men so tipsy they could scarcely stand. They tittered and shoved as she herded them closer together, some trying to press their hands against the breasts and thighs of the nearest women. One man called out, "Only four mummers to pay. We shall get off lightly this year."

Just then five masked men armed with long-barreled pistols entered the ballroom.

"I am the Raven," said the man in front in a rasping voice, "and I shall cost you dearly."

There were screams from the women and cries of outrage from the men, but Noah turned quickly and, aiming his pistol at the bank of windows, fired. The noise was deafening as the glass shattered, and the crowd fell immediately into a terrified silence. He shrugged in mock apology, tucked the pistol into his belt, and pulled out a knife.

"Raise your hands above your heads where we can see them. You mummers, go stand with the others. Except for you!" He pointed his knife at Lydde. "Take your sack around and receive the jewels of the women."

"And if I refuse?" Lydde said defiantly.

"Then I will order my men to shoot. Now do as I say."

The Raven captains steadily trained their weapons on the crowd. Noah had once explained to Lydde that pistols were not accurate, but that trained on a crowd at close range they would leave a gaping hole in someone and likely kill anyone standing behind as well. No one dared move, she was relieved to see. Noah meanwhile had recognized Lord Radford and called him out. The host, resplendent in a red coat, came forward reluctantly, hands in the air. His face was flushed, whether from drink, anger, or fear Lydde couldn't say.

"Turn around," Noah commanded, and when Radford had complied, Noah placed the point of the knife at his back with one hand and gripped his shoulder tightly with the other hand. "Now," Noah said, "you will take me to your strongbox, which you will open and empty into this other sack." One of the masked men tossed a canvas sack to Noah, who caught it deftly with his left hand.

Lydde was busy holding her sack open before the women, who, with faces marked variously by anger or fear, were unclasping necklaces and bracelets, pulling earrings from their lobes, and dropping all petulantly into the sack.

"Sorry, sorry," Lydde kept murmuring, her head bowed.

When she was done, Noah had not returned, and she began to be afraid. She handed the sack of jewelry to one of his captains and backed up to join the front ranks of the captives.

Then Noah and a furious Lord Radford returned, with Noah carrying a noticeably heavier sack. The masked men stepped closer together, and Noah said, "We bid you all a joyous Christ-mass!"

They turned as one to leave when two men entered from the hall, apparently the tardy Greevey and Lord Shepperson. It was hard to tell who was more surprised, the masked men or the newcomers frozen in their tracks, who were not armed but who barred the escape route. The rest happened so quickly Lydde had no time to think. A man on the edge of the crowd took a threatening step forward and at the same time Noah shoved his sack to one of his captains, lunged and grabbed Lydde by the arm, dragging her to him. He held the knife to her throat and took a step backward, forcing her with him.

"If anyone comes after us before we are away," he said, "I will slit this boy's throat." To the captains, more quietly, he said, "A different escape route." And in Lydde's ear he whispered, "Keep your head down."

Then, his captains following, he ran toward the windows, turning sideways as he plunged through. The remains of Lord Radford's French glass shattered and crashed around them as they disappeared into the night.

They fled through the darkness, Lydde clutching desperately to Noah's hand and barely able to keep up, but they soon reached the horses tethered in a grove of trees. Behind them they heard an uproar, the crash of doors being thrown open, and a cry for horses.

"I can hold on more easily if I ride behind," Lydde said.

"No!" Noah hoisted her onto the horse and climbed up behind her. Then they were off and galloping, Lydde clinging to the horse's neck for dear life while Noah's left arm firmly circled her waist.

They rode hard for a time north from Rosewood, turned east onto a narrow track through a wood, then cut back to the southwest. Noah explained each change of direction, speaking in Lydde's ear. After a time the horses slowed and she felt his body relax as it became apparent they had lost any pursuit that might have been mounted. Noah removed his mask.

"They were all unprepared," he said. "It worked well except for that last nasty surprise."

The others had drawn near. "I will leave you here," Noah said, "for I should get back to Norchester before someone from Rosewood arrives to call out the constables. Ingles, you will take the jewelry to our friends in London as before? The rest of you will be in charge of fairly dispersing the coin."

"How much do you think we took?" Ingles asked.

"I would guess at least five hundred pounds from the safebox alone," Noah said.

Ingles whistled. "Some more folk will move to town and set up shop with that."

"Good for them," Noah said. "Oh, and be generous with the poor mummers, who did miss their Christmas collection tonight."

"Wait!" Ingles said. "What about the boy?"

"Ah," Noah said, "this is Lewis, my ward. He it was who made certain the door would be unlocked and who gave us the signal to enter."

"Not a hostage at all, then," said Ingles with a laugh. "And a brave lad."

"Most brave," Noah agreed. "And now, gentlemen, I bid you farewell and godspeed."

He put spur to his horse, which carried them on toward Norchester at a brisk pace. Lydde twisted in her seat to see his face.

"Did you really think I was brave?" she asked.

"You were wonderful," he said, though he didn't look at her but continued to survey the ground ahead.

"And you," she said, "were magnificent. My heart nearly stopped when you came walking in. But would you really have shot those people?"

He was smiling. "Mine was the only pistol loaded. The shot that broke the glass was the only one that could be fired. I would not have the Raven's last act be to kill someone. I am done with that, I hope." He reached into his pocket and pulled out the mask, held out his hand, and then dropped it. "Farewell to the Raven and his threats." Then he pulled the horse to a halt. "Best you take off that costume too before we enter Norchester. Quickly, for I must be back soon."

She slid down and pulled off the beribboned outfit, glad because of the cold that she had kept on her coat underneath all.

"Get back up behind me now," Noah said. "It is more the way a boy would ride with me."

He helped her up and they rode on in silence for a time. Then she said, "Why did you make me ride in front before?"

"Because," he said, "if someone was going to take a gun ball in the back, it was going to be me."

"Why?" she said indignantly. "I can risk that—"

"As well as I can," he interrupted in a teasing tone of voice. "Lydde, I will protect you whether you want me to or no."

She thought a moment, then said, "If you are the one shot in the back, then what will become of me?"

"I'm sure you'll find someone else to talk to death," he said.

She set her hands on his shoulders and leaned forward to see his face. It bore his familiar smirk. She swatted him on the back of the head.

"Ouch! Wait until I get you home, my girl."

"Your *woman,*" she said.

"My woman."

"And what will you do to me?"

For an answer he reached around and she felt her rump pinched for the second time that night.

Chapter 21

Christmas Day

A T THE BISHOP'S Palace they put on their nightshirts and Noah built a fire in the bedroom hearth. Soon a party of horsemen arrived from Rosewood, and Noah, in nightshirt and slippers, opened the door to them. Lord Radford was conspicuously absent. The tardy Lord Shepperson acted as spokesman.

"Good God, Fallam!" he cried. "Where are the constables? We have been pounding away at the jail door and no one answers but a single keeper!"

Noah yawned. "I sent them out toward Bradway looking for an illicit Christmas party and mumming we'd heard rumored," he replied. "I could not accompany them because I still recover from an illness. But I sent the lot of them out, for if the Christmas party is discovered, I intend to clap everyone present in jail."

Lord Shepperson glanced around at his companions, who seemed to be at a loss for words. Noah leaned against the doorframe and raised his candle to their faces. "What brings you out so late?" he asked.

"Why," said Shepperson, "there's been a robbery at Rosewood. That damned Raven and his gang have carried away a great deal of money and jewels."

Noah regarded them suspiciously. "Was there some sort of gathering at Rosewood?"

"Ah. Yes, a family gathering, I believe it was. A small family gathering. I only arrived late myself, after the robbery had taken place."

"I did not know you and Lord Radford were related."

"We are not," Lord Shepperson acknowledged. "Yet I was invited."

"Not a Christmas gathering, was it?"

"No, no," said Lord Shepperson at once. "Certainly not."

"How much was stolen? If this was a small family gathering, I assume the loss was not terrible. At least I hope not, for poor Lord Radford's sake."

"Some of the women were forced to part with jewelry. The few women who were present, of course."

"And nothing else taken?"

"I believe Lord Radford was forced to open his strongbox."

"Lord Radford is a prudent man," Noah observed. "I doubt he kept much in it at one time."

"That I don't know."

"Well, I will look into it. Then I will send to London to learn if any stolen jewelry has turned up. Though I warn you it is difficult to follow such transactions. Good night to you, my lord."

"Oh, one more thing. A lad was kidnapped, a—" Shepperson caught himself just in time, for he had been about to say "a mummer from Little Gallops." Instead he added, "I did not know him—a servant, I surmise. The brigands carried him off and I do not doubt you will find his dead body somewhere on the heath."

"I shall send a constable to look for him after the Sabbath is over," Noah said. Then he shut the door firmly.

.   .   .

PERHAPS it was the adrenaline rush, but that night in bed could not have been more different than the one previous. Noah, returning from speaking with the men from Rosewood, found Lydde hiding on the staircase, listening. He chased her back to the bedroom and, catching her just inside the door, treated her as a conquest of war. She pretended to resist, laughing all the while. He pinned her to the bed. Afterward he apologized.

"I was too rough," he said.

"No. I wanted it rough."

He patted her head and fell quickly into a deep, exhausted sleep, his recent illness and the worries of the past few days catching up to him at last. Lydde had more trouble sleeping. She tried not to move for fear of disturbing him, finally dozed fitfully, but came fully awake at dawn. Noah still slept and she lay watching him, whispered a prayer of thanks that she had found such a man. When she sensed it was time to get ready for church, she shook his shoulder gently. He opened his eyes and they lay for a moment staring at one another.

"Today is the day," he said.

"Yes," she said.

He smiled. "Happy Christmas."

LYDDE stuffed a sack with several changes of clothes for Noah, along with his razor, strop, and comb. Uncle John would bring a bundle from Soane's Croft—a pair of warm dresses and stockings from the attic trunk, and two shifts he had convinced Mother Bunch to sew, telling her they were for a charity case.

Noah stood for a time saying good-bye to his books, touching each on the spine as though memorizing the titles. "I shall miss you, my friends," he said. Then, "It's time."

They walked arm in arm downstairs, out the door for the last time and across the cathedral close. As they went, Noah said, "When we reach Trinity Church you will go straight to John and sit with him. When you say your good-byes, make certain no one hears you or notices any unusual display of emotion. As soon as the service is over I will collect you. We will walk to Mossup's and take two horses straight to the abbey."

"Can't Uncle John come to meet the ship with us?"

"I have no objection, but he may not think it safe. It will put him far from St. Pancras in case he needs to leave quickly. I think he will want to go forward in time as soon as we leave. But the decision is his."

Lydde stopped before they reached the gateway. "I'm frightened," she said. "Let's leave now."

"I doubt the ship has arrived this early, and it would be noticed if I am not in church. Besides, I have a sermon to preach."

"You can preach sermons in Virginia."

"We must give the ship time. Don't worry"—he touched her cheek with his fingertips—"you told me yourself, when you did not know who the Raven was, that Noah Fallam would go to Virginia. Have you forgotten?"

She stared at him, horrified. She had in fact forgotten, and never considered that he might include her remark in his calculations for escape and take more risks because of it. She turned away to hide the expression on her face, but he had noticed.

"What?" he said.

She could barely answer. "Uncle John told me later that it may mean nothing. We may be in a parallel universe here, with different outcomes."

He stared at her, trying to understand what she meant. "You mean it is not certain I will make it to Virginia?"

She shook her head mutely, and tears sprang to her eyes at the look of fear that crossed his face. He looked at the sky a moment, then away, took a deep breath, and squared his shoulders.

"Of course one should never expect a guaranty of safety," he said.

"God would not be thus mocked. There is nothing for it but to go on." He put on the black robe he had been carrying across his arm and turned toward the gateway. "This is the last time I shall have to pretend you are not my wife," he said. "Walk two respectful steps behind me now, and look a properly solemn boy."

Solemnity would not be too difficult, she thought, for either of them. She marveled at the steadiness of his step as they entered the street and joined others walking toward the church. She was terrified at how vulnerable he now was. If Woodcock had heard of the robbery at Rosewood he would know who was responsible. All he need do would be to convince a gang of like-minded men to assault Noah and haul him to jail. But so far everyone they met nodded respectfully as they passed. Then Woodcock himself loomed. He smiled and nodded.

"I look forward to your sermon this morning, Pastor Fallam," he said.

Noah nodded for an answer and walked steadily on, Lydde trailing behind and not daring to glance at Woodcock.

Uncle John waited at the entrance to Trinity Church. Noah waved his arm at Lydde as if dismissing her, and she went at once to Uncle John, who held up his hand to remind her not to hug him. He handed her the bundle of clothes.

"I didn't know if I'd see you again," he said.

"Last night went well," she whispered in his ear. "We got all the money and escaped unscathed."

"Is he ready to go?" Uncle John whispered back.

"He is. We're going straight to the beach from church. Will you go with us, or is this good-bye?"

"I think this better be good-bye. There's something in the air that I don't like. I'm afraid as soon as you two disappear all hell is going to break loose. Better for me to be on my way too. I'll probably be back at Roundbottom Farm before you reach the coast."

They stared at one another. "Tell Aunt Lavinia how much I love her," Lydde said.

He nodded. "I'm going to find you, Lydde. Some way. If you can't make it to the New River Gorge, we'll come east. I've just got to locate the right wormhole."

"A needle in a haystack," she said.

"Maybe not. I've been working on it with the new labyrinth pattern I made from the one in the cathedral. I just need to get back to West Virginia and test it out."

They took their seats at the back of the church beside the aisle. The congregation was more unsettled than usual, people talking among themselves, men even leaning across the center aisle to speak to the women. Then Noah entered the chancel in his robes and climbed into the pulpit. A hush fell over the sanctuary so profound that even the rustle of garments was stilled.

"A blessed Christmas to you all," Noah said.

A ripple of astonishment ran the length of the church. Jacob Wood-cock stood. "Do you dare blaspheme at this late date?" he called out.

Noah ignored him. He was looking over their heads from his high perch in the pulpit through the clear glass windows that had replaced the "papist" stained glass of Trinity Church. Lydde saw the change come over him. She could not see what he saw, that a troop of a dozen helmeted horsemen had entered the far end of North Gate Street. But she saw his death so clearly in his face that she would have stood as well had not Uncle John forcibly held her down. "Give nothing away!" he whispered urgently.

Noah had bowed his head momentarily, then looked up, straight at Lydde.

"I promised someone I love very much," he said in a clear voice, "that I would one day preach a true sermon, from my heart. Today is that day.

"I take as my text the fourth chapter of Luke's gospel. Jesus is bap-tized and undergoes temptation in the wilderness, then reveals him-self for the first time. He says, 'The Spirit of the Lord is upon me, because he hath anointed me to preach the gospel to the poor; he hath sent me to heal the brokenhearted, to preach deliverance to the captives, and recovering of sight to the blind, to set at liberty them that are bruised, to preach the acceptable year of the Lord.' Then Jesus told the people, 'This day is this scripture fulfilled in your ears.'

"What is this 'acceptable year of the Lord'? It is the jubilee year, the time of freedom and justice, of the liberation of the poor and oppressed, indeed the liberation of all of us. It is nothing more nor less than the proclamation of the Kingdom of God, a kingdom which is not *coming,* my friends. No, Jesus says it is already here. We live *at this very moment* in the Kingdom of God. Only we have not eyes to see it."

He was looking toward the windows again and hesitated, temporarily distracted. Then the congregation could hear the hooves of a troop of horses ringing against the cobblestones around Trinity. Lydde began to weep silently. Noah gathered himself and went on.

"Why can we not see the Kingdom of God? Because we avoid living in it. We do not heal broken hearts, we do not deliver captives, we abuse the poor, and we do not free *anyone.*" He was looking at Lydde again. "But also because, though the Kingdom of God is here, it lies just beyond the surface of what we see. It is like another dimension present with us always, though we are separated from it by the thinnest of membranes. But sometimes it trickles through into our wounded world in sublime moments of beauty, of truth, of peace, like water trickling through tiny fissures in a dam. We perceive it when we love. And someday it will burst through in its entirety and its goodness will wash over our world and transform and renew and restore everything we know. Someday—"

Then the back doors opened with a crash and a dozen armed men entered the sanctuary and fanned out along the outer aisles, followed by a short man in a gray coat and hat.

"I am Major-General Elisha Sitwell," he proclaimed, "and I am come to arrest the criminal who styles himself the Raven. Since," he added with a nod toward Noah, who stood frozen in the pulpit, "your Pastor Fallam seems unequal to the task."

Noah stepped down from the pulpit into a deadly silence. "Do you interrupt Sabbath worship, sir?" he said.

"I do," Sitwell replied. "For the Sabbath here cannot be peaceful while crimes like last night's robbery at Rosewood are committed. I will apprehend my criminal, sir, and then you shall have back your peaceful Sabbath."

Sitwell strode halfway down the center aisle and stopped, facing the men's side of the church. "This Raven," he said, "is known to bear a red birthmark on his shoulder. Every man here will therefore remove his coat and shirt and be examined by my constables."

The men looked at one another and began uneasily to pull off their coats and unbutton their shirts. Noah took a step forward. He still looked at Lydde, frozen in her pew, and she saw what he intended to do. She shook her head violently and he answered with a slow, reluctant head shake of his own. At the end of the aisle a Bristol constable was calling for Lydde and Uncle John to comply as the other men were.

"This is not necessary!"

Heads turned toward Pastor Fallam, who was coming down the center aisle.

"And why not?" Sitwell demanded.

Uncle John clapped his hand over Lydde's mouth.

"Because I know who bears the birthmark," Noah said. "It is on my own back. I am the Raven."

Lydde's scream was muffled by Uncle John's hand and the outcry from the congregation.

"Arrest this man!" Elisha Sitwell cried, and four of his constables came around from the sides and grabbed Noah, wrenching his arms behind his back. Sitwell walked slowly toward him.

"You!" he said. "I remember you well from Wexford. I wanted to hang you then, and should have. Has there ever been a more disgusting, despicable act of treachery than this?" He pulled a cudgel from his belt and waved it at the constables. "Tear off the robe of this man who pretends to serve God but in fact serves the Devil. Strip down his coat and shirt and show us the mark of Satan on his back."

They turned Noah roughly, stripping the robe from him and pulling down his coat and shirt to expose the birthmark on his shoulder. Lydde buried her face against Uncle John's arm. Then they pulled Noah back around to face Sitwell. The major-general glared at him a moment, then raised his cudgel and struck Noah a blow to the side of his head that dropped him to his knees. He stayed down, stunned, until the constables hauled him up again. Blood streamed down the right side of his head and face. Sitwell grabbed Noah's chin and turned his head roughly to one side, inspecting the damage he had done, then stepped back as though satisfied and faced the congregation. They sat in stunned silence—save for the weeping of a number of the women—their faces variously mirrors of outrage or distress.

"This man," Sitwell said, pointing at Noah with his cudgel, "is condemned by that birthmark and by the words out of his own mouth. He admits he is a damnable brigand, smuggler, thief, and traitor to the Commonwealth. There is no need for a trial, only a sentencing. Noah Fallam will be lodged in Norchester jail. Tomorrow at dawn he will be led to the place of execution and there he shall be hanged, while yet living his entrails spilled and private parts removed and burned, his head cut off, and his body quartered. His head shall be sent to London Bridge, the rest shall go to the four directions of the Commonwealth as a warning to others of his kind. So say I, Elisha Sitwell, major-general of Bristol District."

He strode back down the aisle, the constables following, with Noah staggering between them. Uncle John stepped into the aisle as Sitwell passed.

"Pardon, sir," he said, "I am a physician. Might I tend to that man's head wound?"

"This man is beyond help," Sitwell said.

Noah was saying as much as he could to Lydde with his eyes:

Farewell. Go back to your time, and know you have been loved for hundreds of years.

Then he was gone, borne out the door of Trinity Church between his captors.

At Soane's Croft Lydde huddled in a corner of the kitchen, weeping in the arms of Mother Bunch, who had at last been told the truth about the odd boy Lewis and Pastor Fallam, her husband. Uncle John watched Lydde a moment, left the room, then returned with a box. He dropped it at her feet with a clatter.

"There's this," he said.

She sat up and stared down at the box, which she recognized as the one Uncle John had carried back from West Virginia.

"Everything in me," said Uncle John, "is saying don't show this to Lydde. Because I know what you'll want to do. And I should simply take you safely back to the New River in the twenty-first century and forget about this place."

She turned her tear-stained face to him. "Except I never could forget him," she said.

"No," Uncle John agreed. He knelt and opened the box to display an array of canisters. "Pepper spray foam for close quarters." He held up one canister, then another. "Pepper spray fogger that reaches up to thirty feet. And a couple of holsters to strap on so we can carry several. The effects of both last about half an hour and the people who get hit will be blind and in pain. Plus they'll be terrified because they'll think it's some kind of witchcraft and they'll think it's permanent. But they won't die."

She wiped her face. "Why didn't you bring back some guns?" she said angrily. "The ones they have here couldn't hit the side of a barn."

He shook his head. "These people have enough problems without inflicting ours on them. Besides, I don't think Noah would want you killing his constables to save his life."

She shut her eyes. "No," she agreed.

"We could get some horses from Mossup's," Uncle John said. "You can hold them nearby while I go in and try to get him out."

"No," Lydde said. "You hold the horses and I'll get him out."

"Lydde, don't let's get into the same arguments you have with Noah."

She stood up. "Listen to me! I'll have an easier time inside. I'll wear one of the dresses. They'll be confused, won't know how to confront me at first. I would have more time to act than you do."

"Lydde—"

"Don't 'Lydde' me! You know I'm right. I'm younger. I'll react more quickly. I'll have the advantage of surprise, not you. Besides, he's in there and I want to be in there with him. If he comes out, I'll come out with him. And if it doesn't work, I'll stay in there with him. That's what I want. Please, Uncle John. He's my husband, not yours."

Uncle John rubbed his hand across his scalp. "Let me think about it," he said after a moment. "I'm going to take a walk."

"Where are you going?" she asked.

But he was already out the door.

An hour later he returned.

"I took a stroll over to Constable Baxter's cottage," he said. "He's upset about Noah. He went over to the jail and scouted things out while I visited with his wife."

Uncle John sat down at the kitchen table, where Mother Bunch picked halfheartedly at a cold roast chicken and Lydde left her plate untouched.

"Baxter learned a few things," Uncle John continued. "It seems Major-General Sitwell and his Bristol constables are having a fine old time tearing apart the inside of the Bishop's Palace and making a bonfire of Noah's blasphemous books."

"Oh," Lydde said, a catch in her voice, "he loves those books."

"Also, they plan, after supper tonight, to torture Noah into revealing the names of his gang members."

"God," Lydde whispered.

"Baxter also told me Noah is in the middle cell on the right. And here"—Uncle John reached into his pocket—"is the key."

THE afternoon was on the wane when a lone figure rode into St. Pancras churchyard with two bundles tied to his saddle and a large puppy sprawled across the horse's neck. John Soane slipped off Lady's back, hauling the dog down after him, and went to knock on the vicarage door of his friend the Reverend Smythe. They talked quietly for a moment, then Mr. Soane, who had retained sole possession of the keys to St. Pancras Church, unlocked the doors and led the old vicar inside.

"You will see Mother Bunch is taken care of?"

"Oh, yes," said the Reverend Smythe. "I shall marry Alis, of course, to head off any scandal."

Uncle John nodded, startled to hear Mother Bunch referred to by her given name.

"If I were you, I'd pack at once," Uncle John said, "and leave for Bradway while all the uproar is going on. I have a feeling the days of this old church are numbered."

"Very sad," said the Reverend Smythe.

"And now I must situate Bounder and be on my way."

They found an old table in the sacristy and carried it down to the crypt, placed it over the cistern so the dog wouldn't fall into it, left Bounder inside, and closed the door. As they climbed the stairs back to the sanctuary, the Reverend Smythe said, "I shall miss you, my friend."

Uncle John put his hand on the old man's shoulder. "I'll come back for the dog," he said, "and it will be best if you don't try to learn where I've gone."

Then Uncle John was on his way once more, riding Lady to the shingle of beach below the abbey with the bundles. There was still no sign of a ship. "God, they should have been here by now," he muttered. He dropped the bundles of clothes far enough away that the tide wouldn't take them. With them he left a note for Simon telling him what had happened. Then he went back as he had come, leaving Lady with the Reverend Smythe and walking the rest of the way back to Mossup's stable.

LYDDE waited at Soane's Croft in an agony of indecision. She wore a dress over her breeches, a cloak with a hood to cover her short hair, and holsters with canisters of pepper gas fogger and foam around her waist. Several times she started to leave. But it was not close enough to dark, when it would be easiest to go undetected. Still she was terrified of waiting too long for fear they would have started torturing Noah. She was counting on his being alone in his cell and able to move on his own.

At last she set out. Few people were out that late Sabbath afternoon and those who were stared at the hooded woman, shawl covering her lower face, who strode alone toward the Pye. When she reached the river she met no one, and by the time she was angling past the market cross, the streets of the town were nearly deserted.

Outside the jail, Lydde paused and took out the canister of pepper foam. She tried the outside door, found it was unlocked, and opened it carefully. A constable in the room where Noah had met with Baxter stepped into the foyer and Lydde sprayed him with the pepper foam, which clung to his face like a mask. Before he could manage a scream, she shoved him back in the room and shut the door. Then she found the key to the cell block on the ring Baxter had given them, turned it, and pulled the door open.

Two men stood in the hall near Noah's cell and turned at her approach. They stared in astonishment. Lydde didn't recognize them and decided they must be Bristol constables.

"Who is this?" one chortled.

She took a step closer.

"A whore," she said.

"Indeed!"

They came toward her.

"No," she said, "a witch." She raised the canister of foam and sprayed them both in the face.

At their howls of pain, a door opened behind her. She had anticipated it—recalling from her previous visit that the jailers hung out in the first room on the left—and she had already moved toward it. When the door swung open, revealing six men, four of them sitting at a table, she hit the closest in the face with foam from her right hand, sprayed the room with fogger from her left, and slammed the door on their screams.

Then she heard Noah's muffled voice behind her crying, "Lydde!"

She ran to the door of his cell, where she barely registered the sight of his battered face pressed against the small barred window. With shaking hands, she dropped her canister of foam and managed to work the key into the lock. She turned it and he tumbled out into the hall.

She took his hand.

"Run!" she cried, and they dashed down the hall, leaping the writhing bodies of the two stricken constables and bursting into the clear evening air.

"To Mossup's!" Lydde yelled, and they sprinted, Noah clutching Lydde's arm so as not to leave her behind. Behind them they heard a man calling out, raising the alarm. Before they reached Mossup's they met Uncle John leading three horses along East Gate Street. They mounted as quickly as they could, Noah stopping to help Lydde.

"Let's go!" Uncle John cried, and they galloped down the street and through East Gate, heading for St. Pancras.

When they reached the turnoff to the church, Uncle John pulled up, as did the others, and dismounted.

"Take care of her!" he called to Noah, who clasped his hand. Then

Uncle John pulled a knife from his belt and handed it over. "Just in case," he said. He smacked the rump of Lydde's horse and watched them ride away into the dusk toward the sea.

At St. Pancras he found the Reverend Smythe waiting.

"Did they get enough of a head start?"

"I don't know," Uncle John said, his voice trembling with pride, "but by God, she got him out."

They stood for a moment listening for sounds of pursuit. Several minutes had passed, by Uncle John's judgment, when six men on horseback thundered past, heading toward the abbey. Uncle John and the Reverend Smythe shrank back against the side of St. Pancras. When the horsemen had disappeared, Uncle John, overcome with emotion, put his hand on his friend's shoulder.

"Do me a favor," he said. "I'm going to the crypt to wait with the dog until I hear from you. Let me know one way or the other. I can't leave otherwise."

The Reverend Smythe covered the other's hand with his.

"Yes," he said. "I will walk into Norchester now."

THEIR horses were running at full speed across the heath and Lydde had trouble holding on. She slipped sideways and managed to right herself by grasping the horse's mane, but the sudden yank caused the animal to pull up and throw her to the ground. She struck her head.

Noah turned his horse and headed back, slipped off his mount, and went to her. She was sitting up, a dazed expression on her face and her forehead red with blood. He gathered her in his arms and looked up. Horsemen appeared on the far horizon.

"Come on," he urged.

She tried to focus on what seemed to be two Noahs floating before her.

"Leave me," she said. "I'll slow you down."

"As if I could," he said, and pulled her up to lean against his horse.

Then, clutching her collar, he mounted, leaned over, and hauled her up by the armpits to ride in front of him.

It was true the horse could not run as fast with the extra weight. Noah cast anxious glances over his shoulder at the pursuing horsemen, who were gaining. Then he was negotiating the hollow that wound down to the shingle and there was a ship offshore and a shallop drawn up on the beach. A group of sailors came alive at the sight of them and began leaping into the shallop, manning the oars.

Simon ran toward them, put his arm around Lydde, and helped Noah drag her to the shallop even as a crowd of horsemen thundered down the gap onto the beach.

"Row!" came the command, and they were thrown back into their seats as the boat shoved off. Behind them the horsemen were dismounting and trying to ready their weapons. Noah held Lydde close and leaned over her as the Bristol constables fired. Their gun balls splashed harmlessly into the surf vacated by the shallop, which the oarsmen expertly carried out into deep water. Soon there was no sound except the rhythmic slapping of the oars.

"My God," Simon said, "you have both been beaten around the head."

"We have," Noah said, and held Lydde.

Lydde mumbled and he leaned over to hear what she said.

"Where are we?"

"We are on our way to the ship," he said.

"Did I get you out?"

He squeezed her shoulders. "You did," he said.

"You should keep talking to her," Simon said, "to keep her awake until we can get her on board."

So Noah whispered in her ear, telling her how magnificent she was, describing her exploits in detail, telling her over and over that he had seen nothing so brave.

Simon, listening, asked, "Did she really do that?"

"She did," Noah said proudly.

. . .

THEY got her on board the pitching ship by tying a rope beneath her arms and pulling her up, Simon ahead and Noah behind to make sure she was not allowed to drop back into the sea. Once on board, they were met by Mary, who showed them to the space between decks that would serve the four of them as a cabin, partitioned by a sheet hung down the middle for a paltry privacy.

For a time the ship was becalmed and all feared a party from shore might try to board. Armed sailors stood watch. But soon after dark a wind filled the sails and they moved out to sea.

The first night a seasick Noah lay on their straw mattress beside Lydde, who slept without moving. He whispered into her ear, reassured only by the warmth of her body and her soft breath against his ear that she was alive.

The next day he went up on deck. Simon and Mary were already out, bracing against a cold wind. They were used to the ship's sharp rocking, while Noah was not. He leaned over the rail to throw up, held at the coattails by Simon, who warned him of the perils of going overboard.

"We have seen the last of England," Noah said later, staring east at the white bank of fog where the coastline had once been.

"We have," Simon said. "But a new world entire lies ahead. It is like a second life."

Noah went back down to their cabin to find Lydde awake and staring at the shaft of sunlight from a small porthole. He stretched out beside her and she smiled at him.

"They didn't kill you," she said, her voice weak.

"No. Do you remember coming into the jail?"

"Yes. I remember riding away from Norchester. And the last I remember is Uncle John giving you a knife. Just in case, he said. What did he mean?"

Groggy though she was, she could see in his face that he was struggling with how much to tell her.

"If we had been captured," he said, "I would have been drawn and quartered, and you would have been tortured and burned at the stake. If we were in danger of apprehension and there was no escape, he meant I was to stab you and then fall on the knife myself."

Lydde was imagining parallel endings in parallel universes: Noah escaping on horseback while she was abandoned to the constables. Both of them caught and executed. Noah killed while she went back through the wormhole. The pair of them trapped on the beach with no ship and no hope, while Noah pressed the point of a knife to her breast, preparing to plunge it in, then kill himself so they might die together and escape further suffering.

"Would you have done it?" she asked.

He looked at her steadily. "Yes," he said.

"Thank you for telling me. And for loving me enough to—"

"Hush!" He covered her eyes with one hand and placed the other on top of her head. "Clear your mind. Think no more on knives."

The motion of the ship and the lingering effects of her concussion made her dizzy even though she was lying down. "It's cold," she murmured.

Noah tucked the blankets more snugly around them and held her close, kissed her forehead. "I will keep you as warm as I can," he promised.

WHEN Uncle John received word that Lydde and Noah had escaped, much to the fury of Elisha Sitwell and Jacob Woodcock, he said a prayer of thanks and went down to the crypt. Bounder greeted him joyously, leaping in the air and licking his face.

"Come on, girl," he said. "I'm afraid I have to add a few years to your life. But you'll get good vet care, rawhide strips, and Milk-Bones. Lavinia will spoil you rotten."

He shoved aside the table, then had an idea.

"Let's give them something else to remember the pepper spray witch by," he told the dog. He hoisted the pup into his arms and dropped into the cistern. The familiar disorientation came and they lay sprawled on the floor of a cave, smelling damp New River smells.

He stood, held the dog close, and stepped back into the vortex of the wormhole.

Again they lay in the crypt room beside the cistern. Uncle John chuckled to think of the wall paintings restored above them.

"Hell," he told Bounder, "they would have burned it anyway."

Then they were gone again to the Gorge and the shelf of rock below the Mystery Hole. Uncle John located the flashlight he kept there and flicked it on. Outside, he could tell by the crack of light near the cliff edge, it was a lovely spring day.

He grabbed the dog, now grown to full size, by the scruff of the neck and crept along until they reached the skeleton stretched out on its bed of stone.

"Still there," Uncle John said aloud. He knelt, the light of the flashlight playing over the bones. He caught the glint of the silver chain and cross, reached in, and lifted the chain carefully with his fingers.

"So," he said, "looks like we were in the past. Maybe it's the eternal recurrence we're dealing with here."

Uncle John continued to move the flashlight back and forth over the old rib cage, certain now that these were the remains of Noah Fallam, his friend and Lydde's beloved. Then the light caught something else. He leaned closer, probing with his fingers until he brought forth the object he had located.

"Oh, God, Noah," he said.

He bowed his head a moment to think and pray. Then he stood and said, "Come on, Bounder."

OUTSIDE, he blinked in the bright sunlight, the dog beside him with a length of twine tied around her neck in a makeshift collar and leash. The blasted stump of Fallam Mountain stretched behind them, hideous as ever. But when they walked toward what had been Montefalco, Uncle John saw that once more the valley fill had shrunk. He had twice breached the barrier with the living dog from the past, and the foundation of Carlo Falcone's house was uncovered once again, looking little different than it had a few days after the fire.

"So," Uncle John said to Bounder, "Lydde is lost in the vast sea of history like the other children. But we'll find her, won't we, girl?"

He led the dog down the mountain to Roundbottom Farm, the tin roof gleaming in the sunshine. On the front porch he paused out of habit to wipe his boots. Then he opened the old screen door with a creak.

"Lavinia!" he called. "I'm home!"